The Radical Novel Reconsidered

A series of paperback reissues of mid-twentieth-century
U.S. left-wing fiction, with new biographical and critical
introductions by contemporary scholars.

Series Editor
Alan Wald, University of Michigan

D0038529

Books in the Series

To Make My Bread
Grace Lumpkin

Moscow Yankee
Myra Page

The People from Heaven
John Sanford

Salome of the Tenements
Anzia Yezierska

MOSCOW YANKEE

MYRA PAGE

MOSCOW YANKEE

Introduction by Barbara Foley

University of Illinois Press · Urbana and Chicago

Introduction © 1995 by the Board of Trustees of the University of Illinois
Manufactured in the United States of America
P   5   4   3   2   1

This book is printed on acid-free paper.

Library of Congress Cataloging-in-Publication Data

Page, Myra, 1897–
Moscow Yankee / Myra Page ; introduction by Barbara Foley.
p.   cm. — (Radical novel reconsidered)
Includes bibliographical references.
ISBN 0-252-06499-2 (paper : acid-free paper)
1. Americans—Travel—Russia—Moscow—Fiction. 2. Women—Soviet
Union—Fiction. I. Title. II. Series.
PS3531.A235M67   1995
813'.54—dc20   95-2992
                                                    CIP

INTRODUCTION

Barbara Foley

During almost all of her long life (1897–1993), Myra Page was a radical activist—a Communist, a unionist, a feminist, an opponent of racism and war. Not long before her death, she lamented from a Yonkers, New York, nursing home that she was being "spread too thin" by her involvement in multiple social causes (Baker 296). Page was also a radical writer, continually composing and publishing poems, short stories, reportage, and novels articulating her leftist concerns. Her writings furnish part of the literary "red line of history" in the twentieth century.

Moscow Yankee (1935), arguably the most important of Page's works, has continuing relevance in the 1990s. Given the recent collapse of Soviet-style socialism, the association of the word "Moscow" with human emancipation will strike many readers—especially younger readers—as a cruel irony. But the continuing inability of capitalism to provide even the most minimal livelihood for many of the globe's inhabitants, as well as the multiple forms of alienation and inequality prevalent even in those sites where capitalism proclaims itself a success, returns many thoughtful people to the left-wing drawing board. *Moscow Yankee* is an invaluable resource, for it gives a glimpse of the joyful commitment experienced by working people who felt themselves involved in the construction of an egalitarian society. The novel reveals the early phases of some of the political and economic policies that would cause Soviet-style socialism ultimately to meet its demise. But it refutes the widely held notion—almost a staple of contemporary bourgeois thought—that egalitarian societies cannot succeed because they fail to take into account the individualism and greed of "human nature." *Moscow Yankee,* which is closely based on Page's own experiences in Moscow during the First Five-Year Plan, provides a compelling portrait of human collectivity. While situated some sixty years ago, Page's novel raises issues of urgent concern to our time; it deserves to be widely read and discussed among those who remain unconvinced that the "free market" furnishes the path to human liberation.

Looking back on the writing of *Moscow Yankee* some fifty years later, Myra Page remarked, "I tried to create a true picture of the people and the life beginning to emerge. The Russians didn't know anything about the novel until I was practically through with it. All I knew was that they wanted me to give a realistic portrayal. *Moscow Yankee* is not a bright Utopian picture at all, nor is it supposed to be. It's a picture of struggle and of people moving. Among the common people, especially, there were many good people behind the movement. The novel is mainly about them" (Baker 184).

When Page began writing *Moscow Yankee* at a Soviet Black Sea resort in 1933, she was well equipped to paint her "picture of struggle and of people moving." Born Dorothy Page Gary in Newport News, Virginia, to liberal, middle-class parents, she had, from early on, reacted strongly against Jim Crow racism and the harsh conditions faced by both white and black local shipyard workers. Though from a relatively privileged class background, she chafed against the restrictions imposed on her as a southern white woman—as a child she was informed that there was no chance of her ever becoming a doctor like her father—and commented in later years that her awareness of "'the woman question, without being very concrete, developed very early'" (Frederickson 11). As a young woman, Page participated in antiracist, humanitarian, and union-organizing activities sponsored by the YWCA, then not simply an inexpensive residence but a "movement of women" for social justice (Baker 67). She moved steadily leftward and, in 1925, joined the fledgling Communist Party of the United States. By the late 1920s she had received an M.A. from Columbia University and a Ph.D. from the University of Minnesota—both degrees in sociology—married fellow Communist John Markey, and begun her long career as a radical writer. Prior to publishing *Moscow Yankee* in 1935, Page had written extensively for the Communist-sponsored press (*Southern Worker, Working Woman, Daily Worker*) and had published a nonacademic version of her doctoral dissertation, *Southern Cotton Mills and Labor* (1929), as well as a pamphlet about life in a "Soviet Middletown," *Soviet Main Street* (1933), and a proletarian novel, *Gathering Storm: A Story of the Black Belt* (1932). The author of *Moscow Yankee* was thus a veteran leftist, a seasoned labor reporter, and an experienced writer of fiction.[1]

Page needed this background, for the task she set herself in *Moscow Yankee* was formidable. She wanted to give her novel—one of very few developed portraits of Soviet socialist construction in the entire canon of American proletarian fiction—the ring of veracity. To this end, she adhered closely to her own observations during a 1931–33 visit to the Soviet Union. A perusal of Page's extensive reportage for the U.S. leftist press, as well as of *Soviet Main Street,* reveals that many of *Moscow Yankee*'s themes, and several of its characters, are drawn directly from her personal experience. The text's documentary feel was noted by appreciative reviewers on the left. The *New Masses* critic Alice Withrow Field declared that "anyone who has lived in Moscow will attest to the fact that the picture is true" (26). Edwin Seaver commented in *Soviet Russia Today* that "there are few Americans who know more about the Russian workers and farmers and the new Socialist world they are building than does Myra Page" (24).

Moscow Yankee's credibility as a register to contemporaneous developments in the Soviet Union was also acknowledged in the mainstream press. The reviewer for the *New York Herald-Tribune Books,* for example, while complaining that the novel was "a little too pat and moralistic," conceded that he did not "mean to criticize it as 'propaganda' or unfaithful to its realism" (Marsh 20). In the 1990s as in the 1930s, much of *Moscow Yankee*'s value consists in its documentation of a process of socialist transformation largely unimaginable to those living in the capitalist United States.[2]

Page wanted not just to document but to move and persuade. As a committed practitioner of literary proletarianism, she espoused the view that "'art is a weapon'" and saw her fiction as a means to winning her readers closer to Communism, calling on writers and critics alike to "free themselves . . . from the old bourgeois methods and approach" ("Author's Field Day," 31–32). Aware, however, that her first novel had been faulted for its mechanistic handling of character and plot, she strove in *Moscow Yankee* to focus more fully on "psychological development" and to make use of the "new stream of consciousness technique" introduced among radical writers by John Dos Passos (letter to Hicks). Aware too that the influential Marxist critic Mike Gold "wasn't keen on women writers, whom he considered sentimentalists," Page "wanted to make sure that *Moscow Yankee* was really down to earth" (Baker 193–94). To convey a vision of human possibility without offering a "bright Utopian picture," to offer a "realistic portrayal" of socialist revolution by means of conventions largely inherited from bourgeois literary tradition—this too was Page's self-appointed challenge. In the 1990s as in the 1930s, *Moscow Yankee* is thus also valuable for what it can tell us about the relationship between left-wing politics and novelistic form.

Soviet Socialist Construction in *Moscow Yankee*

"One thing *is* being deliberately abolished, the unequal status of woman," wrote Page in *Soviet Main Street,* "while the oncoming generations, in rights and status, have at last come into their own" (66–67). Drawing on her observations of Soviet women's rapidly changing status at work and in the family, in *Moscow Yankee* Page offers a portrait of women's contradictory social position in the early phases of socialist construction. The novel's principal exemplar of the "new Soviet woman" is Natasha, a character who was, Page noted, "based on Valya Cohen, a young woman whom I came to know very well" (Baker 191). A factory worker of peasant origins, Natasha is training to be an engineer and throws herself passionately into the project of socialist construction. While possessing abundant physical charms (Page would not go so far as to have an ugly female protagonist), Natasha is tough and wiry in both body and mind and cannot tolerate any assumption of male superiority: her slapping Andy in the face for his offer of silk stockings signals the self-concept of the "new Soviet woman." Natasha is one of the "women heroes of socialist construction" upon whom Page had reported in the 1932 *Daily Worker:* "Resourceful, independent, and with minds largely freed from . . . petty household cares . . . , these women devote their energies to building the new life in factory, club, and community" ("Women Heroes," 4). Throughout *Moscow Yankee*, Page contrasts the Communist Natasha with not only the nefarious and sexually manipulative White Russian Katia Boudnikova but also various American women: Mary Boardman and Edith Crampton, the disgruntled and restless wives of the two American engineers, and Andy's Detroit girlfriend, Elsie, whose whining letters reflect a consciousness defined by commodity fetishism.

The minor character Zena further illustrates women's changing status in Soviet society. A former prostitute turned factory worker, Zena continues to ply her trade with the eager participation of various male co-workers. In the scene where Zena is charged with lateness and low productivity, however, Natasha and Maxim designate the men who have "lured" Zena back to her old ways as the "real criminals" and "traitors," who are "acting the same as White Guards" (191). Prostitution is a crime stemming from the old social order, and its remedy is immersion in the new: Natasha's challenge to a friendly "socialist competition" will presumably eradicate Zena's waywardness. The portrayal of Zena was based on Page's 1931 visit to a "Prophylactoria," or rehabilitation center for former prostitutes, as well as her attendance that year at the First Conference of Former Prostitutes. There she heard a woman testify, "The only card I used to have was a Yellow Ticket [the prostitute's badge and 'passport' under the tsar]. Any man could have me for a ruble. Now I have another card—a red card, my trade union book. Now I bow to no man. And I say hurrah for the Soviet power." Natasha and Zena embody the "oncoming generation" of Soviet women who, "in rights and status, have come into their own" ("The Fallen Woman Rises," 9).[3]

Despite its exhilarating representation of revolutionized gender roles, *Moscow Yankee* also testifies to the tenacity of inherited conceptions of women's intrinsic traits and appropriate roles—not only in Soviet society but also in Page's discourse about that society. Natasha is noteworthy in *Moscow Yankee* for her uniqueness: from the "hysterical New England spinsters" on the Moscow-bound train (19), to the parasitical American wives, to Natasha's superstitious peasant mother, many women in *Moscow Yankee* do not transcend sexist stereotypes. Nor is a sexist division of labor called into question. In the overcrowded apartment building inhabited by the expatriate Scottish radical Mac and his wife, Nan, housewives rather than husbands are blamed for domestic disorder. When the Klarovs have left a pile of dirty dishes in the communal sink, Alicia Klarov is faulted by her neighbor Berta: "That Klarova woman! How much trouble she gives us! . . . Nan and I are forever cleaning up after her" (98). Mac—who functions throughout the novel as a socialist mentor to both Andy and the reader—agrees, thinking to himself that "if Alicia kept this up they'd have to take her before the House Soviet" (98–99). The omission of any mention of Mr. Klarov's role in creating the mess reveals the extent to which inherited assumptions about women's domestic duties—which, unlike overcrowding, will not be alleviated by the construction of new housing—permeate characters and author alike.[4]

While gender issues figure prominently in *Moscow Yankee,* the core of the novel is its representation of developing forces and changing relations of production. The hero, Frank Anderson (Andy)—a refugee from Depression-era Detroit—is converted into a "Moscow Yankee" as much by new conditions for the possibilities of love as by the vision of new possibilities for work. The Red Star automotive production plant

xii

draws its name from a state farm Page toured near Kharkov and is based on the Amo auto and truck factory that she frequently visited during her Moscow stay (Baker 190). The factory foreman, Mikhail, a veteran of the 1905 and the Bolshevik Revolutions, closely resembles Feodor Trefanov, the seasoned Podolsk brigade leader described in *Soviet Main Street*. The American engineer Philip Boardman, who is fascinated with the limitless possibilities opened to industry untrammeled by capitalism, had as his prototype a "hard-headed mechanical engineer . . . [with] a pioneer spirit . . . who decided to stay. . . . the Soviet Union gave him a chance to do what he couldn't do in his own country" (Baker 189). Mac and Nan are based on "a Scottish couple, once active in union and progressive movements in Scotland, [who] were realistic about conditions in Russia and chose to stay" (Baker 189). The participation of Red Star workers in voluntary overtime to meet and surpass production quotas; the celebration of *udarniks,* or exemplary "shock-workers"; the purge of the plant superintendent, Eugene Pankrevich, for bureaucratic and inefficient leadership; the White Russian Alex Turin's attempted sabotage of the factory—these and other aspects of the struggle over production during the First Five-Year Plan replicate common features of Soviet experience in the 1930s and correspond closely with Page's direct observations. "I did very little inventing in *Moscow Yankee,*" Page declared (Baker 187).[5]

Just as important to Page as the epic portrayal of expanding productive forces, however, was the representation of revolutionized productive relations, for these constituted the material foundation of the social order producing the "new Soviet man" and the "new Soviet woman." Andy's growing perception that a mistake at work generates not reprimand or firing but an offer of help from his assembly line *tovarisch* Sasha; that Mikhail is not a "straw boss" but a friend; that injury results not in unemployment but in a paid convalescence by the Black Sea; that government officials and assembly line workers vacation side by side in mansions expropriated from the former rulers—these and comparable insights convince

Andy that, as he says in a letter to Elsie, "working stiffs like me count here. No kidding. . . . plenty my kind are running entire works" (255). Andy's satisfaction at the end of the novel derives from not only his domestic happiness with Natasha but also his discovery of meaningful work that expands his own capacities and contributes to the collective. He and Sasha have devised "a new type of bolt for the upper frame" that has earned them a write-up on the "Board of Inventors" (290). The alterations internal to Andy thus offer a literary projection of the conclusions Page drew about her own experiences:

> The social changes I saw taking place in the Soviet Union received less attention from the outside world than the rapid growth of the Dneiper power station, the Kharkov tractor works or the Magnitorgorsk mills, but they were no less startling and certainly of equal significance. In helping to transform a formerly backward, agrarian country into a highly industrialized one, Russians were changing themselves as well. Of course there were many remnants, very stubborn ones too, of the old life and ugly human traits that remained. Nevertheless, the tendency was increasingly away from the old and toward the new. I believed the Soviet system was helping to create a world that fosters the better aspects of human nature, and that the corroding effects of the old competitive system where the few exploit the many had virtually disappeared. (Baker 198)

Page, eager not to paint a "bright Utopian picture," took care to include in *Moscow Yankee* certain "remnants of the old life and ugly human traits that remained": the inefficiency and waste entailed in drawing "raw" peasants into industrial production (reflected in the episode where a valuable machine is destroyed by a careless worker); the uneven political commitment among the workers (displayed in the theft of Andy's precious hammer); the low quality of consumption (brought out in the factory workers' grumbling about the food in the plant cafeteria); the possibility that Party members may become separated from the masses (signaled through Misha Popov's demotion into the ranks of the workers); the dangers of bureaucratic management (embodied in the top-down policies of Pankrcvich); and the tragic national costs of full-scale industrial development (obliquely conveyed through rumblings of starvation in the Ukraine). The principal role of the Heindricks, idealistic expatriate fellow travelers who become disillusioned with the imperfections of Soviet socialism, is precisely to voice Page's acknowledgment of such flaws; the Heindricks stand in for readers skeptical of the author's generally laudatory representation.

Page takes care, however, to blunt or deflect most of the Heindricks' criticisms. Some of the flaws in socialist construction are shown to derive from the inevitably uneven course of development within the Party, the proletariat, and the peasantry. Rather than offering cause for despair, these flaws are treated as nonantagonistic and thus remediable through increased dedication to the *Pyatiletka,* or Five-Year Plan. Misha helps fight for the Party's position as a rank-and-file worker; Pankrevich is removed from management; the plant cooks engage in a socialist competition to improve the quality of food; the discovery that the hammer thief is a former *bezprizhorni,* or war orphan, alleviates his crime. Other threats to socialist construction derive, by contrast, from the continuing presence in the Soviet Union of the class enemy: the "thieving, speculating" (234) kulaks who withhold grain from the industrial centers to undermine socialist construction; the formerly aristocratic White Russians and their henchmen who, in alignment with capitalist interests overseas, still hope to regain their lost power and property through sabotage and, ultimately, counterrevolution. Contradictions between the socialist U.S.S.R. and such enemies are antagonistic and must be resolved by force, whether through the workers' class-conscious intervention (Ned Folsom's pursuit of the saboteur Alex Turin) or the intervention of the state on the side of the revolution (the O.G.P.U.'s arrest of the kulaks caught smuggling luxury items to the black market). Antagonistic or not, however, contradictions potentially inhibiting socialist construction are, in Page's account, attributable neither to the intrinsic greed of human nature nor to the dominance of a "Stalinist" party but to insufficient commitment to the Five-Year Plan within the Soviet Union, on the one hand, and to sabotage and the threat of capitalist encirclement, on the other.[6]

The Heindricks, still grumping, decide to stay in Moscow; whether Page successfully allays all her readers' skepticism—either in the 1930s or the l990s—is an empirical question, not determinable through textual analysis.[7] What is significant, however, is that the issues noted above are treated as *issues* in *Moscow Yankee*—that is, Page clearly feels it necessary both to air and to dispute them on what could be termed the text's explicit level of doctrinal politics. More problematic, however, is a proposition that remains largely uninterrogated in *Moscow Yankee*—namely, the equation of the development of productive forces with the formation of egalitarian social relations.

Like Soviet-authored novels about the First Five-Year Plan, *Moscow Yankee* is premised on the notion that expanding the Soviet Union's industrial base is the key to building socialism and achieving Communism. Mikhail explains to the impatient Natasha:

> "Yes. Lenin showed us we had to rebuild our life, like we made our October, with men not all good or all bad. Just ordinary humans." Through the struggle, fierce as it was, man was reshaping himself as well. After the First Five Year Plan there'd be the Second Plan, beginning next year and bringing with it an end to classes and all exploitation of man by man. There was the key! All busy at some useful work, and growing like a boundless field on their steppes of ripening grain. After the Second Plan, and Third, a Fourth. And with each fresh generation, man stretching his world and himself further, understand? (139)[8]

The same idea is conveyed in "Look Here, Stalingrad!" a poem constructed out of a *Pravda* news story and inserted, Dos Passos fashion, into the narrative. The workers at Leningrad's Red Putilov steel works have chided their Stalingrad tractor works counterparts for lagging behind production quotas:

Look here Stalingrad
Come through on those tractors!
. . . [You're] making us the laughing stock of the
Exchanges in New York and Europe. . . .

Can't you feel in their scorn
   the swift training of machine guns
   to the east and west!

. . . . Brothers, on to the fight!
   For technique!
      The front of socialist construction
      To work—in a new way! (107–8)

The Stalingrad workers have apparently risen to this challenge to socialist competition:

The whole country waits
For daily reports in *Pravda*
   Yesterday Stalingrad gave forty tractors
   Today forty-six
Tomorrow fifty
      sixty
      sixty-five
Stalingrad is coming through!
Answering Putilov, the whole earth
Not with words
But with
Tractors! (108)

In Mikhail's vision of the Soviet future and in "Look Here, Stalingrad!" "useful labor" and "technique" are portrayed as the key means to socialist advancement. But neither statement clarifies exactly how certain remnants of capitalist social relations of production—the commodification of wage-labor, the division of mental and manual labor—will be eliminated. Indeed, the novel, if anything, valorizes the struggle initiated by the Party, in the persons of Mac and Vasiliev, to refine the division of labor, increase individual accountability, and introduce wage differentials based on productivity. Although they anticipate "stiff opposition, once this fight's launched"—and various workers in their brigade do in fact vigorously resist—they anticipate "no trouble" from management: "'They'll be scared the plant can't pay the wages this is bound to mean. But it's plain horse sense, more and better output. We'll convince them'" (106).

Moreover, the text treats as unproblematic management's plan to construct special apartments for its hundred most-productive *udarniks*—a move also revealing the material incentives being held out to the workers. While it is good news that Crampton will return to the United States and Boardman will stay in Moscow, it is not clear that Boardman's privileging of "science, engineering, efficiency" over Crampton's capitalist fixation on "speed, money, costs" (146) will eliminate top-down management, even if Boardman continually stops to share his expertise with rank-and-file workers. Natasha and Andy are studying to be engineers and will rise in the ranks, and Pankrevich will be supplanted by a more dedicated and motivating superintendent; but the existence of separate ranks of engineers and assembly line workers is not fundamentally called into question. To "work in a new way" means, mainly, to work harder in the "beautiful, quivering nerve center" that is Red Star (22).[9]

In short, just as *Moscow Yankee*'s failure to interrogate received conceptions of women's domestic roles points up Soviet socialism's incomplete achievement with regard to the "woman question," the novel's blithe equation of technique with progress reveals the prevalence of the doctrine of productive forces determinism in Soviet socialist construction. This premise bears comment, because the Soviet Union's failure to achieve an egalitarian society—indeed, its relapse into an authoritarian state capitalism—can be traced in large part to the fetishization of technology. As the Sovietologist Charles Bettelheim has noted, even though the Communist Party of the Soviet Union (CPSU) declared in 1936 that class struggle had come to an end in the Soviet Union, class conflict continued unabated into socialist construction, though reshaped primarily as a struggle over production relations. Even by the early

1930s, however, the course of socialist construction was guided by an economism that tended "to identify the productive forces with the material means of production, thus denying that the principal productive force consists of the producers themselves." This economism "ascribe[d] the major role in the building of socialism not to the initiative of the working people but to the accumulation of new means of production and technical knowledge" (34). To be sure, Page's novel displays plenty of "initiative of working people"; clearly the characters in *Moscow Yankee* are motivated to produce not only trucks but also the "new Soviet man" and the "new Soviet woman." Since this initiative is not translated into altered relations of production but is instead directed toward achieving and surpassing production quotas under existing work conditions, it takes shape as a manifestation of voluntarism rather than as a constitutive feature of socialist construction.

In both its manifest and its subliminal levels of discourse, then, *Moscow Yankee* documents the contradictory realities of Soviet socialist construction. Page did indeed provide a "true picture of the people and the life beginning to emerge"—even truer, perhaps, than she was aware.

Moscow Yankee and the Politics of Novelistic Form

In addition to providing a record of Soviet life during the First Five-Year Plan, *Moscow Yankee* offers a specifically *novelistic* record. Its use of the bildungsroman form to convey its male protagonist's growth into a "new Soviet man" displays both the strengths and the weaknesses of this genre as a carrier of 1930s left-wing doctrine.

The bildungsroman is perhaps the most quintessentially bourgeois of all novelistic modes. Individualistic in its philosophical premises and its narrative structure, this genre routinely features a protagonist who, while often initially rebelling against the strictures of bourgeois society, is eventually reconciled—either happily or reluctantly—to this society's inevitability. In the classical bildungsroman, social contradictions are subordinated to the arousal and fulfillment of narrative expectations surrounding the hero's fate. Conflicting ideological paradigms are permitted articulation but are repressed in a hierarchy of discourses that guarantees the supremacy of one or another hegemonic standpoint. Social criticism is, moreover, conflated with ethical choice, and insoluble social conflicts are papered over in the protagonist's internal moral debates. This personalization of the social is epitomized in the protagonist's quest for an ideal mate: the plot of romantic love involves readers in an emotional and erotic identification with the hero's yearning, and larger questions of social causality and social justice are dissolved in the protagonist's achievement of a selfhood largely defined through the reward of an appropriate life-companion.

It would seem that proletarian writers would have avoided the bildungsroman; however, it was actually the most frequently deployed of all novelistic modes. Proletarian writers used the genre to write novels of "conversion"—that is, narratives tracing a protagonist's development from false consciousness to class consciousness, from alienation and passivity to collectivity and activism. Page's novel exemplifies the conversion plot—initially portrayed with his head wobbling "foolishly from side to side" on the train "charging . . . between two worlds" (3), Andy ends as a purposive participant in a Moscow May Day. While he happily comes to terms with the social order, this reconciliation has involved expunging his belief in the superiority of American capitalism and embracing a new way of life halfway around the globe. Does *Moscow Yankee* thus signal that proletarian writers could use inherited bourgeois literary forms with impunity—that a sufficiently "left" doctrinal politics could predominate over the bourgeois generic politics historically accompanying traditional narrative modes?[10]

To answer this question, we must consider again the narrative structure of *Moscow Yankee*. The main plot-line follows Andy's conversion into the "new Soviet man." Mentors such as Mac, Mikhail, and Sasha function to persuade him—and, over his shoulder, the reader—of the superiority of Soviet socialism, but the principal vehicle for conveying Andy's internal alteration is his relinquishment of the consumerist Elsie for the Bolshevik Natasha. As Page herself subsequently noted, "The main story of *Moscow Yankee* . . . is the relationship between Andy and Natasha," which culminates at the concert where Andy "hears the huge stage orchestra playing music he knows—Dvořák's 'Going Home'" (Baker 188). The central problem in this plot-line is Andy's responsibility to Elsie; its resolution is his decision to break with her and remain in Moscow. This guiding narrative thread is accompanied by a subplot about production in which the principal conflict is between the proponents of socialist efficiency (Boardman, Sasha, Mikhail) and the advocates of capitalist profiteering (Crampton, Katia Boudnikova, Alex Turin). The subplot reaches its climax with the thwarting of Alex's attempt to sabotage Red Star. The two plots are entwined throughout, but especially at the moment of narrative closure: Andy's decision to remain in Moscow has both a personal component—his discovery of the ideal mate with whom to share his awakened class consciousness—and a more broadly social one—his commitment to building a society in which the Cramptons and Boudnikovas will no longer be able to threaten the fledgling socialist state.

If we carefully scrutinize the narrative movement of these plot-lines, however, we note that they are not so much synthesized as juxtaposed. The suspense and vicarious satisfaction involved in each are transferred to the other, but at the expense of actually solving the main problem each has posed. In the love-plot, the dilemma Andy confronts when Elsie announces that she is coming to Moscow derives from his sense of responsibility to his Detroit fiancée. After all, she has not had the privilege of living as a "Moscow Yankee" and cannot therefore be blamed for her false consciousness. Significantly, however, Andy ends up with his Russian beloved without ever having to confront his responsibility to Elsie: when one of his Detroit buddies writes to inform him that Elsie has been unfaithful, he is simply let off the hook. As the *New York Herald-Tribune* reviewer complained, Andy is "never forced to face a vital emotional . . . issue. . . . His way is made too soft for him" (Marsh 20). The reader tends not to notice this narrative opportunism, however, in the flurry surrounding the attempted destruction of Red Star. While the subplot ostensibly functions to politicize Andy's decision to remain in Moscow, it depoliticizes the issue of sexual responsibility. The excitement of the chase compounds the love-plot's suspense but deflects attention from its central issue by conflating the perfidious Elsie with the traitorous Alex.

At the same time, the love-plot depoliticizes the production subplot. The villains in the subplot have been of two kinds: advocates of capitalist-style management (Pankrevich, Crampton) who constitute an internal enemy, and saboteurs of socialist construction (Turin, Boudnikova) who, with their international connections, constitute an external enemy. At the moment of narrative climax, the enemy is wholly externalized: the demonic Alex Turin becomes a synecdoche for all that threatens the nascent workers' state. Because of the strong emotional satisfaction accompanying Andy's reconciliation with Natasha, however, the reader tends not to notice that Mac's and Vasiliev's plan for "more and better output" may not be so different from the policies advocated by Pankrevich and Crampton. Just as Elsie's infidelity displaces any blame for Andy's straying affections, the sabotage attempt displaces accountability for egalitarian socialist construction from the organizers of production. Finding the perfect mate ideologically coincides with the proposition that socialism entails technique plus enthusiasm. The "pink sunset" ending, for which the *New Masses* reviewer faulted Page (Field 26), derives in no small part from the text's mismatch of an individual-centered narrative form with the task of representing the complex and contradictory realities of socialist construction.

Upon analysis of how *Moscow Yankee* positions the reader—to assume certain values, to desire certain outcomes—we discover, in short, that the bildungsroman functions to slough over important social and political contradictions. Before we reach the formalistic conclusion that the bildungsroman genre is the *cause* of *Moscow Yankee*'s rhetorical opportunism, however, we should note that the sites of depoliticization in the novel's plot coincide with the very areas in which, on the level of explicit political discourse, the novel also manifests gaps and evasions—namely, with regard to the "woman question" and the doctrine of productive forces determinism. Elsie is an inappropriate mate for Andy because, as it emerges, she is a narcissistic and manipulative female who would not have benefitted from the Moscow experience in any case. Sexist stereotyping thus conjoins with the pressures of the bildungsroman's romantic plot-line to guarantee that the hero will end up with the "right" woman. Similarly, the subplot's facile displacement of reactionary politics onto the evil White Russians is enabled not only by the primacy of the hero's quest for meaningful selfhood but also by the text's portrayal of the contradiction between top-down control and proletarian empowerment as a nonantagonistic one. The inherited ideological pressure of generic politics is felt most strongly at those places where the text's doctrinal politics contain the heaviest bourgeois residue.

To point up *Moscow Yankee*'s entrapment within bourgeois narrative conventions and its complicity with bourgeois ideology is not, however, to conclude that the novel in any sense "fails" to convey an exhilarating picture of revolutionary possibility. It is all too easy for those of us living in the 1990s to look back on 1930s literary radicals like Page as being hopelessly enmeshed in a naïve, realist epistemology and hopelessly enamored of an authoritarian utopia doomed to tragic defeat.

Actually, I believe, reading *Moscow Yankee* justifies quite the opposite conclusion. As a novel, *Moscow Yankee* demonstrates the considerable flexibility of the bildungsroman as a carrier of radical politics. The focus on Andy's conversion to socialism involves the reader as vicarious partisan. As Rebecca Pitts noted in a review of *Moscow Yankee,* "The book's excitement comes . . . from your sense of looking through Andy's eyes . . . ; you wonder whether he will join the *udarniks* and marry Natasha or go back to Detroit and his American ideals. And with his final acceptance of new friends and new values comes a thrill of participation" (146). Moreover, in proposing that the mate who furnishes Andy's "reward" is a Bolshevik factory worker who instructs him in the ways of socialism, and that Andy's reconciliation with the social order—his "going home" —entails uprooting from Detroit and settling in the Moscow of the First Five-Year Plan, *Moscow Yankee* to a significant degree subverts narrative conventions routinely mobilized to support a bourgeois worldview. It is only when the text explores issues to which it cannot offer persuasively revolutionary answers that it becomes overwhelmed by the ideological inheritance of its encoded generic politics. Both practitioners and readers of radical fiction should realize that there is a good deal of life still left in the bildungsroman: we need not entirely reinvent the literary wheel.

Moreover, as a document of 1930s political radicalism, *Moscow Yankee* reveals the enormous energy and creativity that were released when working people committed themselves to the construction of a society they felt to be their own. Even if the text indicates some of the reasons why control of this society was to slip from their hands, it testifies that ordinary people are more than capable of organizing themselves with humanity, efficiency, and intelligence. Page's characters—and their real-life referents—are part of our heritage. If we are able to learn from their achievements as well as their failures, the project to which they committed themselves is very much part of a history still to be made.

NOTES

1. Page continued to write into old age, primarily publishing short stories and journalism. A novel, *With Sun in Our Blood,* was published in 1950 and reissued under the title *Daughter of the Hills* in 1986. She also wrote a number of children's books.

2. Page's journalism relevant to *Moscow Yankee* includes a 1932 series in the *Daily Worker* and several articles in the magazine *Soviet Russia Today,* on whose editorial board Page served for over two years in the mid-thirties (see the bibliography). For most of these sources, as well as for the vast bulk of my information about the biographical basis of *Moscow Yankee,* I am deep-

ly indebted to Professor Christina Baker, who has shared with me the manuscript of her first-person biography of Page in a manner in keeping with its title, *In a Generous Spirit,* forthcoming from the University of Illinois Press; all references are to the typescript. I wish also to thank Alan Wald and Suzanne Sowinska for editorial and bibliographical suggestions.

3. Page noted in *Soviet Russia Today* that in 1931 there were only four hundred prostitutes in Moscow, out of a population of 3½ million ("The Fallen Woman Rises," 9).

4. For more on women's status in the U.S.S.R., see Page, *Soviet Main Street;* Halle; and Winter. For somewhat different views of the gender politics in 1930s U.S. leftist women's writing, see Foley, especially 213–46; Rabinowitz; Coiner; Lacey; Sowinska; and Rosenfelt. Rabinowitz and Lacey discuss gender and class (and Sowinska also discusses race) in Page's first novel, *Gathering Storm;* Rosenfelt focuses on the gender politics in Page's last novel, *Daughter of the Hills;* Foley covers all three novels. Baker notes that Page excluded from *Moscow Yankee* an episode in the life of Valya Cohen that would have been hard to incorporate into her upbeat tale—namely, Valya's gang rape on a Black Sea beach by a group of anti-Russian Azerbaijanis (192). It is also noteworthy that Valya Cohen was of petit bourgeois rather than peasant origin. She was an accomplished pianist and, with her husband, owned a modest Black Sea dacha (Page, "Your Questions Answered" [Sept. 1935], 21).

5. For Page's experiences with sabotage and spies, see *Soviet Main Street,* 63. For more on politically motivated sabotage in Soviet industry, see Kuznick, 115.

6. For Page's defense of Stalin against the charge of dictatorship, see "Concerning 'Dictators.'" Her concern that "the workers' republic is surrounded by a ring of hostile powers" is articulated in "Your Questions Answered" (March 1935, 14). She later regretted, however, her "unaware[ness] of the other Russia . . . where kulaks were beaten and killed" and her misplaced assumption that the bezprizorni she encountered were war orphans, noting that they must have been "children of the kulaks who were killed or deported" (Baker 172, 176).

7. The historical prototype of Heindrick did not stay in Moscow: "in disgust, he threw his machinist's tools in the Moscow River and left. He had expected Russia to be the land of prom-

ise, and when he didn't find it he returned to the U.S.A. to join the breadlines again" (Baker 189). Sowinska suggests the possibility that Heindrick is based on the Gastonia figure Red Hendricks (letter to author, 14 Feb. 1994).

8. Mikhail here sounds a theme explored by Page in one of her *Soviet Russia Today* pieces—namely, that by the end of the Second Five-Year Plan the U.S.S.R. would attain "the end of exploitation of man by man and the building of a socialist classless society" ("Concerning 'Dictators,'" 15).

9. Page herself, in keeping with the view prevailing among almost all leftists of the time, explicitly defended the institution of unequal wages, arguing that the principle of "from each according to his ability, to each according to his labor" was a necessary principle to follow in the "transitional" period into socialism. She also viewed the multiple chances for upward mobility in Soviet society as proof of its egalitarian nature: "It must always be remarked that opportunities to increase one's skill and qualifications are open to everyone. The unskilled worker of today in Soviet Russia is the skilled worker and engineer of tomorrow" ("Your Questions Answered," [Dec. 1934], 10).

10. For more on the politics of the proletarian bildungsroman, and in particular a discussion of generic and doctrinal politics, see Foley, 321–61. Page claimed to have been influenced by Dos Passos, and she did insert in *Moscow Yankee* some newspaper headlines and songs in a style clearly imitating Dos Passos. Moreover, her adherence to Andy's language in representing his point of view closely resembles Dos Passos's treatment of characters like Joe Williams and Charley Anderson in *U.S.A.* Page worked within the mode of the bildungsroman, however, and did not disperse her narrative into the collective, kaleidoscopic form associated with Dos Passos.

BIBLIOGRAPHY

SELECTED WORKS BY MYRA PAGE

"Author's Field Day." *New Masses* 12 (3 July 1934): 31–32.
"Concerning 'Dictators.'" *Soviet Russia Today* (hereafter *SRT*) 4 (January 1935): 15.
Daughter of the Hills. New York: Feminist Press, 1986. Original-

ly published as *With Sun in Our Blood*. New York: Citadel Press, 1950.

Explorer of Sound: Michael Pupin. New York: J. Messner, 1964.

"The Fallen Woman Rises." *SRT* 3 (March 1934): 9.

Gathering Storm: A Story of the Black Belt. New York: International, 1932.

"A Gift for a Child." *SRT* 4 (December 1935): 13.

"In the Worker's Capital." *Daily Worker,* 10 November 1931: 4.

Interview. Oral History of the American Left. Tapes 1 and 2. Tamiment Library, New York University.

Letter to Granville Hicks, 7 April 1934, box 48, Granville Hicks Papers, Arents Library, Syracuse University.

The Little Giant of Schenectady. New York: Aladdin, 1956.

Moscow Yankee. New York: G. P. Putnam's Sons, 1935.

"Protection on the Job." *SRT* 4 (March 1935): 14.

"Socialism and the Individual." *SRT* 4 (May 1935): 15.

Southern Cotton Mills and Labor. With an Introduction by Bill Dunne. New York: Workers Library, 1929.

Soviet Main Street. Moscow and Leningrad: Co-op Publishing Society of Foreign Workers in the U.S.S.R., 1933.

"Vacations for Everybody." *SRT* 6 (June 1936): 21.

"Who Rules the Soviet Union?" *SRT* 4 (November 1935): 31, 63.

"Who's Behind the Five Year Plans?" *SRT* 4 (February 1935): 15.

"Women Heroes of Socialist Construction." *Daily Worker,* 16 April 1932: 4.

"Your Questions Answered." *SRT* 3 (December 1934): 15.

"Your Questions Answered." *SRT* 4 (March 1935): 14.

"Your Questions Answered." *SRT* 4 (April 1935): 14.

"Your Questions Answered." *SRT* 4 (September 1935): 21.

"Your Questions Answered." *SRT* 4 (October 1935): 16.

REVIEWS OF *MOSCOW YANKEE*

Cournos, John. "Americans in Russia." *New York Times Book Review,* 28 April 1935: 20.

Field, Alice Withrow. "Soviet Tempo in an American Novel." *New Masses* 15 (7 July 1935): 26.

Marsh, Fred T. Review of *Moscow Yankee. New York Herald-Tribune Books,* 7 April 1935: 20.

Pitts, Rebecca. "Worker in a New World." *New Republic* 83 (12 June 1935): 146.

Seaver, Edwin. Review of *Moscow Yankee. SRT,* 4 (November 1935): 34, 63.

OTHER SOURCES

Baker, Christina. *In a Generous Spirit: A First-Person Biography of Myra Page.* (Urbana: University of Illinois Press, forthcoming).

Bettelheim, Charles. *Class Struggles in the U.S.S.R.* Trans. Brian Pearce. Vol 1. London: Monthly Review, 1976.

Coiner, Constance. "Literature of Resistance: The Intersection of Feminism and the Communist Left in Meridel Le Sueur and Tillie Olsen." In *Left Politics and the Literary Profession.* Ed. Lennard J. Davis and Bella Mirabella. New York: Columbia University Press, 1990. 162–85.

Foley, Barbara. *Radical Representations: Politics and Form in U.S. Proletarian Fiction, 1929–1941.* Durham: Duke University Press, 1993.

Frederickson, Mary. "Myra Page: Daughter of the South, Worker for Change." *Southern Changes* 5 (January-February 1983): 10–15.

Halle, Fannina. *Women in Soviet Russia.* Trans. Margaret M. Green. New York: E. P. Dutton, 1938.

Kuznick, Peter J. *Beyond the Laboratory: Scientists as Political Activists in 1930s America.* Chicago: University of Chicago Press, 1987.

Lacey, Candida Ann. "Engendering Conflict: American Women and the Making of a Proletarian Fiction." Ph.D. dissertation. University of Sussex, 1986.

Rabinowitz, Paula. *Labor and Desire: Women's Revolutionary Fiction in Depression America.* Chapel Hill: University of North Carolina Press, 1991.

Rosenfelt, Deborah. "Afterword." In Myra Page, *Daughter of the Hills.* New York: Feminist Press, 1986. 247–68.

Sowinska, Suzanne. "American Women Writers and the Radical Agenda, 1925–1940." Ph.D. dissertation. University of Washington, 1992.

Winter, Ella. *Red Virtue: Human Relations in the New Russia.* New York: Harcourt, Brace, 1933.

MOSCOW YANKEE

A glossary of Russian terms appears on pages 291–92.

1

ROLLICKING, headstrong, the express was charging with its unwilling passenger Frank Anderson between two worlds. With heavy weariness his body sagged toward his neighbor, drooping motionless over the table-prop by the window. A Berlin frau, he'd noted, marcelled to the ears.

Christ, what a train! Jumbled images, spotted red, green and purple, jazzed crazily past his weighted eyelids. His head, slipping free from his body, wobbled foolishly from side to side, keeping time with the click-click of the narrow-gauge tracks.

Her hair reminded him of straw, golden yellow. Virginia haystacks he'd helped gather as a boy. Crinkled mounds he'd got the devil for whooping down.

No man could keep his self-respect with his head careening around like a tailless kite. What if Elsie could see him. Poor little kid, where would she ... Ouch! Another lurch like that and he'd snap his fool neck.

Funny how damn cold it was, and only August. The train was close and dark as hell. An icy chill crept up his legs and licked stubbornly at his spine. If only there was a place to stretch out! Some system to these trains, cooping six and eight in a box! Riding freights was a cinch to this. Guess he wasn't going to care much for Europe.

This sure'd toss the press out of his trousers. Some wash-out. He had to show up for his new job looking like a million.

The woman signaled a move-over with a smart wiggle of her hips westward. He shifted his angle once more toward his other neighbor. With a neat twist his head slipped free altogether. He was back in the Detroit tram, sunk in the fadeout following night shift on the belt. Worn out, relieved as hell to be on the line again. No more hanging around employment offices for him. Sure, back in Detroit. Back to the time before Henry gave him the air. Damn lucky. Now he and Elsie could begin saving up again. This time, he'd . . .

What's that smell? Honeysuckle! And him barely as high as Uncle Jem's knee, sitting next to the buckboard of the old buggy. Jogging along the road to all-day meeting. Dodging Old Pete's tail as he swished flies, fighting for dear life to keep his eyes open. Uncle Jem tickling him, sliding the whip down his collar. Spitting 'baccy at the dusty mulberry bushes. Gidyapping Pete. Joshing. "Ain't sleepy, Andy?" And him teasing for a chance at the reins.

Good Uncle Jem, shoving him back comfortable, head on his knee. Rousing him in time to behold them whirling up in style to the side of the churchyard, buggy clattering. Already Miss Yancey'd be wheezing on the organ *From Whom All Blessings Flow*. Folks hanging back about going inside. Bowing, passing the glad hand. Inquiring in hushed tones how the haying was going, had they seen the new fashions in Sears Roebuck catalogue, and what city gal was that Slim Brown was sporting? In the graveyard behind the church black-veiled figures were wandering in and out, placing flowers, weeding.

Over all the scent of honeysuckle. Sweet. Kinda sad too. Sighing, his head slipped lower. Funny. Uncle Jem's knees had gone soft. Sweet, that . . .

A rough elbow sent him upright. For crying out loud! "Gee, lady. Honest, I didn't mean—" Hell, she couldn't savvy a word of English. Damn crab. As if he'd flopped on her on purpose. His eyes glared screw drivers through the broad back she turned on him. Sappy goof.

He sat rigid, staring. That jolt had scattered icicles all over his body. What time was it? Swell chance to lamp a watchface in this light. Must be all of eight bells. Let's see, that'd make it nine P.M. in the States. What'd Elsie be doing? Moping around the house, writing him a letter? Catfish, more likely she'd be off to a show with another fellow.

He felt mean. Nasty mess, human beings. Look 'em over. Off-guard, at close range. That fellow across the aisle, sprawling, toes out, puffy fingers spread on his beer jug of a stomach. Snoring even—like he was flopped on one of these feather beds that'd nearly smothered him, in the hamburger capital. Kind of a guy that looked rubbed down in olive oil. Polished off with one of those buffers Elsie used to shine up her nails. From what he and his pals could savvy of the fellow's queer jargon, the man was representing a German machine construction firm, on his way to get orders in Moscow. This was his third trip. No, of course he didn't approve of their way of running things. Still, this was no time to be squeamish. Pigs was pigs, and orders orders.

Must be a hick firm, the Detroiter observed contemptuously, that sent its reps third-class. Or it might be the depression. Depression. Steer clear of that, big boy. Prosperity's around the corner. Say, sweetie, pass the bananas.

Businessman. High-class suit he had on. Well, once he had gone in for salesmanship, too. Slinging the bull might be a quicker way of getting that little house Elsie had set her heart on. What the hell! Putting over High Pressure Garters, advancing on the suckers under the slogan which ran in big letters across the firm paper, ALL AMERICA WITH ITS SOCKS UP! Peddling trick umbrellas, World Encyclopædia, Waterbury's-Got-Something-On-Everybody, French in 20 Evenings, Soap and That Skin They Love to Touch, Fire insurance, life insurance, disability insurance. Aw, what the hell! After all, he had some sense of humor. Now if it had been whizbangs or motors. *There* was something to get hot over. But to stick 'em up for garters!

Besides what about Elsie, with him on the road? So back to his six a day at Ford's, shelling out for evening schools, watching his chance to get ahead. Kidding his cutie, kidding himself. Letting things ride.

The Detroiter felt for a light. What big feet that bum had. Looked too damn comfortable. He'd enjoy planting a cool one on those broad slats. He had never liked squareheads anyway. His straw-boss Mike Feldman had been a square-head. Swear you blue in the face, yelling "Step On It! Get 'Em Out!" And when he'd got the can, had Mike so much as said...He could've been an old wrench they were tossing on the scrap heap. Him not yet thirty, going strong, when they...Can it, no use griping. Each fellow for himself, and devil take the hindmost. He'd had the bad break, and Jeez didn't he have company. Half of Detroit.

Well, you had to take it and like it. Crack down or crack out.

And some day things would take a turn. In the meantime ...He fingered the bills in his pocket. Rubles. He and his pals had picked them up in Berlin, ten to a dollar. Not bad. Took Americans to put it over.

Wonder what it was going to be like, where they were heading? Suppose you couldn't believe half you read in the papers.

Guess Morse and the other fellows were hitting it off in the next bunk? He'd have a look. Had to have somebody to talk to. Stumbling over the sleepers, he managed to place a neat one against Beer Jug's exposed shins. Cheered by his swearing, he pulled the door to, blinking at the lights in the corridor. Not a soul stirring.

Morse's door was locked. No answer to his knock. Lucky devils. In there, a regular sawmill. Turning, he flattened his nose against the windowpane. Out there was Poland or Germany. He could barely make out plains, spotted with huts, crouching desolate. Two o'clock his watch said. Three more hours to daylight.

Three hours. Rotten company his thoughts made. Funny world it'd turned out to be. Or was it him? Maybe Elsie was right, he was going off the deep end. Crap, all a fellow wanted was a chance to do his stuff, get ahead. *Life, Liberty and the Pursuit of*...horse-radish! Or was it him?

With one shoulder humped forward, the traveler peered into the galloping void. His egg-shaped blond head reached to the top of the window-sill, one finger rubbed a cheek bone as if bothered with an insatiable itch. The tense line

6

between his wide-set eyes, which were of a peculiar blue, grew deeper as his sandy brows gradually lifted in angry bewilderment. This wasn't the customary *You-telling-me!* or *atta-girl!* look behind which he faced the world.

This toss-up that had happened to him, he hadn't got used to it yet. His bearings were shot. No, by God, they weren't.

If Elsie had only come along. From the gliding plains her clear beauty shone back at him. Poor little kid! After all, maybe it had been harder on her than anybody. She'd broken down, clung hard to him, when he left. Made him promise to come back soon, saying she'd wait. If she'd only been willing to risk it, come along.

That last evening she'd worn his favorite dress. Blue and shiny. He had wanted to take the street car out by the river, where they used to park, when he still had the Ford. She said it wasn't practical. Too far, chilly and all. Maybe it was crazy. Like his . . .

He fingered a smooth tiny object in his coat pocket. He had carried it with him since a boy. Elsie had kidded him about it, called him a hick, until he'd salted it away. Crap. Maybe he was. But he'd sooner pawn his shirt.

When he felt low or tied up inside, this little partner worked magic. Let loose all those things he had no words for. Things that since a boy had welled up in him when he saw brown fields catch fire from the sunset or dogwood come out in the spring.

Elsie said it'd be better if he took up some modern instrument like the saxophone or pipe organ. Those organ babies at the movies pulled big money. Then there'd be something to it. But that thing! She wrinkled her pretty nose in genuine scorn.

She was a smart one, his girl. Always saw the practical side of things. Always planning, urging him on. A guy needed a girl like that. From a slant at her angel-face you'd never guess what an appetite the kid had for good times and swell clothes. Clever, the way she had of making an eight-ninety-five look right off Fifth Avenue. In her imitation fur coat from Gemberg's, snug hat cocked over one eye-brow, she was the berries. Yet this didn't satisfy her. Not Elsie. She wanted the real thing. Tone, high class, his girl. One reason he'd fallen for her.

Poor little kid. When would he be able to get her that eight hundred bucks stunner she had spotted in Shermer's? Well, if that was all he had to worry about....

Kinda silly some of their arguments, looked at from this distance. Like that time she had wanted him to turn in the roadster, not yet paid for, for a Buick sedan. Imagine that hairy square-head, spotting him running around in a rival company's car!

Then, that time he had found her laying it on thick to the other girls at the office. Trying to pass him off as a bond salesman. He'd wondered why it was she had never let him come by the office for her. Only on his off days when he was shined up, hat, gloves, his best suit on. Work days she made him park two blocks off. He'd passed up her lame duck reasons, laughed off her sniffing at the oil-grease smell that clung to him in spite of all the soap and hot water. Until that doll-baby typist had spilt the beans.

It sure made him sore. Jeez, maybe he didn't have a white-collar job and got his hands greasy. Ashamed of him, was she? He was no common laborer, but an A-1 mechanic, pulling his six a day. She could take it or leave it. But nix on that bond salesman stuff.

Wasn't he going to night school mainly to please her? Missing out two dates a week, digging into their savings, just to get on? It sure made him sore.

She had cried down his collar, asked him to forget it, that Dumb Dora had mixed things up. Wasn't he her Sweetie? And she had let him love her up more than usual.

She had wanted him to take up law but he had told her technical stuff like engineering was more in his line. Men knew better about such things. After six years at night school, cramming those law books, suppose he did get by the state exams. It took pull and capital to get on as a lawyer. Look at what had happened to Fred Murphy. Cool-

8

ing his heels in an empty office, piling up rent, waiting for customers. Until he'd had a lucky break. Got himself married to that shyster's daughter and in on the pickings from the bootleg and divorce business.

Elsie's Old Man had about as much connections as a chickenwire with the Bell Telephone. Some ways, Elsie wasn't so practical.

Getting a bit lighter outside. Every station they passed even at this hour had its *Polizei* on the platforms. Queer cut to their uniforms. Neat little gardens around the houses. Whitewash looked fresh. Guess it was still Germany.

Jeez, they'd had some sweet times together, parked along the river. Before he'd had to cash in on the car. Elsie was no cold one. But careful, always. A nice girl, proper ideas and all that. They'd lie close together on the back seat and talk in whispers. She'd plan out each room's furnishings, he only half listening, lacing his fingers through her hair until she told him to mind out crazy, you're ruining my wave that cost two bits and he'd tell her he was going to dress her in seal and diamonds, the way a girl her style deserved. Guess he had piled it on heavy. But did she fall for it! Sweet bug.

Elsie was a smart one, you had to hand it to her. Sometimes parked by the river her sweetness'd go over him so, he'd near lose his senses. Not Elsie. She'd always break away before. Them going together steady close to two years, and not once. Though one time she nearly. Kinda wish she had. Then maybe she'd have to give in and marry him. Not keep putting off, "Big boy, wait. Wait until..."

Until. He knew. Until he'd been promoted, got the little house and a cold thousand salted away in the First National. Well, they had waited.

Jeez, for all her sweetness she knew how to drive a bargain and stick by it. Elsie was a planner. Even before the Big Bust he had begun worrying, seeing them getting close to a stalemate. Not only law took capital and pull. This preparatory course he was taking meant a couple of years longer. After that, even if they put off marrying indefinitely, sunk all their savings into his going at this school business full-time, earned his keep evenings—with all the best breaks it would be close to eight years before he finished. And then?

Nope. Chances were, with luck and another fiver on the belt, he might get to be a straw-boss, like Feldman. Speeding up the line, hated like hell for it. Drawing ten bucks. This would never satisfy Elsie. Up-street she was. He had to admire her for it.

Still. Engineer hell. So long as things were going pretty, he'd done his share of kidding. Besides who knew? Hadn't Ford started out in a small way? Elsie argued. Well, Elsie was smart. In some ways, though, not too smart. After all she was a girl. It was okay, a fellow had to feel himself the master. He would never let himself in for being bossed around the way Elsie's Dad was. Poor worm, letting the Old Woman walk right over him.

He had never liked the Old Woman. That old saying like-mother-like-daughter gave him the willies. He had put up with her, though, for Elsie's sake. Even brought her Week-end Chocolates when he came over for Sunday dinner.

Elsie had been square. Never thrown him over, as many girls might when things went hooey. Stuck by him though she had her chances to do better. She had changed some, cooling off those last months, when he'd had no jack even for movies or a dance at the Savoy. They had had to sit home in the parlor. He had felt like a beggar. Him who had always stood treat, been the one to fork out for good times. Now, on the rocks. Dropping in on friends accidentally around mealtime. Bumming loans he had no way of paying back.

He had made up his mind. Before he hit the breadline he'd join the Army.

The Old Woman had stared through him, hinted broadly. He'd swear her shriveled breasts were marked with dollar signs. Throwing up to him how Elsie had turned down swell chances, and couldn't he work in the insurance line.... Puking old hag! Not his fault was it? He had no mortgage on Ford's or General Motors jobs.

It was her work, bringing that Hal Mortimer over for dinner. Nearly sunk him when he dropped in offhand that Thursday, and found that fish sitting in his old place. Was Elsie's face red! It was all an accident, she'd explained behind the hall door, the only time honest and Ma had thought it good policy with Mister Mortimer head of her department and all, he had come by and Ma had asked him only what could she do really and this was the first and only time honest, and if her Big Time would snap out of it, behave decent—after Mister Mortimer had gone she would stay on with Andy in the parlor and you know ...

The first lines of reddish amber fired the horizon, dimming Elsie's image. He blinked. Crap, a little jazz would go great now. Wish the boys would snap out of it. They'd start the old Vic, make things lively. He shook his watch, listened to make sure it had not stopped on him. Longest bulleyed night he'd ever spent.

Queer, riding along this way, hour after hour. Usually he liked it. Gave him a sense of, well, you know. Kinda footloose, free. Going places, doing things. Ready for any kind of adventure. Now, he hated it.

He, Frank Anderson, better known as Andy, was being torn up by the roots. Hurled from one half the world to the other. How could he like it?

He slipped his hand into his pocket and drew out his old reliable. Breathing softly, sliding his feet in rhythm, he began a lively croon picked up from his Mammy. She said she had heard the colored folks sing it when she was a little girl down among the 'baccy leaves.

> *When I was young I had to wait*
> *On Marsa's table 'n pass the plate;*
> *Fill up his bottle when he got dry*
> *And brush away that blue tail fly.*
>
> *Jim crack corn, I doan care, doan care,*
> *Jim crack corn, I doan care, doan care,*
> *Jim crack corn, I doan care,*
> *For Marsa's gone away!*

His shuffling feet drove away the cold. Taking in his breath, he wheezed

> *I got the blues*
> *I got the bl-u-es*
> *Those dog-gone sun-day bl-u-es*

You telling me? Oh honey . . .

When a door opened down the corridor he did not notice. There was something about those dark firs. He drew plaintive notes from the keys between his lips.

> *Oh meet me tonight on the mountain*
> *Oh meet me when the moon's at the full*
> *And I will tell you my story*
> *The saddest story that ever—*

What was that? Deftly he slipped the instrument in his side pocket. Old Hothead, by crap. Well, he was better'n nobody. He grinned warmly at the little fellow shuffling forward in his house-slippers. "Say, you get up before breakfast, don't you?"

Gustav Heindrick ran a hand over his hair, which rose in sandy clouds from his low forehead, adding at least half a foot to his scant height. Andy suspected him of wearing it straightup in the old rah-rah fashion for just this purpose. Unruly stuff it was, needed a bit of Stay-Put. Heindrick had a nervous way of playing with his watch chain, clipping his finger nails.

"Who could sleep in that bread-box?" he retorted. "Didn't I hear some music or something, when I came out? You were whistling, or what?"

Andy gave an incredulous shrug. "Who me? Your brains are cloud-hopping."

"Nothing of the kind!" Heindrick straightened his collar. "I'm not like some people. Soon as I get up my wits are about me." He looked out of the window. "Who could sleep? My boy, I'm too excited. This is going to be a great day. You can't imagine!"

The Detroiter studied his ruddy, set features. A queer one. Still believed in Santy. "More bedtime stories?" he teased. "Go ahead, warm me up. Though I admit I'd rather have a beer or coffee."

"My boy, just the thing! I'll get my little woman and thermos bottle. We'll have some hot tea with a bit of brandy in it." With a broad wink he clattered off. He knew Anderson's type. One of those fair-weather tow-headed Americans you saw on the billboards. Well-slung, trim set of a T-square to his shoulders. Sure, he knew the type. Hard muscles, clear skin and eyes. But a light-weight. Cocky. Always wisecracking. Ignoramus who thought Karl Marx one of the famous vaudeville brothers, and Lenin came from Ireland. Time this Hundred-Percenter got some education. That was where he and his little woman came in.

Sure, Freda would get up any morning to do a bit of propaganda.

Gustav Heindrick considered himself a born agitator, a professional revolutionist whom hard-fisted necessity had chained to his bench. A skilled craftsman, he had learned his trade in the Old Country long before the machine had taken all the art from the industry. Before he was out of short pants he was in the Union and in the Social Democratic Party. On May First he marched with his father near the head of the parade. When the war broke he had migrated to America to escape the draft. Yes, he had been a rebel all his life. He had begun, his friends said, by protesting the quality of his mother's milk. On the boat coming over he had tried to organize a protest against the bad food until those black mountains rolling under the ship had laid him low. Thereupon he poured his protests upon the heedless sea.

Along the crown of his head ran a jagged white line. Heindrick's wife had pointed it out to Andy with proud solemnity. "Look! See what those Jersey Cossacks did to my man! Just for demanding help for the poor unemployed."

Heindrick had worked steadily all of his seventeen years in the States. Yes, he had worked hard and confined his agitation to outside the shop. He and Freda bought a little house with a garden, gave generously of their earnings to the movement and always had some comrade or organizer getting free lodging out at their place. Their evenings were crowded with meetings of some fraternal order, mutual benefit society, the union or radical gathering. They read revolutionary classics, shook their heads over these dumb American workers, and almost despaired of the time when there would be Socialism in the United States. More than a year since the crisis started! Those Henry Dubbs driven to breadlines. Still no outbreaks! The Heindricks couldn't understand it. Americans were dumb.

Their white hope was Soviet Russia. Here in the States maybe they were nothing. After seventeen years, still foreigners. Hunkies.

But in Russia *their* kind were the cream of the earth. There all worries ended, everybody was equal with fine things for all. With a group of like-minded friends around his hearty table consuming beer and those delicious doughnuts that only his Freda knew how to make, Gus would wax eloquent until Freda told him he had real poetry in his soul.

When some disgruntled engineer who had returned from Russia came to Newark to lecture, Freda thrilled at the power in her husband's voice as Gus rose and denounced him from the audience.

Ach, the Heindricks sighed, only to go to that country! Finally their chance had come, although hardly in the way they had planned it. During a mine strike, Gus had housed a West Virginia miner brought to him by a comrade. Another Sacco-Vanzetti case. Apprehended, the Heindricks were faced with deportation, or worse. Returned to that fascist butcher! Never! They had made arrangements. Russia needed skilled workmen. They had sold their home, contributed heavily from their savings to the movement they were leaving forever, and rejoicing, set sail once more for a Land of Promise.

Several times on the trip across the Atlantic Gus had risen from his bunk to go below with his wife to make sure their trunks were safe. They had two big ones and a small steamer crammed tight. Afterwards his head swam more awful than ever, but his beaming wife soothed it with alcohol. Did he remember, she asked, if they'd put the electric toaster in for certain and that lamp shade from Stern's? And did he think the plugs would fit Russian connections, else how would they use their iron, coffee percolator and all. If her china broke she'd never get over it—especially those with the bluebirds on it. How carefully she had wrapped it, each piece separate . . .

Soon Heindrick reappeared in the corridor, bringing with him a lidded basket and his sleepy-eyed wife. With quick pats over her hair and person she gave Andy a limp handshake, dived into the basket. Such a nicelooker he was. Her boy Gilbert could have been so tall, if he had lived.

Munching bologna sandwiches washed down with steaming tea, Andy listened politely to their warm recital. The woman and he were seated on corridor stools and Gus leaned against the doorframe between. The sun was a red orange pushing above the dark green. Gradually the train awoke, stumbled into the corridor.

At the first sound of the Victrola the Detroiter gave one of his quick smiles. "See you later, friends. Thanks for a swell feed." The Heindricks exchanged disappointed glances.

Through the long morning the Americans danced up and down the corridors. Passengers gathered to watch and some joined in. One record finished, another went on. For lack of girls they jigged singly or in male pairs. "Come on, Morse," Andy seized his redheaded friend. "Be my tootsie." With his reddish lashes and florid skin Morse looked as though he was always in a stew. He dared Andy to take on the Berlin frau. Oh, yeah? He wasn't cuckoo.

Between times they gazed out over the strange bleak landscape. Miserable huts with thatched roofs, miles on end of beanvines and spuds. Must be a poor country, Poland. At every station they raced out on the platform to look things over. Surrounded by eager tradesmen they played the Big Americans, tried to figure prices and were glad of Hothead's help in changing over a dollar bill into that cock-eyed currency.

Of course the old boy knew nothing about the rubles.

15

They had only let Abrams that New York journalist in on that. Pretty slick, eh?

Everywhere officers in gray uniforms walked stiffly about. "Whew!" Morse said. "You'd think a war was on or something." Where'd Poland get all the money? Hothead treated all around to tea with brandy, even the dark-eyed chaps who stood off to themselves watching the dancing but not talking to anybody. They seemed afraid of something, Andy thought, and relieved when the officials had finished his once-over of passports.

Freda refilled cups and glasses. "Before midnight," her husband said and lifted his glass high, "we shall be in our true Fatherland."

Smacking his lips, putting down his glass, Morse looked him up and down. "Say, where do you get that stuff? I ain't giving up the Stars and Stripes so quick, myself. But maybe as a foreigner—"

Heindrick's cheeks quivered. "Oh, you! You—"

"Don't mind him," Tim Martin broke in. "Sure, Morse is a dyed-in-the-wool, a red-hater. But me, I'm open-minded." His tone was smooth, convincing. His near-sighted light eyes and round face looked innocence itself. Heindrick's hesitation vanished. Wowy, Andy whispered, now the fun's started. Shame to take such easy money. As Tim drew him on, Andy's face muscles ached from the effort to hold them steady. Twice overcome, he ran coughing up the aisle after a drink. Once he got going, Tim was a scream. Trouble was, he oftener got the dumps.

Finally Tim rose, made Gus a sweeping bow. "Really, I think you're a wonder. Honest, no kidding. Best show I've seen since Loews'. Come on boys, shell out!" Hilarious, the crowd threw cigarettes, nickels and confetti into the cap as he passed them. "Say, is his face red!"

"And oh baby, there's free love in Russia!" Morse did the hooche-kooche. "Mae West and plenty! Well boys, take a tip. I got my prophylactic kit ready." He turned on the Vic and hooked his arms through Andy's and Tim's. "Here's a song and dance dedicated to old Hothead, who, so help me,

16

believes in fairies." Side-stepping, they chanted with the record:

> In the Blue Rock Candy Mountains
> Where the hens lay soft-boiled eggs
> And the bluebird sings
> By the lemonade springs
> And the cops have wooden legs.

Afterwards, Andy felt sorry for the little fellow. "Don't mind our kidding," he told him. Heindrick refused to answer. "Honest, you know how it is—"

Fact was, Hothead was a nice chap. Only his eyes were full of moonbeams, his feet off the ground. Well . . .

During the afternoon Andy set about remaking friends with the Heindricks, then seized an opportunity to stretch out full length on a train bench while people were in the corridor. When he woke it was already dark. Evenings came quick in this part of the world. Pounced down on you like. Andy shivered, brushed down his trousers, went for company. Goddam this train.

They were nearing the Polish-Russian frontier. Excitement grew contagious. Andy's nerves were quivering, irritated by Hothead's high humor. Karl Abrams, the New York journalist, stood by the window, debating. Should he report those rubles? His sympathies and connections he had not revealed to those chaps. But those bootleg rubles. Well, these boys didn't know the difference. Besides, they didn't have much. Better let them get away with it than start them off on the wrong foot. He knew his Yanks. It was those speculators peddling sneak-thief rubles that he'd like to get his hands on.

Last stop before the border. Polish guards, their smart sabers clicking, made their final trip through the compartments. Morse gave a sailor's hitch to his trousers. "Well, what next?" he demanded. "Where do we go from here?"

Others in khaki, red stars on their caps, came on the train and asked for passports. Andy stared. Were they? He saw the Heindricks seize them by both hands, Freda openly weeping. One of the Italians gave a cheer and quickly kissed an embarrassed guard on both cheeks. As the train moved forward and passed under an archway, many passengers began singing some tune in several languages. Damn fanatics, Andy thought. He looked the guards over. Not bad lookers. No long whiskers or clicking sabers about them. Just ordinary guys.

At the little Russian station every one filed out for baggage inspection. "Where're your fireworks and brassband?" Morse jibed Hothead. Too excited to mind him, Gus busied himself shaking hands all around and running back and forth to make sure their trunks were safe.

One was missing! "Those Polish blackguards!" Freda declared she wouldn't leave the station until it was found. The examiner of Andy's bags was a woman wearing a heavy jacket with a red scarf wound about her head. Going through in a methodical manner, at sight of his tool kit she straightened up, offered her hand. Morse's phonograph records caused a sensation. To his amazement they wrote a list of them into his passport. Through an interpreter they explained that when he left the country he must take them with him. No importing of bourgeois jazz into Russia.

"I'll be stewed for a prune!" Morse pushed back his hat. "Andy, can you beat it! Imagine a country without jazz. Same as no ham and eggs. What'd they do for music anyway, Sousa's band?"

The engine sounded a warning whistle. "All aboard, fellows!" Lugging their bags, Morse and the others made for the train. The Heindricks, who were speaking in broken German to a group of examiners, refused to move. A second whistle. Lingering passengers hurried. Gus and Freda would not budge. Only as the train got under way they scurried up the steps, panting, protesting. "Oh, my percolator, toaster, iron . . . all—all. Those scoundrels!"

Andy found four bunks to a compartment with mattresses and sheets! Would he hit that hay! But what kind of business was this? Housed in his section were a Russian couple, a whiskered farmer and his wife, and the yellow-haired Berlin frau! He ducked out into Morse's compartment.

There an old woman and her daughter were parked sedately in the lower berths. What kind of a system was this? Cross-eyed Mama! Streamlines, and how! The frozen Diana from Berlin like every one else seemed to be taking things for granted. Well, it was okay with him. He waited in the hall with the other man while the women prepared to turn in. The fellow drew out a bag of seedy tobacco, tore off a newspaper and made a light. He offered Andy one. The American fished out a real light over which the stranger bowed and ah-ed. Hotdiggety, travel and see Europe!

Down the hall, two New England spinsters were hysterically insisting on a place to themselves. Of all things! Their roommates were Red Army men. Heaven alone knew what might happen, in the dead of night. They should never have come on this trip, if they had dreamed. For ladies to sleep— they had read all about those villains. The fact that the men had books and were reading was only a clever ruse.

The Russians had much trouble in understanding what it was they wanted. Finally, with suppressed smiles the Armymen arranged to exchange places with the old woman and her daughter from Morse's section. Mollified, the New Englanders reëntered their compartment. Virtue for another night was secure.

When the farmer disappeared into Number 5 Andy ventured after him. In the berth under his own he spied a mop of marcelled hair against the pillow. He swung up to his bunk. In the darkness he shed his outer clothes, stopping long enough to crease his trousers before sounding off.

The train was an iron cradle rocking him across the sleeping plains.

Screams and angry voices sent him bolt upright. Thieves! In the darkness he sprang down and seized hold of a dark figure by the window. Women's screams grew louder. The thief squirmed madly and fought to get free. Andy's grip tightened. "Turn on the light!" he called. Bastard!

"*Ach! mein Gott! Lass mich los!*"

The Russian farmer scrambled for the switch. "*Chom delaet?*" he shouted hoarsely.

"The light! The light!" Andy gasped. "I got him!"

The current was off. From the next compartment people came running. The door flew open. Hearing the tumult, the spinsters drew the sheets tighter under their chins. Why had they ever ventured to leave Beacon Hill?

"A light! A light!" A trainman's lamp pierced the darkness of compartment 5.

Andy's arms dropped and he fell back astonished. Standing before him, rubbing her sore shoulders, the German woman pulled her wrapper closer about her and burst into tears. Confusion, babble in many languages. The American threw his topcoat over his underwear. Sniffling loudly, the frau rescued her coat from the floor, where it had slid during the night. She had thought some robber. *Ach mein Gott!* The strong wind of laughter swept down the corridor. Morse's guffaws sounded above the rest. "Say bo, some like 'em tough!"

As the car resettled for the night Andy in his bunk swore under his breath. From beneath came muffled sounds of exasperated crying. That woman was a hoodoo. If ever he saw her in Moscow, he'd sure beat it the other way.

Some one was jamming his ribs. "Fall out, cow's tail!" Tim peered up at him. "In three hours we'll be in Moscow."

The sun struck Andy full in the eye. Sitting up, he fastened his garters. *All America With Its Socks Up.* Oh, yeah?

Tim clucked. "Have we got old Hothead going! Asking where the angels and gold streets are hiding. In the village we just passed we saw some fellows in straw boots, and a drunk. Say, Hothead's mug is a knockout!"

Andy twisted his necktie. "What's it like outside?"

"What you expect? Come on, shake a leg. Your frau baby is eating breakfast in the diner. Going to join her?" Tim's good-natured face was creased in a perpetual smirk. Shouting, he plucked a long yellow hair from Andy's coat-sleeve. The Detroiter pushed by into the corridor.

Through the open window the sun streamed in, warming the breeze that slowly fanned away his drowsiness. A vapid yellow heat seethed above the green fields and low time-worn villages. But always behind the dinginess some huge brick structure was rising. The train raced on. Christ, what a lot of building!

The hallway was full of people talking Russian, German, Italian, the devil knew what. This language business was going to be a mess.

2

THE shop was a thundering vortex of machines and men. Through its wide skylights the pale yellow sky of a Russian winter drifted down through cranes and pulleys and finally settled on the swinging arms of workmen and the broad asphalt aisles. Amid the hoarse and strident clamor the persistent click-click of the steel-tread conveyor rhythmically dominated all. Nothing could halt it: everything was timed and controlled by its speed.

The grotesque skeletons which it picked up and carried were transformed under the eye into coherent high-geared mammoths; gawky ribbed metal sprouted axles, steering gears, gray fenders. Black shiny motors and double-tread tires descended on endless revolving lines from floors overhead: bodies and hoods smelling of fresh paint swung down and fastened into place. Dozens of blue caps and women's red kerchiefs moved along the line, climbed over the monsters, pried into their vitals, fitting screwing mastering the vast mechanism of assembling two-and-a-half ton trucks.

The main line was the beautiful quivering nerve center of this automobile plant, its hard final testing ground, where all the synchronized movements of countless parts of metal rubber lumber engines and men were registered, and every misfire courted disaster. Don Bas, the Urals and far-off Archangel had contributed to this giant twenty-thousand-handed labor. Tashkent and Vladivostok were waiting for these trucks. Day and night through the shed's unceasing labor, the steel-tread conveyor thrust hungrily forward.

Andy was part of it. Back on the belt. Reversing chassis, tightening frames. To get there he had gone a third of the way round the globe. Christ, stiffs like him had to go where work was. This was his second day. His shirt was clawing his damp chest and sides as he raced to keep up. This Moscow conveyor was slower than Ford's, but work a heluva lot different. A man's job was less specialized and the whole line shorter. A guy didn't keep plastering one dizzy nut on, a thousand times over, but did several jobs in one. Right at first, it proved a fast one. Trucks anyway were a new one on him.

Anxious, his eyes on the menacing succession of chassis bearing down on him, his haste tripped him. Damn it, his fingers were all thumbs. Pretending to need a screw or nut, he glanced back repeatedly, keeping a sharp lookout for the straw-boss. Eight months off the line, had he lost his speed? His shoulder muscles were flabby, aching. And no mistaking it, the fellows next down the line were slowing up, waiting. He was misfiring, a good three minutes behind. Jackass, step on it. Giv'er the works.

Sasha Smenov watched his workmate drop nuts, look furtively behind him, and was more concerned than amused. What was bothering the Amerikanets? As they swung the next frame over, he called reassuringly, *"Nichevo, tovarisch, nichevo!"* and much more that was so much Greek to Andy. The way the guy said it, sounded like a song and dance. Who cared? The numbskull had even offered him a smoke.

If only he had a drink of water or the lunch bell'd sound! Where was that wrench? Right by him only a minute ago. Sasha was using the automatic. Down the line he could see the sprayers, masks up, waiting. He had to have that wrench. Damn it, he was close to holding the whole line! Stooping, he searched along the conveyor. He had to have that wrench, and quick. Him, an A-1 mechanic—

"Seen my wrench?" he demanded of his partner.

"Shto?" Sasha questioned.

"Wrench!" Andy shouted more loudly. The fellow must be deaf. "Wrench! Wrench!"

Under his shock of brown hair, Sasha's broad countenance grew troubled. *"Tovarisch, ne ponimayu." Ne ponimayu*—the American had reason to know that lingo —no savvy. He darted again under the conveyor. Jeez, he'd be jamming the whole works. Down the line another car ran off the belt. No savvy, horse manure.

Crossing over to his side, Sasha followed his movements. *"Shto?"* He tapped the Amerikanets on the arm.

Crouched on his knees, Andy gestured "wrench—wrench." He made semi-circles with his wrist and forefingers. Fool, for two cents he'd spit in his eye.

"Ah—" Sasha's eyes crinkled. *"Gou-ech-ni kluch!"* He leapt over to his side of the belt and handed his partner his own. Andy worked feverishly. What if . . . Sasha, his half of the chassis completed, climbed back to take up the search. *"Nichevo!"* he repeated, *"nichevo!"* Andy glowered. For two cents he'd. . . . Turning around for a nut he had dropped, he encountered the solid bulk of Mikhail. His muscles refused to move. The straw-boss! Now they'd catch it. Holding the line!

Mikhail nodded, said something in a booming voice and pulled Sasha by the shoulder. *"Vot! Vot!"* Grinning, the lad held out the lost tool. Hastily Andy exchanged wrenches with him, his face burning, and turned back to his work. Was his workmate a plain fool? The Big Cheese catching them with the goods, and that kid laughing. Hyena!

He could hear the two talking behind him and the old man chuckle. As Sasha vaulted back to his place, Andy felt a hand on his shoulder. Instinctively he braced himself, rammed his ears against the bawling-out due him. Old Mike Feldman all over again, yelling "Hell! Step on it! What's the matter withya? By Jesus, plenty outside wanting your place!" Maybe he'd get the air right off.

The steady line of motors and tires circled in dark arcs overhead. The hand pressed his shoulder firmly. *"Nichevo, tovarisch,"* the strange words came quietly. Mikhail stared at him over his glasses. His eyes were a light hazel and peered straight through Andy. *"Ti haroshee rabochee."* The words burned into the Detroiter's memory. What the hell did they mean? So help me, what kind of a calldown was this?

Mikhail turned away. Andy stepped on it. He'd show 'em he knew how to get 'em out. Jumping spark plugs! If he could only talk to them, explain how it was. He had the jimmies today. By tomorrow he'd be into the gait swell. "Just gimme a chance. Honest! After I've come all this way, you gotta."

What a break. What a lousy break.

The chassis was done. Sasha and he prepared to swing the next.

At last he dared make an excuse for glancing back. The straw-boss was gone!

A close call, that one. And what'd those phoney words mean? Perhaps after work he had to report to the office. Perhaps... Springing on the support, he fastened the chassis. Lotta things here he couldn't savvy. Like those sprayers, openly reading the paper. Fast workers, those two young bulls kept a jump ahead of the conveyor. But pull a news sheet out of your jeans in a Detroit shop and you'd head straight for the bughouse.

Where Morse worked everybody smoked during work-hours. All through the plant, except around motors. Queer, nobody quit when the bossman showed up. And did some of the hicks spit on the floor! Blew their noses right through their thumbs and forefingers. Acted like they had the run of the place, didn't care who knew it. Damn breezy.

Well, this was Russia.

What a jitter that strawboss'd given him. Aw, forget it.

Something else he wasn't sure of, who were the spotters? Worse rats than a boss. This guy Sasha now seemed a good sort, but who could tell? Awful chummy with that foreman. Matter of fact, that Big Potato Mikhail acted chummy with everybody. Even shook hands when he first came round, checking up. Kinda goofy, the whole thing.

Well, as for him, he'd watch his step. Old Mike wasn't gonna catch him rawhanded again. He was no bootlicker.

He'd mind his job, let the boss mind his. Foremen were the devil, popping up when you never expected them. Always at the wrong time. But he was no baby at this game. Not him.

Why was there so many greenhands about the shop? Piles of scrap? As for the girls, that was a new wrinkle on the belt which he liked. Not bad looking janes. Had to make time. And what was all this red bunting strung along the walls, full of cockeyed lettering? Fellows bunching after work, yesterday, arguing, holding some kind of meeting? Imagine that in Detroit!

The whole thing was beyond him. Like that big shindig they'd pulled off for them last week, when their bunch had first come in. Music, speeches, handshaking and how! Russians were strong on that. They'd made all twenty of them sit on the stage. Guys in Moscow seemed to have a big idea of a stiff just because he knew how to turn out autos. Sure wish Elsie could've seen it. Him playing Jimmie Walker and Lindbergh in one. And had Morse and Tim lapped it up. Looked kinda foolish too, facing all that mob. Hothead, the old fool, had stood up and shot off his jaw and got choked up, and everybody gave him a big hand. He would.

Only thing familiar about this damn place was the stinks in the toilet, and the line of gray trucks rumbling off the conveyor. Those trucks gave him a substantial feeling. Three meals a day and once more on his own.

If he could just hold on.

The assembly slowed down, came to a full halt. *"Obed!"* his workmate sang out. Andy knew what that meant: grub. Packing their tools, they made for the washroom, then hurried to the restaurant to be among the first served. Tim and Morse joined them. "Ah, *tovarisch*—comrades!" Sasha's roughened palm swung out and then down, closing in on theirs with a resounding smack.

The girl passed steaming bowls of soup down the long table. *"Borscht!"* Sasha repeated. He had decided to teach these Amerikantsi some Russian. Then they'd feel more at home. And from them he'd learn English. Real International, they'd be. They seemed kinda stiff now, but it'd wear off quick. Think of it, honest-to-god American workers, from Ford's. Later, when they could really talk together, how many questions he had to ask. Many things he'd tell his new comrades, show them.

For him it was a new experience, deep, exciting.

Three years previous to this, Sasha Smenov had never been out of his native township. Harvesting, sowing, village gatherings, rounded out his existence. Moscow was red star beckoning two hundred miles to the northeast. When the first tractors had come to the state farm nearby, with half the village he had treked over to see. There and then he determined to run one. Some day.... Then, the *Comsomolets* had come to little Alexandrovska to recruit extra workers for the factory. Sasha had scrawled his name, high on the list. To learn to make autos!

Once it had been enough to drive one, cutting deep straight furrows in the rich black earth. Enough no longer. He must make them. He'd be no peasant, but a worker, wear leather boots, city clothes, go to the kino whenever he fancied. His old mother wept, made the sign of the cross over him. On top of the basket she packed for his journey she placed their best goose. Joyfully Sasha had smoothed its white feathers. To behold Moscow, the Red Square, and where Our Lenin was lying! Ride streetcars, visit the Kremlin, become educated, a full-fledged proletarian.

All the way to the Capital that obstinate goose had acted as contrary as an old bull. He had thought rashly of letting her out of the window. Was it worth it, to arrive in Moscow with country written all over him! Peasant thrift was too much for him and he forced the silly fowl lower into his basket. The nasty bird had chosen the tram, of all places, to begin squawking. He could cheerfully have wrung its long neck. When some passenger offered him five roubles for it, Sasha took him up quickly. Good riddance! He should have bargained though for seven or eight.

Well, he had done all he had planned, and more. Completed the factory school, discarded his bark shoes long ago.

His horizons were pushing out. To make autos, that also was insufficient. He was going to invent improvements. Secretly he was working on something. Now these Amerikanets were good mechanics. He could learn a lot from them, once they could talk together. And they'd find he knew a thing or two. They'd see. Needn't think Russians were know-nothings, backward. Nothing of the kind.

He wouldn't mind giving Europe, America, the East, the once over. Not to stay, of course, only to see for himself. Lend them a hand, any time they were ready to start their October.

He smiled across at Andy and his companions with frank admiration. Yes, America was a cultured country. It was good these tovarische had come to help with the *Pyatiletka*.

But how was it, with so many unemployed and things half as bad there as you heard, that these Amerikantsi always came in such fine clothes? He fingered his own coarse jacket.

"*Borscht poanglishky?*" he queried.

"Soup." Andy glumly surveyed the beets spuds and carrot moons swimming in a sea of red. "Goulash," Tim insisted. Morse dipped rapidly. "Slum gullion," he announced. The tidal line in the soup bowls dropped noisily. Fifteen hundred, Andy estimated, served at one swoop. The whole twenty-two thousand at the plant eating twice during the course of a day. Quite a system, but why not cafeteria? Would go faster, fewer waits.

Sasha held up a dark crust. *Kleb! Bread,* the Americans said. The game bored them, Morse turned to the other Americans. "What's new?"

"I damn near got the gate this morning." Andy stopped short, looking across at his workmate. "Tell you later." Morse and Tim exchanged glances. They were on.

Soup bowls stacked, the tables grew restless for their next course. "No hurry," Morse grumbled. "Not if they pass out that godawful mush—*Kasha*—like yesterday. Already I puke at it. Twelve months, Jesus!"

As they left the dining room, the Russian linked his arms

through theirs and began humming the *Internationale* under his breath. Signing with elbows and head for them to join in, he stopped short. Well, now! Could it be? They looked blank. Could it be, they didn't know! But surely.... What the devil! His mind grappled. Ignorant as that! Impossible!

He began again—

> *'Tis the final conflict—*
> *Let each stand in his place—*

Morse made a toothpick from a matchend. This cabbage had a way of winding around your molars. With a squint at the Russian humming so loud, he signaled across to his friend "What's griping this nut?"

The four pairs of grease-splotched workboots crunched the brittle gravel in hard strokes. Desperately, fighting off the blues, Sasha's voice rolled on. Passersby hailed them, raced by. The Russian gave a characteristic hump to his thick shoulders. Well, and so they couldn't talk together, and they couldn't sing. That's how it was. So then ... well, what under the sun *could* they do?

He eyed Morse, who was smirking broadly. That cabbage! No, comrade.

Above the hard rust-colored brick sheds running for long blocks on either side of them there hovered the biting lift of late fall. Abruptly a fluttering shadow spread over them. Andy paused to look up. A flock of sparrows on the wing.

Sasha also looked. With a broad smile he began to explain. Those birds were heading for the Volga. For fall grain and heavy pickings. Devil's mother! His workmate was staring at him, not savvying a word! He raised his voice. Louder, louder. Suddenly they both laughed, broke off.

Well, what could they do together?

Tim left them at the next turn and headed for the construction job at the far end of the yard. A new carshed was being added. The job? Couldn't say he liked it. As builders these guys were hams. And he felt like a deat and dumb mute. He needed some one to jaw with. Well, solong.

At the far end of the conveyor, Sasha drew Andy over to where Ned Folson was making ready to run a finished truck into the yard. He asked the Negro, "Find out what's troubling him, will you? Anything wrong, or what?" Ned translated. Andy shook his head. Nope. Everything jake.

Puzzled, Sasha screwed his cap to one side. Cagey, was he? For what?

Andy hesitated. One thing he'd like to know. What was the dope on that *nichevo* line?

Ned's white teeth flashed against his dark skin. "The hardest-worked term in the whole Russian lingo. Like *tovarisch*—comrade, the word you learn right off. *Nichevo* can mean a dozen things. Take it easy, who cares, okay, nothing doing—and well, *nichevo* is *nichevo!* You'll pick it up in no time yourself."

"I see. One thing more." Feigning indifference, Andy repeated the phrase Mikhail had used on him. "Somebody's been feeding you a hot one," Ned countered. *"Rabochee,* that's what you are—a worker." As for whether he was *haroshee,* good ... Well, they'd see!

"Anyway," he added with the largess of an oldtimer, "any little thing I can do to help you out, say the word. Know how it is, was new once myself." Springing into his truck he threw on the engine. He wasn't too anxious though. These white fellows from the States gave him a pain. Thought themselves the cat's pajamas.

Andy hurried up the belt to his place, wanting to shout. Wait till he told the boys. He'd spread it on thick. Calldown, me eye! What was that strawboss' game, kidding like that? Riding him for a fall? What was that word—*nichevo!*

Mounting the frame, he signaled Sasha. "Atta boy! Let'er have it." He'd show 'em, by Jesus. Watch me, baby. Over she goes!

His mate laughed happily. *"Atta buoy!"* he imitated, and

swung with all his easy might. The conveyor rolled on, a monstrous earthworm eating the circular miles.

"Atta buoy!" What could they do together? Sasha whistled. This, and how!

3

FROM beneath her crooked elbows slipped one pudgy
moist bag, then another. Mary Boardman gave a vexed
cry. As she made frantic reaches after them, she jammed her
neighbors in their backs and tightly padded sides. With
a ripping squeak a third parcel scattered its fat little balls
of plaid-wrapped bonbons over muddy boots and seasoned
rubbers and rolled into the secure dark niches of the
crowded homebound car. Andy retrieved her bags and made
valiant efforts to rescue the candies. He bobbed down beneath overcoats and umbrellas, snatched blindly at trouser
legs and full skirts in his quest for the sweets. Crap, this
was worse than grubbing for spuds!

With a grateful flash the woman moved over to make
room for him on the seat beside her. How splendid of him.
She just had to have those candies for her party tonight.
He was also an American, wasn't he? And working where?
At *Red Star!* What a coincidence. Yes, her husband was
employed there, in the tool and die shop. Very responsible
position. No doubt Mr. Anderson had heard of him: Boardman was the name, Philip Boardman. Andy nodded. Of
course. (Why in hell should he? Only in town a week.
Did this dame think her mealticket was the whole works!)
Oh, of course. Everybody at *Red Star* knew Mr. Boardman.

Mary transferred a generous share of her bundles to his
lap and chatted with half-whimsical plaintiveness, as the
car spun along, of the trials of a day's shopping in Moscow.
(Should she, she pondered, invite this young man over for
one of her parties? Often an extra was sorely needed, and

he seemed quite eligible. Perhaps she had better have Phil make inquiries, look him up.) At their car stop, when he offered to help carry her bundles as far as her door, she agreed readily. How good he was. With this icy pavement and everything she could never manage, alone. Did he mind if she took his arm? And in what department was he employed at *Red Star?* On the assembly? But...Why, he was an engineer, of course. A mechanic? Why, she had been sure. She had thought...How, how interesting.

Andy felt her hand loosening under his coatsleeve, the subtle change in her manner. Damn her, for a copper he'd unload her bundles on her right here in the street. What'd she think, anyway? And him with his stomach like a raw persimmon.... To her random attempts at conversation over the last blocks he replied in gruff monosyllables. Talk about your democracy. The thing reminded him uncomfortably of the bond salesman affair with Elsie. He gave over her parcels without a word, walked off. Last time he'd rustle bundles for her, nervy snob.

Exhausted, and for some unaccountable reason annoyed with herself, Mary thrust her packages into the soapy hands of Nura, the housemaid, or *nanya* as the Russians called them, and dropped on the divan. Had she cleaned every room thoroughly, put Junior to bed? Oh, the woman was too stupid about English, she had to pantomime everything for her!

Satisfied by Nura's emphatic nods and affirmative *da-da,* Mary disappeared into the darkened bedroom, a half hour before Phil and dinner were due. If only this headache would wear off. The swish-swish of Nura's final scrubbing of the kitchen brought a pleasant drowsiness. Life in this country was puzzling. To think how near she had come to inviting that laborer for one of her parties.

Philip Boardman, blowing rapidly from his run up the stairs, flipped the moist snow from his leather jacket. With methodical exactness he removed his muffled cap and dripping goloshes and thrust them toward the quick-fingered Nura, absentmindedly brushed his wife's slim cheek, and rinsed his hands for his waiting meal. "Well, how's Mary?

Had a good day?" He slipped into his seat, gliding a blunt hand over his thinning hair, as his eyes darted about, head immobile.

"You're late," she reminded him coldly. "After you'd promised."

So that was why the soup was cold? Thrusting out his elbow, he pushed back his left cuff. Six o'clock. On the dot, as usual. What's wrong? Mary knew he was never late, a principle of his.

"What's wrong! Where's your memory!" Her voice caught. The Cramptons, Stuarts and MacKensies coming over for the evening, she and the *nanya* spending all day rushing to prepare for them, and he— What's up! Hadn't he agreed that morning for supper three-quarters of an hour early? Mary moved about the room, long fingers dusting this, fingering that. It was so difficult, here, to give a satisfying party. Choices at the store were limited, yet she had wanted it to be original, different. It had been free day at the nursery and Junior had been his worst. Three solid hours she had spent in that blessed store, because she couldn't trust N'ura to buy the right candies, or anything else. The girl was a peasant, with impossible tastes. Of course, it wasn't as though she could talk with her. The servant problem here was the worst yet.

What a day she had spent, queuing up for sweets, cream, wine and voucher checks. And the streetcars! Unspeakable. Really, she had never imagined such a country. How was it that Philip didn't have one of *Red Star's* cars at his disposal, like the Cramptons? Surely he was important enough, wasn't he? Even if he wasn't chief engineer for the whole die shop, like Henry Crampton.

Frowning, Philip reached for his second dish. So Crampton was coming over. He loathed that man, all the more because he had to keep up the appearances of friendship. Friendship for that windbag! Well, one had to be practical, sociable, and all the rest of it. Mary was right. Hadn't they learned the social game, those years in General Motors? It had helped, too, to push him ahead. But Crampton! Something about that man, with manners more rubbed down than his shiny patentleathers, something that ... well, he, Boardman was as good a Yankee as any, but the way that four-flusher was putting over the Great American Bluff! Pretending he knew dies. Why, he had forgotten long ago more than Crampton had ever been able to get through his skull.

Mary's swarm of words suddenly dropped to the floor. "Philip! You're not listening!"

"Of course I am. What an idea!"

"You are not! Tell me what I was talking about, then."

"Oh, the crowd at the store—"

"So that's the last you heard. What a man!" Studying him, her mood shifted. Was something worrying him? He looked harried, worn out.

He pushed back his chair and motioned Nura to clear the table. "Nothing. I am okay. Where're the kids?"

She brought his houseslippers. Joe and Bella had been sent over to the Hoskins for the evening, Junior was in bed. "Five minutes for a smoke, dear, before you begin getting ready. Philip, you are working too hard at the plant. Your mind is there, even when you aren't. No use denying it, I can tell. What on earth is getting into you?" She sighed. Work that absorbed you! she almost envied him.

"Whoop-pee!" Door banging wide, a round human ball threw itself headlong into the man's lap. "Junior!" Mary made a reach for him as Nura hurried out from the kitchen. Head burrowed in his father's stomach, pajamaed legs flying, Junior prepared for vigorous defense. "Pop! Don't let 'em!"

Laughing, Philip warded off the attackers. "Only five minutes, Mary. That's a go, son?" He settled the small figure astride his knees. The boy's cheeks were flushed with first sleep, his lips moist, eyes wide, dancing. His father trotted him on his knees. "What's my boy been doing today?"

Junior dimpled. "Shooting Bujwah!"

"What!" Philip shot a startled glance at his wife.

"It's that day nursery," she retorted quickly. "I am sorry

we ever agreed to send him. What ideas he picks up from those children! It's terrible." Next term he would be old enough, thank heaven, to enter the English school.

"But I don't wanta," Junior protested. "I like where I am. Every day we get eats and play games. I learn the kids CowboynIndians, and they learn me shooting Bujwahn-Whites." He caught hold of the foot of each pajama leg and pulled them at arm's length.

"Junior, stop that!" Mary caught his hands. They were too big for him as it was. Phil must let Nura put him to bed. He was sleepy, and cross, and there was still so much to do, before the Cramptons and others came over.

Her husband turned the child's face toward him. "Just a minute, Mary." Playing Cowboy and Indians, that was one thing. But this other.... "Junior, these Bujwah, who might they be?"

Sliding between his father's knees and thrusting out his stomach, Junior strutted back and forth. "That's a Bujwah! A fat guy, what hurts poor folks like my Pop and me. Bing! Bing! Kill the Whites!"

Philip lifted him again to his knees. "But we're not poor folks."

Junior was puzzled. "You ain't a Bujwah?"

Mary, who was straightening a picture, whirled around. "Junior, how many times has Mother told you not to say ain't! *Are not*. Really, Phil, I don't believe we'll ever be able to raise the child properly in this country." Her head ached so and she did want the party to be a success, and Junior ought to be asleep, really.

"Are not, Mamma," Junior caroled obediently as he aimed a tight fist at his father's vest. "You ain't no Bujwah, Pop. Where's your fat belly?" At his father's quick guffaw he jumped back, trying to outlaugh him. "Mamma, did you hear what I said, Mamma?"

Boardman felt his side. "My boy, that's a good one." Crampton now: if you put that test to him! Bloated squash! His son was a realist. Fine, it would take him a long way. He placed Junior across his shoulder, and started for the darkened bedroom. Mary hastened from the bathroom, her curling-tongs swinging. "Phil, you're not going to take a nap! You have to shave and everything. Really, you're too aggravating."

Already he was dozing off, his son against his shoulder. "Call me in twenty minutes, Mary. I'm a fast dresser."

Carefully she put in her waves, smeared cold cream, prepared her make-up. In Detroit she would have gone to a beauty parlor, but here one learned to do many things for herself. It was better than waiting in one of those slow *orchereds* at the hairdresser's. She leaned closer to the mirror, her brows drawn tightly. Those telltale lines about her mouth and eyes were deepening. Was that why these last months Phil had paid her so little attention? Or could it be ... ? She pushed the thought aside. No, he had never been that kind. Yet, in this country, anything might happen. And to her he meant—and he knew it. A man had so much, a woman so little. It wasn't fair. Heavens, her skin! This awful diet was ruining it.

Seven-thirty! Philip yawned. No mistaking the phosphorus watch hands glowing in the darkness. Mary must have forgotten him. Cautiously he slipped away from Junior, shoes in hand, and crept into the living room. In the bathroom his wife was singing "For Your Black Eyes." By quick work, he could just make it. He reached for his scarf and jacket, shuffled Russian-fashion into his rubbers. Nura pulled his arm, gesturing emphatically in all directions. "You have forgotten?" she asked him, in Russian.

"No, no!" His vocabulary failed him. "Factory. Back soon." When she turned toward the bathroom, he pulled her back. "No! Back soon." Chuckling, he was down the stairs before Mary, Japanese kimono thrown about her, had responded to Nura's insistent knocking.

Outside the blue night closed around him. It was warm, for all its sharpness and fierce blanket of stars. The many-eyed factory glittered against the fresh snow and beckoned silently. He walked briskly, breath cutting his nostrils. Those after-dinner naps always set him up. Never make the grade, otherwise. These Russians are husky, he thought; these Russians, seemingly they can stand anything.

The frozen sidewalk narrowed and curved senselessly. Reconstruction had not yet reached here. Modern apartments gave way to two-story logged structures, typically Russian, with frescoed roofs and gay window framings. A line of boarded carts on wooden runners carrying hay moved slowly down the street. Workmen from the neighborhood and their wives were clearing sidewalks in front of their homes. The women wore dark shawls wound securely about their heads and shoulders, short skirts and navy jackets. As they chipped and scraped the hard ice their voices rang out. Good-natured untroubled people, Boardman thought. Perhaps a trifle heavy. Still, no nerve ends sticking out all over them. Being among them often dissolved his restlessness. He could not comprehend this. Nor them. He felt passion, something deepgoing in these people. Once he had the language better, he would probe into it.

Mary was right: what was getting into him?

Streetcars clanged by, their windowpanes frosted. Passengers had cleared peepholes in order to peer out for their stops. Every car was jammed. Movie crowds. People hung about the cars' rear platforms like hornets to a swinging nest. Dangerous as it was, no regulations and fines could halt it. Work on the new subway was only at its beginning. Well, Philip reminded himself, what could you expect when a metropolis doubled its population in less than a decade?

The guard at the factory gate, a bulky shadow in long goatskin, was shifting his weight from one foot to the other and trying to keep warm. With a brisk nod in his direction, Boardman swung across the plant yard. Would he be in time? If those kids had started in without him! No, they'd wait. Russians always did. One thing they had plenty of: time. Still, it hurt his American reputation for promptness.

It was not his shift, but he couldn't see those youngsters ruin another die. It hurt them as much as it did him. They were ready to come at any hour, if the American *spetz* had a mind to show them something.

In the doorway of the shop he loosened his jacket and rammed his cap into a pocket. At the droning of lathes and the sight of forge fires, his head went up and his step quickened. A setter catching the scent.

He felt in his pocket for his English-Russian dictionary. During the day there was an interpreter whose time was divided between the three foreign specialists working in the die shop. One of Philip's grudges against Crampton was the other's needless monopolizing of her time. It hampered his own work. At times such as this, Boardman had to rely upon himself. She never worked overtime, that girl: not unless there was a pair of silk stockings in it. Sometimes Natasha, one of the turners who was studying English at the Institute, gave him a lift. Nice girl, Natasha. She never got in the way.

Somehow, though, his lads and he always managed to understand one another. Where repeated demonstrations or gestures failed, he resorted to a fast line of swearing. Even though it was in English they immediately came through.

He stepped aside to let an electric handcar rush past. Its driver waved a greasy hand in his direction. "Hi there Meester Boardman!" Myths were growing up about Boardman. This cryptic jumping jack terribly efficient American. . . . What a man! Forever in and out of the shop, always ready to give a fellow a tip. Workmen from other departments were beginning to come to him to ask technical advice. The die men termed him affectionately "our swearing Amerikanets." He was even accumulating a rich vocabulary in Russian.

Boardman passed down a crowded side-aisle. Supplies, stacked up unused, stared reproachfully at him from the corner. Over in the storehouse were many new dies, he knew, also lying unused. By Jove, if he only had some authority! Or if Crampton cared a whoop about anything but his five hundred per. The shop super, a Russian, seemed sunk in a jovial *nichevo* attitude.

When would BRIZ, that department for inventions and suggestions, get around to acting on his rationalization suggestions? So polite they had been, cordial, seemingly impressed, and what have you. Yet they did exactly nothing. Ninnies! But these youngsters. . . .

Just as he had thought, he found Kolya and his companions idling about the waiting press, smoking and arguing over a blueprint in a book spread before them. "Ah, Meester Boardman. You didn't forget, eh?" They shook hands with gusto. The American warmed. Great kids. Real farmers when he had taken hold of them, but quick to catch on. They would make A-1 mechanics, some day.

The die was in place. They had been afraid to lower the press. Last week Kolya and his helper had smashed one. But the *Amerikanets* knew, to a thousandth of a millimeter. Ah, technique! What their country had to master.

Boardman placed a practiced hand on the control levers. Kolya and Alex, crouching flat, turned fascinated gazes upward, toward the swiftly descending press. The engineer worked at high speed. He jumped about, the boys thought, like a quick-limbed panther. At the exact moment, lever wheels reversed quickly and the press, for all its weight, settled softly as a bird on the form below. "Hurrah!" Kolya held out his thumb and sprinkled on imaginary salt with a free hand. "First rate!" Boardman smiled back at the boys happily. They didn't need words, these three. The lads pressed their fingers carefully about the die's edge.

Eight-thirty. Mary Boardman met her arriving guests with forced gayety. What was Philip thinking of to run off! After all, this affair had been arranged for him. What would the others think? "Oh dear Edith Crampton, it was so sweet of you and your husband to come! You know the Stuarts and the Lewises, don't you? Come right in: here, Nura, take their wraps. You won't mind if our living room is a bit crowded, will you? These Russians simply do not know how to build along American lines!"

"Not at all." Edith Crampton surveyed the place. "Really, you have given it quite the New York style, haven't you?" Mary glowed. It was true: the only Russian objects were rugs from Tashkent and a gay-patterned shawl draped over the piano. "My husband?" Mary gave a light shrug. "The rascal has stepped out, for cigarettes or something. What a dream of a dress, Eleanor Stuart! Do tell us the secret, where did you find such a modiste in all Moscow?"

Wordless, her fresh head-shawl pinned neatly and her full moon still glowing from its recent scrubbing under the kitchen faucet, Nura hustled away coats and rubbers, and stole curious glances at the foreign women's costumes and toilets. Whatever made them paint their nails that blood red!

Frederick Lewis took one of the cigarettes Mary offered him. "Have you heard the latest? The Murphys are going back."

"No! Lucky devils!"

"Things ought to pick up in the States, in the Spring." Crampton bit down on the end of his cigar. Yes, Murphy no doubt had saved up a pretty penny. "Say, Mrs. Boardman, what about those decorations over there?" He gestured toward trays of caviar sandwiches and glowing white vodka. "Now that's a Russian touch of which I highly approve!"

Mary laughed. Yes, help themselves, please! Something to warm them, after the frost outside. Where under broad heaven was Phil?! She glanced at the waiting bridge tables. Surely he would return before the Tompkins and MacIntyres arrived! She slipped into the kitchen to whisper in monosyllables to Nura, then returned to her guests and started the Victrola. Maybe a bracer would ease her head.

Eight-fifty. "Meester Boardman, before you go. One short minute?" Kolya held out the blue print. Boardman's vocabulary soon was exhausted. Where was Natasha? He led the way over to her machine.

Nura stamped her foot at the factory gateman: either he must let her through to Meester Boardman, or go himself. He was needed at home. No ordinary matter was it, when his son was ill? She had no pass: what of it? Doubtfully the guard looked about for counsel. Pesky skirt! Get on with her. He had strict orders.

Nine-ten. Henry Crampton looked openly at his watch. "Well, Mrs. Boardman, and what about your husband? With his reputation for being on the dot!" All the guests had arrived: the twelfth place for bridge stood waiting.

Mary's laugh was unsuccessful. "He is impossible really, isn't he? Always at the shop. But I expect him any minute now." Crampton puffed slowly. "One can overdo a good thing." She sensed an undercurrent in his words. Could it be he had a dislike for Philip? He continued, "I make it a point to keep strictly to hours. I expect my men to."

She bit her lip. It would never do to anger her husband's superior, but wouldn't she like to tell him!

Seeing her discomfort, Edith interjected that she and Henry had a scheme for New Year's costumes that they would never guess. Really, it was going to be the hit of the ball. Frederick Lewis was surprised how badly his little joke had gone off, about Boardman perhaps busying himself with that beautiful interpreter, Katerina Boudnikova. Just where had he slipped?

Mary fumbled at a deck of cards. Oh, just wait until she got hold of Phil. With arduous lightness, she rattled on, flattered. Oh dear.... Footsteps! Somewhat shamefaced, Boardman paused in the doorway. Behind him loomed the triumphant figure of Nura. "Hello folks!" he said. "Mary, old timer, awful sorry to be late. Something urgent came up. Be with you in three shakes." He disappeared into the bedroom to reappear, in his bathrobe, clothes over his arm, in a quick dart for the shower. Mary prayed fervently that the Victrola might drown the sounds of his splashing.

Ten-ten. Philip found himself drowsing over the cards. Damn it, he had trumped his partner's ace. That Edith Crampton would never forgive him, empty-headed woman. Mary's sweetness was icy, distant. He'd had just enough of that wine to make him groggy, after a few more, he'd spruce up. It was a relief when tables were finally cleared and cloths spread for refreshments.

By two, the last couple had tripped gayly down the stairs. Philip slipped an arm about his wife. "Old Scout, forgive me this once? We are going to the *Bolshoi* Theatre next free day. I got tickets this afternoon at the plant." Her shoulders were shaking convulsively. Phil was a wretch.

... He didn't care. And she was tired out. Couldn't he take her back home—away from this dreary country?

Sparks from the forge shop shunted along the floor until snuffed out like candles by the wind. Natasha, standing by her lathes, gazed across at their steady shower. Lights overhead threw her figure into bold relief against the whirring machines in the aisle beyond. The brown eyes beneath her red kerchief, always candid, reflected her present troubled mood. Uncle Peter was drinking again. Lazy lout! She glimpsed him as he pottered about his machine. Now he would spoil some work. Her chin set firmly: too firmly, some thought, for one so young. One detail completed, she prepared her machine for the next, then examined her products; for once, exact.

"Natasha!" Her neighbor, Lucia, called over to her. "Lend me your machine rag. Did you hear? A new lot of *Amerikantsi* have come here to work."

"Yes, I know. About twenty." She handed Lucia the cloth. The girl waved it before her. She had seen three of the Americans in the restaurant yesterday, such pretty ones! What a swing to their walk! Didn't Natasha think it would be fun to step out with them?

"Silly!" Natasha retorted.

"You're the silly one," Lucia answered, tossing her yellow head. Soon she came over to the other girl's machine. She was going this free day with their collective to the *Bolshoi?*

Natasha rubbed the side of her machine. "Can't, this time."

"Oh, but they are playing *Red Poppy!*"

"Really?" Natasha sighed. It would be a treat, especially the dance of the sailors and coolies. Softly she hummed the air.

"What will you do?" her friend insisted. "Laundry?"

"Really, Lucia, you're a little goose. Do you think I couldn't put that off! No, I must study. Would you believe it, my brain's fairly swimming with figures from the technicum." Bright, darting fish she must string in ordered lines. But Red Poppy! Why weren't there more hours in the day! And she still had that awful problem to do. But next week, she would go, no matter what.

Eleven o'clock. Giving her lathe a final pat, she joined the crowd that was flowing out of the shop into the crisp blue night.

4

"**N**O use, kid. Gotta see a doc." Andy's disconsolate grin turned on his friend. No telling what godawful thing they'd caught.

Morse was stubborn. Poop on these fakirs. What good'd any Long Whiskers do? Relieve them of twenty berries. (Christ, what a bellyache!) Feed them pink pills, castor oil. Nix on the hooey.

"But I tell you we got something awful. My stomach's a bag of stones."

"And mine-oooh!" Groaning, Morse hugged himself like a bloated Humpty Dumpty with tender concern. Say, he was gonna lay off that vodka stuff. Strongest bootleg he'd ever smacked. He dropped back on the cot. "Jesus, wish I was in the States, don't you?"

"With a job, sure." Andy lowered his voice. "Listen, buddy, I ain't fooling. Honest. We gotta see a doc." His belly, joints, even his head was on fire. Russia was full of goofy Chinese diseases. Mysterious fadeouts. Anything might happen.

His companion drew his knees gently toward his chin. "Aw, pipe down. Easy come, easy go with you, eh? I'm holding on to my jack. Give old Nature a chance. Jumping Jesus! Got some cascarets?"

"What you take me for, a lousy quack?" Furtively Andy scratched his chest. If Morse really knew! He wanted to ask his pal if he too.... He didn't dare.

Even the soup line in Detroit'd be better than dropping off with some hell's blight. All day at work he brooded. What was the disease? Cholera. Knocked 'em off like flies.

He'd fix that chiseler, Morse. Rattle his guts. He remembered pictures of the Black Plague in England given in his grammar school books. Middle Ages. Russia was still like that. Maybe Moscow was in for an epidemic.

The more he brooded over his tale for Morse, the more depressed and convinced he became. His tongue felt swollen, fuzzy.

Sasha tried to cheer him and called *"Nichevo, tovarisch!"* and made funny signals for all the world like some big kid with his fist and hairy forearms. How that jackass could always be in good humor was beyond Andy. It jarred his dark mood. You facing some godawful cavein, and a chap playing monkeyshines with you across the belt. Not fitting. Though, of course, he'd hardly expect the Russian to notice it. Not yet. Not until he grew purple, choking.

At lunchtime the Americans pushed aside their plates. The thermometer in Sasha's eyes dropped. What was up? Sick? Pale around the gills. They must see a doc. Morse caught the last word. "You know he's right." His voice sank. "I'm busting out. On my chest and legs."

His friend started. What color? Kinda purple?

"You telling me! Why?"

"Itchy?" At the other's nod, Andy declared solemnly, "It's the same as mine. Now, you see. I told you."

Morse ran his handkerchief over his wet palms and face. "Oh, you and your lousy toldmes. My head's splitting. Honest to God, what you think we got?"

"The plague." Typhus, or cholera. Came to the same thing. Seeing his pupils expanding, with morose pleasure Andy went the whole hog, repeating all he remembered from Poe's story of the Black Plague and newspaper reports of famine. "They say at the end," he mournfully concluded, "your tongue puffs up and you smother. You go black like from gas or drowning."

Morse glared resentfully. "I caught it off you."

"You didn't either," his friend retorted. "I got it off you. Just because I broke out first ain't no sign. You got the bellyache before me, remember?"

46

"Nothing of the kind! Aw, to hell with it." Morse loosened his belt.

Sasha took them to Ned. "Go with them to the dispensary," he asked, "translate for them."

But his work? The driver felt he couldn't lay off, for the testing department was jammed as it was. Of course if the Yanks needed his help.... Sasha brought Mikhail. While work relief was being arranged, the two Americans slouched against a pile of tires.

Ned led them toward the plant's nearest dispensary. Personally he thought this pair of boobs were running a bluff, their downcast looks cagey. Still, they did look pasty. To Andy's queries about typhus he made short reply. It was a silent trip. Morse was figuring how much they'd be docked; Andy was wondering if they'd ship their bodies back, and how Elsie'd take it. Poor little kid....

In the outer room of the doctor's office several patients were waiting with a queer stolid endurance. One man's jaw, Andy noticed, was bandaged to double size. Toothache. He'd give a new job to swap places. A woman's plaintive monotone drifted about the quiet of the deathly white room. Sickening odors of disinfectant and the nurse moving about bore in on the Americans. Quickly they slumped onto the empty bench. So help me, they were doomed. No doubt this fellow with them was running a big risk. Would Sasha come down with it, and Tim? Had these other guys been bit by the same louse?

Gravely the doctor listened to Ned's relaying of their symptoms and night watches. The kindly gaze fixed on them seemed to be deeply impressed. Morse forgot about fakirs. So help me, here was his judge.

According to instructions they exhibited tongues, gripped thermometers under armpits, balanced on scales, and stripped off their shirts, revealing dark blotches around their waists. While the physician pressed some queer-fangled instrument about their chests and back, they breathed in and out with painful exactness.

This clinched it. He handled them like interesting specimens. Dead men.

Indicating with a swoop of his white linen arm that they might redress, the doctor began covering some cardboard sheets with small characters. He wrote deliberately, reading after each sentence, and saying "tak-tak." The patients awaited his verdict. What a slow ham.

Innumerable questions. Their family name, given name, patronymic. What's that? Americans didn't use their father's given name, also? How curious! Then how was it possible not to confuse people? How to identify this Frank Anderson from any other. He must be Frank Frankovich or Frank Petrovich Anderson. No? Well, *tak-tak*.

Morse glowered. Another minute he'd yank him by his starched shoulders, shake the truth out of him. What difference did it make whether he'd had red measles or whooping cough as a kid, if he was going to pass out tomorrow!

The doctor reversed his file cards and began putting his next question. Ned shifted his feet. He was bored, and restless to get back. When he relayed the query, had they ever had smallpox or typhoid, Andy broke in. "Tell him to cut short the quizzing and come out with it. What've we got?"

Slowly their judge put away his glasses, placed the cards under correct numbers in his file, and wrote out a prescription. Ned listened attentively to all the murmured details of his diagnosis. Suddenly his close-cropped head went back and his quick laughter rattled among the bottles.

"Say, you know what's the matter with you boys? All you got's the plain old-fashioned hives!" Common ailment among foreigners, the doctor commented, when they first came, due to change of climate and diet. Morse gulped, thumped Andy. "See? I told you."

Ned handed them a slip of paper. Take it over there to that window, the plant drugstore, and they'd get their swig of dynamite. He wanted to get back to his trucks.

"And the doc?" Morse asked. That fakir! "When do we fork out for him, and how much?" Andy interrupted. Yes, and what was that hooey he'd said about their getting paid for time out, today and tomorrow?

Still chuckling, Ned made for the stairway. Feature that,

time out for hives! "We got a social insurance system here that covers the doc and everything. Sure, wages besides. But don't you be pulling any tricks, they're wise to that." He knew these guys, be trying some gag in no time. "Say, Andy, your face's going purple!"

"Aw, cut it!"

"Well, so long. And get your paper-wads ready." Ned ran toward his waiting trucks. Suspiciously, Andy and Morse shook the bottle given them. The label was Chinese, but there was no mistaking the taste. Andy gagged, spat out his sample. Morse groaned. "What'd I tell you?" Hell fire and castor oil!

Shaking the bottle like a mastiff, Morse declared, "Andy, so help me, if ever I sign up again for a lousy job like this here, I'm a sonofabitch."

> *Oh when I die*
> *Don't bury me a-tall*

Morse sprawled triangle-fashion on Andy's cot, Tim's bowlegs hung abjectly over the arm of a rocker as hoarse tortured notes rebounded from the walls in piercing succession. "Say, you nuts!" Andy's hands clapped to his ears. "I'd as soon have the damn hives again!"

Slouched by the window, chin on his knees, he watched the children dashing up and down on their skates and bobsleds. He wished these punks would scram. Mulberry clouds of cigarette smoke spiraled about the blue ceiling. Their last packs of Luckies.

Jeez, free days were the worst of all. "Go on, enjoy yourself." He'd try sarcasm. Christ, when was that contest going to end!

Shouting, tripping, the kids were up and at it again, racing like mad. One boy had his skates tied on with rope. Funny ones, kids were. Little Molly Cotton Tails, bundled to the ears. Lot nicer than grownups.

Andy flipped his dead butt to the floor. "How you guess these Russian kids learn this cockeyed lingo so quick?"

Personally he was in favor of one language for the whole world. Be much simpler.

Morse agreed. Sure. One language: English.

At my head and shoes
A bottle of booze

Outside the sun was glimmering; the horizon was banked with mounds of freshly picked cotton. Andy peered up the street. That lousy postman was late. "Say, wailing catfish!"

Abruptly, as children bored with a cranky toy, his friends dropped the ditty and looked about for something else. What day of the week was it, Monday or Tuesday? Saturday, Andy said. Morse scoffed. Catfish, it was Wednesday. Sure, because payday fell on a Saturday this time, and that was four days ago. Tim whistled. Dancing Mamas! Some system where you didn't even know what day it was. This sixday week was a phoney idea. Anyway, he was bored stiff.

Morse gave his fat womanish chest an approving slap. He'd won this song bout, eh, Andy? Five inch expansion to his windbag, by actual measure. If they didn't believe it, and there was some measuring tape about this chicken coop, he'd prove it.

"Ah, you're dizzy!" Tim snapped his fingers. "Five inches, me grandmother." Grimly, eagerly, they seized on the argument. With conviction of an expert on human anatomy Tim declared it impossible for human lungs to expand beyond four inches. Andy supported him, what did Morse think he was, a Schmeling or Gene Tunney! He wagered the average for heavyweights was no more than five.

Just feel, Morse demanded. He placed their hands on each side of his chest, and breathed in until his face reddened with strain. Tim looked blank. Feel anything quiver? Dolefully Andy shook his head. Morse flung them off. A pair of pikers, they were. Hell's bells, how about string! He began rummaging through the wardrobe. Socks collars shirts tossed high.

50

Andy jerked him back. "Say, quit messing my things!" Tim was pulling his suitcase from under the bed. Andy swooped down on him. "Say, where you fellows think you are? In a bawd house?" Leave off, he'd get the string. From the lower shelf he produced some neatly wound twine, tied with a slip knot. What an old maid, the others jibed, you'd think he had some sweetie about the place. Grumbling, Andy restacked his socks and shirts. Crap, it took Morse for a quick one on the sweetie pickup. Not him.

The twine kept slipping, but they stuck at it until they had measured the expanse. For want of a ruler, they used thumbnails as an inch rule. Six, it measured. Tim said a thumbnail equalled a half-inch, Morse said it equalled a full three-quarters. In the midst of their fury, Andy laughed. "Aw, let's can it!" What a free day. Now if he was in Detroit, with these spondulicks in his pocket . . .

Morse thumped on the cot. "And they call this a red town. Dead as a cockroach. Work! work! Construction! Tempo! Technique! Horse manure! And on a free day, what do they offer us?" Jumping up, he stepped gingerly, mimicking a high female treble. "Comrades, tomorrow we shall make an excursion to the Museum of the Revolution . . . Hell! What's that Foreign Section think we are, a bunch of tourists, or school kids? What we need is a coupla bottles of their moonshine, and some redhot mamas."

"Say, put the lid on can't you? Always crabbing." Andy locked his wardrobe, and Tim felt for his pack of cards. Now for some poker. Too late. Andy exhibited his watch face. Time for dinner. And where in hell was that postman anyway!

As they went out Andy asked, "Tim, how's your work going?" His buddy scowled. Like the mischief! Think these Russians knew the building game? As carpenters they were a bunch of shoemakers. Their tools and methods were way behind the times, he could do more in a morning than any three of them.

Ned Folson passed them on the stairs. "Better step on it, boys," he called amiably, "all the tenderloin will be gone." Andy gave an incredulous snort. Oh yeah? With onions and french-fried to boot. He pushed Morse, who was practicing a Charlie Chaplin descent down the stairs. When outside, Tim inquired "Who was that Ace of Spades?" Andy gave a shrug. Just one of the suitcase brigade from Detroit. Used to work, so he claimed, for General Motors. Seemed to have a big pull here.

Tim whistled. "That guy a spetz, with foreign store book, and all? I'll be damned! Cheeky way he has of hailing you like a long lost friend." Morse agreed. He'd never liked niggers himself. Beat the devil how the Russians made up to them. Chinks, dagos, hunkies and white men all mixing as one. What was the big idea?

Search me, Andy said. Over here they got to feel their oats or something. Tim told them it was no use trying to figure it out, the Russians were half-civilized and didn't know no better. Think of that guy in his checked suit and spats passing off as a Big Cheese! Taking a handful of snow, he hardened it between his gloves. Cheer up, the first ten years'd be the hardest. Morse seized him by the back of the collar. "Say, Sour Face, you gimme the jimmies." Ten years! Tim's ball smashed against Andy's cheek, and snow flew fast as they speeded toward the restaurant.

Ned Folson clogged it about his room, practicing up. Good chance that tonight he and his friend Gil would show 'em a few turns. They'd a big evening ahead at the Moscow Artists' Club. He tried his voice

> *Water boy —*
> *Where are you hiding?*

Top shape. Still clogging, he lay out his best suit, fresh shirt. Now just what was it that had gotten that rise out of him, on the stairs? Nothing tangible. But those new guys from the States were all alike. Except Mac. He was in a class to himself.

These last years among the Russians, Ned had nearly forgotten the old swift resentments that would course over him, back home, and rush bitter words to his mouth. Words that often he had to choke back. Yep, forgotten, until he ran up against some hundred percenter. Well, if those guys thought they could pull that whiteman stuff here, they had another guess coming. He for one would enjoy showing 'em how.

Aw, forget it. They'd a big evening on. And he felt pretty good, the way his pal Gil Wilson was getting ahead. When Gil had had his tryout, choosing a passage from "Othello" to deliver, the Russians had thrown their arms about him, their eyes unashamed and wet. Fine people. With deep feelings and not afraid to show them. Not cold, like Anglo-Saxons. More like his own race. Warm, quick to laugh or to weep with you, share with you whatever they had.

He had known Wilson since boyhood days in Memphis, where they had played penny-ante with coca-cola tops and chopped kindling for the white folks, together. Even then Gil had made the gang play Stage 'n Actors. They had dressed up in any old clothes they had been able to find in their Mas' closets. For the Grand Opening Night in the backyard admission had been by pennies, marbles, pins, or what-have-you, and when news circulated about Memphis of a boom in Detroit, their families had made the long trip north. Only he and Wilson knew the ceaseless pinching it had cost their parents to see them through grammar school. Later, he had entered trade school and Wilson's talent came to the attention of a well-to-do member of their race. With this man's aid, his friend had finished at one of the best theatrical institutes in the country. It had proved of no use. On the American stage no big parts were open to Negroes.

Wilson, longing to play "Othello," found himself playing parts of butler or comedian. "Othello"? Why that would mean playing opposite a white girl! See what a furore Charles Gilpin's rumored appearance in it had created. *Emperor Jones* was the topnotch a man could aspire to, if his face happened to be black.

Ned gave a final buff to his patent leathers. Tomorrow morning, even if they had been up to all hours, he would pull Gil out for a run up the Boulevard. He chuckled, remembering the stir their last sprint had caused. Half of the early travelers had stopped to watch the two erect black figures in short trunks, their arms crooked, speeding up the avenue from Salonika to Nikitsky. Ah, these *Amerikantsi,* great ones for sport.

As Andy walked back from the dining room with his companions, the white puffs banked on the horizon were climbing merrily up the blue wickets of the sky. From corniced rooves spilled a steady drip-drip of snow melting under the sun's pale ardor.

Before Andy's eyes ran the mail box, beckoning and taunting. Don't count on it, don't count on it, he kept saying to himself. Mail is slow. Besides, she has a lot to do beside writing you letters. That box has cheated me often and plenty. Surely this time...His hand rattled about the empty tinder. Well, he was not letting on to these suckers, and even joined in their ragging. He thought he'd have a turn up the block, he said, before hitting the hay. Let the bozos snooze away the whole afternoon, if they wanted. As for him.... Their sallies tagged after him, a cur dog at his heels.

He wished he had a dog. Something to pal around with. To talk to, without being afraid of getting the big ha-ha. He was fed up with humans. With things in general. Guess he was plain homesick. For bacon and eggs, a Harold Lloyd movie, and little Elsie to make a fuss over. Poor kid, was she having a rough time of it, too?

The Moscow river was frozen. A man was crossing the ice leading a cart and horse. Andy surveyed the river's winding course. If he followed it far enough, it'd surely bring him into the center of town. He would walk himself dead tired, drop across his cot in a deep sleep. Maybe he'd be late meeting the boys for the Big Show. What of it! People looked padded in their bulging heavy coats. An old woman, bent to the level of the basket over her arm, came toward him. Mumbling to herself, she stopped to peer about, then addressed a rapid flow of words at Andy. As she stood waiting with an expectant leer for his answer, squinting up at him, her face was as wrinkled and season-marked as last

54

year's June apple. Andy stepped to one side. *"Ne ponimayu,"* he chanted the familiar formula. "No savvy."

"Oi Ne ponimaete!" she echoed. Her curious gaze grew fixed and her head bobbed at him as if he were a worm to be plucked in her beak. Quickly he pushed by her, gave a savage jab at the snow. Hundreds of people, not one he could talk to. Signs books newspapers everywhere, not one he could read. Jeez, he'd never thought how it must be for foreigners in the States. He'd had his share too in making fun of their lingo. Folks here were friendly enough to the stranger. Sometimes, like Sasha, they came close to being a nuisance. Still, it was damn hard.

Ne ponimayu—no savvy. The phrase hung on the frost, glanced from the dazzling windowpanes at him. *Ne ponimayu.* Nitwit. Numbskull. Sparkling, lively world. And you! *Ne ponimayu!*

Must be a lot of strangers in Moscow. Anybody would stop you anywhere in this berg to ask questions. Each time he went out some one hailed him. To vary the monotony, he sometimes replied in English. Just to see their startled look, and give 'em as good as they sent. Andy walked on. The streets in this old part of town curved about themselves and sidewalks were barely wide enough for two persons to pass each other. Squatty white houses were mixed in with pancake structures of blue, salmon pink, or dusky yellow. This section, he figured, was being squeezed from both sides, as the town's center pushed out to new communities that had sprung up in the city's outskirts around the factories.

He zigzagged up the streets running from the river, past apple women and booths selling straw flowers and cigarettes. Above crouching structures rose a few modern buildings and countless onion-shaped domes of churches.

Andy had a fancy for these domes. Real eastern they were, judging from pictures he remembered of Turkey and Asia Minor in his geography. Fat strong onions. Often they boasted golden stars on a blue foundation, and all were topped by gilded crosses. Some churches he had passed on earlier ramblings had had a disused appearance. On others he had made out the word "Museum." A group of elderly people were crossing themselves as they passed through a shabby entrance. Could it be? Incredulous, he followed them. A dreary voice boomed against the columns, and lighted tapers glimmered from the altar. He tiptoed out. For crying out loud! A church doing business in Moscow.

Outside, he stopped to decode a street sign. Thumbing his pocket dictionary, he wrestled with the queer letters. What in the devil made the Russians play somersaults with the alphabet! Got a fellow twisted. Now if he could work out some quick system.

Another queue. What were all these people waiting for? Baskets of all sizes bobbed half way down the block. What the! Breadlines. The *Detroit Journal* had been right. He crossed over to join. The queue crept forward by inches. Women stamped their feet, while tongues and heads wagged. Ignoring their protests against his crashing the line, Andy worked his way inside the shop ... This was no bread but a meat line. Customers were queued up before counters and cashier windows. He thought he had never seen such slow-moving clerks.

Every queue he saw, he walked out of his way to inspect. At the next shop, women and a few men were waiting their turn to purchase packages of monstrous dill pickles! Lines, lines all over Moscow. For newspapers, macaroni, ice-skates, confetti. Mostly, for daily bread rations. And not handouts either, but pay-as-you-go.

These Russians had the patience of Job. Why, though, must it take forever to serve the public? Some of those clerks and store managers should get it in the neck. What they needed was an A. and P. system. If he knew the language, he'd propose installing one. Ought to be able to make a swell thing out of it. Go over big.

This cross-eyed language! Maybe after you got the alphabet it came easier. He needed a system. He had learned the capitals of Europe and the line of presidents from Washington to Roosevelt as a schoolboy by putting them into jingles. Why not try it on this? Humming to himself, stopping occasionally to refer to his dictionary, he finished the first couplet.

He had come again to the river. In the distance shone the peaked towers and turret walls of the Kremlin. He leaned on the iron railing running along the bank to scrawl four lines on the back of an envelope. Not bad. Laughing, he began the next. His fingers were so stiffened with cold he could scarcely read his own writing. He walked on, pausing to scratch out, rewrite. Wait till the boys heard this one! A knockout.

At last. Seven letters in three verses. Not bad. He said them over, in a sing-song beat:

> *When you go to Moscow*
> *Leave your alphabet behind*
> *Since "C" is "S" in Moscow*
> *And that ain't half the line.*
>
> *"P" is "R" in ruskky,*
> *"B" not "B" but "V".*
> *Every carrot top is "J"*
> *"M" both "M" and "T".*
>
> *In this cock-eyed language*
> *"H" is always "N";*
> *While "Y" is "OO" and "W" "sh"*
> *And so on without end.*

It had taken him a solid hour. But wait till he pulled it on Morse and the boys! ... As he spanned the next curve of the river, he noticed the low houses were beginning to add stories, the streets to widen and straighten themselves. Traffic signals appeared on main corners, manned by solemn-faced militiamen in white gloves. He was nearing the center of the city. Across from him along the white silenced river there stretched a huge buff building, paralleling the bank for a full three blocks. Against its fresh walls fluttered more of those red banners. Just beyond was the beginning of the ancient Chinese Wall that surrounded the Old City. He longed to go in there, but was afraid of losing his way. He wasn't going to chance being picked up as a vagrant. Not him. Must be quite a history to this wall and town. They said it was built before Columbus discovered America.

He walked on until abreast of the Kremlin. The aged brick of its score of towers had an indescribable glow in the late afternoon sun. Their green peaks wore crescents which glistened from a dozen angles. Here and there sturdy onion-topped domes punctured a turbulent iridescent sky. To his right and left, over bridges which arched the slumbering river a dense traffic poured incessantly. Boulevards running along the banks were thick with cars, wagons on sleighs, and black specks of humanity.

Andy surveyed the Kremlin. Its beauty held him. From here the old czars had ruled for centuries. The golden eagles which crested the towers were reminders of those times. To overthrow this stronghold had surely taken revolt from within. Well, it must have happened, for now there was a new government in the Kremlin. Above its main building on a central commanding hill there floated its symbol, a scarlet flag.

This power in the Kremlin was almost as much a mystery to him as the one preceding it. In there lived a guy named Stalin. Before him was Lenin. The American papers called them dictators. He was against that: all types of Mussolinis. Yet, when Sasha had pointed out their photographs in the clubroom, there was no mistaking what he thought. Sasha was hardly a fellow to take to dictators. The things he had seen at the plant, too, somehow didn't fit in with the Big Stick theory. Jeez, what a headache. "No savvy."

He watched the flag rippling, and he started to hum:

> *When you come to Moscow—*
> *Leave your alphabet behind—*

Some one touched his arm. Andy started. A man in uniform. The secret police. The dread O. G. P. U.!

What must he do? Maybe he had broken some law. Would the fellow arrest him, send him off to one of those dungeons? Ship him north to a lumber camp? In the States he had been picked up once as a vagrant and had actually done three days on the North Carolina chain gang before his people had arranged to get him off. Probably they had the same racket here for getting free labor. There had been a lot in the papers.

The O. G. P. U. man grinned at him, pushing his questions. His revolver swung in a leather belt about his hips, he looked strong as a young bull. The American made several steps backwards. *"Ne pon-e-ma-yu. Ne pon-e-ma-yu."*

"Oi—ne pon-ne-ma-ete!" There was secret malice, Andy thought, in the man's way of reëchoing of his words. Taking advantage of people passing, he sidled away. When the policeman called after him, instinctively his hands raised, then dropped as he dodged into the crowd and around the first corner.

Regretfully Sergei Mertsov gazed after his vanished figure. What a pity that *inostranets* would not talk with him. Only three months in the Red Army, Sergei was enjoying his first week-end in the Capital. He had wanted to ask that *Amerikanets* (he felt sure he was a Yankee, by the cut of his clothes) if skyscrapers really ran as high as forty stories, and with elevators operating clear to the top. Were there ever tie-ups on the subway, and was it true that there was a roadway under the Hudson?

Crossing the bridge, the American hastened across the Red Square. He dared not halt even for a look at the curious old Saint Basil Cathedral whose designer was rumored to have had his eyes blinded because Ivan the Terrible wanted this the one temple of its kind in the entire world, nor at the auction block where slaves had been sold and Stenka Razin, or so they said, had lost his head for defying the czar. Nor even at Lenin's tomb, where some day he planned to wait his turn in the long line going inside. He made his way toward the Grand Hotel. Around the corner he would get his 59 car and head for home.

He walked in circles. That carline had certainly been to the left. Discouraged, he stopped before a bookshop, to eye its display. Pretty covers these books had. He had nothing to read. What he would give for a copy of *Liberty* or *Popular Mechanics*.

"Have you a match?" a bystander asked him. Andy beamed. English! As he lit his cigarette, the stranger inquired through narrowed lids, "You have been long in Moscow?" Andy nodded, "About ten weeks." The man was well-dressed, but spoke with a slight accent. "How do you like it here?" he queried. "It is much better in America I suppose?"

"Oh I don't know," the Detroiter answered. "Could be a lot worse here. Say, would you help me find my car stop? Somehow I missed the street."

"Of course. In just a minute. It is interesting to exchange opinions ... Ah, if Americans knew how difficult it was for us Russians now." They were suffering untold agonies. He gestured darkly. Had the newcomer seen the misery right here in the Capital? What did he mean, Andy queried, were there jobless, souplines? Where? He'd like to see. His companion shrugged the query aside. No, everybody had to work or starve. It was other things. He lowered his voice and glanced quickly around them. But in the provinces! Had the gentleman by any chance been to the Ukraine, Georgia? No? Ah, there there was the real hell, Dante's *Inferno* gave only half. Whole villages were destitute, starving. ... Aghast at his description, Andy forgot his straying car.

Why? the Russian demanded. Why this tragedy? There was hate in his gesture toward the Kremlin. "You Americans believe in freedom, do you not? Democracy? So do I. But let me tell you that today those demanding liberty and justice in our sad country are sentenced to exile. If not worse. Ah, ugly, ugly things are going on in my Russia. My soul aches for my beautiful country."

As they walked up the street to the carline, the stranger clung to his arm, whispering rapidly. "Write home," he urged, "you can speak out where I can not. You are an American—free! While I ... I ... " There was hopelessness in the lift to his sleek shoulders. "All the world must hear our cries, deliver our enslaved nation."

Andy made a successful rush into the crowd that was clammering aboard the packed street car. Only then he wondered, "Why did I forget to ask that man who he was?" And why was he so keen on shooting off his jaw?

But his new acquaintance had disappeared and was by now accosting a man coming out of *Torgsin's*. "Could you oblige me with a match? Thank you. You are from America or England? And have you been long in Moscow? No? But do you know—?"

In Sixty Days

DEAR ANDY,

It's lonesome here without you, things are just the same but more, Ford's laying off by the hundreds there's talk of a new model but nobody knows. Guess it's gonna be different though because President Hoover made a Big Announcement from the White House about *Prosperity in Sixty Days*. Guess you heard about it, was in all the papers even Europe. Everybody sure was glad because its kind of depressing the way it is. Poor Bill got the air last week, Ma's been crying all over the place, he's been to Flint General Motors everywhere the same as you but what's the use. So it was Big News about this *Prosperity in Sixty Days*.

U. S. STEEL DROPS 10 PTS.
Suicides on Increase

MUSSOLINI CALLED HIT-RUN DRIVER
Demands Apology Gen. Butler

FIRST GRADE WHEAT HITS NEW LOW

PEACHES SUES DADDY BROWNING
LONDON CLAIMS WALL ST. PLAYING EXCHANGE
Fifteen Million Unemployed

(Clothes lines of To Rent Signs are strung across America. Jobless men and families are building shacktowns in New York, Atlanta, Boston.

Congress declares in interest world peace England, Japan and all of Europe should reduce their military programs.

Nobody knows who'll get the sack next, somebody must have started a tornado out in Kansas.

But it's nothing anyways with *Prosperity in Sixty Days*.

First Hoover saw it Just Around the Corner but

(Now it's *Certain in Sixty Days*.)

And Andy, is it True all they say about Russian women you know what I Mean. Last Sunday a man visited our church, he'd been in Russia and he told awful things how he'd seen old men and nursing mothers shot down in Cold Blood for crossing themselves. You better be careful never let them get your passport because what could you do with no American Consul or anything? It's sure lonesome here without you, I never go out anywheres now that is hardly ever. Mama keeps asking that Hal Mortimer over but I'll never like him honest and if you come back I'll give him the gobye so quick he won't know what's happened. The papers are full of sales real bargains if you've got the dough. I got a few things but everybody is getting careful even me imagine, nobody can tell who'll get the solong next, it gives you the creeps. Mama's started going to church regular and

FIVE YEAR PLAN DECLARED FAILURE

Rumors Discontent British Navy Denied

MURDERER ESCAPES CAPTORS

Ford Says Jobs for All

STALIN ASSASSINATED

Mary Ashford Has Face Lifted

BRITISH FLEET MUTINIES!

U. S. BANK CLOSES: EXAMINER ACCUSES REDS

Al Capone Said Behind Chi Milk Racket

JOBLESS VET JUMPS OFF BRIDGE "NEW WAR WILL END DEPRESSION"

Gen. Guardmore Startles Peace Convention

REPS. CAPITAL LABOR MEET IN WASH.

Pledge Coöp. End Depression

And Andy, don't you think everything considered you'd better plan on coming home soon baby? To get in on the first rush seeing as how we're going to have whoop-pee and
Prosperity
in Sixty Days!

5

AS she gave over her machine and prepared to leave,
Natasha heard angry voices behind her, near the giant
drop hammer. What was wrong with the *Amerikantsi?*
Through their rapid talk ran an undisguised heat. Too bad
her English was too limited to follow them, for by what she
could catch they were arguing about the shop.

With a long easy gait she moved around her lathe and
toward the voices. The second crew was already at work.
Outside the sky was drawing on its speckled gray coat, although it was barely four o'clock. On day shift this week,
she had waited to make sure that chump Leon didn't run
their new cutter too hard. Just let him, she'd give him what
for.

As she came by, the two engineers broke off. Boardman's
hello was abrupt, overcheerful. With a gay nod the girl
passed on to the washroom and lockers, slipped off her black
work apron and began scrubbing the machine grease from
her hands. Now just what could those two be quarreling
over? Did they know what was wrong in the shop, for that
matter care? She must hurry or she'd be late for her swim.
Boardman was genuine, no doubting that. Look how he
worked. Energetic, demanding, always exact. If only more
Russian engineers were like that! And could he swear!

She slid the red cotton kerchief from her bob, wet and
combed her hair. It was nice having the washroom to herself,
nobody elbowing and pushing for turn. That other enginner,
Meester Crampton, who knew? He must have the stuff
though, entrusted with buying machinery abroad. So much
precious *valuta* spent on these foreign *spetz*, it was hard

telling if they gave all they could. Not always their fault either. That blockhead of a super Eugene Pankrevich would never know how to handle them, draw them in.

Natasha jammed on her tam. "Well, see here my girl," she scolded herself, "we can't depend on foreign engineers alone or Russian either. It's up to us youth. We gotta speed up preparing our new forces, hundred thousands of them, understand?" A whole generation of young Soviet engineers, imagine! If only she weren't such a dunce at calculus!

She ran down the stairs. Tomorrow she'd try to draw Meester Boardman out, see what's wrong. Maybe her brigade could help.

She crossed the yard, along the freight track and on past the double line of trucks drawn up by the assembly shop. She asked the gateman the time. Four-ten! Exhibiting her pass, she hurried through the exit along the treacherously smooth pavement toward the plant gym. At four-thirty she must be in the pool.

She would be late. Hang it, she was always being late. She never stayed off days as many did, but to come five or ten minutes after her shift had started: that often happened. Naughty girl, Natashka, she scolded herself, where's your discipline? See here, get a hand to yourself. It was terrible always running five or ten minutes behind, and never able to catch up with yourself.

Once she had a watch, it'd be a lot easier to be prompt. Just think of glancing down at your wrist any hour of the day, and knowing to the exact second what time it was! Well, she'd have a watch. If not in the first, then in the second *Pyatiletka*. Be nicer, though, if she could have it right away. She had such a dear picked out in a Commission shop on Tverskaya. But it cost like all blazes.

At five-thirty her time in the pool would be up. She hated missing even three minutes of her biweekly swim, and especially now with the swimming match due next month. Her team was coming up against a strong one, *Dynamo's*. After that, with luck, the All-Moscow finals, perhaps even the All-Union. And hurrah for *Red Star!* Natasha skipped through lines trudging forward into the steam baths, and maneuvered for her chance to give in her wraps and get a locker key. Already she was experiencing that afterglow of her first plunge, and the delicious feel of her body gliding through the clear azure water.

Dressing quarters were fast emptying. "Come on, Natashka, you late thing!" Lydia, in a tight scarlet suit pattered across the damp tiling toward her. "A fine Captain you are, always late!"

"Oh, am I?" She colored. "I'll be ready in no time." Lydia was mean. This wasn't team night, but general. Besides, if Lydia did as much outside work as she did! Maybe she thought she'd make a good captain herself? Happy shouts and the swishing spank of bodies as they broke the rippling surface reëchoed from the pool through the moist closeness of the dressing rooms and the gurgling drip-drip of the showers. Natasha danced with impatience, and kicked her shoes free. Quickly she shed her blouse, skirt and scant underthings; ducked under the shower. From warm to cold, a quick rubdown and into her suit. Hers was black, close-fitting. Above her firm, breasts glowed her life-saver's award (she certainly hoped nobody thought her cocky about it) interwoven with their team's emblem, a red star.

She gave Lydia a gay push, "Well, piglet, come on there!" and made a dash for the pool. With a running surface dive into its glittering depths, she began long even strokes about its length. Gone all fatigue from her day's work; all thoughts of shop studies Mama's nagging for the moment, forgotten. She swam five times round, practicing sidestroke overarm and her latest feat, the Australian crawl. That needed work, she still lost power when she brought her left arm forward. Finally she pulled up on the tile runway by Lydia and sat, hands under her knees, singing contentedly to herself a popular air

O'er the wave
O'er the sea

Here today
Tomorrow there!

Andy's companion nudged him. "Say, will you stop it! Popeyes! Get your peepers glued, if you ain't careful."

"Save your worries." With a damp elbow Andy thrust back. "You're old frogeyes yourself. Some beauty, eh?" And could she swim! He'd been following her smooth circles about the pool.

They were off on another lively discussion of Russian girls. A bit stocky about the legs and hips. Not slim like Americans. (Skinny, Morse called it, but Andy, remembering Elsie, hotly disagreed.) Not fleshy, either, like the Germans. Shoulders? And how! Morse rolled his eyes. "And those elephant hips and—"

The Detroiter pushed him headlong into the pool, and jumped in after to save himself from being pulled in feet first. They lazed about the tank. An eye on the observation benches, Morse generously entertained with porpoise dips. Slowly he arched to the bottom, came up for air and again lunged into its transparent depths. Yep, the benches were pointing, taking it all in. With a final gasp, he flopped over on his back, a plump shapeless jellyfish that drifted with the shallow waves made by divers off the deep end. His eyes roved about the wall's crimson runners and trophies. These cockeyed Russkies even had slogans about swimming! Feature that. He bet they got born with slogans too. What a riot!

Andy reclimbed to the runway, longing for a smoke. Self-conscious of his long underpinnings, which Morse dubbed a pair of ragweeds that had shot up too fast, he squatted on the blue tile. His lanky arms hugged his chest and thick shoulders. Long summers of boyhood work on the farm had developed these, at least, to a gratifying size.

Beneath his soaked mop of hair his sharp blue gaze fastened on the diving board. Kind of a disadvantage to first meet a girl in your bathing suit. He was no Doug Fairbanks. More like a skinned eel. Halfchoked, Morse came alongside. "Honest, with your calf's eyes, you'll drown me yet. She sure's hit you a knockout."

"Aw, wailing catfish." Andy thumped his knee. "So you

dare me, eh? I'm on! I'll date that jane before we leave the tank, how do you like that?"

Natasha and Lydia had joined the divers. Beginning with the low springboard they soon mounted to higher rungs to take off like a line of starlings busily playing a fast game of catch-who-catch-can. Caps and sleek heads bobbed to the surface like so many red and blue corks on a fish pond. As they clambered back up the ladders, their young muscles rippled beneath their tanned water-gilded skins. Half bird half fish, Natasha soared and dipped, then impatiently waited her next turn. To her the pool was an oversmall piece of her beloved Volga.

Five years it was since she'd had a swim through its ample brown heart. Five years since her family had moved to Moscow, and she had cut her braids, donned city shoes, and entered *Red Star's* factory school.

Moscow and *Red Star* had left little of the shy-eyed country girl in Natasha. Resting easily, head back, on the highest stand, water running in exciting streams from her tingling shoulders and hips to the runways beneath, life coursed in glad even beats through her veins. She felt herself mistress, or at least equal of all she surveyed; the world, a gay comrade, marching ahead arm in arm.

Ned Folson's dusky wet arms wriggled against his vivid green suit. His fingers snapped while his feet slid under him to the beat of his latest jazz hit. Attaboy, what'd they say for a jack knife from the top stand?

Morse gripped down on his chattering teeth and prayed for that dark baby to misstep. Hit the water flatter'n a pancake, burn his guts. Serve him right the way he was showing off. He was a poor diver himself. When you got up there, the surface looked godawful miles below. And could it sting! He glanced toward the benches. As soon as he got his breath, he'd porpoise again. Then they'd have something to ogle about. Good anyway for reducing your spread.

Andy was intent on tracking the girl in the black suit and red cap. Whenever her turn came on the spring board, he noticed she wasted no time posing. He rather wished she did. How in hell was he going to meet her? How could he talk with her, if he did! The bunch was grouping around that Ned Folson while he pantomimed some dive form. Damn his time, he knew some water tricks himself. Since kneehigh to a grasshopper he'd been in the water, paddling about in the old swimming hole. "Watch me, baby," he told Morse, "here's where I muscle in."

With a running start Ned somersaulted hands about his knees. Morse groaned: he'd hit the water clean. Others followed in quick succession. Sasha made a bad takeoff and struck the water a resounding smack. The benches shouted their convulsed approval, while the divers, blowing noisily, overarmed it back to the stand. With a last dig at Morse, Andy slid frog-fashion into the tank. As he glided below the surface toward the deep end, eyes open, he spied the girl in the black suit just ahead of him shooting up from the tank's bottom. Doubletiming it, he threw his body full in her path.

He hadn't intended for her to crack into him full on. The blow knocked his wind. She came up gulping and made a blind dash for the edge. Tagging her up the ladder, he tried to apologize, but his few Russian words failed him. Only one remained, "Kharosho" (good), and it hardly made sense.

Swimmers crowded round them. What'd happened? Nobody hurt? Ned eyed the Detroiter with obvious disgust. "Say, why didn't you look where you were going?"

Andy pretended not to hear. "Tell her I'm damn sorry. Honest. Sure, it was all my fault." Natasha waved his excuses aside. (Gawky dunce!) *"Nichevo!* No matter." Her smile broke over him. Gee, she was even prettier than he'd thought.

"You speak English?" he asked happily.

"Very little. I study."

He liked even her accent. Oh boy, what a break!

Soon after, she left for the dressing room. What a clumsy boob. One of those newcomers. Nice eyes, though. Sort of. Here she'd lost ten minutes by being late, and now another ten at this end. And she'd got an aching head to boot, and all that calculus to do! The devil with him!

Hastily throwing on his clothes, Andy started for the

entrance. "Not bad, eh, Morse? I said I would, didn't I?"

"You get your date?" Morse was fumbling with his collar. Contrary thing. He was going out with his friend even if it stayed off and his tie too. He wasn't missing the take-off. Not him. "Well, did you date her?" he repeated. Andy bluffed, "Sure thing."

As Natasha came through the doorway, he winked at his friend. "Beat it." But Morse was a staunch cottonwood rooted in the cement. Andy scowled. "Numbskull. No horning in." Cap creased between his fists, he stepped in her path. "I hope you don't feel sore at me for that whack in the pool?" She didn't understand, so he repeated, tapping his forehead, asking if her head hurt. Lydia, who was walking with her, giggled. He looked so funny, talking with his hands. The girls started up the blue-shadowed street, he keeping resolutely by her side, Morse trailing behind. With a frantic hand reversed behind him, Andy signaled the fool to clear off. What'd he want to do, jimmy the works!

Conversation lagged. How in samhill, Andy wondered, could he crack the ice. At the third corner, Lydia still giggling into her fuzzy tan collar, left them. He felt awkward. This damn language! "Where do you live?" he asked in English. "Can I walk home with you?" She answered, in Russian, that she was taking the car. (Now that she had a chance to practice her English, her tongue was tied!) Under the glow of the street lamps she looked pale and once she slipped on a frozen ridge of snow. Impulsively he took her arm. "Gee, I feel rotten. You got a head on, eh?"

"*Nichevo!* It is nothing. Please, speak not so fast. Why you not know Russian?" It was hard, he countered, and he had no teacher. Maybe she'd give him lessons? She'd be glad to if she had time, she said, but there were classes at the plant for foreigners, didn't he know? (Of course, it wouldn't be a bad idea, she told herself, to exchange lessons with him. Still ...) If he wanted, she'd see he got notice.

He crumpled his lip. One blind alley. Had the girl no followup? Besides, he suspected her of maneuvering to free her arm. It was rounder, harder than he'd imagined. Make two of Elsie's. He held more firmly. Lord, he felt lonesome.

70

There were blue lights over the snow, a sad feel to the air. Why wouldn't this girl take to him, as he had to her? The tight ball of cotton on the crown of her red stocking cap caught his eye. Like a kid's cap but devilish cute on her. Picture Elsie in such a thing! Not her style.

Never mind Elsie. She was having her fun with that Mortimer fop. He'd have a fling on his own. The type Morse had picked up he didn't care for, but this girl... "What's your name?"

"Natasha Safonova." Natasha. Nat, he'd call her, when he knew her better. What shoulders! What if she already had a steady? Lights from the apartments twinkled around them, their boots crunched with a gentle squeesh-squeesh against the snow. In several homes shades were not drawn; he could see a family at supper, in another flat a mother putting her baby to bed. Lord, he felt lonesome. He could pass out tomorrow, and not a soul in all this town or whole country would give a hang.

She asked him, "You a worker?" (His eyes were nice. And what a friendly grin.)

He nodded. From Detroit.

She turned to glance up at him. (Did he like it here, she wondered, or find it dull?) "From Ford's?" "Sure thing." (He was not saying how long back.)

Her interest roused. An American worker. There must be a lot he could tell her. Perhaps he had helped lead strikes, gone on hunger marches! "Communist?" she asked eagerly.

"Who, me?" Andy flipped a light. "Not me, baby. I got more sense." But what a look she gave him. Just where'd he missed fire? It couldn't be that this kid was a bolshy!

"More sense!" Natasha echoed. His bantering hard tone, the careless way he had said it! Why... "You Americans!" she hesitated. "I think I not understand you."

They walked on. These Americans, she puzzled. In some ways so clever. Machinery they knew inside out. They were cultured, literate. But in politics! Why he, a worker, acted like a Communist was the last thing he'd be! She couldn't make him out. She had grown up in a world where revolution was an accepted everyday fact. Of the old days she had only a child's vague memories, and a deep loathing. With her and her friends, to be a Communist was a thing to strive for, dream about. And here this stranger! It was clear he came from another world. Boardman and Crampton were engineers, old school intellectuals: their attitudes were easier to understand. But her companion ... after all he was a worker! She drew him out, tried to argue but their vocabularies soon petered out. His talk, that is as much as she could follow, was the queerest yet. What a hodge-podge! Partly what she'd expect from a worker, but more what she might hear from any ordinary bourgeois. It was strange, disturbing. Her cheeks grew hot.

The silence hung between them. Andy searched desperately for some topic of small talk. How did you make time with a Russian girl? Ignoring his discomfort, she tried to remember all she had studied about America. So this was what her professor had meant. All those fairy tales and promises they put over on the masses. But was this man so dumb, he couldn't see through them! Democracy! Square deal!

"Do many American workers talk like you?" she asked.

"Sure. All but a few hotheads." (She barely reached to his shoulder. There was a cute tip to the end of her pinched nose.)

She quickened her step. "No. I think. How to say? ... You *must* be wrong!" (What a fine overcoat he had. But she knew about those things, America had technique. In a few years they'd have it, too, and an output equal to any.)

He laughed at her stubbornness. "Have it your own way, lady. Guess I know my U.S.A."

"But after years of crisis! No, you must be wrong." She was provoked, upset. His talk made the world revolution seem so many years off. If she just had the words! She'd ask her English professor this very night, thumb her dictionary, convince this young fool.

They had come to her stop. "My tram." She ran forward, relieved to end their trying walk. Keeping up with her, he demanded, "Let me ride home with you." "But I told you, I have class." The crowd moving into the car threatened to swallow her. Persistent, he elbowed his way in. Then when could he see her?

Turning on the step, she gave an abrupt wave. He looked too cocky. These Americans, she knew them. They thought every Russian girl'd eat out of their hand. "Oh, at shop or in pool. I'm veery busy. Well, *poka!* So long!"

Andy let the crowd jostle him aside. Wowee, that was a cold one. But he'd haunt that tank like a fish. Gee, he felt lonesome. Well, who cared? And just what story should he make up to tell Morse and Tim?

"What's so funny?" her neighbor in the car asked her. Natasha sobered, had she been laughing aloud? But that Yankee, how droll he'd looked standing there in the cold with his cap lifted. America must be a funny country. Some day she would go and see for herself.

6

HENRY CRAMPTON secured the rugs around his wife's knees, then under his interpreter's, Katerina Boudnikova, his hands tremulous at even this slight impact. He trusted Edith hadn't noticed. Women had a nasty way of snooping. Silly idea of the wife's, anyway, to use up his one free day from that blasted dieshop, hunting those ungodly pictures of gawky madonnas known as icons. He had refused point blank until Katia's enthusiasm had led him to change his mind. Guess it was cultured and all that, and the costume idea was pretty hot. He nodded to the chauffeur, "Be off."

Squinting up at the monstrous lemon that hung above a turreted roof, Sergei released his brakes. What could be taking these *Amerikantsi* back to that village? Very inconvenient, these trips. The State's automobiles had more important work to do, not to mention himself, than tour Meester Crampton's wife about the country.

As they rounded corners and skimmed boulevards he honked incessantly. Hang these pedestrians. It was either this or slow down to a horse gait. Furred creatures with bulging arms blew like horses on the cold muffled air and wandered jay-fashion across avenues, looking neither to right nor left. Some used thoroughfare borders for footpaths, as they had once used the main road through their village. At the horn's shriek they ran for cover, scattered like a brood of turkeys before the unforeseen leap of a yelping fox.

Sergei's brakes came down, sudden, firm. Crampton lurched forward, his arms clasped convulsively from both sides. Not three feet ahead of the machine stood a young farmer, rooted in the ice. The chauffeur leaned out to scold, "Citizen, what's the matter with you! Are you deaf, blind! See that traffic signal?" The boy shook a clenched first. "Oh you! I shall have you run in. Near went right over me, you did. What's a traffic signal against the life of a human being, you swine!"

Sergei flushed. "But I tell you! What a fool you are!" Served him right, if his brakes hadn't worked. "Well, get on with you. Are you stuck?"

Crampton thumped the driver between his shoulders and motioned him to go on. But the angry pedestrian had leaped to the running board to shake his reddened knuckles under Sergei's blunt nose. "The likes of you, driving a state auto! I'll have you run in!" "Oh you will, eh?" Cars and wagon-sleds blocked in their rear honked a discordant chorus: a whistle sounded, and the militiaman came over. "Citizens, what's this!"

Simultaneously, without taking breath, Sergei and his accuser rushed to enlighten him. "Hey, citizens! Pipe down!" Motioning them to the curb, he signaled traffic ahead. Crampton looked at his watch and spoke with gruff authority. Katia whispered a hurried explanation—to no avail. The militiaman was young and seeing that full duty was done. Edith pouted. One of those dreadful Russian arguments over nothing. Now they'd be late getting back for the theater. This *would* happen, just when they were starting out. And all these chubby inquisitive faces poking around them. Silly dolts! Pulling her fur collar closer about her face, she beat a rat-a-tat-tat with her chilled feet. Oh, for sunshine and her own kind.

It was just as she supposed: endless heated discussion, including several bystanders, everybody made to show their documents and Sergei his driver's license. Why was Henry so helpless! She'd put an end to this. She leaned forward to concentrate her charms on the militiamen (she'd handled traffic cops before) and gestured prettily, trying to impress him by her foreign tongue.

Crampton pulled her back. "No use, woman! Once Russians start, gotta let 'em have it out." Look at 'em! By God, at the drop of a hat they held a Soviet and no stopping them.

"Oh, hello there, Crampton!" From the edge of the crowd Philip Boardman tipped his hat with a mock flourish. With him was a stooped dark man with furred turban and close-clipped Vandyke, obviously a Russian. Quickly Crampton turned aside, pretending not to hear. That grinning ape! Popping up now.

Edith nudged him. "There's Phil! Maybe he can help us."

"That sucker! A swell lot he'd do!"

"Hush, he's coming over!" But she must have been mistaken, for when she looked again Boardman and his companion had gone.

With a final warning to both Sergei and the farmer, the militiaman sent them on their way. The engineer leaned close to his driver's ear. *"Tempo!"* he shouted. He'd heard the Russians use the word in the shop. He wished the drive over and himself back home near the radio, with a good cigar and detective yarn.

Willingly enough Sergei gave her more gas. The smooth asphalt was tempting. That numbskull had no call to give him a warning, though. Hadn't he been driving three years, and not an accident? Besides, he was sure of his brakes. Every morning he tested them. Moscow was overrun with peasants and they expected you to make *tempo!* Well, traffic was picking up a bit, these last months. And he'd do his share. Gleefully he pressed down on the accelerator. He liked the feel of the machine's leap forward as she clipped through the biting rush of air.

Henry sucked his cheek uneasily. So Murphy was going back! Lucky devil. Well, another couple of winters and he'd have enough saved up to see his way clear to pulling out. Even if the firm didn't come through with a transfer back home, he'd find another way to swing it. Edith wanted to get back and so did he. A little place outside Chicago, and take it easy for awhile. They'd put Henry Junior and Bella in good schools. Especially Bella. The child was nearly twelve and a regular tomboy. A few years in finishing school would polish her off, set her right. She was a great kid, more like her Dad than anybody else. Their firstborn. If she'd only been a boy he might have made something out of her. Oh well...

He looked across at Katerina. From her cold exterior you'd never guess the fire in the woman. You'd never guess.

Edith Crampton gestured toward the packages on the car floor, and her husband gathered them by her on the car seat. Quickly she examined their contents; the butter was intact. Four kilos of butter, about nine pounds and a thousand roubles certainly ought to be enough for her intended purchases. If not, there were meat and confetti. Sergei was watching her through the mirror on the windshield. Now what could she be planning on doing with that? She slipped the packages under the robe and settled against the cushions. It was pleasant, driving this way, not too cold, and the wind swept cobwebs from one's brain.

She spoke in undertones with her husband about their mission. It was an unnecessary precaution for Sergei knew even less of their language than they knew of his (the one thing they knew being how to bargain in Russian, with a "How much?" and "Very dear!"). As for Miss Boudnikova, she was an icon enthusiast and full partner to the trip. It was her kindness that had put Edith on the trail of this exceptionally rare icon, a Bougletov which dated back to the thirteenth century and was worth several times the thousand roubles she must pay for it. A real bargain!

The thoroughfare was reaching beyond the city, houses scattering and traffic becoming less dense. On a dull afternoon such as this, Edith Crampton found something foreboding, somber, in the landscape. Those blue-gray shadows cast by dark silent firs along the snow, that brown dead underbrush—it was too much like Minnesota, where she had spent her bleak unhappy girlhood. From all that only marriage to Henry had delivered her. Yet, had it? This scene made her doubt, feel caught like a rabbit in the snow. How could any one find beauty in the Russian countryside?

Those things she had so desired as a girl: had she achieved them? Children, material comforts, a home. Yes. But there had been something more. Elusive troubled yearnings that now escaped, now tortured her, led her at times to do foolish things. Anything to drive the taste of ashes from her throat, to keep her from lying awake nights. What was it? As a girl, she had dreamed ... She was thankful that there would be gay Tschaikovsky and dancing, this evening. They had taken a box at the ballet with friends. Now if Henry—he was such a phlegmatic creature, one had to know just how to manage him. Well, she knew.

Glancing across at her, Katia fairly surmised her thoughts. And to think that she, a Boudnikov, had once stood in awe of these Americans. For all their *savoir-faire,* in some ways they were as gullible as any *babushka.* Edith Crampton, she had soon discovered, knew as little about icons as she knew about tangos and permanents. The most flimsy substitute put her in ecstasies. Still, it would be well if the priest today had carried out all instructions. Atmosphere counted for so much, and nothing must go amiss. And Henry at the last moment might prove obstinate. Too bad that his wife had insisted on his coming along.

"Perhaps we should have helped your American friend?" Mark Koshevnikov asked in his punctilious English, as he and Philip Boardman hurried on. His pronounced Oxford accent at first had irritated Boardman but now it amused him. He laughed. "That boob! Crampton'll crawl out, he always does. Anyway, you said we were late."

Boob? the Russian queried. What a versatile language, this English. Until he had met these Americans he had flattered himself he had a fair grasp of the tongue. Why, he had read Shakespeare Dickens Jack London and many scientific books. But slang, *patois!* What a rich speech! He much preferred Americanese to British, it was so strong, clearcut. And what colorful epigrams and figures of speech! Well now, Russian too had its racy vernacular. Interesting subject, come to think of it, comparative philology. Yes, yes, of course they must hurry, or they'd never get in.

Resolutely Philip took his friend by the arm. Just like

Mark, when he got engrossed in a subject he forgot everything, even where he was.

Philip had first met Mark Koshevnikov at a metallurgical conference, where the Russian's report had impressed him by its daring and insight into one of engineering science's most difficult fields. Since then Philip had spent many keen-edged hours in Koshevnikov's study, exchanging experiences and views. There was a human quality to the man, his graying temples and serene twinkle, an eagerness in his long sensitive fingers that drew the American to him. He couldn't quite explain it, but there it was. To talk with him was like exploring yourself. Their discussions near the tiers of books and perking samovar had long ago extended beyond metallurgy and dies.

Often Vera Koshevnikov, his plump jolly wife, would burst in on them with her mass of wiry gray hair and mobile acid-bitten fingers with a "Well now, Mark, aren't you two done yet! An end to your serious talk! Let's eat!" To his amazement, Philip had learned she was a practicing chemist. Somehow it was incongruous, this motherly creature minding test-tubes! Behind her there usually tripped one of their shy between-age girls, with her dark braids and tray of homemade cookies and pink and green candies. There were plates of steaming hot rolls stuffed with chopped meat and rice, and occasionally nuts or apples and wine from the South. Mark would clip the huge lumps of sugar into small bits with the old-fashioned tongs and try to match Vera's stories of bear hunts and fishing exploits. They'd ask about America, or start a folk song ... and before any one knew it, it was past midnight and Philip hurrying to leave.

More than once Vera had asked, "Why don't you bring your wife sometime?" But he always made excuse. Mary would think these little gatherings a bore.

Over innumerable glasses of scorching tea sucked through the green candies, Mark had spoken with complete frankness about himself, the many problems and perspectives in his work and that of the whole country. "Snags? Medieval backwardness? Red tape? Of course, we have all! But we are building, transforming! In ten years, the world won't know Russia."

In the early years of the Soviet power, he said, he had been doubtful, confused. Methods and objectives were quite new to him, and largely contrary to his traditions and somewhat cloistered life. If not actively hostile, he had been passive, sullen, waiting for he knew not what. Well, the gigantic ventures of the *Pyatiletka* had won him completely. That, and the new type of man with whom his work brought him in daily contact in the shop. He hadn't believed such things possible, yet here it was. Anything that could do this for the people, for Russia's degraded masses was not to be passed by. Doubts gone, he could not stand apart. To build! To build! What engineer had not dreamed so—to clear wastes, drain swamps, plumb depths, risk hides—to build!

Since then, in these last years he had tasted life to the full.

Last free day, Boardman had been over the machine construction works with Koshevnikov where his friend was working as chief engineer. He found it equipped and operating as well as the best in the States. How much better it would be, he couldn't help thinking, if he left *Red Star* and cast dies here. But if the Russian had a similar thought, he gave no hint of it. Queer too, with all the competition and high pressure there was between plants here, each trying to excel the record of the other. "Socialist competition" they called it. And Boardman knew Mark could use an engineer like himself. Well, he'd never broach it himself. Not yet.

This present morning, Mark had rung him up at the plant. "You have—how to say? Crazes in America, no? So do we. What? No, not a bear hunt. Later, later. Well, decide. Will we go? Listen, for once when there's a free-day I can take, you must come! No excuses! Yes, the explorer himself! Then in half an hour? Good!"

So they were on their way to hear a report of the latest scientific expedition into the Arctic. They had reached the town's center, where subway excavation derricks towered over streams of traffic and dense moving crowds. Philip gaped at the solid human thicket ringing the House of Columns. Damn the mob, they'd never get in. Billboards flashed down at them giant likenesses of the famous explorers, surrounded by photographs of dog teams, aeroplanes, ice floes, polar bears. Mark tightened the Detroiter's arm in an enthusiastic vise. "You've played futball, yes? Come!"

Further in, long lines were inching toward the boxoffices and worried militiamen were begging, "Citizens! Quiet! Citizens, order!" Once through the thicket's circumference, the pressure lightened. Mark waved his special passes at the guard, smiling with delight. How had he got them? Philip demanded. Well, to tell the truth, this *udarnik* business applied to engineers and scientists as well as machine workers. He had *won* them, understand? A special reward.

Within the entrance, they tossed their overcoats and rubbers to the cloakroom attendant and raced up the red-carpeted marble stairs two at a jump. Just in time! Doors of the main hall were closing. As they reached their seats Philip looked about him and tried to imagine scenes long past. This room had made history. Under the czar, as a Club of Nobles its marble pillars had echoed with the brilliant oratory or the gay balls of a now vanished aristocracy. Here Lenin had lain in state while a burdened multitude treked through the bitter winter to mourn at his bier. And here science and youth were welcoming home their explorers of the far north. Galleries and floor were crowded, there was a gala feeling in the air.

Philip turned to his friend. "Some bear hunt, this!"

The Cramptons' machine jolted over frozen ruts, coming at last to a halt before the high gateway of an old village church. The Americans climbed out, carrying their packages, and started with their interpreter down the pathway. Sergei lifted his cap and reflectively scratched his head. Exactly what was up? He'd just have a look. At the sound of his boots on the flagstones, the Cramptons motioned him back. Hm, so that was it, was it? He turned around, waiting until they had gone inside.

Blackbirds were cawing about the belfries. In the burial ground beyond the church, time with sardonic mirth had thrust gravestones like so many tilted dominoes into the moldy earth. Three old women, black crows whose beaks and sharp eyes were turned on the strangers, crouched on their sticks by a freshly dug grave.

Sergei walked along the side of the church until he reached a window that gave upon the altar. The interior was dark, he could barely distinguish four figures, his passengers and another—a priest. As the holy man repeatedly bowed, his black flowing robes swept the aisle and the heavy gold cross fastened about his neck swung to and fro. There was something intimate and confiding in the way he stroked his vibrant white beard.

Standing so as not to be observed, the driver speculated on their conversation and how much was in the roll of bills they gave him for the picture. The old scoundrel was obviously protesting their offer with his hands, eyes and whole body. With a final sad shaking of his beard, he produced a dark bundle, and packages exchanged hands. More bowing. Sergei spat volubly.

The priest was showing his callers about the cathedral, holding a lighted tallow up to sacred pictures covering walls columns and ceiling, long ago grown dim with age and dust.

Sergei, who had seen enough, retook his place by the wheel. That woman was half-mad for these musty places. But this was going too far. Passing across a wad of bills to that relic, that anti-government skunk! And scarce as butter was, the country rationing every bit, exporting it in exchange for needed machinery, his kids able to eat twice what they were getting: these two were trading off eight pounds of it to that old scarecrow! That parasite. And for what? Surely they knew he'd send his agents to the open market to speculate on it. That foreign store needed a good check-up, must be leaks there somewhere. He'd like to call it to the proper persons' attention, express his opinions to Meester Crampton, outright. He was sure the American didn't understand.

Well-pleased, his passengers returned with two large parcels but of quite another shape than those they had taken in. As they stepped into the car they looked questioningly toward Sergei. His back was immobile, expressive only of that Russian stolidity which Edith found so provoking. She caressed her parcel. Icons were her passion: antiques of all kinds. And this one was a real jewel. But she could never rest until she possessed one of those golden crosses that swung in the candle-lit dusk against his pure white beard.

Katia also was well pleased. If adroitly managed, these trips could become quite a thing. The Cramptons had friends. But one must be careful. Above all things, careful.

The return trip was made in even shorter time than when going. Half-frightened, Edith wondered what had come over the chauffeur to make him tear along at such a furious gait.

7

AS the noon bell sounded Mikhail came over to the conveyor where Sasha and his workmate were examining a new type air-driver installed that morning. The department chief dug in his loose workjacket and held out his cigarettes. Andy took one, then at his urging, another. What's the game? Sasha helped himself liberally.

Mikhail puffed slowly as he asked the Amerikanets, "Well, how's it going?" His eyes narrowed with warm quizzicality. He liked this yellow mop, a cocky young fellow. But he couldn't make him out. Not quite.

Andy shrugged. *"Nichevo."*

"You like it here?"

"Nichevo." The American gave a disarming grin. Just what's this foreman driving at? The whole three months this mug had been tramping on his tail. He knocked his cigarette against his thumbnail and took a light from Sasha.

Old Mikhail's gaze was fixed on him. And where he lived, was it all right? If it wasn't, he knew how to speak up. Did he need anything?

Again, *"Nichevo."* Gurgling sounds rumbled from the depths of Mikhail's thick chest and shook his shoulders, whole body. Taking off his glasses, he wiped them and hooked them again behind his ears. "Well now, my lad!" he said in Russian, "the only word you know, eh?" Except *da-da,* and *ne ponimayu.* "Never mind, you'll get the language before you know it." His next question Andy couldn't get, so Sasha illustrated by pulling his face down, then broadening it and throwing up his chest. Which? How did he feel? Andy smiled. Fine. Okay! (What the hell was this, a cross exam? Gonna give him the works? Like fun.)

Mikhail seemed satisfied. *Lodna*: good. Remember, if he needed anything, just say so. Andy nodded. (Oh, yeah?)

"I'm looking out for him," his workmate added. "You can bet a new truck on that."

As the older man's solid bulk disappeared in a broad waddling gait, Sasha puzzled, "Now why is it that Andre doesn't like our Mikhail?" Aloud he asked, "Mikhail a good *tovarisch*, eh?" The American jerked his head vigorously in the affirmative, "*Da-da.*" Sasha, however, wasn't deceived. Mikhail and he had talked it over between themselves. But why was it?

The shop was emptying. The two beltmen walked past rows of stilled machines which glistened like a forest of oak trunks after a quick spring rain. Through its heart flowed the conveyor, a cypress-dyed river that was bearing metal Samsons to the far parts of the land.

Yesterday Andy had gone to his first Russian class. Morse and Tim told him he was haywire to bother with it. Earlier he'd figured the same. Going back in nine months to the States, all this brain storm'd be for nothing. Well, in the meantime it might come in handy. Want of it cramped his style. Besides, he was ashamed to tell Natasha he wasn't going. These women! Always after a fellow to study this or that. Now if it was airplanes or diesels—but grammar!

Another day ended. The Detroiter packed his worktools, made off. He knew his workmate was standing, looking after him. Sasha the poor sap worked overtime whenever the belt jammed. The way these guys ganged up. Looked sideways at him as he walked down the aisle. Well, who cared? What funeral was it of his if the Company ran behind schedule? He was giving them a fair day's work for a fair day's pay. Why *should* he work over?

He'd done enough of that in Detroit. That sowbelly, Mike Feldman'd come around about quitting time and tap you on the wing. "Boys, we're staying on tonight. Rush orders." To say no meant landing once more in the suitcase brigade. Here, he'd found it was up to you. For the first time in his twenty-eight years, he felt downright sure of his job. Too crack a mechanic for them to give him the air so easy. And he was going to enjoy this seven hour day and easy life, while he'd the chance and a girl to share it. That bow-legged Sasha was a plain fool.

Look how he'd fallen for that old gag. A boob pin. The guy was all broke out with it. Strutted around getting the glad hand from the fellows. *Udarnik* badge they called it. And what might that mean? That he was a "full-fledged member of an *udarnik* brigade, a shock trooper, in the front ranks building Socialism."

Oh yeah? This Socialism, what was it anyway? Could you eat it, see it? A lot of bull. Here they were, living hard, working overtime. And they took it and liked it. Gave it high-sounding names. Horse manure.

Now for a dip with Natasha and a grand feed after. He was going to show this girl one big time. What a knockout she'd look in some of those silk togs he'd lamped in the Foreign Store. He half-ran to the dieshop so's not to miss her on her way out.

Say honey, you got my sparkplugs going, know it? Watch out cutie, I'm heading your way!

He needn't have hurried. Dark smears across her cheek, head scarf awry, she was busy adjusting a spare machine for a new detail. Nothing doing, she told him briefly, she was staying on until three hundred of these screws were done. They had to have them tonight in the body department. Tonight! Sure, she'd like a movie. Another time. Today, everything'd gone fooey. She was in no mood for joking.

"Aw," he begged, "come on. Be a sport. Forget it. What's the big idea?"

Nearby Boardman was running back and forth and swearing a blue streak. Some steel blocks he'd ordered were cut a whole millimeter too small. Ruined! Work was at a standstill. Goddamit, this lousy dieshop took the booby prize.

In his rush the engineer brushed against the assembly-man. "Say, Anderson," he called irritably, "after a job? Then what you hanging around here for, blocking the aisle!

Natasha, tell these dumb-bells," he gestured with disgust to the two men he'd brought with him, "tell the jackasses just what it is I want."

Andy scowled. "Say, watch who you're shoving!" Damn snoot. Like his wife. And shining up to Nat was he. He needed a jab in the slats.

Cross with herself and her brigade for falling behind, the girl pushed by her visitor without so much as a smile. He saw how busy she was? Another time.

Forcing a whistle, Andy strolled off. Have it her own way. Ride her high horse all she wanted. She'd plunge for a fall.

Would she call after him? He looked back. Boardman had gone. She was regulating the feeder and Andy already was forgotten. Hell, he was going to find another sweetie and drop this lemon. Not making time here. A flat tire that skirt. She treated him like he'd been another girl. Maybe a Russian way for stringing a fellow? Well, he'd show her. He knew a few passes himself.

What got into these Russkies anyhow? Crazy lubbers always putting on the gas. Driving themselves more than anybody, far as he could see. What'd they get out of it? Breaking their backs for the firm. What the diff if the company turned out forty, fifty or sixty trucks a day? Not their hard luck. Phoney the whole thing. And to think they made him feel out of it. A lot he cared!

Nine more months. He'd go cuckoo. Just wouldn't he whoop to sight that old New York skyline. If there was anything in this boom talk. He was going home, drop Elsie a line. Tune in on his old reliable. She knew how to make a fellow feel right.

The glowering sky swooped down on him. Didn't Moscow ever have sun in winter! What he'd give for some news. Who'd won the Thanksgiving games, what new movies were on. The one American paper at the plant was a new one on him. Full of labor stuff but only one measly sport column. Crap, Elsie's letter could wait. He was sending two to her one. Better hop a car for the foreign library downtown, they had all the home papers and magazines there. He didn't feel up to Tim's and Morse's crabbing. They'd sink a hearse.

The library was a curious but friendly sort of place, housed in what had once been a small cathedral with its oven domes and Greek crosses. Sonia Magidson, one of its staff, came each week to *Red Star* to bring books and lead a reading circle. She was a pretty young thing but grave as an owl. Andy liked to drop by her table canyoned with books. When she wasn't there, he'd stop for a little kidding with the blond girl on the desk.

Tonight neither was in, so he pored over scores, games, reports and murder cases. When his snickers over the funnies bounced across the quiet of the room, a reader sitting across from him put down his book and came around to enjoy them over his shoulder.

As Andy left, he found the other man standing in the doorway pulling on heavy woolen mitts. "Hello!" he said, "what part of the States you hail from?"

"Detroit. And you?"

"The old Hog City. I've been here nearly three years. You a newcomer? Good! You can give me some late dope on things back there. I say, if you don't mind I'll walk your way a bit?" They decided on a turn about the Square. His new acquaintance had seen the Detroiter in the plant gym, evidently they worked at the same plant? He was a repairman in *Red Star's* tool-making department: his name, Clarence MacGregor, or Mac for short.

In the late dusk, the snow-drenched buildings and Square had a blue eerie light and the still frost hummed in their lungs.

Andy found himself liking this fellow, right off. A tight black tam was pulled close to his eyes, a brilliant plaid scarf wound about his throat. Laughter wrinkles ran along the borders of his pug nose and from the corners of his gray eyes back to his pointed ears. Altogether there was something breezy and amusing about him. Andy felt as natural and at home with him as a worn baseball mitt. "You know," he ventured, "with your cap and scarf and that brogue of yours I'd never take you for a guy from the States. More like ..."

"Scotland, eh?" Mac added. "Right-o!" His wife Nan and he had been eight years from the old country when the blizzard broke. Sure, and he was Scotch-Irish American, Russian, and what have you. Internationalist. His little girl though, had been born in Chi. They trudged around Constitution Square on which the library faced, past the Municipal Soviet to the irongray walls of the Lenin Institute and then reversed the circle, buoyed by the feeling that comes when one human senses in another one of his kin.

"What's that for?" Andy thumbed at the needle monument in the center of the Square. Mac led him over. "To the revolutionary heroes of 1905-1917," he translated. "Bet you never noticed this." He pointed to copper plates that encircled its base. The Constitution adopted by the first Soviet of Workers' Peasants' and Soldiers' Deputies. Here any citizen might come and read his rights. "Some idea, eh?" If the light was better, he'd translate it for him. A document, he figured, that meant for this century what the Declaration of Independence had meant in its time. Even more.

Suddenly he clutched his overcoat pocket. Cats, he'd forgotten! What was Andy doing this evening, maybe he'd like to lamp a good movie?

"Would I! But those queues. And I can't savvy the darn titles."

Mac took him by the arm. Romp on it, just in time for the next show. They swung into the rear end of a bus. When they found lines extended half a block in front of the *Udarnik,* the Detroiter scowled. "Let's beat it!" Hold it, his friend cautioned, he had tickets. Nan had planned to come along but got tied up with a meeting. Hadn't his buddy caught on to getting his tickets ahead, through the Union at the plant? So that was it? Andy clipped his heels. It was swell walking right in. Made you feel the cat's pajamas.

He'd never been in this new *Kino.* Some hangout. Its plain lines struck him as too modern, but Mac said it was quite the thing. The schedule of film showings, they found, had been changed, they had almost an hour to wait before the house emptied and the next show began. Mac swore good-naturedly and led the way to the restaurant in the basement where he treated to fancy cakes and coffee and drummed on the tablecloth in double time with the music. Andy brought hot chocolate and more cookies from the buffet and plumped two red apples before his new friend. Jeez, it was great having money in your pocket. Prices here were stiff but things tasty. He chewed heartily. "Swell joint, eh?"

"*Nichevo*," Mac answered. "Come on up and see the exhibits, might as well kill time that way."

The foyer was lined with huge glass cases of graphs, statistics, and photographs about oil, transport, Moscow reconstruction, mining, machinery and public schools. Music drifted up the stairs. Andy stepped restlessly. If they'd just reel out some good old jazz! They wandered through the reading rooms and out again to the upper foyer in search of a free checkerboard table. In many booths chess was being played. A national sport, Mac said. Andy thought it looked a bit slow. Checkers were more his speed.

"Mister Anderson! Andy!" He felt himself seized about the waist in a convulsive wiry embrace. He whirled. Old Hothead, by God! There was genuine warmth to his welcome. He'd seen the Heindricks but once since their journey into the country together. As he introduced them to MacGregor, the excited couple turned to the men sitting by them in the booth. "*Inostrani*"! They whispered the modern open-sesame and gestured toward their companions. Not unwillingly the Russians offered their seats and started off. With the air of a host Gus Heindrick motioned for his guests to seat themselves. "Say, wait a minute!" Mac spoke directly in Russian to the men who gave a jolly *nichevo* and left. Andy saw that Mac hadn't liked it. These two didn't click. For his part, he wished the movie buzzer would ring.

Gus fixed his near-sighted gaze on the Detroiter. "Well, how's it going? It's hard here, eh?"

"Oh, not so bad. And you?"

Freda and Gus sighed in unison. "Oh, it's hard for us! We had no idea." Yes, they had a goodsized room but what a place! Plastering cracked although the house was built only last year. And water bugs! Freda shuddered. Never, for ten blessed years had she been bothered with such things. She had scrubbed and spread powder: only the Old Scratch knew what it was going to be like in the spring. They missed their garden, little friendly gatherings, street demonstrations, and the chain store around the corner. She paused. So far only one thing had been as they had dreamed it: the November celebrations in Red Square. Ah, if all days could be like that!

At the shop? Shadows trembled above Heindrick's cloud of hair. Waste, inefficiency, bureaucrats: was this socialism! Take what had happened to him just last week. He was a skilled machinist, wasn't he, Russia needed his type bad. He'd come with such enthusiasm, but how they killed it out of you! Last week, he had needed some pieces of sandpaper to polish off some tools he'd been making. Just ordinary sandpaper that you got at home for ten or twenty cents. It ought to be a simple matter, you think, to get it? More complicated than a balky mule. My God, just wait till they heard! You think his department had any sandpaper? Not a sheet. He must get it from another section half way across the whole works. This, mind you, in one of the largest electric plants in the whole country. Well, he left his work, losing valuable time, on the trail of that paper. When he came there, the office girl told him to go back for a requisition sheet. Sure, didn't he know? Transferring supplies from one sector to another meant she needed a record.

Well, so he had gone back to his shop for that requisition sheet for the sandpaper. Mother of Jesus, the girl who had to make it out was gone! He paced the floor thin before she came.

He ran with the paper back to the supply room. A half-hour wasted, and his work standing. "All right," that simp of a woman told him, "now please, the bill." He groaned and turned his overall pockets inside out. Not a cent on him. She was unconcerned. Never mind, she wouldn't take his money anyway. He must take this bill she was making out to his department to have it stamped and signed. Didn't he know?

Gus stormed at her. Why in Himmel hadn't she told him before. Think of all the time wasted. And they talked about Socialism!

"How should I know you needed telling!" she retorted. "We work on a cost accounting system here. Go back, bring the signed sheet, and you'll get your sandpaper." So once more he'd gone back to his sector with the slip to get that damn sandpaper to polish those tools. Was he sore.

And what did they think, that sly eel of a girl had disappeared! Everybody he asked said she'd just been there but left. He protested and repeated his troubles to everybody he met in his broken Russian, and waited. Just imagine what a bawling out he'd get for filling his order two hours late!

At last that blockhead had showed up, calm as you please. Why was he so excited? At that Gus had grasped his head, exploded, and fled. Papers clutched in a defiant fist, his short legs flew across the plant yard. That Supplies female was busy with another order but he refused to wait. "Give me the sandpaper!" he cried, fluttering his bills under her nose. She examined it, it wasn't stamped. He must take it back before—

Immediately Heindrick began a demonstration: not outside the shop as in America, but right on the spot. What had he to fear? These fools! Brainless flappers. And they called it Socialism! "Aw pipe down, comrade," the girl told him, "can't you see I'm going over with it myself? Here, sign this, take your sandpaper, and go."

So, exactly two hours and five minutes after he had left his bench he returned. Five roubles of his time, paid by the firm, spent to get thirty kopecks' worth of paper. Was that Socialism?!

"No, it's stupidity," Mac agreed. But what was he doing to help get rid of the red tape there, besides hollering? Gus' hands and eyes lifted. What could he do? What *was* there to do? When you talked, nobody listened. It was terrible. His wife sat at home, weeping, while he ... Sometimes he thought he should lose his mind. To think, after all these years!

Andy felt sorry for the little couple. It must be tough,

all right, to be let down like that. But how Mac was going for Hothead! "And in the States you called yourself a Red, —eh?" Was this all he had learned from twenty years in the movement! To see no further than the end of his prickly short nose! Many of his fellow countrymen did better. Did Heindrick think the Russian workers didn't know these drawbacks better than any? That they weren't busting their suspenders getting rid of these crazy hangovers of an old system? Wearing their nerves thin? What was needed though was fighters, organizers, not squealers!

Freda was offended. "What right you got to speak to my husband like this? He's given everything, everything for the movement! Why, look on the crown of his head. That scar—and you dare!" Andy blessed the gong's sounding. Why should Mac get so hot under the collar? It wasn't his funeral.

Their seats luckily were right in the center. The Scotchman translated titles in such a distinct voice that those in front looked around in protest. *Inostrani tovarisch,* he explained. They turned back. For a few shots he read more quietly, then gradually his voice soared to its old pitch. Andy at first was self-conscious, not fancying the rôle of youngster with its Ma at the movies, but soon he forgot everything else in the picture. It was a real thriller. After the show he insisted on Mac going back to the café. When they chanced on the Heindricks, Andy urged, "Come on, have a drink on me." He remembered how they'd fed him coming over. Sure, this was his treat. Aside, he cautioned Mac, "No arguments."

Wisecracking, going back for seconds all round, he was the only hilarious one at the table. Jeez, it was swell, having dough, a job. If only Elsie was here. That young snip out in the dieshop could go pick dandelions for all he cared.

Mac was fidgeting and cracking his finger joints. Freda sipped her hot cocoa gingerly. Ah, for some good coffee like they had in the States. The orchestra was playing a lively march, she leaned forward to make herself heard. If only they hadn't lost their percolator and trunk coming over what good coffee she'd make them. Real American coffee. Her lips tightened. Andy worried. He knew what was coming. Would Mac let them tell the story of their lost trunk clear to the end?

At the height of Freda listing her lost possessions, Mac rose to go. "Time I was home," he said abruptly, "got a full day tomorrow."

Andy followed. Try and laugh that off!

With a promise to the Heindricks that he'd sure be over one evening soon, he trailed the rude Scotchman.

"Excuse me!" Mac jerked on his tam, knotted his scarf. "I can't stand their brand. Moscow's no place for them. They think a blanket of roses should've fallen from the sky, and their job is to lie back and enjoy the view. That's their Socialism!"

Andy started to break in but changed his mind.

"I know 'em," Mac went on. "They're all wet! You don't build a new world overnight. Or without plenty of sweat. Point is, Andy, we're on our way. Get me? When you know where you're heading, who minds the bumps!" He'd plenty reason to know the weak spots in organization here. Who wouldn't after two years' work! But he and his Russian pals weren't trifling time away, whining. They were knuckling under to change a few things. "Yep," he told his uneasy companion, "keep your eyes peeled for news of our tool shop. In fact, before we're done our whole auto works may get into the scrap."

"What you mean?" At his friend's explanation Andy cautioned, "Keep away from that stuff. And boy, I don't mean maybe. Say, you're sure heading for a land on your bean. Drop it! Honest." Going in for a scrap with the straw bosses, probably the whole administration! By crap, he was going to keep clear of it himself.

Eyes sparkling, Mac knotted his scarf and hugged his bulging brief case under one arm. Its weight warmed him. It held ammunition for several weeks captured during a raid that afternoon on his old haunt, the foreign book store. "Sure somebody's going to land on their bean," he agreed readily, "but it'll not be me or my comrades, or any honest worker. A few hotair artists and boobs. Just stand by,

94

buddy, watch the fireworks. It's going to be interesting. And hot!"

The Detroiter narrowed his gaze. And he had taken this chap for such a level-headed fellow! Almost as looney as Hothead. Sure he would keep a lookout for the fireworks. From a safe distance!

Outside, a fresh snow was whitening sidewalks and over-coats. Behind its moving curtain hung the dim jagged outline of the Kremlin. "Pretty, eh?" Mac hooked his companion's arm. As they paused, soft flakes settled on lashes and hands. With a gruff wrist the Chicagoan cuffed away several flakes on the tip of his flat nose. A night truck with heavy limbed shovelers was clearing the avenue: in its rear hooded men with monstrous twig brooms were whisking the sleety asphalt of fine rice mounds. "Several thousand of those sweepers in Moscow," Mac commented. "Winter and summer sweeping, sweeping. Some day machinery will free them for industry. Every time I see them slinging those brooms, I think of the seven maids with seven mops, trying to sweep clear the sea."

Andy felt curious, drawn to his queer friend. "Say," he volunteered, "I'll take you up soon about dropping over."

"Do," Mac urged. "Bring your pals if you like." He'd see how they lived, real à la Moscow, not like foreigners. For once Andy was sorry that his car came so soon.

8

QUIETLY Mac unlocked the door and made his way
along the darkened hall, past the Chestakovs' room to
his own. Nan was asleep: she had left the light burning for
him and the window closed. With her fair short hair lying
tousled about the pillow, one slight arm around little Lucy,
she might have been taken for the child's older sister.

Not bothering to remove his coat, he reached in his port-
folio for his new books and pamphlets. Where was that one
on Siberia? There was pioneering for you! Siberia, the new
West! Maybe some day Nan and he would go there. A fellow had to step out. Still, there was plenty of pioneer work
right here in Moscow. He had ridden by his stop on the
way home, reading, but it had been worth the bloody extra
walk in the cold. He'd just finish this off before turning in.
As he emptied his briefcase on the table, he whistled under
his breath. What a stack they made. He must remember to
salt them away in the bookshelf before Nan spotted them.

In the midnight quiet of the apartment house, the sleepers'
even breathing was punctuated by rapid turning of pages.
Mac, having given up Siberia, was at Dnieprostroi. Ah, there
was a job to stir a man's soul! Grappling with a maddened
river, welding 40,000 hicks into a working unit. The room
grew close. Eyes fastened on his book, he maneuvered out
of his coat, tossed his scarf on the bed. Nan roused. "Mac!
What time is it? It's stifling in here!"

Guiltily he closed his book. "Hello, old scout. Be ready
for bed in no time, and the window open." She sat up
gingerly, so as not to wake Lucy. "Was it a good movie?"

"Not bad. How was your meeting?" (From long habit

they spoke in whispers, as Lucy was a light sleeper.) Dull, she'd thought. Honest, would she ever, ever get settled here? He unlaced his shoes. "Sure. Takes time. Say, a swell looker went with me on your ticket."

She yawned sleepily. Oh yeah? Tell her another.

Pulling off his shirt, his gaze fell on the stacked books. How to clear that table before . . . ? He placed himself between them and her bed, playing for time. "Well, my movie pal turned out to be not a bad chap. Raw and all that, but good company." One hand behind him was easing his incriminating evidence across the table's uneven surface. Nan fenced against the light: would he hurry up! It was two o'clock. How he kept going on such hours was beyond her.

With an ominous thud, a solid object bounded against the floor. Quickly he picked it up and started with an armful of his purchase toward the bookshelf. Lucy cried out, and Nan, soothing her, turned on him. "Why Clarence Mac-Gregor, you must have spent at least forty roubles!"

Hurriedly he cleared the table. Now, buddy, no time to start an argument. Wake Lucy again. (Clarence was it? Bloody nonsense!)

"I don't care if I do!" Her voice rose angrily. Forty roubles. Enough to buy two pounds of extra butter for the baby in the open market. Really, Mac was not fair to the kid. Last month it was the same. Books, books! Selfish, that's all. Her impatient words rushed about him like bees from a robbed hive. Well, couldn't he say something?

"Gee, Nan—" Aw, hell, she knew well enough. Socks, underwear were flung in a heap, trousers carefully folded over the back of a chair. She knew well enough. Wordless, he slid into his pajamas. Why must they fuss over such things? Let her rave: not a peep she'd get out of him. Him, neglecting the kid! The air was unbearable. He switched off the light and threw open the upper window.

Overhead the flecked midnight was glittering down on a heedless world. That sky. While the cold rushed in, he stood there gazing out. . . . Must be great to fly at night. See how men, during the day, had been changing the face of the earth.

Hearing his cot screech, Nan lay still. The fresh cold air felt good against her flushed cheeks. "Mac?"

From the darkness: "'Huh?"

"You forgot something, didn't you?"

"Er . . . maybe." The alarm clock ticked on, unconcerned, in the stillness . . . Oh well, if he was so stubborn! Shut up like a clam. Not even willing to say goodnight.

From the darkness: "Nan?"

"Huh?" Already her feet were searching happily along the cold floor for her house-slippers.

With an answering shout, Mac plunged for the cackling alarm clock, banged to the window, and leaped back for a five minute nap. Six A.M. always came two hours too soon. Nan pulled on her stockings and bathrobe, lit the heater in the bathroom and the light under the tea kettle, and took Lucy on her shoulder. "Get up, lazy!" she called to her husband, "your turn to take Lucy to the nursery."

"Right-o." She heard his heavy tread about the room and across the kitchen sink for a washup. The Chestakovs were already dressed, their kettle purring. Eyes puffed, shawl thrown hastily over her disorderly hair, Berta Chestakov was bustling about preparing her husband's *kasha* and herring. With loud raps on the Klarovs' door, she returned to the kitchen. "Look at that sink!" she scolded. "That Klarova woman!" Sink and shelf were crowded with soiled dishes. Filling a pail with them, Berta placed them squarely before the offending woman's door. Mac grinned and mopped his head with a rough towel. This living three families in one flat was no joke.

"How much trouble she gives us!" Berta grumpled. "Nan and I are forever cleaning up after her." Did he think that Alicia Klarova took her turn at scrubbing the kitchen floor? Not her. Nan was a slip, but she knew how to push her elbows. "I may be only a plain know-nothing, but Alicia for all her brains is a dirty snob!" Berta made a spitting gesture off the palm of her hand.

Mac frowned at the dirty circles about the sink, which Berta was vigorously attacking. Yes, he agreed, if Alicia kept this up they'd have to take her before the House Soviet. Soon dressed, he made tea and cut bread while Nan set a hurried table in their room. While Lucy gulped her milk, stuffed bread and butter, she chattered rapidly in Russian to her sleepy-eyed parents. Mac had bundled her into her wraps and the three left the house together. "Nan, you'll call for her after work?" he asked. He had a brigade meeting. Lucy skipped gayly, swinging onto a hand of each. She liked kindergarten, singing games and eating lunch off little tables and chairs that were made just to fit.

Leaving her at the kindergarten, Mac walked briskly on to the plant. Its buildings rose in cleancut squares and oblongs against a leaden sky. Swell place, he reflected, hurrying through the long shed to his section of the machine shop. Swell place, and run like the mischief. On three cylinders instead of six.

Misha was before him, his work tools already laid out. "Hi there, comrade. What's new?"

"*Nichevo,*" Mac opened his locker. "And you?"

A slow smile crept across Misha's angular countenance as he searched his pockets. He had been working on a scheme. His workmate made a quick reach for the rumpled papers he produced. "Let's have a look!"

"Not so fast, *tovarisch.*" The Russian smoothed them out on the iron work table. "These cost me not a few hours. What we need is a plan, right? So here it is, a scheme for reorganizing our fitters' work." Here was what he'd propose to their brigade, Mac must add his ideas.

Through skylights a gray but steadily brightening light cast shadows on lathes, drills and men and women moving up aisles to their machines. At the power's roar, the brigaders straightened up. What the devil! Well, they could finish at noon hour.

Ivan's loose frame blocked their way down the passage. "What the hell's got into you repairmen!"

"What's up now?"

"A pretty stew! Only six fitters showed up on the third shift last night. But every goldern work-key signed off, that's what!"

"No need to bellow at us, Ivan," Misha told him shortly. "We can hear you." It was true, the man's full voice fairly drowned the lathe's rumbling. Was Ivan sure, Misha asked, who was in, and who wasn't?

Was he! He had checked up, himself.

Misha Popov took out his pad. "Give us the list. We'll do some checking up ourselves." Damn these loafers. Beginning with his blackened thumb, Ivan named them off with a last sneer, "Some crew, you repairmen."

Misha's glance was contemptuous. Not all the men's fault. Rotten organization all through this shop. "We repairmen are taking steps to stiffen our ranks. Time you, as assistant manager, did something besides bellowing. Now listen here, Ivan . . ." Together, they started off toward the far end of the shed.

Mac began his work on an old drill they had decided to recondition. Peach of a chap, Misha. Ugly as an old scarecrow, pock marked and droop mouthed, his tongue with the wicked edge of a razor. But when it came to brains, Misha had more than his share. And nobody knew that better than Misha. He could draw circles around the Ivans. Still, he had few friends about the shop. What was it?

And what, Mac asked himself once more, what could Misha have done last year to bring disgrace swooping down on him? With his talents, Party record and energy, Misha Popov had risen quickly from the ranks. Completing one school after another, he had been in his second year of the land's highest university, the Institute of Red Professors, when something had happened. Just what, Mac could only guess. He knew Misha had been excluded from the Institute and Party, and had returned to his old repairman's job, silent, morose.

Such drastic measures, Mac knew, only followed on grave offense. Word went round that the Party figured Misha Popov needed to renew his proletarian experience. Oh well, it was none of his business to nose into his friends' affairs. If the Party found him in the wrong he was wrong, and that was that. Some political question, no doubt. But what? Misha seemed so right. Mac felt in his friend a fierce stubbornness, perhaps resentment: a hurt and self-searching that could unburden itself to no one. Sure, Misha was taking up this brigade fight because, as an old war horse, he couldn't help it. But it was more than that. Misha was out to conquer, above all, himself: put himself on the up and up with his fellows. And that was a thing as big in its way as conquering Siberian wastes. What a century! Well, Misha knew he could count on him. Only... Mac's old worry cropped up. Maybe he was a slacker, ought to be back there. Hell! Resolutely he set his mind on other things. But if he thought...

As Mac left his repair work to give his section of operating lathes their daily once-over, he stopped behind a man smoking, inattentive by his machine. "See here!" he cautioned. "Watch out or you'll wreck her." What kind of a worker was he, anyway! Acted more like a doorkeeper than a turner! (This namby-pamby entrusted with such a beauty! His fingers itched to shove the fellow aside, take on the job himself.) He watched the machine churning, revolving, cutting, feeding, everything timed in perfect rhythm. A wonder! MAG, as Misha and he affectionately termed her. Only four in the whole shop, bought last winter in Germany for real gold. And worth it. MAG turned out fine steel parts that had no equal. Just look at her, with what precision she was cutting teeth in this screw. Like a human, was MAG, with brains, nerves, eyes. Little darling.

Ouch! He sprang for the lever. With a soft purr the machine came to a full stop. "Idiot!" Mac whirled on Peter. "You'll ruin her!"

Furious, the turner threw on the power. "Say, who do you think you are! This is my machine, ain't it?" Mac danced with anger. Did he think he was going to let him spoil her! "Listen, you boob, I told you before about letting her pound on her end like that. Oh, you'll wreck her!" Bloody swine.

Peter tossed his butt aside. So the handyman was worrying over having to fix her, eh? Well, he was no supervisor, just a repairman, see? Pavel, the young worker operating the MAG next to Peter's, came over. Mac was right, he said, a hundred times right. He understood as well as the fitter what had happened: The machine, allowed to run beyond her right length, had pounded against the brace end, sending a jolt thundering through its delicate mechanisms. A few more shocks like that, and she'd snap her safety screw. Then, three weeks she'd stand idle, while they took her to bits and set her to rights again.

He had been keeping an eye out, but Peter was balky as a mule. He'd no business there at all.

"You're a lad after me own heart," Mac squeezed his arm. "Look at your machine, trim as a bell. You got some feeling for our MAGs. But that ... that ..."

Peter blew an indifferent ring in his direction. "Do your job, windbag, and I'll do mine." Mac went in search of the section manager. He was not around. Nobody in this shop ever was around, when you wanted them. What the rest said about the repairmen. Pretty kettle of fish.

During midafternoon Ivan came for Mac. Where had he been hiding?

The repairman straightened up and wiped his hands on some scraps of rag. "Fixing up this milling machine that broke down because some greenhand forgot she needed oil. What's on your chest?"

"One of our German machines shot to pieces."

MAG! Not waiting to hear more, Mac darted up the aisle. Peter was sitting on an idle machine end, downcast, smoking. "Not my fault," he remarked sourly.

"You'll find out soon enough whose fault it is," his workmate retorted. This would come up before the whole department meeting: Peter be taken off the machines for good.

Mac ran a tortured hand over MAG's stilled body.

Work over, Misha joined him on the way to their shop's Red Corner. Vasiliev, the oldest repairman in the shop, was waiting for them. Specs pushed up, banding his high narrow forehead, he was scanning the wall paper. With an appreciative grunt, he beckoned them over. "Just have a look at this." Under a cartoon depicting a well-fed sow standing by *Red Star's* restaurant table and giving dignified refusal to the manager's offer of borscht, were written these words: "Not even a pig would relish the meals our manager serves us!"

"Pretty hot, eh?" Vasiliev chuckled. "Now, Misha, we really need to broaden our fight to include this front, too. Better meals." And more quarters, young Pavel added. With several other lads he had been sleeping on tables and couches in the *Comsomol* office for nearly six weeks. All the administration had given them so far was promises. The boys were getting fed up with it, what'd they take them for anyway! Everybody knew Moscow was crowded, rooms scarcer than hen's teeth, but that was no reason for the Housing Committee to go to sleep on the job, was it? Falling back on the excuse of "objective difficulties"! If anybody thought just because they were young and *Comsomoletz* they were going to put up with it, they had another think coming. And damn quick.

"Funds on hand to build, all right," Vasiliev observed dryly, but no lumber no bricks no labor, and above all no will. Well, they were going to see to that. Good, Misha agreed, soon as they'd straightened out their repairmen. They had to prove themselves first. Unless they wanted the razz from the whole shop.

Grouping around one end of the long table with its red cambric cover, the brigade set to work. As the oldest and most experienced, Vasiliev took the lead. Busy all afternoon teaching beginners his favorite methods, devised in the course of three decades at the trade, his eyes were still watering from so much close work. From an inside pocket he whipped out a rumpled handkerchief and drew it rapidly across his eyes, forehead and gray stubbled cheeks. "All right! We're agreed on what's wrong, eh? Now as to what's to be done."

Simply, wasting no words, he placed his points. As it was, every man was expected to know and care after every blasted lathe, milling machine and drill. Actually nobody knew any type well. Better division of labor and fixed personal responsibility would do away with this state of affairs. "We'll divide into brigades, six each, two to a shift.

Each brigade responsible for only one set of specified machines. What do you think?"

Mac gave his everpresent tam an absentminded push over one eye. Right-o! As it was, he rarely got a chance to come back twice to the same machine. This way, he'd soon learn their individual whims and weak spots and just what was needed to keep them in trim. He winked at Misha. "Oh boy, we'll take on the MAGS!" Okay? With real study of the old girl they'd be able to find ways of reconditioning her in much shorter order, reduce her breakdowns to a minimum.

Vasiliev's corrugated thumb and its stubbed mates rapped on the bright cambric. Years ago, when still an apprentice, he'd had them chewed off by a greedy unguarded machine. Second point, he continued, a better system of wages. At present, whether a man worked badly or well, kept his machines in fine shape or like the devil—no matter, he drew the same wages each month. All rubbish! They needed a new plan that rewarded good work and penalized bad.

"And that," Mac interrupted, "is where Misha comes in." With a slow flush, his morose workmate drew out his papers. Yes, he had a plan.

Knotted fist gripping a blunted pencil, Vasiliev's tongue worked laboriously in one cheek as he added items which Mac, Pavel and others proposed. "Now lads, I think we're ready to take up our plan with the *Triangle?* And then for a general repairmen's meeting tomorrow after work." Misha promised to get exact figures from the office on time lost through machinery standing idle and waiting for repairs.

As they disbanded, Vasiliev took the Scotchman's arm. "You know," the older worker commented, "I think our Pavel has real talent. No? What'd you think of proposing him for a scholarship? And see here, my lad. As one Party man to another, we're heading for a stiff opposition, once this fight's launched. You know that? Good! For my part, I feel ripe for a scrap."

Fitters straddled machines and sat humped on tool boxes, listening to Vasiliev. The old chap had a way of putting things, Mac noted, kind of got the men on the right side. That was lucky, he'd prepare the way for Misha. "We repairmen are the talk of the shop," he told them. "What fine lads we are! Never can find you fellows they say. And when it comes to the night shift—half manages to sleep through, but get their cards punched just the same! How's that?" He mentioned names and dates.

"Who's been squealing?" some one demanded.

"Ha, the shoe pinches, eh?"

"That's right, show the roaches up!"

"Say, where were *you* last night!"

"Quiet!" Vasiliev called. "Comrades, a man can hardly squeal on himself? Here we are, looking after nobody's business but our own. Who profits by this loafing? In his own heart, I know not one of us is satisfied with the way things are going. Not so much our fault as poor organization. We've called you together to propose a new plan of work." If all three shifts accepted it, then a committee'd be elected to take it up with management.

"What's this! Our present scheme's okay!"

"Let's hear!"

"Leave sleeping dogs lie."

A repairman swung around on the dissenters. "Never mind, you Smart Alecs. We need a new system for guys like you!"

"Quiet, quiet, comrades! Nobody can hear."

Cleaning his spectacles, Vasiliev unfolded a sheet of figures. Listen to this: they had 2300 hours of excess idle time on machinery this quarter. A fine record! Cries of "Impossible!" "Must be a mistake!" No mistake, Vasiliev answered, figures straight from the books. "Four thousand dollars thrown to the winds! by us! Bravo! We can feel proud of that! For this money we could've given our country eight extra trucks. Think it over. Now as to our proposals—"

"Sure! Let's have it!"

"A lot of hoxus. Nothing'll come of it."

"Quiet! Quiet!" Cigarette smoke circled among machines

across eyes glittering at the speaker, considering disagreeing speculating, each to himself.

When Misha rose to speak, Mac saw the men stiffen against him. The poor crow had a way of antagonizing, in spite of everything. What was it? At mention of fines for going below norms, a fitter sitting near the back pushed his way in. "There's the trick. I knew it!" His neighbor joined him. "Take money right out of our pockets! I guess not!"

"Oh, you loafers!" Pavel scoffed. "See who's the first to raise objections!" "Scared, eh?" "All the same, there's something to it." Stubbornly the brigade defended and explained: a minimum wage was guaranteed.

One questioner asked, "What'll management think of the scheme?" Vasiliev laughed. "Tell you the truth, we'll have some trouble convincing them. You see, they'll be scared the plant can't pay the higher wages this is bound to mean. But it's plain horse sense, more and better output. We'll convince them."

Discussion was long, heated. Among suggestions from the floor was one for blueprints of all types of machine, and Vasiliev added it to his list. Good! "Well," he asked finally, "want to vote now, or wait until next meeting? No need to rush it." It was agreed that every man was to get the plan and proposals in writing and take final vote at the next meeting.

Afterwards, Vasiliev took his brigade comrades home with him for a celebration. He knew his repairmen. Some'd hold out to the bitter end. But it was clear that on the first round, victory was theirs.

And down in Stalingrad they had a big scrap on. Had Mac read today's papers? Sure, things were stirring and high time, too.

LOOK HERE, STALINGRAD!

Look hear Stalingrad
Come through on those tractors!
What's the matter down there
Forgetting the job you took on
   in face of the whole world?
Pretty mess you're making of things
Give an account of yourselves!

> (So wrote *Red Putilov's* steel workers of Leningrad
> in an open letter to the tractor plant on the Volga:
> fiery words blazoned across the face of *Pravda*)

Remember how you vied with Kharkov Rostov Cheliabinsk
   for the site of our first tractor plant?
How your one-horse town woke to life when you won?
And now—what're you doing?
Bringing disgrace on us all!
Making us the laughing stock of the Exchanges
   in New York and Europe.
"Stalingrad's a white elephant," they say,
"Russians build but can't run their giants."
They are wrong? Prove it!

Can't you feel in their scorn
   the swift training of machine guns
   to the east and west!
On guard, comrades—
To work in a new way!
This year we open five hundred new giants
Clear Siberia's wastes for Magnitogorski Kuznetstroi
And you, proletariat of Stalingrad?
You hear our black earth crying out for steel horses!
For shame!
We *Red Putilovets* call you
   As once we called in nineteen-five -seventeen
   To the barricades! To our October!

Brothers, on to the fight!
  For technique!
  The front of socialist construction
To work—in a new way!

Shame hovers low over Stalin's town.
Along the Volga floats the black banner.
  Shop meetings, heated discussion
  Fresh brigades forming and
Finally these words back to *Red Putilov*:
"Dear Comrades, you are right
We shall answer
Not with words
But Tractors."

The whole country waits
For daily reports in *Pravda*.
  Yesterday Stalingrad gave forty tractors
  Today forty-six
  Tomorrow fifty
            sixty
            sixty-five
Stalingrad is coming through!
Answering Putilov, the whole earth
Not with words
But with
Tractors!

9

GYPSIES, Cossacks, Spanish dancers whirled across polished spacious floors of the Metropole's ballroom, as the room's gay-colored kaleidoscope constantly reshaped itself into fresh, brilliant designs. Beneath its frame of gilt-trimmed marble columns stood rows of small tables, crowded with baskets of fruit, bright favors, wine bottles, and slender, crystal tumblers.

New Year's Eve, and Moscow's foreign colony celebrating. Henry and Edith Crampton were joyous, secretive. He, as the fat monk, a pillow stuffed under his belt accentuating his natural rotundity; she as the demure nun, sheer linen drawn across her forehead under her black hood, setting off her delicate, regular features, were the acknowledged hit of the evening. Between dance numbers their table was besieged by curious, admiring friends. "Come on, tell us how you got those costumes." "Is there a place in Moscow where you can rent them? You borrowed them from some actor?" To all questions they presented a smiling reticence, Henry Crampton roaring good naturedly, "You'd never guess. A military secret!"

Mary Boardman felt envious. Philip, uncomfortable in the Mephistopheles outfit she had forced on him, was getting what pleasure he could from his elastic, padded tail. Mary had chosen to come as a witch, but the costume had proven neither original nor suited to her slender type. Its one advantage, that it gave her an excuse for letting her reddish masses of brown hair flow loose about her angular shoulders.

Henry Crampton had the next number with his interpreter, Katerina Boudnikova. Holding her as tightly against him as his pillow allowed, he murmured, "You're looking wonderful this evening, wonderful!" As gypsy, she wore a green clinging affair softer than spiderweb. Her green earrings dangled coyly as she whispered, "And you, you are so pious, I am afraid of you!" He gave her a playful squeeze. "Pious, am I? Be careful!" This woman was strong wine, making his whole body tingle. Heady as the perfume she used. He wanted to reach down and bite the green halfmoon in her blueblack hair. Damn shame that a creature with her breeding should be condemned to the life she was. A cruel unfeeling country, this, with values turned upside down.

She had told him her story, one evening when the orchestra's tragic music had moved strange depths in both. Mere memory of it raced his pulse. She had sat, dark eyes moist, staring at unseen shadows, her voice sometimes singing out, again dying away on the moan of the violins. Henry sighed. It had been one of those moments.

Not yet thirty, she had already lived, she told him, ah how many lifetimes. Her childhood had been uneventful, happy. Her mother had been threatened with disinheritance because of her willful marriage to one whom they considered beneath her, for, although, wealthy, Katia's father had not sprung from the aristocracy. Nevertheless there had been an early reconciliation, and Peter Boudnikov had been able to give his children every advantage that Russian culture offered. They had spent several winters in Paris and Venice. Ah, Rome by moonlight! She had been considered especially gifted in languages by their French governess, with no ear for music but talented in art. She had been engaged to a young army officer, Alexander Kriskov, well-connected, with a future before him. Life the taunter had promised all, only to snatch everything. Alexander ... killed in the war ... Her family tossed penniless to one side by the revolution, robbed of property, position, everything! Even half of their house had been confiscated and converted into quarters for the most ordinary trash. To Bolsheviks, nothing was sacred.

Her poor father, who once commanded several large

stores, was now reduced to keeping books for a state shop; her mother, to creeping out to part with one treasured belonging after another. Ah, what humiliations they had suffered. When scarcely eighteen, she had been forced to find means of earning her bread. How? The stage, of course, had been a possibility. She had scored several successes in school dramatics. But no: her talent, such as it was, was not above average. And for art! (Hands clasped, her dreamy voice rang out with the melodramatic fullness of well-rehearsed lines.) To Art, one gave all or nothing. To be a great artist was to live to the utmost. To be only average, a mediocrity... impossible! She had rather serve like her broken old father behind a counter tracing senseless figures than desecrate man's highest calling. (A pause. Her figure dropped back.)

So she had taken this work, utilizing her gift for languages. Dull, uninspiring, it was true. Yet it let one live. And with people like Henry Crampton to work for—life was smiling on her again!

Touched by her confidence in him, he had covered her hands with his own, vowing to be her friend, her helper, always. Why had there been such a tragic, almost mocking quality in the smile she had given him? Could there have been some discreet gaps in her story?

The waltz theme of the Metropole orchestra was low, persuasive. Crampton stumbled against his partner's arched feet and collided violently with a couple dancing near them. With a "Sorry, old man," and "Too early in the evening for that!" they limped once more into step. Katia reiterated softly, "Yes, I am in awe of my black-robed godmother." He gripped her palms until she winced. Their secret make-believe: he was the godmother who brought surprises and good news from afar into poor little Cinderella's scullery. He had learned more about the intricacies of women's finery in this last month with Katia, than in all his years with Edith. Maybe he was reaching the age where such things mattered? Or maybe....

Katia gestured toward Philip Boardman. What had been troubling his assistant these past days? Henry scowled:

"Why bring that up!" As quickly his look softened. "Guess he's jealous, eh?" Her answering jest was only on the surface. She had worked enough with Philip Boardman to realize that something was brewing, and she had no intention of being a passive witness. One must know how and by what means it was possible to act, and still not risk . . . This pillow was a godsend. As he sought furtively to press her harder against him, she was searching the dancers, speculating. To break Henry Crampton away from his wife, get him to take her back with him to America? She would prefer a more promising candidate. But where? They sidled endlessly about the dense throng of bodies.

Mary Boardman fingered her sherbet glass. Why, she asked herself, why must Agatha carry on her highbrow talk, even here! Such a bore, really! Had the woman no sense of fitness, consideration for others?

Unconscious object of her friend's impatience, Dr. Agatha Lloyd was intent on her point. Her words came in a smooth incessant flow, gliding like a practiced swimmer who has learned to get a maximum of strokes with minimum pauses for breath. "Tell me, Mister Spenser, you are a radical journalist, I believe: then you can explain many things here which are not clear to me. Now I am a scientist, a doctor, so I am particularly interested in these aspects, you understand. Why is it that Bolsheviks say that science in capitalist countries is serving the interests of the bourgeoisie? Many, many of my friends are scientists; research workers, biologists, doctors like myself. I know they have no such desire; they are liberals, you understand. Science I hold is above classes, that is, pure science. Am I wrong?"

Gazing idly over her piquant earnest countenance and full bosom, Alfred Spenser began a routine explanation: It was not a question of the individual desires of the scientist. The whole social situation determined the objective rôle of science in capitalist society. There were certain contradictory factors, however. . . . He caught Boardman's eye, sent a mute appeal: "Deliver me from this woman!" Philip flipped the tail of his devil's costume in Spenser's direction and pulled Mary to the dance floor. "What on earth possesses her!"

112

his wife exclaimed. "It's like a fatal disease with Agatha."

Agatha Lloyd had become a byword in the English-speaking colony, most foreigners fled at her approach. Agatha knew this. It hurt her, yet she kept on. When she wanted a thing, she went after it. Nothing should stand in her way, not oceans nor continents, and most certainly not some person's whims. She had come to Moscow for a specific purpose: let all situations and purposes be subordinated to this end.

She was persistent? Persistency, like mental discipline, was a characteristic that she valued above all others. Such traits had enabled her to force her way to the front in a profession still traditionally dominated by men. She had literally made her place as a leading physician in Sydney. In the course of it she had met Terry Merrick, a young anthropologist whom the postwar radicalism sweeping Australia had caught in its tide. The one irrational act of her thirty-odd years had been her marriage to him.

They had argued, labored passionately to convince one another. The Socialist point of view she found comprehensible, intelligent. But the Communist! "Hopelessly bourgeois," he had finally called her. And to him, she knew, a streetwalker was more deserving of tolerance, pity. She, a good liberal, wellknown for her medical social work, dubbed hopelessly bourgeois! Nonsense! Simply because she loved him was no reason for committing mental prostitution was it? She must be genuinely convinced.

In the months after his departure for an indefinite stay in England, she had realized how deeply she loved, yes, and envied him. Envied him his passionate certainty, his readiness to put his revolutionary conviction before everything—career, wife, perhaps even life itself. How could anything in the world come to be so unquestioned, so intimate a part of one's inner existence?

Terry had been hard ... unbelievably hard. Destroyed her old faiths (the crisis, his ally), and left her without new. Deliberately, carefully, she decided. She forsook her substantial practice for eighteen months, purchased a suitcase of books on Communism, and sailed for Russia. She told all inquirers with frank, half-amused irony, "Yes, I came here to make myself over from a bourgeois. Moscow is the modern Mecca, is it not? If I am to find mental poise and new conviction at all, where else but here?"

She assumed as a matter of course that every one must help her. Not of course in any material sense: she was well able to manage that, even serving as a volunteer in a large Moscow clinic for sake of the experience. Yet spiritually, intellectually, she sought on all sides. Her Russian as yet too poor to enable her freely to talk with the natives or to understand them, she was constrained to mingle primarily with the Capital's English-speaking residents.

"Life here is hardly what I expected," she confided to Philip, on one of her frequent visits to the Boardmans' home. "Yet, it is even more absorbing. Daily new ideas and customs bombard me. I am forever meeting people, points of view from all corners of the earth. Of course, it is hard, very hard for one at my age to try and make herself over. Sometimes I am worn out with the struggle. Nevertheless, I make progress!" Would it take her months, years, perhaps forever, before she dared communicate with Terry? "At last I have hopes of coming to read the pulsebeat of history as you do." But more practically, without illusions as to persons or circumstance. And not until she was honestly sure.

Spenser's lecture on science faltered, came to an abrupt end. Noting the next question forming on Doctor Lloyd's lips, he asked desperately, "Oh say, won't you dance? This is a swell number." She one-stepped abominably, he knew, but what the hell. He would certainly get even with Boardman for this.

"All right," she replied shortly, "but you know as well as I that we shall only fall over one another's feet. First, may I make one inquiry, only one"—she ignored his protest—"tell me how is it that you became a revolutionist?" She was secretly amused at the change that went over him. His body, which gave one the impression that his clothes were fast becoming too snug for him, relaxed gently. Was she really interested? he inquired. It was a long story. "Shall

114

we have drinks? I always talk better with a little cognac handy."

Agatha, when occasion warranted, was a good listener. While he talked, she made mental notes along the margins of his story. Here was a man, not yet forty, who looked back fondly and often to the brave bold days of fourteen-eighteen, when as a gentleman hobo he had fallen in with a group of fellow-wanderers of all shades of opinion, and ended in San Quentin for the cause of free speech and opposition to Wilson's war. His term out, he had lavished funds received from his useful though Republican sister on a big fling for the boys, first thoughtfully purchasing a new suit and dispatching a telegram to his sister for quick reënforcements. Her husband, a Dutch-American in the hardware business, was well able to afford it. Spenser had always approved of Nietzsche's theory: let the lesser gods support their Supermen.

Since then he had worked on various radical papers, developed quite a style as a columnist, covered England, Ireland, the Continent, and had arrived at last in Moscow to represent one of America's liberal magazines. He was fast becoming one of the permanent landmarks of American gatherings, cultivating an aloof slightly cynical air as befitting one in the know; writing witty lightweight columns for his journal of scenes about Moscow; and preferring, so rumor had it, affairs with young boys to most women. His reputation as a connoisseur of Russian wines he valued, as of Italian, French—in fact, in this regard also he was an internationalist. When new rumors concerning the foreign store or liquidation of the Black Exchange, or new steps contemplated by the Party were circulating, Spenser always possessed an inside tip from ... well, sources close to the Kremlin. It was his right as veteran revolutionary. If, later, the tips proved unfounded, then the fault lay higher up. Let Arthur Mackay, the correspondent for the *New York Examiner,* be *popularly* referred to as Washington's unofficial representative in Moscow. He would scorn such a rôle. But as the Red Capital's interpreter and best known columnist, let no one excel him. His sketches always dealt with scenes on street, tramway, queues, and occasionally some public gathering or club. He had no flare for factory, union, or village studies. When necessary, he could deliver stirring addresses on perspectives of the World October. And on one recurring theme, as Agatha Lloyd had discovered, he was always prepared to speak.

Mary and Philip, the dance over, found Spenser and Agatha in animated conversation. The columnist fixed on his listener an examiner's look. "Have you," he demanded, "read my book?" Philip jerked his wife's arm. "Come on. I can't stand that old gag. Why in hell doesn't he write a new book, or quit bellyaching about the one he accidentally delivered some ten years back? Whew!" Agatha was noting down the book's title on the back of an old program Spenser gave her.

Mentally she was rounding off her other notes. Exactly what place had a man like this alongside of Terry? Yet the same movement embraced them both. Back in Sydney, she had heard the Spensers referred to as drawing-room bolshies. Somehow she hadn't expected to find them here. Another shock. Yet, why not? When you thought it over, where a more likely place for some of them to drift than here, where they might find easy living, with prestige as a foreign comrade, at least for a time, until the Russians, for all their courtesy to foreigners, found them out. And for all she knew, a man like Spenser might even be useful in some queer way.

It was puzzling, discouraging: just when she thought she had her feet on solid ground, this smooth Spenser had to set her doubting everything. What a little fool she had been to expect him to discuss seriously with her about science! Rising, she said, "Thank you. This has been an enlightening hour."

Spenser bowed. "I trust I have not bored you."

"Not at all. Quite the reverse." But Diogenes with his lantern would not knock at this door again. Further up the table line she noted Gilbert Sims, sitting alone, a disconsolate droop to his shoulders. Near him were several empty bottles. She took a chair by him, asking, "Well, how is it going with our famous stage designer?"

116

"Rotten," he answered. "Socrates better not come around me now. Always feel this way when I am half-lit. Fed-up to the gills, philosophical and all that. What I need is a good souse, or a bump under a cold shower. Oh, well, if you *will* stay. I saw you hobnobbing with Spenser. Did he tell you how they're putting the screws on him, after him to do social work? Imagine Spense leading a workers' class in journalism, helping edit a shop paper! They got his goat and tagged his number and I only wish they'd get mine. Then I'd have to snap out of it.

"Bad habit, thinking about yourself and the world in general. You don't think so? Well, you ought to know. Just what I've been doing." He motioned toward the dance floor. "Thinking what a sorry bunch, especially one G. Sims. Living in a great country, with the biggest happenings in history going on—and about as cut off as a lake-surrounded island. By Christ, that scene'd make a good drop curtain, get me? Our crowd might be a colony in the Philippines or India, for all it matters. Not that bad, you say? Maybe not. I told you I was seeing everything in dark hues. For pete's sake, quit interrupting me, Agatha, else I'll clam up, and then what about your devilish notebook?"

Breaking match sticks into half-inch pieces, he shaped a five-pointed star on the cloth. "Now take me: I do my job each day, and that ends it. All my free hours, I spend mixing with my old New York Chicago crowd. Never among Russians. I can't savvy their lingo: in fact, I can't savvy them. Great people, I admire them. I agree with their scheme. But I am cut off. My own doing: somehow I can't snap out of it, chasing around with the same bunch, drinking the same drinks, singing the same tunes. God, what a head!" The match sticks were tossed into a mound. "Sure, plenty of good chaps, I admit. Useful and all that. But you get what I mean? Not enough into things. Phil Boardman, now, is getting a big kick out of puttering around his shop, hobnobbing with the Russkies, and that architect Frank Williams is on the lark of his life. But I ... Why, you ask, do I stay on? Oh, I like my job. No economic worries. And what could I do now, with two youngsters and twelve million jobless back home? I'm not a fighter. Not a coward, either, just easygoing. . . . Hell, let's call quits on this wool-gathering. But between us, I am going to snap out of it, get into things more or head for the States. Well, what you say, Socrates, how about a couple of bracers? Let Diogenes put down his lantern and fill my cup."

10

As she hastened back to her lathe, hands full of shining disks, Natasha came full upon them, without warning. They were standing in a dim neglected corner, almost hid in the indigo shadows cast by pyramided boxes of dusty metal scrap. Zena was pressed against the brick wall, one arm of her wooer a tightening vise about her waist, the other fumbling in her loosened blouse. Playfully she warded him off, ruddy cheeks vibrating with suppressed mirth. Behind them roared the myriad-colored high noon of the shop's labor.

Roughly the man threw his full length against her, her giggling smothered under his wet mouth. Natasha halted, her brown eyes shot with copper glints. "Zena!" Her voice was level, matter-of-fact, "Your work's waiting."

The couple whirled. "So it's you, Turin! What a fine pair you are!" With a dark flush the woman broke away. Her purple-flowered blouse refastened, she tossed her disheveled head. "And what business is it of yours, I'd like to know! Why you butting in?" Her powerful arms swung defiantly as she swished past the younger woman and lumbered toward her machine.

"Zena, we'll talk later." Natasha turned on the man smearing the back of his hand across his lips. Her voice darted at him. What a swell fellow he was! Bravo! So this was the work that brought Alex Turin from the assembly to the dieshop. Idler! Beast! "Just you try it again, I'll report you for sure." For shame, taking advantage of a weaknatured woman.

Turin hitched his trousers, buttoned his jacket. "Old

busybody," he sneered, "poking your snout into other people's affairs." His arched nose and high white forehead appeared swollen, ready to burst. "No instincts of your own, eh? Maybe you need some loving up yourself!" Pretty bitch.

Eyes narrowed, she stepped toward him. Fool! Keep his dirty mouth to himself, and get out—quick.

Suddenly he heeled about, made for the exit. *Muzhik's* daughter! He'd like to give her pretty shoulders what-for.

By the old stairway which shambled up to the buffet and manager's office, he chanced to meet Katia Boudnikova. Had she been looking for him? His heart skipped, racing like an idling motor, and his angry mood slipped from him to the pockmarked floor. Startled, she looked past him. No one was near. As she stepped aside, inadvertently she dropped her glove.

As he stooped to retrieve it he wiped his hands quickly on his jacket, and wormed the small paper concealed among the glove's fingers into his own. "Katia, darling!" he whispered, "when may I come to you?" Above her lavender freshly-starched frock her distant face appeared as a magnolia that had bloomed unexpectedly in this dingy shop. Her perfume, triumphing over stench of oil and grease, swept him out of himself. For the moment he forgot where he was, even his despised workjacket. God, the old days!

"Well," her tone was vexed, hurried, "give me my glove!" Alex was keeping her, inexcusably. The past was long dead, and this was dangerous. "Can't you hear! Give me my glove."

He was silent. In his eyes was that glazed stare she had come to dread. Once again he was Alexander Kriskov, and back in the drawing room with its shaded lights. His heels clicked smartly as he bent over her unguarded limp palm.

Quickly she tore it from him. Imbecile! He forgot himself! Her red-heeled slippers sounded a frightened tattoo up the stairs.

Turin threw the glove after her, strode out. Let the bitches swallow her and this whole blighted country. Forgot himself, had he? Yes, so he had. That he no longer wore gold braid to dazzle her, make him the catch of the season. That his career and fortune were smeared out by the dirty rags of the proletariat. Forgot himself. Bah, Russia had become an outcast, a pariah among nations, the butt of fools.

A sweaty truckdriver, was he? And she, private interpreter, lip and soul mistress to those foreign devils. Heartless, scheming creature, he knew her too well.

She was afraid. He, never . . . not of the whole Bolshevik pack.

His boots kicked out at walls, trucks, everything he passed. *"Tovarische!"* Dog's lice. Beneath his coarse jacket beat still the heart of a soldier. Let others compromise, weaken. He knew how to hate; how to remember, destroy.

So, Katia, my pretty one, you think you can spurn me? Be careful, my hour will strike. Honor, Civilization demand it. Do you think the upstarts can ride the saddle forever? Illiterate swine. My lovely witch, some day you'll come fawning back to me. Shall I take you? Be careful.

The note read, Alex Turin carefully destroyed it. With his dirty roubles, this Sokolov thought he'd command whom he liked. Low bourgeois, in other days he'd have dealt with the man properly. Now—well, let him pay well.

With a scowl, Turin jumped to one side as Ned drove a truck from the conveyor into the yard.

Before entering the office, Katia paused to regain her breath. Suppose some one had seen! Sentimental dunce, Alexander Turin. As if there were any going back to the old days. One had to take life as it came.

This was the last note she intended delivering for Sokolov, let him say what he pleased. She had to sever all connections with these people, while there was time.

If only Crampton could be induced to take her with him, abroad. To Paris, New York!

Poor Alexandrushka! Was he losing his wits? Living in dreams, fancies that might cost him dear. If only she dared hope. No, no, the thing was to live life as it came.

Philip Boardman was pacing the office. "Five minutes late, Miss Boudnikova," he said genially. And why so pale? Had she met a ghost on the stairs?

121

Did he believe in ghosts? she inquired. Her gayety struck him as a bit off-key. A black cat had startled her, she said, she had run all the way up. Silly woman, wasn't she?

She held out her hand for his drawings. "May I look at them? Won't you take pity, explain them to a poor ignorant female?" Gently she edged her soft weight against him.

With terse brevity he explained the main points of his diagrams. This crank shaft die he was proposing, would mean freeing the plant of a costly import. It required exactness, steel of a high order, for it was one of the biggest jobs in the shop.

"How very interesting!" she exclaimed. He saw that she had comprehended nothing. She pressed his thigh with her own. "Such a clever energetic man!" Much more promising, she reflected, than Crampton, although too matter of fact.... Coldblooded.

Philip pressed back. "Not half so clever, my dear, as you!"

Did she imagine a shaft behind his raillery? (She had yet to meet the man she couldn't subdue.) Didn't Mr. Boardman think it a good plan to show these first to Mr. Crampton? He would be *so* interested!

Yes, Philip thought, and how! He moved away, rolled the blueprints into a firm cylinder. He hardly thought it necessary, he said, to bother Crampton with them. She was persistent. Oh, but he must! The chief would surely recommend that it be pushed right through. (How was she to get these to Crampton, without arousing suspicion?) This Boardman made her uncomfortable, a veritable jumping-jack on a string of perpetual motion.

They were already late for their appointment in BRIZ, he reminded her crisply. Should they go? She apologized in admiring undertones as they walked over for her presumption in suggesting anything to him. It was her desire for his good: he was so talented, so useful to their backward industry.

Boardman pursed his lips. BRIZ no doubt would accept these as it had his earlier ones, with polite enthusiastic passivity. He'd like to take them up by their collars and shake them for the bunch of sleepy kittens they were.

Later in the day, Katia found herself alone in the office with Crampton. She endured his kiss, throwing back her head in a pretty submissive gesture. This man was a boor, really. "Now, grandfather," she reproved. Plenty of time for this, after work. She wanted to report her visit with Boardman to BRIZ.

He spat out the end of his cigar. "And—?"

"Well," she defended, "how could I get hold of the drawings? I did try."

"Trying's not enough." He resumed his curt business manner. She should have stopped him. Lousy hog, plainly after his job. They had to see those drawings, and that was all there was to it. Now for a plan...

Natasha, meanwhile, eyes on her whirring lathe, drummed her fist to its rhythm on one polished end. She was puzzled, angry. The whole die shop in a tangle, its *udarnik* workers straining every nerve to see her through on the plan, and people like Turin and Zena idling about! It made her blood boil! What was wrong, anyway? Here it was: motors, body, tire departments running like welltimed clocks, dies and castings holding up the whole works. Impossible! Why was it? Were they worse workers? No. Then... oh the devil take it.

She glimpsed Zena's swarthy countenance three aisles down, scowling and fussing around her machine. Was the woman slipping into her old ways? Hardly. They'd put an end to street-walking, long ago. But what made her keep so much to herself? A brooder. And was she quick on a comeback, easily offended! Come to think of it, she didn't know Zena. Who in the shop did? So far the woman had warded off all attempts to draw her into the common life of the shop. What went on in the mind of a person like that? Was she unhappy? After this, the girl decided, she was going to make friends.

A die man passing near Zena's machine stopped to jibe, "Oi, our girl's rosy apples are washed out. Must have slept badly. What kept her awake?" Not got married had she? That'd be sad news for all the men in the shop. Nothing of the kind, his companion leered, Zena'd got a Five Year Plan all her own. She was fulfilling and overfulfilling, and how! It made her groggy by day.

"Leave off!" Kolya, Boardman's young helper, stopped on his way by, face reddened. Shut up, fools! Let Zena be, no place anyway for such talk in their shop.

Zena snapped her fingers under her taunter's nose. "Ah, shut up, Kolya. See how I take care of these gas birds myself." Elbows crooked on her broad hips, her rasping voice raised for all her neighbors to hear. "You pie face lout, all you are is a bull in heat! Who'd sleep with rats like you!" She stared malignantly after their retreating backs, her elbows and lips working.

Kolya pulled her arm. They were old fogies, she was to pay no attention to them. This was a new grinder on her machine, wasn't it?

She whirled irritably. He pretended not to notice her short answers, twitchy lips. How was her youngster? he asked. A fine boy, he had seen Zena with him once in the bread store.

Her scowl melted, she gave Kolya a vigorous thrust in his ribs. That boy! the same little devil. Learning so fast he'd soon outknow his Ma. "Now get along with you, lad," she told him, "can't you see you're making all the girls jealous of me? Besides, I'm behind with this work." Now if all were like Kolya ... to hell with it.

Early the next morning, before her shift had come to the shop, Zena sought out the manager. "Eugene Ivanovich, I must have two days off."

But why? he asked. She knew the rush now.

Her reddened eyes filled appealingly, threatened to overflow. She must. Her baby.... Sobbing, she drew closer. She must bury her child. Eugene Pankrevich, moved, patted her heaving shoulders. There, there. Of course. He had not known. Poor woman.

Her feet dragged her heavy body out of the shop. Once outside, her gait quickened. She chose the longer route home to avoid any early comers. Slowly her lowered eyelids curved upwards. What luck! A fair day!

Something good'll come from this. Andy threw open his door with gusto, stepped aside to let Natasha enter ahead of him. She looked about with frank interest. Such a large room, and all to himself? She had thought he lived with his American friends.

Such few books, she noted to herself. On the walls, crimson and mauve pennants, Andy in uniform, a fading snapshot of a pugtailed dog, and a sepia-colored photograph of a wide-eyed girl.

Andy wound the victrola, set the needle. *Happy Days Are Here Again.* He had borrowed the vic from Morse, in anticipation of her visit. "Sure, I got a place all to myself. Why not?" (Pretty kettle, if he lived with Morse. That jane of his was around all hours. How Tim stood it, he didn't know.)

It was better by yourself, she agreed. Quiet, chances for study.

Andy whistled. Study! My God, what a girl! "And yours?" he asked curiously. Her home, she answered, was crowded and their family large. It made no difference, except sometimes it was hard to keep her mind on her books. Her kid brother was a bothersome scamp.

Andy laughed. "Well, any time you wanta move in with me, just say the word." He meant it.

She eyed him coolly. "You Americans have queer ways of joke." He decided to lay off.

Who was the lovely girl in the picture, she asked, his wife or sister? He hedged. (Boy, he had to wriggle out of this, somehow. A bad slip, leaving it out.) "Oh, that?" he said, loud. That was Elsie. Confused, he let her think her his sister.

Natasha was curious. She knew no American girls and this one was uncommonly pretty. What did she do? Andy wanted to change the subject. Elsie was a typist, and a histepper. He knew Natasha would want the last word explained. She was set on learning English. Anything, but to talk now about Elsie.

"Say, take off your things!" he invited. "Make yourself at home." He placed his hands on her shoulders to help her off with her coat and ran his fingers along its bronze fur collar. He'd like to bury his face in that fiery brown hair. Hold on, he told himself. Take it easy. Gotta learn the ropes with these Russian girls.

She jumped to the edge of his desk, and let her feet swing. Thanks, she had little time, where was the technical book he had promised to loan her? He slid a few onesteps toward her. "Get it in a minute. Say, can you dance? Come on, take off your coat. I'll show you how." He laughed nervously. Had to carry this off, like an old hand.

No, she couldn't dance. She only knew village dances. But she'd like to see this American foxtrot. Come on, once, he urged. Well, after him? Braced against the table, she smiled at his jigging figure, snapping fingers. A sandy lock was falling into his eyes. How much unchained energy the man had. She liked his cleancut vigor, boisterous good humor. She'd really like to try a dance, but she'd stumble all over him like a cow. Some time though.

"Andy," she asked suddenly, "what your plans?"

His dancing came to a quick stop. "How you mean, plans?"

"I mean, what you working toward?"

His gaze hardened. Plans! How could a fellow have plans with the world like a crazy house. But why bring that up? His mouth twisted with one of his three-cornered grins. Come on, try jazzing. Just once.

Flushing, she tried a few steps, broke away. Another time, honest.

She examined the Victrola. Beat the devil, he thought, how these Russians loved machines. He lit her cigarette, flipped the dead match between his thumb and forefinger. "Say, you got a regular?"

"A what?"

"A regular. A steady. You know ..." he explained.

She smiled. No, she hadn't. (How many personal questions he asked. Well, she might like to ask a few herself.) He was relieved. "Why not? A pretty girl like you."

He brought her his book. She opened it, surprised: why, this wasn't on motors, but his book to the foreign store. Sure, he said, but he couldn't make out some of the items in it. She'd help him out? She read them off: he had the right to the following purchases each month. (Gosh, what a lot of things these foreigners got! She wouldn't mind, when she, everybody had ...)

"See how little I buy," he offered. "But what a lot a fellow could get if he had any use for it." He hesitated. Not as if he had a wife or girl or somebody like that. Seemed a pity, didn't it. He brought over a box of chocolates. She ate rapidly, with relish. A sweet tooth, he noted. He'd remember that. And lamp it, cotton mitts on swell legs like that!

"You don't happen to need anything?" he ventured. "You know, in the way of supplies or silk folderols?" At her expression, he added quickly, "Or anybody who does?" She returned him the look. (Damn his impudence, did he think just because she wore cotton stockings! In another minute she'd give him a piece of her mind.) No, she answered quietly, she didn't. He tossed the book on the table, bit down on a caramel. Jumping Jesus! The damn thing was cementing his jaw. This girl sure had a line all her own. Had him guessing. Was she shy or what? Not helping him out at all.

Natasha watched him, puzzled, her temper rising. Funny, these cocky Americans. She'd heard they knew how to be pals with a girl.

What time was it? she queried. Five-thirty! She must leave for class, would he please look up the books? He put on another record. "Here's a good one." With a flippant drawl, he hummed with the singer

Um-huh Um-huh Wanta take a walk?
Um-huh Um-huh Think it's gonna rain

She turned from the picture in time to see him take the key from the lock. (Not going to have Morse butt in at the wrong time.) "You got the walk of a good dancer," he proposed. "Come on, you'll catch on easy." He one-stepped near her with a gliding leisurely motion, stopped before her, and held out his arms for a dance. She shook her head, stood up to go.

He stepped nearer, breath coming fast. "Gee, kid, you sure got me going. How is it?"

She didn't understand his words, yet their meaning flamed from his eyes, eager body. His arms closed about her. "Honest, Nat, you sure are sweet." He thrust the book at her. "Silk and whatever you want—"

She slapped it against his face. *Durak!* Fool! Did he treat girls in America like this! "What you take me, eh? A bitch? You fool!"

Ruefully he rubbed his cheek, brain in a whirl. "Say, you got me wrong!"

"Wrong, eh? We even then. And I think, I think . . . you *svollitch*. What you take me, eh! Sell myself for a pair of silk stockings, eh? Fool! I hate you. Well, what you stare at? Give me key." (She wanted to wail, pummel him good. What vulgar rot he had in his dumb head.)

Wordless, he placed it on top of the book on motors and held them both out to her. The door closed behind her with a resounding bang.

Caught in a scratched groove, the record was running down. The harsh glare of electric lights traveled mercilessly across rumpled rugs. Andy's slouched figure, the half-empty box of chocolates and the lazily spinning disk, while the whining voice crooned on a constantly descending key:

Um-huh   Um-huh Wanta take a walk?
Um-huh   Um-huh Think it's gonna rain

Some prefer the talkies
I prefer the walkies

Something good'll come from this!

11

KOLYA was in search of the *Amerikanets*. Boardman was not to be found. Courteous, suave in his black embroidered smock, from behind his oak glass-top desk Eugene Pankrevich, dieshop superintendent, was informing the engineer that he had called him in to discuss certain important matters. Yes, certain matters regarding his work.

A light from the street played across the manager's bald crown, Katia's yellow knitted frock and the wide part above her low forehead. Evidently, Pankrevich continued, certain unclarities existed for Boardman as to what was expected of him as a foreign specialist? Katia Boudnikova translated in measured tones, with an insinuating glance at Henry Crampton who sat to one side, chewing on an unlit cigar.

Meester Boardman, the dieshop superintendent reminded, had been employed here with the definite understanding that he was to get out dies. It seemed that he was taking on another function: that of instruction. This latter, it was reported, was seriously hampering his production labors. In the future, might they expect him to confine his attention to his main task?

Philip cut the translation short. Thanks, he remarked brusquely, he was able to understand this quite well, by himself. Pankrevich and Crampton needn't think they could pawn off any of the poor running of this die shop at his door!

In his opinion, Crampton interjected, his assistant's anarchistic behavior was a significant factor in the shop's falling behind program. Boardman was forever hobnobbing with the youngsters and stopping any time day or night to jaw with them. It spoiled discipline.

Boardman paled. Sure he was helping the lads, but not at cost of output. He knew his duties. Where were the facts! He broke off. What was the use. "And when workers come to me for technical aid, what am I to do?" he demanded. "Tell them I have orders not to help them? In plain words, that's what you mean?"

Pankrevich fingered his engraved metal inkwell. No, no, of course not. But it was true, wasn't it, that in the last week the American had been receiving visitors and calls for help, not only from die shop men, but also from other departments? Some repairmen had been over, no? And foundrymen? Unless there was a halt to this thing, where might it end? Of course the American engineer's willingness was commendable. As soon as he had the language sufficiently, they would be glad if he gave a course in the *technicum*. This present method, however.... He shrugged. "Yes, tell them when they come bothering you, that your instructions are to get out production. There are ample instructors here for any technical help a worker may need."

Boardman's fist smashed against the table, spattering ink over glass top and the manager's slowmoving hands. "Pankrevich, you sonofabitch, you never wanted me in the dieshop from the beginning. Tried to pawn me off on the foundry. Afraid I'd show you up, eh? You jellyfish, softy! You're a plain bureaucrat." He seized Katia's wrist. Translate every word he was saying. "You two make a good lousy team. Crampton's pulled the damn wool over your eyes for fair!" He turned on the chief engineer. "As for you, I'll show you up yet."

As Crampton jerked to his feet, Katia placed herself quickly in his path. Philip whirled aside: the worn stairs shook under his quick tread to the main floor of the shop. Kolya was waiting for him.

Gradually his work calmed him. With cool fury he surveyed the situation, made his resolve. Sure he'd tell the lads ... in his own good time and by God, with a bang.

Later in the afternoon when Maxim came over, as he often did, to inquire, "Well, how's it going?" Philip hesitated. Should he? This toolshaper who had taken on duties as Party secretary for their shop seemed a real guy. Should he unload to him? No, damn if he was going to bellyache about another American. "Okay," he replied gruffly, "couldn't be better." God, this battle was getting his nerve. And Mary like a sore thumb nagging to go home.

Maxim ruffled his shaggy brows, walked off. This Boardman was a good fellow but offish. Stood on his dignity, did he? Well now.... "Couldn't be better." Humph! The engineer knew as well as he did that was the bunk. Humph. What a job he had. Things weren't going too well around here. A good thing this brigade begun in the repair section had spread out to include the whole plant. Together with Natasha, Vasiliev, Mac and a man from the assembly, yesterday he had been down to the paper *For Soviet Machines*. They'd got what they wanted too, endorsement as an official brigade of the magazine, and they'd talked over plans with the editor for a rousing checkup campaign on *Red Star's* production and weak points. Still ruminating over Boardman and die shop problems, he hurried on to meet Vasiliev. They had an important appointment to keep, had to be on time.

A kettle left over the fire too long is sure to boil over: the housing department ought to know that. So old Vasiliev observed, as he vainly endeavored to rub oilspots from his coat sleeve. Slipping off his jacket, he ran dismayed fingers along the tear under the left shoulder. Maxim was restless. "Come on, you're all right. Everybody's waiting." He helped the turner into his coat. Dubiously, elbows crooked, Vasiliev shook his lean head. Really, he shouldn't go, look at that tear! Why couldn't the delegation give them time to dress proper. His first trip to the Kremlin, and in a split work jacket. Oh, what his wife'd say, when she heard!

"Never mind," Maxim consoled him. "No one will notice. What you think, Loganov never wore a ripped jacket himself! No nonsense: this housing business can't wait." When his shopmates had elected him that noon, they hadn't expected him to go back on them or dillydally about his clothes.

Vasiliev eyed Maxim. The other's fists were ingrained

with a grime no washing could erase, his nails broken, his shoes scarred. His face was covered with reddish stubble. "Come on," he repeated, "ain't this our country?"

All right. Anyway, he'd keep on his overcoat on the pretext he was chilled. Most of the others, he thought, looked more trim than Maxim and he did. All were near his age. He felt proud as he walked with them to the carline, not one but had twenty years' record in industry. As he swung onto a car strap, he laughed in his companion's ear. "I remember that delegation we sent into our manager thirty years ago. How I scrubbed, brushed up! Donned my Sunday clothes. We bowed ourselves in, cap in hand, backed out. And that goldern super had the brass to turn us down!"

Two freshcheeked guards at the Kremlin's southgate stopped them. Maxim produced documents: delegation from *Red Star* to see Loganov. The Armyman picked up his phone. "He's expecting you?" "Yes, we called from the plant." Soon they were following their guide over the bridgeway to the inner gate.

Beneath them, along the turreted rosebrick walls, ran a garden through which muffled foot-travelers were hurrying homeward after their day's work. Three armymen were strolling back and forth under the iced branches, arms linked and singing a marchsong. Vasiliev looked closely at the walls mounted by greencapped turrets, and tinted by age with soft iridescent colors. Within the outer Kremlin walls the wind whistled a lusty northwester, catching them as they rounded a bend, full in the face. They were atop the hill. Below them glimmered dusky Moscow with its darting fireflies of electric lights. The line of black oldfashioned cannon which they passed Maxim said had been captured from Napoleon on his famous retreat from Moscow. From across the river municipal apartments blinked their thousand eyes at Vasiliev and his comrades.

He felt the full weight of this moment. Fourteen years it was, since he had battled outside the Kremlin in the Red Square, with the czar's troops mowing hell into them. His rifle had balked. So he had made a run with his comrades at those devils spitting death at them, against the walls.

Fourteen years. . . . His breath wheezed through a barrage of coarse hairs frozen rigid in his nostrils. That dogged wind had swept inside his head.

The guard led them inside the central government building, where the sudden warmth thawed his stiff hands and rigid nostrils and made his nose drip. While fumbling for his handkerchief, Vasiliev eyed the red velvet carpets, marble stairway, and gilded columns. A painting of brilliant reds and blues covered the entire wall of the stairway landing. Vasiliev nudged Maxim, some place they'd fallen heir to!

They gave the hallman their rubbers and caps. "And your overcoats, citizens," he asked. Vasiliev held back. Impossible! He felt chilled through, he protested, even while the close heat sent the blood to his face. The doorman insisted until Vasiliev reluctantly gave in. All the way up the broad stairs through the hallways he held his arms tightly against his body. Where was that rip, under his right or left? As they went in he'd be facing Loganov, his torn back would not be noticed. Coming out he'd take it sideways, never once turn round. Most important, he must keep his arms down.

Loganov came around his desk to greet them. Vasiliev shook hands guardedly, remembering his tear, but gazed at Loganov with affectionate curiosity. This was not the first time he had seen the country's leading statesman, a man close to Stalin, although never before had he observed him at such close range. Loganov, as one of *Red Star's* elected representatives in the Moscow Soviet, often came to the plant to report and investigate. He was an unpretentious man, Vasiliev knew, whose voice was so low that it was sometimes hard to distinguish his words. As a public speaker he was mediocre. Yet Vasiliev, like his mates, found it worthwhile straining to listen, for their representative had a way of going after the point.

Loganov's face was that of a student, but his hands and wrists those of an active man. Middleage was thinning his hair. From behind his glasses he directed toward the world his direct contemplative glance.

His workroom, except for its ancient inlaid floors, oriental rug and mahogany desk, was almost bare. By his desk hung a gigantic map of the country with red and blue dots and triangles marking off construction points of the Five Year Plan. Like a boy he pushed all the buttons for them, to show how the various industries and new towns flashed up, all the way from Vladivostok to Leningrad.

Briefly Maxim explained their mission. Coming here was a matter of last resort: they knew how busy he was, but this was an emergency. They needed Loganov's help in getting a consignment of bricks and lumber from Archangel to Moscow, so that work on apartments could be begun, at once. The plant's housing program was no program, but a disgrace. No apartments had been completed in the last five months. Funds were abundant. First, there had been no labor, then no weather. Now, with winter soon to break, spring near and labor available, their bricks and lumber were stranded! After repeated telegrams the shipment had been located in Archangel. Pleading or cursing the transport office got no results: their carloads of bricks refused to budge. Nevertheless, before May first *Red Star* must have new apartments ready for a hundred of their best *udarniks,* and dormitories to house youth. Vasiliev told of Pavel sleeping in the clubroom. Loganov listened, made notes. "So you want a special order for your shipment to be given right of way? Good. It'll go off within an hour." His secretary was called to take the dispatch and Vasiliev thought the interview over. It had hardly begun.

Loganov put his papers to one side, folded his hands on the desk before him. "Now comrades, how are things in your plant? I've been too occupied lately to keep in close touch. First in Siberia, then Ukraine." He addressed Vasiliev. "Not going too well at *Red Star* lately? What's wrong? How's the mood of the workers?"

"Dissatisfied," the old repairman's answer was prompt. "We work hard, still our plant falls behind on its program. We feel management's not up to it. And of course there are other things, these hitches never come singly. Meals— we have the worst cooks in Moscow! And of course housing. But we are setting about things proper." Gray hair bristling, he told about their brigade.

In his eyes there was an answering gleam, as Loganov leaned across his desk. It was the end of a long day, fatigue pressed his body into his chair. At eight there was an important committee meeting and and he needed to run over his report. He forgot everything. Tell him, he urged, what had their brigade uncovered to date? (Devil take all the routine, he ought to get out to the plant more.) Vasiliev's description was pointed, vivid. Unconsciously he rose from his chair, his arms swung in emphasis, when unexpectedly he heard something rip and Maxim chuckle. Abashed, he dropped in his chair. He too had forgotten. Had Loganov noticed?

It was seven before they wrung hands, made their departure. Not until he was getting into his overcoat did Vasiliev realize what he had done. He stopped short, his overcoat half on and sleeves dangling. "Maxim! I'm a son of a bitch!" His friend tossed his scarf about his throat. What's wrong: they'd got what they'd come for, hadn't they? "What's wrong!" Vasiliev ejaculated. "Do you know, it went clean out of my head. I turned my back full on Loganov. I'm a squash if he didn't get an eyeful of my naked old ribs!" The wind raced to meet them, roaring and beating them back. Vasiliev sunk into his collar. Maria would surely chide him when she heard. Well, what of it? He and the others massed together as they forced the gusty northwester before them, down the runway.

The sky threw blue and rose shadows along the snow's powdered crystal. The still crisp air nipped at the Detroiter's pug nose and cramped toes.

He was tired of this beginners' pond. The rest of *Red Star's* crowd were further down the line. With other learners he had grasped a common pole and pushed back and forth until he knew this skating trick by heart. With perilous lunges he made for the next rink, clung to rails, collided with passersby and resisted an overwhelming desire to sit peacefully for a moment on the ice or proceed on all fours.

Now if the Russians went in for baseball, he'd show them a thing or two. But this! For crying out loud.

At last he reached his destination and slipped thankfully onto a bench that bordered the rink. His ankles throbbed from the unaccustomed exercise, his army sweater was splotched white with his attempts to master the ice. He cupped his nose in his gloves, warming it with his breath, while his skates slid uselessly to and fro. It looked simple enough, until you got started. The way these Russians went at it, every muscle under control. Some flew along like they had hold of an invisible sail. Among the skaters he spotted Mac's Scotch plaid flapping against Nan's red tam. Sasha, all heaviness gone, was bent at a sixty degree angle, hands clasped behind him, like a black hawk tracing light arcs around the pond.

How long, Andy wondered, before the bunch'd head for home? He was getting chilled through. Guess he should have stayed for Morse's poker party. Tim's griping, though, was getting on his nerves. Such a squareshooter, what was getting into him? Full of pip. Morse was a big false-alarm but Tim was the goods. His pal.

At sight of his comrade's humped figure, Sasha swept a wide curve to the right and came up before him on a deft sidestroke of his skates. Dubiously Andy accepted his offer of a turn about the ice. His forearm muscles were soon aching with his stern grip on his mate. It seemed they were in everyone's way, everybody in theirs, one imminent headon miraculously avoided after another. He stepped gingerly, on guard against that fearful way his feet had of gliding away from him. The ice's smoothness had vanished. Treacherous cracks, sudden holes loomed at every stroke. Damn those guys who took running starts on the tips of their skates, they had chipped the whole pond! His gaze fastened on the sliding glassy surface, Andy was dimly aware of his friend's clever maneuvering against constant disaster. When they passed Natasha skating with old Mikhail, Sasha smiled at his companion's unexpected burst of confidence that nearly swept them both off their feet. He stroked faster, keeping Andy to his quickened tempo.

The learner set his square jaw. Let hell freeze over, he'd skate or crack his skull. Cripes, what call had he to get jealous. No strings on her. She could flirt with that straw-boss, old enough to be her Dad, or whoever she pleased. Snotty skirt. He pushed too vigorously, with a dizzy swerve backwards. Resigned to a hearty sprawl on the ice, he found Sasha holding him firmly until he'd regained his balance and they could stroke more evenly.

Andy ignored his indignant ankles, stiffened wrists and the dazzling red beams across his eyes. By Jeez, he was swinging into the gait!

Natasha paced her stride with Mikhail's slower one. To-day the horizon wore a peculiar green tint. The ice, as yet, wasn't too chopped for good skating. When it was, they'd skate down the canal to the next pond while this was being reflooded.

Andy, she noticed, was still ashamed. She had accepted his apologies, tried to forget it. He hadn't. Well, let him rue it a bit longer, do him no harm.

A half-smile rippled unconsciously about her lips.

Mikhail nodded toward the pair. "You know him, eh?" Natasha gave a nonchalant shrug. Sure, a little. (Not much this old wizard of a Mikhail let by him.)

"Good fellow, eh?" he queried. Actually he felt sore at the boy. Why, the young whipper treated him as if.... And he was beginning to guess why. He gave an exasperated cluck. The thing took him back thirty years. To memories he'd sooner forget. To a youth spent—well....

Natasha tried to dismiss Zena from her mind, but couldn't. Thoughtless of her, as usual, not to make sure the woman was coming along. How'd Zena live anyway, spend her free time? She'd have to make friends, draw her into a brigade.

What a varied lot humanity was, anyhow. And here it was, with such people their country had to do Five Years in Four, reshape their whole life. She tried to clear her thought, relay it to Mikhail for his help. A habit of long-standing of hers, to talk over with him things that worried her. He had been her first teacher at factory school when she'd entered as a raw country kid, not knowing how to manage her hands and tongue, and her hair only recently minus braids still feeling all ends.

She liked to ask Mikhail about the times of the czar and rich nobility. Like a jumbled fairytale it sounded, of ogres and slaves. But a look at her bent Mother reminded her that the jumble had really existed. And their plant, their very own plant, had belonged not to the workers but one man, a millionaire. Imagine. Queer, and rather disgusting she thought. What amazed her was why they'd put up with it so long! Often she tried to imagine it all, gave it up, only to come back to it again. No wonder that Andy . . . Rubbish!

"How is it?" she asked Mikhail. "On the one hand, people like you, Maxim and Kolya. On the other hand, the Zenas, Turins, and that snout of a Pankrevich. What a hodgepodge!"

Listening to her, Mikhail's lined face grew pensive. His chin rested against his leather jacket, worn smooth from long usage. It meant much to him, these confidences of youth. Kept him young.

"Of course," she added, "in the first line are the old guard." Everybody knew that. Old workers like himself, passing on their skill, great experience. And how they did it! With the same passion that must have carried them through all those underground years.

"Yes," he interrupted her, "but don't forget. In the first line, also—the youth." Fresh generations, their revolution's best fruits. "You, Sasha, Kolya—our shop's full of 'em! Right?" Tell the truth, they warmed his old blood. After all, here was the living proof, what they'd fought for since nineteen three.

For awhile they skated on, not speaking, drawing in their thoughts with the crisp needled air. "All right," she began once more, "the old guard and the youth. But what about all the others? The inbetweens?" Along with thousands of *udarniks,* plenty of no-cares and drags. Look at the millions of villagers, loaded down with their crazy old ways. Crafty, each thinking only of his pig and himself.

"You say we're rewelding them? All right. But what load-

138

stones. What a costly affair for our Five Year Plan! Enough to break your heart!" In short, she didn't have his patience.

"Dear Natasha, you know why?" The genial tug of his arm took the edge from his words. "Because I am old, and you—you are young. I see the perspectives," he continued quietly, "the distance from which we've come. You read *Lower Depths*? Good. Man's a queer bird, but even in the worst, there's a spark. From the outset, we've been betting everything on that. We knew men could come together, working men, coöperate, smash their chains, start anew. We bet high.... And we're winning. Right?"

They circled the rink again before he continued.

"Yes, Lenin showed us we had to rebuild our life, like we made our October, with men not all good nor all bad. Just ordinary humans." Through the struggle, fierce as it was, man was reshaping himself as well. After the First Five Year Plan there'd be the Second Plan, beginning next year and bringing with it an end to classes and all exploitation of man by man. There was the key! All busy at some useful work, and growing like a boundless field on their steppes of ripening grain. After the Second Plan, a Third, a Fourth. And with each fresh generation, man stretching his world and himself further, understand?

"Natasha," he exclaimed suddenly, "we live in a great age. And you, still so young. You'll see greater things yet. Maybe I too? Perhaps. Not one country only, but a freed human race."

As he drew breath, he turned to smile into her intent frost-reddened face. "Serious talk, eh, for a skate?" They broke off and quickened their pace, while music bounded over the ice like rain on a wind-frenzied lake.

Arm locked in Sasha's, Andy laboriously clinked his way into the buffet for biscuits and steaming tea. "In a few weeks you'll be skating like an oldtimer," his mate encouraged. Andy nodded. Sure thing, he would. He was going to skim circles around that Natasha with her stubborn chin and laughing eyes. Run on his toes, double with her about the pond. See if he didn't.

When they returned to the ice, he traveled with a dash,

then less surely. Have a rest, Sasha advised, and he'd come back for him later. So once again the beltman watched from the sidelines. Natasha with that engineer, Boardman, was skating in a foursome with Mac and Nan. Didn't they ever tire of those endless circles? Should think they'd grow dizzy, at that speed. Land on their nuts.

Swinging his feet, he reflected on women—Soviet style. They were hard ones. Since that night in his room, except for a harassed apology, he had kept clear of her. A flat tire.

Hell, what could a fellow do, when a girl answered your "Gimme a kiss" with a calm "But why?" Try and swipe one. Elsie was a real sport. In her own way. This girl was colder than the frozen glass she was skimming. What the hell, she think a man stepped out with a girl just to talk sports, socialism and revolution!

A disgusted back turned on the quartet, he faced toward the pond reserved for experts. A woman's figure outlined in angora-trimmed white wool, her costume fitted tightly about her shoulders and waist and flaring out in a cone skirt, was marking perfect figure 8's. She seemed to swing on transparent pulleys, with uncanny grace. A snowbird flying through the air. Near her a man in a skintight outfit was skating like a black crow with one leg that first dangled then shot out and under him as he reversed in midair. Soon the snowbird and crow had coupled, and were whirling each other around the waist, practicing figures more complicated than any which the southernbred Andy had witnessed, even on the screen.

"Well, how's our *Amerikanets?*" he heard a gay voice behind him. Natasha! Friends again. Good old world! He'd greet her in style. He rose on his skates and shot off at a giddy angle, planning to execute a sweeping curve, like Sasha's, and come up on a deft sidestroke squarely in front of her. But his left foot raced ahead, and his arm beat the air. Careening desperately to the right in an attempt to save himself, he succeeded in landing squarely in front of her, feet first. Skaters flying by skimmed his legs, called to him to clear off. Angered by her amused snicker, he engineered a quick rise. When she offered her hand, with dignity he refused. What'd she think he was, anyway, just learning to walk! Then take it easy. He threw himself to his feet, then through a dull haze heard the ice crack under him, as he spun on his stomach like a top.

Natasha leaned against the bench, clicked her skates in merriment, and doubled over. Sitting up on the cold surface, shamefaced, he grinned back at her. Good old world. She patted the seat by her, and carefully he slid over, crawled alongside.

"You're too ambitious for one day." With vigorous whangs she brushed powdered snow from his shoulders. "Anyway, with that will you'll soon learn. Catch your breath, and we'll have a skate together." An agreeable sight he made, with his fair skin and rough-woven jersey matching the blue in his eyes. She suspected he had known this when he bought it.

"Come on," she offered her hands. He would bear down too hard on her, he protested. She had no idea! Try it, she invited. They kept well to the edge of the circle while she showed him how to arch, balance his body slightly forward, and bear down on his stroke just enough, not directing it either in, in pigeon-toed fashion, or in too outward a manner.

He marveled at the power in her grip. Curiously he tested it, bore down harder. A girl had no business with so much strength. Not womanly. Oxen not girls were meant for heavy work. Yet, contrariwise, he liked it. Her dark hair slipping free of her cap whisked his cheek. His ankles, by some magic, ceased aching. Only his shoulder and side throbbed from that last fall. When Sasha flashed by with Lydia, his mate managed a hi-sign. Attaboy! Morse and Tim didn't guess what they'd missed. Fancy strip poker in a close room, against this!

"To the Lenin hills, for ski-ing!" Kolya gave the signal. Andy laced on his street shoes with concealed relief. But ski-ing! He had seen movies of that. Swift headover tumbles into snowbanks. Feet straddled, long skiis tilted skyward, he'd lie on his back unable to rise. How'd he ever be able to swing frames with Sasha tomorrow? *Nichevo!* This was

great sport. When he joined his crowd starting for the to-
boggan, his skateless feet propelled him stiffly with the
peculiar sensation of walking on stilts, but grateful nevertheless for solid leather and not-too-smooth underfooting.
He kept by Natasha, Mikhail on her left. The older man
called across to the American, but Andy made scant re-
sponse. That strawboss was still making up to him. Queer
bird. His resistance stiffened.

The forest moved toward them on muffled tread. An early
moon was climbing the breathless sky, and the woods
reëchoed with Sasha's singing:

> *Mighty and strong*
> *Our song of labor*
> *Power in us sweeping*
> *Stormy and free*

Tramping lines rounded out the full deep harmonies:

> *Where terror we'd strike*
> *There our song travels*
> *To others our theme*
> *Heralds the free*
> *Breath of the dawn*

> *Listen! For you*
> *Clarion notes*
> *In our rhythms*
> *Our ocean song*
> *Song of spring sowing*

Andy stole glances at those around him. Natasha had forgotten everything. Their voices rang through distant tree-
tops. She sang without effort, not releasing her full power
until some high note demanded a swelling chord. Andy
followed the air and tried to catch the words. These mass
harmonies reminded him of the Negro's, but with different
more martial beats to the rhythm.

They had come to an opening in the woods. Nearer still

142

the white mantled hills approached and gave back their
singing:

> *Mighty and strong*
> *Our song of labor*
> *Power in us sweeping*
> *Stormy and free—*
> *Who will deny*
> *Our glorious singing*
> *Sweeping high onward*
> *Vast waves o'er the sea!*

12

ANDY whistled with a will. No bolt dropping or wrong slings to his work today. He was racing Sasha to see who could complete his half of the chassis first. Sure thing, he won. Why not? Tonight he was having his first date with Nat. Other times had been mere pickups, chance meetings. This was the real thing, theater tickets and a big feed after. Movies had the edge for him, but he imagined she'd prefer a show. Some heavy upstage stuff. Well, that was jake with him. With a low chuckle, he challenged his workmate to a record on the next chassis. Old Mikhail, who was passing by, stopped to watch. Andy flipped his wrench. Who cared? Later on, when he rummaged his toolbox for his large hammer, it wasn't there. Nowhere about the belt. Sasha, nor any of the boys working near him had seen it. None of them, he was sure, had walked off with it. All the same, it was gone. Swiped! By whom?

At noon his mates started a checkup. Such petty thieving had to be stopped! When a union committeeman came to learn any clues, Andy recalled having seen a man from the testing section fooling about the upper end of the conveyor yesterday. Together they went up to ask Ned Folsom. Near him worked the man Andy had seen. Ned disagreed: he'd never liked the guy, himself. Still, he hardly thought Alex Turin guilty.

When questioned, Turin was furious. How could they suspect *him* of such an act! With a dramatic flourish he opened his locker; no hammer there. Andy apologized, returned to his work. Might as well chalk this up as a loss. His best hammer. Tools had a way of disappearing in Detroit, too.

"Borrowed," for keeps. To hell with it. Tonight he was having . . . All the same, his best hammer. Made him sore.

Turin accepted the American's excuses with sullen disdain. Damn Yankee: bloodsucker. He, a petty thief! Why should anybody risk trouble over a miserable forty rubles that the hammer'd bring in the market. What fools they were. They took him for the peasant he pretended? Good. A piece of bad luck, though, his visit to the conveyor being noticed. It might jeopardize some of his future work.

By three, Andy's hammer was back in his kit. His surprised glance clung to the young culprit who had come, accompanied by the committeeman and Mikhail, to return it in person and declare that this was the last time, honest. Mikhail appeared more upset by the incident than Karl, the guilty boy. Sasha told Andy afterwards that Karl was a former *bezprizhorni* whom Mikhail had befriended, persuaded to give up his hoboing and join their ranks. This was the boy's one slip in five months: the foreign-make hammer had been too much for him.

Andy rubbed his thumb over its worn handle. Who would have thought of going about it that way? These Russians sure had a new line. And that old straw-boss had seemed real worked up.

Work over, he was soon home. Now for the final jerks and the big date ahead. He'd begin with a stiff rub under the shower. Sandy hair dripping, he took a fresh razorblade from its packet. Two hours to go and he'd be meeting his Topnotcher at the club. Morse needn't try nosing in, either, to watch the takeoff.

Face distorted with his effort to offer even surfaces to his blade, his reflection stared back at him with friendly interest. Critically he examined the results. Okay. An unusually clean shave. But try and get a straight part to his mop of hair. He went over his ties, undecided between a red and a striped purple one. Elsie had accused him of loud tastes. He suspected his tonight's date didn't care whether he wore orange or black. Hot diggety, he bet she would too.

Natasha with Kolya meanwhile was waiting about the

145

shop, waiting for results from the *Amerikanets'* experiment. He had to swing it, the old sow's ear, he had to. What a boost for their shop, onto the red board, and for once off the black. If Boardman proved these parts could be made here, think of all the gold saved. How much they could buy with it—more MAGS from Germany, more combines from the States. Silently they stood, watching. If he just could!

Using Soviet metal and his own die, Boardman was stamping dressing wheels for emeries. Imagine, more than a thousand of these babies used up every day throughout the plant —and all of them imported from abroad, for pure gold. Damn it, he'd show them. He'd show them.

If only once he had a chance to show how this shop could be run. Never in all those years in America . . . Always it had been sweating his men, sweating himself. For what? It all got jammed somewhere. When he had come out of Cornell he'd been stuffed full of nice theories and pep for his job. Then his super with his "Forget that bunk! Engineering's a business, like any other, get me?" Sure, down to hard nails, brass tacks. All those years, he'd been often forced to do shoddy work. Always that nightmare of "What's the cheapest? the quickest?" Science, engineering, efficiency —bull! Speed, that's what counted. Speed, money, costs, more speed!

He'd show this louse Crampton. All that twenty-five years of swallowing cockeyed orders, but now he'd show them.

In this test more was at stake, he felt, than these wheels. More than putting it over on Crampton. What in God's name was happening to him anyhow? . . . Roughly, he forced his whole attention on his work.

The last die he'd designed for a new-shaped lid to the gasoline tank had been smashed in the testing. Since then, he tested out his new designs himself.

Diemen going about their work contrived to run over for spare moments to watch; also Pankrevich, who happened to be on the floor. Ah, an experiment! The manager became infected with the general excitement. If Meester Boardman proved these dressing wheels could be produced here, what a saving. Also something for him, Pankrevich, to report in

146

large letters at the next meeting of dopartment managers. They'd premium the *Amerikanets,* have quite a big meeting, a Red Letter Day, all round.

Philip worked with brisk assurance. That pig Crampton had declared these wheels impossible to produce here. Russian steel was not hard or tempered enough, he said, their work not sufficiently exact. And the damp-battery was staying on after hours, imagine! Just to enjoy his subordinate's failure. Philip gripped his steel. Let him, the bastard. All the pike cared for was greenbacks, prestige. And a tight fist on his job.

Beckoning Kolya, Boardman held up a finished wheel. Neat, eh? Observers closed in to watch its measurement: her teeth proved exact to a hundredth of a millimeter. Exultant, Natasha's eyes and arms danced. "Wait!" Crampton snapped, "test them out." That steel could never hold. Scientifically, he knew he was in the right. Would the Russian steel prove strong enough to smooth the roughened emery and not itself be worn down by the stone, leaving the emery as rough as it was before?

"Oh yeah?" his fellow-engineer wheezed slowly. "We'll see."

Under his cool direction, Natasha and then Kolya stamped off more wheels. All measured exact. With featheredged wheels fastened into the forked instrument for dressing emeries, the real test began. Restlessness gone, the engineer waited, almost motionless by the whirring machine. He wasn't, Kolya noted, even swearing. A bad sign? Torn between pride and misgivings, he watched his swearing *Amerikanets* toss a cigarette aside, light another, eyes narrowed to fine slits. Maybe it wasn't going to hold?

Kolya twisted his coatsleeve, walked around and around the sparking disks.

In the toolhardening sector, Maxim's black outline moved across redgold fires as he stoked and jammed his iron tongs into the flame. Whenever he could manage it, along with his Party work, he gave the lads on his old job a lift.

An electric car rumbled near Natasha. She longed to leap on, take control, anything to be busy. If the dressing wheels only held! Red Putilov steel: it must. "Five Years in Four." Dammit, why couldn't things go faster?

Her crimson scarf roved among giant drill presses and milling machines. Tonight she was going to a show with that nice *Amerikanets,* and her favorite actor in the leading rôle. If the steel only held! This driller she was watching knew his stuff, real skill. That's how it went, now here, now there. But faster, they must learn faster!

Kolya's triumphant shout bounded toward her. She ran back. Bravo! Hurrah for *Red Star!* Darling Boardman—the steel held!

Skepticism gone, Pankrevich shook the engineer's hand with genuine warmth. Crampton had disappeared. Seizing their swearing *Amerikanets* by the shoulders, Kolya and Natasha spun him around, jigged him in dizzy circles, even threatened to toss him above their heads. Several workmen and girls stopped their machines to run over, discipline for the moment to the winds. Hurrah—the *Amerikanets!* Science! Soviet industry, no stopping her. The steel held!

Embarrassed, restless again, Philip tried to escape. Hang them, with their hurrahs and pawgrabbing, they got you all hot.

Quickly shop routine reasserted itself. Kolya and Natasha were examining the tested pin wheels when a workman from the jig fixtures department approached the engineer to ask for some technical advice. Boardman looked up. What a break! Pankrevich was within earshot. "Can you spare me five minutes on my problem?" the workman repeated. The engineer's reply was distinct, carrying: "No, I can't help you. I am forbidden. Those are my orders." His companions stirred. Orders, what did he mean, orders?

Philip gestured toward the superintendent. "Am I right? Those are orders?" Uneasily Eugene Pankrevich shifted his weight. Perhaps Meester Boardman had not clearly understood their conversation; management had requested him to give his attention exclusively to increasing output. That was all. The girl listened to his halting explanation with open amazement. That was all!

As Philip started off, Natasha followed. "And this, my

148

girl," his tone was caustic, "this is how we foreign specialists are encouraged to transfer our technical knowledge to you." God, he'd almost forgot that sonofabitch.

Natasha held his arm. Wait! They must have this cleared up, right away. Would the engineer have time to come with them to give a detailed statement of what had taken place? She sent Kolya for Maxim. Tomorrow, after work, there was to be a meeting of their Party group with the director and plant committee on their dieshop's functioning; then Pankrevich, as a Party man, must account for several things, including such methods of handling a foreign *spetz*.

(What if this delayed her in meeting Andy? She hoped not. Devil take it, something was always coming up. But what could she do: Boardman could never manage the language alone.)

Philip looked at his watch. Quarter after six. Mary and supper were waiting, Junior demanding his Dad for his bedtime romp. *Nichevo!* He went with Natasha into the office, where Pankrevich and Maxim joined them. Occasionally when his rapid flow of ungrammatical Russian halted, in search of a term, Natasha and his dictionary came to his aid. She was racing against time. At the engineer's reference to rationalization proposals pigeon-holed, Pankrevich interposed, disagreeing. Maxim Sotnikov looked at him coolly. "Comrade Pankrevich, don't interrupt." Heavy brows pressed together, he added brusquely, "The facts are against you. You can make your excuses to our meeting tomorrow." Natasha wanted to thump his jacket. Good old Maxim. Just didn't he take that highhat down a peg!

Her unit had made a good choice in Maxim. He was from the tool hardening sector, a plodder and a bit slow, with shoulder muscles that threatened to rend his jacket and a matter of fact honesty that spared no one, least of all himself.

Andy reached the club ahead of the time agreed. He fingered his tickets, ran through magazines on the table. Where was that girl? A real Russian, bound to be late. Going to the entrance, he peered down the dimly lighted street. No sign of her. Crap, she knew how long it took to reach the center. Sure made him sore to be kept in a corner, shifting one freshly pressed trousers leg after the other and waiting on a tardy date. Who'd she think she was! Greta Garbo?

Natasha gave a startled look at the engineer's wristwatch. Already six-forty, a pretty mess. She was going to miss out on the show. And her favorite actor. And Andy. She must get word to him, but it was no use trying to phone. If she left at once, there'd still be time, theaters began at half past seven. She looked at Maxim, bit her lip. Excusing herself, she looked about for some one to carry a message. No one was about. What a pity. What could she do? She couldn't leave now. Well, when she explained, he'd realize how she just couldn't leave. And to think how all day she had been looking forward to that play.

With each dragging moment, Andy's fury mounted. He would wait, he swore, exactly forty-five minutes. Not one second over. What was this, anyway? A run-around? Trying to string him along, was she, let him down? He'd wait long enough to hear what she had to say for herself. Then leave her cold.

Jumping Jesus, Morse and Tim!

He made a dash for the club's rear exit, dodged along side-streets. Two crumpled theater tickets tossed in the air. They fluttered with a doleful swoop until the wind snatched and dashed them gleefully against a lamp-post. Exasperated, he caught them as they fell toward the ground, wound them into vicious hard balls, and pelted them at an ashcan. Cock-eyed world.

As they came into the restaurant for their lunch, the Detroiter noticed a line of photographs along the wall, and a crowd of diners circling beneath them. He nudged Sasha. Why all the fireworks? Had Moscow discovered a new Lindy? Maybe movie stars! The Russian gave an incredulous grunt, walked over to see.

Under the likeness of a rawboned, curlyhaired Tartar with melancholy whiskers was written:

COMRADE POGOROVSKY, FIRST COOK TODAY IN CHARGE OF BORSCHT.

His neighbor, a snubnosed, jolly woman, was introduced as Dora Ivanova, responsible for the second course. Joking among themselves, truckdrivers diemen turners and assemblers milled around the photographs. So these were the ones who fixed their grub! All honor to good cooks, devil take poor ones. "Well, Comrade Pogorovsky, we shall sample your *borscht* today, and if it is rainwater!"

Andy queried his workmate, "What's the big idea?" These Russkies were always coming out with some new wrinkle. In answer, Sasha drew out that morning's edition of *Red Star Trucks.* Nothing less than a socialist competition among the cooks. It had started, he said, with that article in their wallpaper *Conveyor,* remember? A chap on the belt had written it and eight of them signed: *We Eat Borscht and Make Sour Faces.* Sure, Andy remembered that. A hot one. He'd even considered adding his John Hancock to it. (But he knew better. Get in dutch with the boss! Not him.)

As far as he was concerned today, the whole globe wore a sour face. Tim a perpetual grouch, Morse forever with a morningafter head on, and Natasha as calm as you please about the date she'd broken. Things in the States were still going haywire. Sure, both goldern hemispheres wore a sour face.

The *Conveyor* article, his friend continued, had been brought to *Pravda's* attention by correspondents in the shop, and a brigade from the staff of the country's central paper had come to investigate the kitchen, organize a campaign for better meals. This, he took it, was the opening round.

Their *borscht* consumed, angry diners demanded to see the cook. Somewhat startled, white cap at a precarious angle which Andy was sure required glue, the chef, fumbling his stained apron, appeared in the doorway. At the head of the table a bucketshaped machinist rose to his squat height to remark gravely that he had been delegated to make a report. Today the *borscht* had been far too sour. For their part, they were working hard at their jobs to fulfill the

Pyatiletka. Why was it the cooks couldn't do their share, give them decent meals? A checkup showed ample supplies, yet who'd suspect from that dishwater the tons of carrots and cabbage that had gone into the soup! At a gruff voice's interjection, "What are you anyway, cooks or hogfeeders!" the chef mumbled something into his drooping whiskers and vanished into the kitchen.

With angry fervor his scooper attacked mounds of light-green cabbage and goldenskinned carrots, while automatic choppers and peelers sung over their prey and spun fluffy hills into the yawning vats. Tomorrow, so he'd been informed, they were going to call him again. Let them! This time, he vowed, they should thank him. Yes, by the blasted saints, the whole dining room. He, Alexander Pogorovsky, a cook for fifteen years, told he couldn't concoct a decent stew! Because they made trucks, those guys thought they knew everything! (His knife wielded flashing arcs over bloodred pyramids of beets.) So they had come around at last to noticing the cooks, eh! He'd show them. His was as good a craft as anybody's. A thousand devils on them and their "the *borscht* is too sour."

As Andy and Sasha crossed the yard toward their assembly-shop, Mac and Ned joined them. Their subcommittee, the Scotchman said, had been collecting the lowdown on breakage, and was it hot stuff! He jabbed the Detroiter in the side. "Still an onlooker, eh? A wailing Job in overalls, predicting dire fate for us all. Well, hold on, old boy, in six months you won't know our plant."

Andy listened, clamped his jaws. In six months he would be on the high seas.

Mac showed them his last pay envelope: "Quite a jump, eh? The turners say they can't recognize our repairmen, so Johnny-on-the-Spot, that's us! Our new system's a humdinger. And does it jack up the laggards!" Of course his brigade had made a few enemies in the change-over: some of the lazy ones who'd liked the old carefree system. *Nichevo*, they'd get over it. As for general management of the department, it was as weak as ever. "A bit of spring cleaning, fellows," he added with easy assurance, "can be good for more than houses." Andy shrugged. That crazy bird was at it again.

Mac walked with the others through their shed. Why the crape? he jibed Andy. Come over tonight, they'd cheer him up. His friend brightened. Should he bring his pals? Mac hesitated: do as he liked. Did Morse and Tim really like his kind of a party? Nan wouldn't stand for a lot of booze. Besides ... his arm through Ned's tightened. Sure, bring the other two Americans along, provided they knew how to act decent to his friends.

Andy understood. Oh well, he said, those simps probably had heavy dates on, anyway.

Last time he had taken his friends over to Mac's, there had been some snappy crossfire between them and Ned, and their grumbling and wisecracks must have got under his skin. "To hear you talk," he'd burst out, "anybody'd think America before the crisis was some kind of a paradise." Hell, if they'd happened to've been born with dark skins (which they evidently thanked their lucky stars they weren't) and had lived in that hellhole known as the South's Black Belt, then they'd have something to talk about! Or if they'd been among the millions of foreign-born sweating their lives out in steel mills and mines, or poor whites in cotton mills— anybody but who they were! Part of American labor's upper tenth, dumb enough to believe they'd the world by the tail! Until the crisis gave 'em the laugh.

As it was, they'd better clamp down. They didn't appreciate a good thing when they had it. Spoiled, that's what they were, gone soft. Fat to their gills.

"I suppose it's beyond you," he'd said, "how I can be proud, yes actually proud, of being a Negro? More than that, I know how damn lucky I am, if you don't, to be over here."

And Mac had backed him up. They sure were thick.

Anyway, Andy had kinda liked Ned for his frank blow-off. The fellow had grit. And he handled trucks, you had to admit, like a duck in water.

With a solong to Mac and Ned, Andy and his workmate entered their shed. As they neared the conveyor, the Detroiter reread the chalked figures on the blackboard standing nearby. Jumping sparkplugs, yesterday that gang of bums on second shift had topped theirs! Twenty trucks against their seventeen. He motioned to Sasha. "Those figures right?"

His friend gave a characteristic hitch to his shoulders. *Nichevo*, today they'd make a comeback, right? All afternoon the pair worked at top speed. What the Russian called *udarnik tempo*. His mate scoffed, call it what he liked. He was just plain mad. By now they knew one another's movements like the right hand the left.

Andy looked down the line. Attaboy! They were well ahead of the game. So were the sprayers. Glistening steel-blue, a body was lowering from the floor above, while motors and tires swung in slow circles, like gulls in full flight. The men handling them, though, were behind schedule. Andy scowled. Lousy snails. His mate and he counted eighteen chassis. Eighteen, and barely an hour to go. By God, they'd never top those other boys at this rate.

When the bell for change of shifts whanged, the Detroiter hung back. Slowly he went for a drink, returned. Eighteen. They needed twenty-one. His companion, he saw, was staying on. He would. That damn brigade had evidently decided to work over. Let them. Damn if he would.

He began gathering his kit together. Well and why didn't the sucker give him a look, say something?

But at times like this, Sasha had long ago ceased looking after the American's carefree disappearing form. If that's how it was, that's how it was.

The American idled his hammer. Made him sore how they took for granted he'd walk out on them. "Say, got a place for an extra, today?"

His mate grinned, jumped up. Sure thing, why not? Say, this was fine! They were well up on chassis, though. Twenty-one already on their way down the belt, only needed finishing off. Say, wait until he asked Mikhail?

At the old man's pleased glance, Andy winced. What the hell! He wasn't doing it for him. In fact, just why was he doing it? Acting the sucker. A fool thing. But just this once.

154

He'd nothing pressing, outside. Hell, you couldn't let 'em get away with it. Gotta give 'em a run for their money. A lousy eighteen, when they needed twenty-one.

His fingers raked impatiently through his hair. Say, he knew a thing or two about connecting motors. Fact was, he knew about every lousy job on the belt. How about giving those motor boys a hand?

Just the thing! Mikhail hooked his arm, led him over. A man lying face up under a car waved his greeting. Ah, the *Amerikanets!* Suddenly Andy wanted to bolt, shout he didn't know what.

The eighteenth truck, he saw, was being driven by Ned into the yard. Now for three more babies to match it.

On his way to fit on doubletread tires, Sasha passed his workmate's towhead screwed inside a lifted hood. His slap resounded on his damp shoulder. Some assemblyman, their Andy. These boys better keep their eyes peeled, learn a few tricks from the Yankee. *To overtake and surpass!* That was their slogan.

Andy connected wires, adjusted tappets, whistling. Who cared?

He was one of the gang.

13

W HEN he reached home, it was nearly six. Pinned to his door was a note from Morse:

Come quick Urgent

He raced down the stairs across to their rooms. Maybe only some sap joke of Morse's but you never could tell. Might be bad news from home?

Tim fallen off the scaffolding? Or some lucky break?

He found his friends dashing about a room hit by a Kansas tornado. Beds and chairs were sunk under hills of socks underwear trousers, tables and windowsills choked with half-empty bottles ties striped pajamas. With faithful glee the Victrola was reeling a jazz version of *Be It Ever So Humble.*

Andy stepped between the bags lying about the floor. "What's the big noise?" Arms full of dirty clothes, Morse was puffing like an Irishwoman redfaced over her wash. At sight of his visitor all dropped to the floor. "Old horse, doublequick it back to your room!" he shouted. "Get your junk packed." Oh baby, they were heading for home. The good old land of pork and beans, classy gals. He waltzed Andy round. No more cutlets, ears aching for English. No more cockeyed Bolshies but beefsteaks, ham and eggs! Broadway. Sweet mama. Detroit! Whoopee, what a party they'd sling!

Andy loosened his hold, sank on the bed. What was up? Six months to go before their contract expired. What exactly was up? Morse made him move off his best suit. Christ, had his earflaps gone back on him? What he meant they were going home! Wait till he heard. Tim had gotten a raw deal. Downright rotten. The sooner they knocked the dust of this lousy berg from their steppers the better. Tomorrow they'd make the company fix it up. No Russian tomorrow either. And he didn't mean maybe.

Andy turned to his buddy. "Tim, get down to brass tacks." His head spun dizzy arcs, tossed between hope and sickening dread. Home! Sacked ... Handouts ... but home! Waltzing Elsie at the Savoy ... If only ... Tim stalked from door to window, recounting the latest as he booted luggage to one side. Andy's stare was fixed on a spot along the tan wall where the walker's shadow passed and repassed across the light. Jeez, what a turn. Crimson blotches stamped Tim's prominent cheekbones, his gaze fell heavier than his tread. By God, he was an American with a sense of justice and fair play. They had been outraged. Beyond repair. But one thing to do—go home. He was fed up to the gills.

Nobody could say he hadn't shot square. His pals knew that, even if he'd never liked it here. Everything was *Zavtra*—tomorrow. Waits, red tape, one bullheaded idea after the other. His stomach acted like a raw heel, his job a madhouse. One day it was no lumber, the next no nails. Building equipment was about zero and methods a lousy thirty years behind. No modern system for division of labor for these birds. Why, they expected him a skilled carpenter who'd worked on some of the biggest construction jobs in the States to do all sorts of common labor for himself. Everything short of carrying off shavings! As for the foreman, he didn't give a hang about learning new methods. Not that bum.

Andy waited. Good old Tim. But he'd heard all this a dozen times before. What was new?

All the same, Tim added, he had done the right thing. More than he'd say for that pack of hams he worked with. Dogs in the manger most of them, plain hicks with the straw sticking out of their ears. Couldn't turn out first class work but envied his. He was sure they grudged him his higher pay. Imagine that, and them making window frames like windmills and housedoors roughfinished enough for a barn. Well what the, they were Russians for crying out loud! Damn farmers, their coats little better than gunny sacks and fitting worse than Alec's old shirt. Their legs were wrapped in yards of dirty cloth. Think of putting mutts like that, ordinary daylaborers, on skilled work like masonry! Only these cockeyed Russians would try it.

At first these bums had tried making up to him, acted like he was their longlost brother from Egypt. Imagine, him! Admiring his better tools and clothes, asking a dozen questions. Damn foreigners. He hadn't come here to hobnob with ditchdiggers.

Then they had turned meaner than a pack of Satans. Sly as hell with it too. They jammed his arms accidental-like when he was planing. They swiped his best boards when nobody was looking and even some of his tools, they spit near his shoes. Especially they got a big kick out of wisecracks made loud enough for him to hear about stuckup foreigners wagehogs *valuta*. "Some of these Yankees think they got the world sewed up in a pig's sack." Oh, he knew enough of their brogue to get the point. They saw to that. They mimicked his walk and dubbed his trousers pigeon wings! They asked him things in a flood of Russian, then pretended he was a dummy for not understanding. A pain in the ass. They even mooched his cigarettes with a sneer about *Torgsin* and his being able to afford it.

What? Well, yes, there had been a few decent fellows. But what did they count when the rest ganged up against him? The Satans were clever. Whenever anybody else was around, they drew in their tails. Sweet as you please. God, how they burned him up.

That morning had come the blowoff. For a long time they had been passing him up bad lumber, he was wise to that. The planer he used made them snake-eyed, he knew they planned to wreck it. Theirs were crude things, just clumsy horsetroughs. After he'd complained to the foreman, for a time he'd had no trouble. Today though, the nails had been hidden in the boards too damn well: before he knew it, he'd jammed his planer.

158

He'd thrown it at the devils, given them a piece of his mind in good old American, and quit 'em cold. The foreman and one of the fellows had run after him but it did no good. He was through.

At the gate the guard demanded his pass. It was unsigned. Tim'd have to go back and get it signed, the buzzard said, before he'd let him through. He placed his gun across the entrance, so Tim closed in. "Oh, you won't, eh?" His fist gave him a swift one on the nose, crumpled him flat.

Tim had gone straight to the downtown office and demanded a ticket on the first boat home. All the apologies and arguments of the Building Trust and Auto Industry combined could never change him. He was quits. Take their lousy job. Him for the States. He hoped the guard had a busted nose.

Morse offered Andy his pack of cigarettes. "So you see how things stand. We gotta back up our buddy. Anyway, I'm sick of the place." His liver had gone bad on him for life. First thing in the morning he was giving notice. Gonna scram. Hotcha! *Be It Ever So Humble.*

Andy studied his burning tobacco. What about their contracts? Damn that record!

Morse ground a butt beneath his heel. Contracts hell! The company paid their fares home and that was that. So long Moscow, hello New York! "Step on it kid," he told his friend, "Pack up, get ready for the big shoveoff."

"So it's final, eh?" Andy asked. If only he could clear his brains, think! "And when we get to the States, what about jobs! Our savings? Gone in three months. Honest, boys, I'm homesick as any." (What he'd give to drop in on Elsie! Stroll down main street. See his old pals.) "But we gotta be practical. That's all." Tim had a real grievance, no doubt of that. A lousy shame. But why let a bunch of nitwits run him off? Be a good sport. The Building Trust had offered him other work. Take it. "Come on, act sensible! Shake down a peg. You can't go off your bean like that." As for equipment, everybody knew the strenuous efforts the country was making to put itself on a machine basis. You had to see their side of it too. Give 'em an even break.

Andy hesitated, "As far as Morse and I go, we ain't no grounds for quitting them. They've been decent and then some, right from the start. Christ, Tim, you know I'd like to hit the trail with you."

Morse threw out his arms. "What's getting into you! You put a bargain with a bunch of reds ahead of sticking by a friend? Guess we're free to come and go as we choose."

Tim's comments were weighted. No, he'd never expect Andy to give up a soft thing. Not just to back him up. Of course not. Nothing of the kind. Andy was afraid to go home, take his chance on a job? People looked at friendship good sportsmanship different, that was all.

"Aw, Tim!" Andy began, but broke off.

"Crap," Morse offered, "things are bound to pick up soon." In the meantime they had saved up some berries. Tim and he had a scheme for opening an oil station. If Andy wanted they'd make it a threesome. Times like this fellows had to stand together. What he meant, divvy their losses and split their gains. And you know.

Andy smoked his nickel-case empty. A present from Elsie. Its snap clicked open and shut, open and shut. Detroit! His old girl. A run down to see Uncle Jem in Virginia. Could he ever make a go of it there on the farm? Perhaps the oil station ...

His companions began packing. Andy roamed over gaping bags to the window. Outside it was foggy. The great Russian bear crouched on its white haunches, asleep. Andy rested his forehead against the pane. To head west? To stay on? Sasha, Mac in his tam, Feldman swearing "Get 'em out," Elsie gurgling him one big welcome, Natasha and for some reason old Mikhail crowded near him by the window. They reeled a fast merry-go-round through his tired brain. To be left behind or leave? He wanted neither. To go and to stay. He wanted both. Hell, he was a half-and-half, torn between two separate worlds. But if only he could wake up tomorrow in Detroit!

"Well?" Morse called. "What you mooning over there for?

160

Get a move on. Which is it? Make up your mind, yes or no."

Andy slipped on his coat. He couldn't. Not tonight. He'd let them know in the morning. They knew how it was, kind of sudden. Had to come up for air.

"Okay. As you like." Morse sat on the lid of his bag, striving to force it to. He was sure Andy'd not be letting them down. Think of the old boat steaming up to Manhattan with Tim and him but no Andy on board. Nothing doing. It'd be a threesome. And he didn't mean maybe.

Andy tramped until his feet refused to carry him further. Streets, deserted at this hour except for occasional latecomers, held an ominous silence as his troubled footsteps crunched along the tracked snow. A weather-beaten *droshky* waiting for stray passengers shuddered with the regularity of its snoring driver. He had curled himself up in his sheepskin, dug in under the horsehair blanket. Andy passed shopwindows of mechanical toys. Dress goods. Warehouses. Bundled gruff nightwatchmen on their rounds.

America! Should he? His very bones ached, tugging both ways. His memory was playing tricks with him, bringing up all the sweet things, letting the rest go. America! Elsie! But . . . Back on the belt. The damn strawboss. Dirty snitchers. Besides, who could get a goddam job! . . .

He walked until mocking stars faded from a lowering sky and the east streaked with yellow. Were those planets inhabited? If so, was life there as damn complicated as here? Well, you had to learn to take the breaks as they came. Head on. And no looking back. Christ, he was tired.

On his way home, he halted by a showcase of musical instruments. Violins horns guitars and those inevitable accordions. How dead they looked at this hour. If suddenly they woke up, what a howl they could set loose. Or what swell music. That was how it was. He'd like to try out one of those accordions. Squeeze 'em, tap his foot like Sasha. Tomorrow he must ask how much.

And tomorrow he must get some things to send Elsie. Cute figure she'd cut in one of those Ukranian dresses and a pair of embroidered boots. Tomorrow? It was already today. Well, six months might pass in no time. Until then.

He slept in his clothes, alarm clock close to his pillow. So far he had a clear record for not being late.

His friends refused to believe him. "Quit your kidding." Morse was sore, "No time to lose." Convinced finally that Andy meant to remain, he linked his arm in Tim's, expressed his full opinion of deserters whose three meals per came before friendship, and walked out. The last days before their departure they openly avoided him. Well, who cared? Several times he was on the verge of rushing into the office to demand a return ticket. America! Home!

Andy purchased gifts for all those back home, unlocked his suitcase, and packed his things. So in case, at the last minute.

The waiting room at the station was close, pressing your chest. Its bustling eddies swirled round them as travelers, arriving and departing, elbowed their way through. Morse was in high spirits, Tim sulky. Grudgingly they took the packages and a note for Elsie. Their bags were bursting as it was. The representative of the State Trust who had come to see them off observed with an amused twinkle their swearing attempts to fit them in.

Andy eyed the station clock. The hands were going backwards. Would that bell never sound! He labored to match Morse's rapid sallies, but his comebacks fell with a hollow ring, striking on his ears like from some distance far off.

The tracks, when they went outside, gleamed at them, wet with fog. Steel ribbons they were, running back toward the land from whence he had come. Mists of a midwinter thaw stung their bones, blurred green and red lights and moving throngs. Everybody, Andy brooded, seemed to have somewhere they were heading. Friends to meet them. Everybody but him. He was a half and half. The stupid bat of the old legend. Neither fish nor fowl. Engines puffed restlessly, a siren whistled along the wind. Crap, who cared?

Collar up, hands thrust deep into his overcoat pockets, he watched Tim and Morse aboard and their train gather steam. The Russian said something to him, but he didn't hear. His gaze strained after the long monster disappearing into the raw mist. Its last sounds, as he stood listening, were swallowed by the wretched night, blended with hoarse shouts of an arriving train. With jocular indifference an incoming crowd jostled him about the platform. Shivering with the damp, he reversed his steps. Cars at this hour were overflowing, it was a relief to throw all his energies into tackling his way in. He'd biff the first stiff who spoke to him right on his snout.

In the center of town he had to make a transfer. He knocked left foot against right and stared ahead into the blurry drizzle. The damn thing was trickling inside his scarf, probably running green and purple streaks down his jerky spine. "Street car!" Padded creatures, their bundles baskets and briefcases jamming, splashed about in the slush. Madly he plunged in, slipped on icy ridges of packed snow hidden under murky pools ... Snakes, number 6! Close behind though with people hanging on the steps loomed his. He had joined the trail hastening to meet it halfway up the block, when he noticed a handsomely dressed woman standing to one side. By the cut of her clothes, an American. As he wrestled for a foothold he looked back to see how she was faring. Maybe loan her a free arm. She had vanished.

From behind came a steady pressure and cries of "Citizens, move up!" He felt a dozen elbows, heavy feet. With grim pleasure he pushed back. Some fellow with a huge sack between his legs had jammed the doorway. Face flushed and clanging her bell, the conductoress motioned to the last hangers on to let go. The car must start. They had a schedule, she wasn't getting listed on the blackboard for tardiness. But it was dangerous to hang on that way. Let go! She knew her instructions: either they let go or she blew her whistle.

Protesting to the last, a few were loosened. Slowly the groaning car was underway. A man suspended on the rear gestured wildly with a brief case. The conductoress motioned to him with her plump arms through the window: despairingly he motioned back. He couldn't get on or off!

Passengers took immediate sides. He must get off. (Sharp prods in his exposed ribs.) ... But was the woman a fool! She had no business starting the car until he was well on. Suddenly the bell clanged, the crowd lurched forward in the stopped car, and the suspended individual was helped to the frozen asphalt by a militiaman who immediately fined the man three roubles for breaking traffic rules. He knew well enough, no hanging on cars!

Wedged in near the back, Andy glimpsed the foreign woman seated calmly in a front seat. A slick one, that. She'd pulled the old *ne ponimayu* gag and comfortably boarded the car from the front. To top it off, she had a place reserved for invalids and women with kids.

Something familiar about her puzzled him. The way she carried herself or ... Stubbornly he worked his way forward to lamp her face. The car gathered speed and rounded a bend with gusto. Two girls near him, busily conversing, were swept off their feet into the laps of a pair of aviators seated down the aisle.

"Sit down, do!" they told their unexpected guests. "Make yourselves comfortable." The car laughed heartily while the girls righted themselves. "Never mind, lassies," a youth braced against the window frame called over to them. "Remember, this is socialism!" A passenger of serious mien looked up from the book which he had been managing with great adroitness to read. "And never mind your Smart Alec talk, my young flip! Remember our subway is already started. Do you know how many new cars and buses Moscow added to its traffic system this past year? Do you know ... "

The youth pretended amazement. Say, that was fine! After this, he'd ride home on statistics: save fare and wear and tear on clothes. Did the citizen know how many buttons he'd torn off, how many scoldings he'd got for rips in his coat? There were statistics for you!

Again the passengers laughed, Andy with them. A ride in a Moscow car was better than a three-ring circus. Halfway up the blocked aisle he had his first full view of the woman passenger. Holy cats! Yellow hair, marcelled! He plunged toward the rear.

Gradually the car emptied. From a rear seat he watched his Berlin frau descend at the Kalinin works. Her *Mann* must be a specialist there. Jeez, what a nightride from the

164

border that had been! Would it slay the boys when they heard! When?...When hell froze over.

The next was his stop. He was first on the platform and dropped to the bottom step, ready for a running jump, as the car slowed down. Against orders. In town if they caught you, you were fined three roubles with a caution besides. Mac had told him of dropping off once right into the arms of a militiaman. Imagine that. Out here there'd hardly be one around. If he rode on to the regular stop he had an extra block to walk back.

The damp haze plunged its fingers through his overcoat as if paper, twisted his spine. He was in for a cold. Hang it all, in ten minutes he'd be home. And was he going to pound the hay! Tomorrow'd be another day.

The motor woman, who rode her car like a ship's masthead, sounded her tocsin, slowed her car by a notch. Another. Andy jumped. Ice, car, houses revolved about him as he fell. His full weight crushed against his left foot: he felt something snap, then hurl him headlong into a yawning black void.

14

THE bare wintry limbs of a solitary oak, framed by the frosted pane, rubbed themselves mournfully. Since early morning Andy's tired gaze had been fastened on their crooked beckoning fingers. As soon as his head was clearer and the nurse not around he ought to make a break for the exit. Had to devise some kind of a crutch. He gave his bummed ankle a resentful twitch: pain ripped up his side and whanged his head.

Subdued, he lay motionless, eyes on the tree. Its lank arms were reaching up for a fast hold on the sky. Its grasp slipped, cried out, reached again. Andy repeated under his breath, as he had done as a boy when he'd come down with the measles, *goddammit, goddammit.* Of last night he remembered nothing except loud demands to the ambulance doctor to take him home. Then, smothering drafts of chloroform and a heavy sleep. And a greeneyed witch who had ridden her broom all night on his hurt leg. *Goddam it.*

He had a dread of hospitals. Their knockout smells of ether dove to his lower guts with sickening thuds of disaster. Bills bellyache bills. How in hell was he to get out of here? *Goddammit.* Here, when he'd had a good job. Shit that ice. He'd be sunk with debts. All going out, nothing coming in. Lousy break.

His unknown room-mate had his shoulder and arm bandaged. What sort of bung up had he had? No chance to ask, for the man slept like a baby. Only woke in time to be fed. Didn't the fellow have a worry or pain about him!

The old witch was hammering his ankle until he wanted to tear off the bandage. High noon. Things in the shop in full swing. Tim and Morse on the high seas.

He imagined he heard the city humming. What he'd give now for a stroll down breezy Tverskaya! Wonder who was paired up with Sasha? *Goddammit.* Bet the boys'd whistle when they heard where he was. How long before he could get out? Must be some way of making loans here. This'd clear him of three or four hundred jack before he was done and the devil knew what else besides. Jeez, what a washup.

With a soft click the door opened. No doubt that white-robed sister with faint odors of disinfectant about her quick hands. He feigned sleep, then sniffed. No listerine to that smell. Good old machine oil. Or was he plain off his nut?

Someone called his nickname. Starting, he hoisted himself by his elbows. Sasha! Never had that round face with its trail of brown seeds looped from nose to ears looked so good. Sasha!

His workmate pulled his chair close to the bed. Word had come that morning, everybody was sorrier than the deuce. Just what had happened, and how bad was it?

Andy tried to give a sporting account of his fall. What he'd aimed for was one of Mac's Highland flings on the ice. In spite of all he could do, his voice came in thin hoarse whispers. Ran the scale like he had the goslings! Dirty traitor ... Provoked, his voice trailed off.

Sasha edged his scrupulously scrubbed hand over the pillow. His buddy was white as a sheet. He wanted to fondle him like he would his kid brother. Better not, might fuss the American. You could never tell about these Yankees, they weren't ones to show their feelings or make a fuss.

"A rough tumble eh, *tovarisch?* What you trying to do anyway?" he bantered gently. "Learn to ski all over again?" Never mind, he was lucky not to have snapped a pin. As it was, it needed only a few weeks to mend those torn ligaments. "Say," he added, "the belt don't seem right without you, honest."

Gingerly the Detroiter shifted his weight. Who had his place?

Sasha righted his covers. Nobody had his place. What did he think! Mikhail was putting on a chap by the name of Seenya until Andy came back. The boy swung chassis like a hen paddled water. Whenever Andy was ready to go it again, his place was waiting.

The sick man looked up. "Honest?" He hadn't been sure.

His friend was examining the room. Sure thing. Was it all right here? They took good care of you? He left to speak with the nurse, hurried back. His noon hour was soon up but he was coming over tomorrow after work. "You never said how you like it here?" he asked again.

Andy worked his shoulder against the pillow. "Okay I guess. Must cost like all high water."

"*Nichevo!*" the word flew out with hearty emphasis. "You should worry about that!"

The American's gaze fretted over the tree. Tell Mac to come over. He must see him. (He'd wait and talk brass tacks with him. At times, Sasha with his bag of *nichevos* was an easy-going fool. A nice one for all that.)

As his workmate's screeching boots tiptoed through the doorway, Andy's gaze followed him. The boy's jacket was a halfsize too large for him. His trousers hadn't seen a press iron since they were handed across the counter. Inside of his boots were thick red socks of which their owner was secretly very proud. Cap slung on at a cheerful angle, his eyes were clear; steady with what Andy termed an up-and-coming look that had impressed him in workers here. You had a feeling that they and life had come to terms. Were pals.

Andy smiled. Sasha was the real thing. He longed to catch up with him, face him once more across the belt. Hear that Russian voice shouting in English, "Atta buoy! Dis es how!"

Dozing fitfully, he battled with the old vixen to let up on his lame hip. Uneasy with pain and old fears, he dreamed again of chasing the belt. Fingers slipping. Tramping for work. Now he was running on the sea chasing that boat. Heigh, Tim! Wait! Wait! ... He was loco, he'd drown like a rat. God, he was skating the waves. (And he'd never believed that Jesus yarn.) Tim, can't you hear me? Throw me a belt-line. Here! Over here.

But it's Feldman. That sonofabitch! Got me on the hip,

eh? Under the pin? No you don't. You speed crank, quit those jerks. I ain't working your belt, see. Let go!... Where's the ship? Feldman! God, I'm gone nuts or what. I ain't got a job. Tramp you fool, tramp. Hunt till your guts dry up.

Elsie, you ain't letting me down easy? Come out straight with it...Feldman, I'll do any job you say. You know I'm as good all-round speedy man as you got on the line...

Don't bawl, Elsie. Our granddads now, they had to rough it. Come on, give it a try....Christ, I'm all washed up with this tramping. My poor leg. Ain't there some way? Ain't there?

Starting upright, shuddering with fever, Andy awoke. What a nightmare. Well, for him it had passed over. At least for awhile. But for millions of his buddies back there ...Wasn't there a way? Would he get caught again? Why couldn't America snap out of it?

For a long hour he listened to the tree purring in the wind.

Funny, this country had no jobless army. On the streets, you didn't run into that godawful drove of young "forgotten men." Some beggars, sure. But more jobs than men. Things booming. Just why this was, he wasn't sure. Things here had their tough side but it was different. Different as hell.

He was sure of it now: Tim and Morse had been crazy to leave.

Before dusk Mac had come, with Lucy on his shoulder. While she explored the room's strange fascinating plateaus and low corners he talked with his friend. Like a good motor he was humming with news. He slipped a book from his pocket, placed it on the table. By tomorrow Andy'd feel up to reading. Straight fact, he envied him all this timeout for books. Thought he'd smash a bloody ankle himself.

When the sick man broached the matter of loans, stating why, Mac looked at him quizzically. "See here, buddy, it's time you wised up." Where'd he think he was anyway? Working for Pierpont or Ford? "See here, your rights as a worker were read you when you first came. Didn't you take it in?"

"That bull?"

"Bull, me eye! Get this, bo." His expenses here were on the State. Sure, accidents came under the social insurance system, why not?

The Detroiter whistled. Wouldn't that blow you. Not to have to worry over those bills. Mac said he'd draw his wages besides. Seeing was believing on that. Sure they'd read some stuff to them when he came, but he'd tossed it aside as some more company line. Besides a crack on the ice, his own fault. Who'd ever thought anybody else'd foot the bills for that?

So this was what they meant by their Socialism stuff. For crying out loud!

Climbing onto her father's lap, Lucy pulled insistently at his blunt nose and pointed ears. Suppertime! Come on home. He tied the strings of her cap, buttoned his coat. Yes, they must go. Tonight he had a meeting at the Moscow Soviet on the public schools. Their plant had taken patronage over the City Department of Education. Some job! Well, cheerio. His brisk step timed to Lucy's patter re-echoed down the silent corridors.

Andy lay thinking. Wise up. His head was on the blink. But savvy that. Two billion a year on stiffs like him. And Mac said they weren't giving him nothing. All coming to him. Well bo, for once you *are* telling me!

Wise up. Well, he would. Not easy. This was a tough nut to crack. The next morning he woke early, to go it again. Same as pulling a whole auto to pieces. Trying to reassemble her on a new design. He needed more blueprints. Some parts were missing, others didn't fit. His head throbbed. Still it was like Mac said. If you had a choice, who'd take a balky 1910 model against a reliable Supersix? Try and make any grade these days with a prewar jit. Just didn't go.

He rustled the leaves of his book. Wise up. You telling me?

Same old world. People living dying loving working. Same, but how changed. A fellow had to hustle to keep up. Had to know his stuff.

(Days in bed are long ones. A man's body, irked at first by its enforced idleness, slips gradually into a soothed quiet.

His mind no longer closed in by routine, may roam at will. Imagination may play tricks, or again thought grow clearer. So it was with Andy. His nightmares gave way to confused dreams of characters and ideas in Mac's books. Often they came alive and leapt out of their pages across his cot.)

It was godawful, not knowing. The whole world in flux. He thumbed some American papers Mac had brought him. BUY NOW, plastered everywhere. *Bring Back Good Times.* A chicken in every pot.

Sure. Okay. But find the buyers! Was Morgan gonna shop with GimmeaDime Rockefeller, Hoover with Silent Cal?

BUY NOW—lemons   raisins   ovaltine!

"NO Home Complete Without a Frigidaire"

"More rubber heels"   Jesus!

Andy turned the page. Government telling the dirt farmers to plow under their cotton, every third row. Hell, and them burning corn and wheat. Some way to boost the market for BUY NOWs! Was it him or what? His eye fell on a reader's letter:

Editor, *Detroit Times,*
DEAR SIR:
Other day your paper ran a swell cartoon, "Spend Like An American." I'm one of those. My people came to Ben Franklin's state in 1758. One was army teamster at Valley Forge. Last week I earned seventy cents, the week before three-fifty, four weeks no work at all.
Point is, I still have sixty cents. I want to take your tip, spend like an American. What in hell's the best way? One tooth is gone from my lower plate, shall I get a new one? I want, you get me, to do the right thing. My watch face is cracked, shall I replace it? Should I pay for my home or buy a car? Can you advise me? And soon, before the sixty's gone.
                    Yours in suspense,
                    EARL JAYSON STROCK.

Boy, that was tellin' em! And Detroit buddy what's happening to you? He stared at the headlines:

FIVE THOUSAND MARCH ON RIVER ROUGE PLANT DEMAND WORK: FOUR KILLED MANY WOUNDED

He read it through, lay back to stare at the tree.

Those fellows, they'd been ready to Buy Now. But how can you when you draw all the deuces, somebody else all the aces from the pack. Those fellows, they'd taken old Tight Lip at face value. About Jobs for All Who Want Them.

Poor devils. Desperate, tramping past fire hose and tear gas. Machine guns ripping. Calling on Henry to give 'em jobs.

If he'd been in Detroit he might have been one of them. Marching. Shot.

Dopey world. Old organ-grinder cracked but wheezing out the same tune—BUY NOW AND BRING BACK. Jeez, a big horselaugh when you gave it the onceover, wised up. Or a big heartbreak.

Well Mac boy, what you say? Call quits, shuffle a new deal. And no third party calling trumps. Just you me and our kind, playing it straight.

BUY NOW. The whole world on the bargain counter. Damaged goods and no customers. *My Country 'Tis of Thee . . . buy now!* Over here they didn't say it. Just went to it and not enough to go round. If all goods dumped in Great Lake and Seaboard harbors were shipped here, they'd be gone in a week's time, he bet.

Dopey world. Why couldn't America snap out of it? Ask him another. A big snag somewhere. No fooling. Well, he wasn't Jesus, born to set it right. So, as the Russkies said, *spakoini nochi,* and turn off the brainworks for a snooze.

During Andy's weeks in bed, Mac came often to bring more books, Sasha returned from a weekend visit to his village cousins with a covered basket under his arm. Raising the lid, he dangled a freshly baked chicken before his mate's nose. That ought to go down good, yes? As Andy crunched greedily, Sasha gave him a lively account of the cook's progress in their factory kitchen.

Competition between pots and skillets was waxing apace. *Red Star* cooks had challenged those at *Spartacus* plant to a ten-day competition. The issue? Who could make the best *borscht!* Sure, judges had been chosen and conditions as to size of kettles and quantity of beets onions potatoes and carrots carefully defined. Winners would be premiumed. Pogorovsky, the chef with drooping whiskers, was leading *Red Star's* brigade: a furious general set on victory. The opening day honors had gone to *Spartacus,* for *Red Star* diners had received no soup at all! Vinegar had given out and how, argued Pogorovsky, could you make decent soup without vinegar? The second day they had lost again. Sasha and his mates had voted their *borscht* entirely too sour.

Pogorovsky had given his mates no peace until their shop had won five days straight. Under the battle cry, "Bad *borscht* means bad Communists in the kitchen!" the cooks were advancing with their pans in midair. Astonishing too, how much their meals had improved.

They were still laughing over the picture of Pogorovsky's recklessly tipped cap and wilting mustaches storming among his bright kettles, when Sasha remembered a message he had to give.

Today he'd met Natasha, she was coming over.

Andy flushed. Needn't bother herself, that girl.

Ah, well now, Sasha argued. She'd been out of town; sent out to the village to help organize study circles. Why act mad?

When his visitor had left, Andy hobbled over to the window. His tree stood close by, like an old friend. Day after tomorrow he was going home. It'd be swell to be out.

That girl was a pain in the neck. She'd never come. Just get his wind up, jangle his pistons for nothing. Nerts on her. No whippersnapper was gonna play fast and loose with him. That was all off.

He reached for his pencil and half-empty pad.

DEAR ELSIE:

Honey girl lamp me now and bust out weeping. Your Big
Time lying in state with a game leg. (That'd bring a letter
p.d.q. He finished particulars, chewed his pencil.) You
talk about being jealous. No cause. How'd I see any girl
after you? Anyway these Russian gals are fat cows. Beefy,
all shoulders and hips. Cold as ice, and talk about for-
getful! If Tim or Morse try to tell you different don't
listen. They'll be stringing you for a sinker.

What about you? You ain't letting that Hal Mortimer
in for a big drag? You know I ain't the selfish kind, I
know you can't sit home twiddling your thumbs for me.
But sweetheart not Mortimer. He's a bad one. I don't
say this for meanness but like to my own sister. He ain't
keeping you on for nothing after so many've been fired.
And he ain't the marrying kind.

Cats, what's the use! The lead snapped between his
fingers as he returned to bed. The evening crept up on yellow paws.

Slow heavy footfalls halted by his door, entered.

Jumping liver, the strawboss! Andy gave a stiff nod,
sparred for time. Why in hell had the piker come? Here he
was, gummed up. Caught with his pants down. The old mug
had him in a clinch and knew it. Damn the breed. He braced
himself. The man's deliberate gestures, his sideglances
proved he had something on his chest.

All the while Mikhail was asking him how he felt and
then about his life in Detroit and Ford's, Andy sensed the
old crow was leading up to something. Crafty, that's what.
Why didn't he shoot his jaw? There were deep puffs under
his eyes, a worn stoop to his relaxed shoulders. Andy fought
against a sudden grudging feeling. Well, you had to give the
devil his due. The old fellow never stinted himself, that was
certain. Somehow when you came down to it, he didn't fit
into the 1910 model either. Not of the speednuts stripe....
Crap, was he going softy! Watch it, Andy.

Mikhail was putting questions about foremen and plant
managers. The American's face burned. Just as if the

174

sucker'd read his thoughts! Uneasily he plucked his covers. He longed to say, "Out with it! Spring your cold dose." Maybe he'd come to say they were keeping on the new man after all?

But since when had foremen traveled halfway across town to tell an ordinary truckpusher that! Never could tell, maybe the way they did things here. Of course, he had his contract. Plenty more jobs too. No worry about that. Still, he'd miss Sasha and the boys. Besides, in the dieshop— Could it be the old weasel just wanted to ... nuts! Must be some reason behind it. Why didn't he spit it?

Mikhail took out his cigarettes, then remembered where he was, put them back in his pocket. This was harder than he'd thought, the boy was obstinate as a mule. His distrust cut deep. Somehow he had to get round it, open up man to man. But devil take it, how to begin?

A saber cut beneath Mikhail's left eye had begun twitching. His rough thumb tried to still it. Andy noticed the thing had gone a livid brown. That meant the old louse was worked up. A jam on the belt.

The Russian sat there, thumbing his cheek. After all, he reminded himself, he was a man of few words. Always better to let your acts do your speaking. But here he was, where to act meant to speak out. And blast it, if he knew where to catch hold.

Impatient to be over with it, the invalid asked in his broken Russian, "Come about anything particular?"

The puffs under his supervisor's eyes wagged from side to side. Nope. That was, nothing in particular. Just to see how the sick man was. Say, they'd be glad when he got back on the line.

Covertly Andy watched the twitching scar. He had always been curious about it. And just sitting and slow talk was getting too much. He'd just ask him, "Say, how'd you come by that cut?"

"Oh that?" his visitor smiled, sensing his cue. That was a souvenir from General Wrangel, given him back in nineteen-twenty. "His dogs had just started in on me, trying to get information about our Red Partisan troop movements when our forces surprised them. So I escaped with this scratch."

Andy asked, "You were through the Civil War days?" (Somehow he had never fancied the strawboss in this rôle, a Red Partisan trooper, standing the worst gaff.)

Mikhail's indignation boomed at him. "Where else would I be! What kind of a worker, with our young Soviet power in danger and me—behind the lines!" (Devil's mother, this lad made him sore.)

The American craned on an elbow. "What was it like?" Almost before he knew it, Mikhail was reliving those days. Grimy daring months on end: canteens often empty, but such comrades. Death riding at their elbows but bothering them less than the damn lice in their shirts. Those who had been through those days would never forget.

Did the American understand all his words? If not, stop him and he'd explain. Listening until the witch relented of her hold on his leg, Andy studied the heavy weather-beaten features and ruminated: so this chap had been an ordinary working stiff. Well, for that matter so had Feld-man. But try and lamp that speedcrank taking a gun, risking his hide to get the common fellow a new deal. Not on your life.... This latest strawboss of his was a new brand. Model '33. He got mad sure. And that crazy scar twitched. But never once had he yelled or ripped a fast line of swears at them, speeding the hell to get out trucks. Had to give the old boy his due. He was human. And even if he had tried, quick as lightning the whole shop'd give him the works. Wise up, Andy. A new deal and no hooey.

But by Jesus if a fellow really believed that! ...

Mikhail had begun telling about his youth and life in the old days, losing his diffidence as he talked, for Andy made a good listener. "In a little Ukrainian village half a century ago a farm woman was carried in from the fields. And so I was born. Our mud and straw hut was about the most down-at-heel of them all. But we had the best sun-flowers. Bless my head, I was weaned on the seeds.

"At eight years I was put minding the landlord's hog and sheep. Fat swine himself! Well, in our family the member who claimed the most care was a blear-eyed sack of bones. But for all my mother could do, the old bitch never managed to calf. I used to pull at her dry old tits. Well, that's how it was. What I carry with me of those days is my Mother's terrible weeping. Storming home from a village brawl, a rough beard stinking of manure and *Kvas* would beat and curse us all until his misery was spent. But why am I telling you this?"

Andy propped on an elbow. "Sure. Go on." He'd been raised in the country himself. The older man's eyes crinkled. Really? He'd like to hear about that. And had there been a blacksmith shop? "I used to sneak away from the goats," he continued, "to watch our smithy at work. Hidden under a barrow I'd watch the old shanks heat his tongs and wait for the strokes on his anvil. Plink! Plonk! I can hear him and see those sparks yet. Queer how a thing like that sticks by you, when so much else fades.

"Someday, I boasted to my Mother, I wasn't going to be a dumb farmhand in bark shoes, but a blacksmith.'Is that so?' she scolded, 'You're playing hookey, again!' And she boxed my ears. The old man's beatings grew worse so I ran away. My poor Mother crossed the river soon after and I never went back. Beating my way to Kharkov, I got help from her brother who apprenticed me to a locksmith.

"Ever been to Kharkov? Ah, there's a city for you. A thousand blacksmith shops, an Arabian nights to me. I never tired of roaming her streets, though my fun was dimmed with shame of my rags and because I couldn't read even the corner-signs that I passed." (Andy grinned, he'd felt that way in Moscow not so long ago himself.)

"My master," Mikhail looked at him dubiously, "was a devil. Cheated me, fed me on swill. Once more I decided to run away. I was now thirteen. I loved my Uncle, who did what he could for me. Then he got bad lungs, and he had no one else so I had to stay. A forlorn sight he made, coughing and mumbling his prayers before his icon.

"When he died I set out for Moscow where by luck and bluff I got a job, in the railway yards as machinist helper. Always into mischief, I was the bane of the place. The foreman swore at us, goaded us. One day when he broke a leather strap over my back, a big-limbed fellow by the name of Andreyev Oborin jumped to my aid. We were both fired and Andreyev took me home with him. His place was small, but his wife took me in, like the fifth of her children. Andreyev found work in a tool shop, and later took me there to work with him. He taught me to read. In fact, he opened my eyes.

"Andreyev was a man with a ready laugh but a quiet tongue. Right under the beaked noses of the czar's watchmen he carried out his dangerous work. When police got on his trail, we moved to Petrograd."

"Why the cops?" Andy asked.

"Secret meetings of revolutionists at our place," Mikhail answered. "At first they wouldn't let me come. Great secrecy was needed and they thought me too young. But I quit my pranks and carried through some tasks they gave me that required caution and good judgment. So Andreyev persuaded them, 'Let the lad come.' Believe me, I was more proud than if all the czars of Imperial Russia had requested my presence! You're following me? Good.

"So, at fifteen I became partner in plans to destroy all the dogs and misery that weighed me down even in my sleep. Plans to seize the levers of history, turn mankind on new paths. Here was something to live by. Yes, if need be, die by. Understand?"

Andy wondered. Never in his life had he felt that way. About anything or anybody. Not even Elsie. Not sure he wanted to.

"There were eight in our group," Mikhail went on. "One was a student whose hate for the autocracy was burning him up. Another was a woman from the nobility who'd broken with her family to stay by us. Her stiff blouse and high collar looked queer among our rough shirts, but she was all right. The rest of us were workers from our plant and a cloth mill nearby. Once Lenin came to us to discuss plans for our press. He was well known among us, even then. His bright little eyes squinted at us while he put and answered questions, advanced plans. You know there was something about Ilyich. In later years I saw him often, not always at close range. But whether I saw him or not, I always felt him there, leading us on. Am I speaking too fast? I'll slow up.

"Well, the devils got Andreyev and packed him off to Siberia. But he escaped, in time for the 1905 days. He was like a man on fire. At the heat of the street fighting I felt him keel against me, plugged through the lung. Don't mind me.... Andreyev was father, brother, comrade to me. I vowed to do what I could to carry on his work.

"During the black years after our defeat, I was arrested many times, and served my turn in Siberia in the snow deserts where Andreyev, Stalin and many more were sent. Deserts that we transform today with our Kuznetstroi and Cheliabinsk tractor works and thousands of new towns, clubs and theaters. I have been there, seen for myself. Imagine how I felt.

"Well, when I came back to Moscow I had to change my name and job plenty. But in spite of all the rulers could do, our movement spread!"

Mikhail halted to explain a phrase, then continued. "Sometime if you like I'll take you to see an underground printing press. Sure, right here in our district. It was placed in a small dugout far below ground. We reached it by way of a narrow tunnel running from a closet in a comrade's bedroom, and lit up by candles. Air? Well, we just drew our breath. You couldn't work many hours at the time. Overhead, as a disguise, our comrade ran a small food and beer shop. Often, while one of the czar's rats was having his vodka in the shop overhead, we were safely below him running leaflets off our handpress ... and him trying to track down their source! How we laughed at that saphead among ourselves.

"Finally came 1917. The great days of February to October. Our Moscow metal plant's millionaire owner fled to Paris where he still occupies himself issuing silly proclamations about what he'll do when his kind 'frees' Russia. Would I like to get these hands on that son of a bitch!

"As for his slavedrivers, from foreman to super we gave

them short notice. The meanest, we slung in a wheel-barrow, rode him off the conveyor, and dumped out the gate. He scurried like a rat. Another, we handed a kopeck and told him to ride so far he'd never come back."

Andy thumped his knees. What a picnic! Christ, lamp Mike Feldman being rode off the belt!

Halting, Mikhail let his slow gaze rest on Andy's. "Well, that's my story. Nothing much. But enough so." He paused. Oh, no use the boy's denying it. He knew what'd been troubling him. He'd figured it out. "For you see," he added with a wry smile, "I spent most of my life under the Feldmans and cockroach bosses myself. But see here, my boy. Over Feldman and his kind were higherups, right? It was for them he drove you, right? And over me, backing me?"

Andy stared. He'd never thought of that.

"Well, who?" his foreman persisted. "Millionaires? Not on your life! Over me, flesh of my flesh. My class and yours. The same that trained me, put me at my post. Can take me down!" Mikhail leaned forward, the bags under his eyes twitching. "Well?" His scarred fists wedged in an anxious grip. "Well?"

The Ford beltman gave a slow amazed nod. Flesh of his flesh. So what?

From under his pillow he drew a packet, gave it an agitated jerk.

"Here," he offered, "have a smoke."

15

PHILIP BOARDMAN was covering rectangular sheets with neat calculations on an imaginary problem in mathematics while Mary swept listless fingers over the keyboard. Rose folds of her shawl trailed the brightly waxed floor. Head propped against a disconsolate elbow, the man solved equations with absorbed rapidity. This relaxed him when nothing else could.

Mary was making Hungarian goulash of the *Blue Danube,* damn it, why couldn't she end. He'd had a rotten day. The shop's tangle was no better, if anything, worse. Things must change soon, he told himself. But how slow. It wore down your nerve. He'd like to chuck the whole works. Today when he had gone again to BRIZ to inquire about his proposal on the crankshaft die, he found the Bureau's chief had left for his vacation while his dumb assistant was amazed to learn that such a proposal had ever been made! Of course, he would look up the drawings immediately and if Meester Boardman would be so good as to call again in a week's time . . . which meant begin all over again. Lazy hams. Moss grew all over that office, the very room smelled musty.

Algebraic formulæ brushed aside, Philip stretched full length on the sofa. As Mary turned in his direction, automatically he raised himself, placed the evening paper under his guilty shoes. If Junior were awake, he and his Dad could have a hilarious pillow fight. The boy's questions, however, were not so easy to handle.

His wife had half-risen to come sit by him. "Play me some more waltzes, Mary," he asked hastily. Sighing, she complied. In five minutes, she knew, his cigarette done, he would be asleep. Gradually he relaxed. She might play on for hours, with any one to listen. Poor woman. But he couldn't talk with her...Not now. He was worn out, depressed. Curious situation: Mary and he had so much to talk over, yet he was at a loss to know where to begin, what to say. So far, attempts always ended up in argument, accusations, tears.

If only the human equation were as easy to solve as mathematics! Too many variables here, unknown Xs and Ys. Divide multiply subtract as you liked, the damn thing never came out. His eyes closed. The sea was coming closer closer, flipping his sides. X over Y...Z raised to the ninth power...Drowning the waltz. Gratefully he slipped into its green lapping billows.

A bell's jangling and women's voices pricked him awake. That Agatha Lloyd had come to plumb the whys and wheretos of existence. Without even waiting to say hello he made his escape. What Mary and Agatha found in each other was a conundrum in itself.

Contrary to what his wife supposed, Philip did not direct his steps toward the plant. Times such as this he went to his friend. He found Mark Koshevnikov in his vividly splashed Georgian houserobe sipping tea and enjoying a new book on machine construction just received from Germany. Mark knew five languages fluently, although in German and English he was at his best. With his poor command of Russian, Philip felt apologetic, half-educated. Outside his own field, he was a small town hick. Well, these Europeans were like that, versatile, cosmopolitan. Take Mark: with curios from all parts of the world and a dozen hobbies. And he'd discuss trends in art and theater or international politics with as apt interest as he would the spectrum or latest theories in physics.

It was his views on people and the social *milieu* that the American found most provocative of all. There was nothing his companion relished so much as a friendly penetrative argument. Systematically he came at it from all angles, as you might study a skyscraper under construction from varying points of the compass.

As he poured his visitor a glass of steaming amber liquid, Mark launched into an enthusiastic account of the book. "What gets me," he broke off suddenly, "it is such a highly developed country, this Germany—and what an archaic social system. Can you account for it? And your America, Philipovich, is no different. Now this bombastic talk of Hitler and his Nazis about seizing power, war. Fantastic? But the whole thing smells bad, bad."

The other engineer thumbed his unlighted cigarette. "Boloney. Hitler is a false alarm."

Mark frowned. "I'm not so sure."

Philip smoked hard. "I am. You and your press here make me tired. All this talk of Fascism or Communism. What about Democracy? I tell you, she isn't licked yet. The Americans, and yes the Germans too, aren't giving up their rights so quick."

Mark ran a quick palm over his gay-colored knee. "Do you know, I used to believe as you do. But realities, my friend—"

"Your realities! With you everything is always classes, classes. I believe in the people."

"So do we, friend. Workingpeople—and the kind of democracy they set up. But you're tired—" Mark broke off. It was true, tonight Boardman felt no zest for these mental gymnastics. When the Russian queried, "Something on your mind?" he opened up. Previously, in a guarded way and avoiding all but a passing reference to Crampton, Philip had confided in his friend. Mark comprehended far more than his companion suspected. With a patience often pointed with humorous asides, he explained Russian ways and advised his American friend. Phenomena like Pankrevich were hangovers of the old days, when take-it-easy bureaucratic methods could get by.

Philip had grown to depend on Mark: his visits were as frequent as their mutually rushed lives allowed. For his part, Mark found the American stimulating—both as engineer and man. And he was experiencing that keen unworded pleasure that one human has when aiding another to find himself, unfold.

In describing his latest encounter with BRIZ, Philip's tone grew bitter, flat. The waste in *Red Star* was tremendous. Not only in materials, but in enthusiasm and energies of men.

Mark drew his chair closer to the table. "Maybe you'd like to come to us? Chuck it there?" Philip snorted. "You asking me!"

"As you know," Mark went on, his mind evidently busy with something else, "we've set out on some pioneer work, designing new types of lathes. Just the thing you'd like. And we could use a man of your abilities to fine advantage. Couldn't we! Well now, if things get too hot for you at *Red Star,* come to us." He put down his glass, paused. "See here, Philip. Maybe you won't like what I say. If not, forget it?"

Boardman tossed his butt in the fireplace. "Shoot."

"All right. You are something by nature I never was, my friend. A fighter. Recent years have taught me the value of that. You're not going to toss it aside?"

"What do you mean?"

"Surely you know. Frankly, as much as I'd like having you, I'd be disappointed to see you make a change."

The American gave a disconcerted shrug. Why?

His friend ruffled his close clipped gray beard between his long fingers. "You'd be running away, admitting defeat. That's not like you." As for the dieshop, it would come through. He knew people in the Heavy Industry Department. "And I happen to know that the Party and State have the entire workings of *Red Star* under the spotlight. Things there are abnormal, it can't last. Go to it, push your ideas and criticisms, stick by your guns. But whatever you do, devil take it man, don't go stale. You see, I know you Americans. But Philipovich don't."

They talked until the samovar emptied.

Next morning found him tackling his job with his old agile spirit. By God, he was getting his second wind. In the conference of union members with management after work he took a seat near the front where he could hear and see whatever came up. All the crossfires and byplays. These production conferences were peppy affairs. Some foreigners thought them a bore, a drag on work. Not he. With the exception of Henry Crampton who had left early, the entire staff and working crew were on hand. Diemen, turners and millers crowded benches and lined the walls. And there was Eugene Pankrevich. Ah, my dear fellow, you wear a harassed look. These recurrent discussions of why the past month's program hasn't been fulfilled are trying, eh? Yes, to say the least. Just watch us!

It was true that Eugene Pankrevich was worried. He knew he repeated himself, his reports bore a stale sameness, the old exhortations: yet that magic formula for pulling his shop out of its rut never appeared. Like a flea on a dog, you put your hand on it, but it stayed one jump ahead. The whole business was vexing, yes, in the extreme. To crown it all, that plainspoken wiseacre Boardman had chosen to sit right under his nose.

What he, Pankrevich, needed was a vacation. Also more congenial work. For example, in some planning section or department of finance, where you made programs and let some one else worry over carrying them out. But first of all, a vacation. In the Crimea during grape season. Ah, the luscious golds of Yalta's landscape! The tang to those grapes—so sweet, almost bitter.

In hesitant bewilderment, Eugene Pankrevich shifted his gaze from one face to the next. As he talked, he fingered the embroidered edge of his blouse and tried to explain away disagreeable facts. Why the dieshop was the weakest link in *Red Star's* revolving chain, slowing down the whole plant. A virtual House that Jack Built, with a less happy ending. Even periodic overtime volunteered by *udarnik* brigades couldn't mend all gaps. Somehow somewhere they must hit upon the correct formulæ.

Philip viewed the superintendent with frank contempt. Once, before his talks with Mark about Russia's past history, her feudal remnants and present struggle for fresh cadres, he had been at a loss to understand how a pompous fool like Pankrevich had come to hold such a post. Well, he had scored one against this ninny: Pankrevich had rescinded his orders about no instruction to workers asking his technical advice, rescinded with apologies and tremulous voice.

The engineer's attention wandered from Pankrevich's pointless recital and oratorical entreaties to his problems at work, to Mary, to Junior. The wife was certainly unhappy and making every one else so. His enmity with Crampton was cutting into her social whirl. Trouble was, she had nothing to take her interest. Ill-tempered, touchy, she put him on edge. He felt sorry for her: yet what could a man do?

His intent gaze fastened on Natasha whose bobbed head was thrown back, revealing the steady pulse in her throat. She was waiting, he knew, for the manager to end and discussion begin. Her tree-green blouse fell in strong beautiful lines about her shoulders. A woman as different from Mary, he reflected, as steel from silk. Sure of herself, and of what she wanted. Mary's nervous energy racked the entire household. Highstrung himself, Natasha's composure and sunny disposition were reassuring. The girl's energies seemed to flow in organized sure channels. Organized: that was the word. An organized personality. Mary wasn't. What was it that Natasha got out of life that Mary lacked? These Bolshies had a complete theory worked out about women: he needed to go into it, when he had time. Mary was getting beyond him. Locking herself in her room for long crying spells, jealous over nothing, imagining God knew what. Even accusing him of not talking with her. Well, if she resented his concern with the shop, what was there to talk about! On the slightest excuse she flew out at Junior and blamed her husband for wanting to eat and sleep in the shop. To tell the truth, often he wished he did.

He didn't know, he admitted, how to help her. As for discussing his personal problems with any one, he was not a man to do that. Just letting things ride. Dangerous? He knew it. But when a man doesn't know what action to take, where to turn?

Junior: one subject on which Mary and he had had some bitter disputes. In earlier years, he had always made it a policy to give her a free hand with the children. That was her job; his, to bring home the bacon. Yet this division of labor had somehow worked out poorly with the older children. They wern't growing up into the persons he had taken for granted they would be. Instead, they were self-satisfied young saps. What was life here doing to them? He didn't know. He, their father, was unknown to them, and they to him. Ridiculous, tragic. He was a stranger in his own family. Laugh that off!

With Junior, it must be different. They were pals. The boy must get a different training, better grasp on the world. How, where? He wasn't up to it, that was clear. And Mary ... Well, they had agreed on transferring him from the Russian school. Those kids there, judging by Junior's reactions when he came home, were real dyed-in-the-wool reds. He wasn't ready to see his young son a watertight Bolshy. On the other hand, the influence of the older American boys at the English school wasn't doing the kid any good. Only last week Junior had demanded of him, "Pop, you got a big office to yourself? How many men under you? It's bigger than Crampton's office, ain't it?" This was the doing of that lousy Crampton boy. Like his father, he judged the universe in terms of dollars and cents, the biggest, the most costly. One man pitted against the other, lording it over his inferiors: an outlook that the Russians termed bourgeois. His Junior was picking it up fast.

When it came to scratch, he'd rather have Junior squealing over his game of fighting the Whites, than joining gleefully in snubbing a fellow pupil, as had happened last week, because the child's clothes were patched and she ate with her knife. Imagine! He had talked with Junior quite plainly about that. His boy, a snob! Hell, he had no time nor skill in these matters, always had relied on Mary and the school. Until lately he hadn't realized that his wife's conceptions were not far removed from these newly acquired ones of his son. Nor had he realized how incoherent and unformulated were his own. As for the school, no doubt the teachers were doing their best. But with a boy, what a gang says counted ten to one against any one else. He had to find Junior the right companions, have him make his Dad his confidant, pal.

Shifting his slight frame restlessly about on the wooden bench, eyeing his diemen, Philip Boardman recognized his task. Work, engineering science were not enough. In the science and art of living, Mary and he were children. There were whole libraries of knowledge and philosophy of which he was ignorant as hell. Cornell graduate, and dumb! Dies, he knew. But in social science he was an illiterate. He must begin school all over again, study. Man, his human relations, what the best thinkers had written about him, to what destiny he was heading. Study, so he could chart a new course, sight a reliable North Star. Then Junior's simplest questions wouldn't set him adrift, confound him.

What was this? His attention was recalled by a stir running through the conference like cornstalks mustered by a sudden wind. Pankrevich had ended, Maxim risen to speak. "Let's come down to concrete facts," he said. "Where we have breaks, how to mend them."

Philip's attention snapped back. "Now you're talking!" This man was a force, worth twenty Pankreviches.

Later, during the discussion, Philip took the floor. His listeners encouraged him: never mind the poor Russian, they'd get his points. He saw Pankrevich wince. Was he playing the fool? Philip cleared his throat. Good! He knew where some of the breaks were. Loose labor discipline: Several had mentioned that. People stayed off when they chose, came in late, and walked around during workhours, leaving their machines whenever they pleased. For instance, take the question of the tieup on small parts for bodies, two weeks ago. He had something to say about that! It happened that one necessary detail, number 2634, was made on a special set of lathes where several raw or irresponsible turners were working. Who? Well, for one, Zena. She had missed work, to his knowledge, three times that month and been late five.

Zena felt the gaze of the shop directed at her. Uneasily she plucked at the purple roses in her waist. Philip had intended citing her only as an example in passing when events took an unexpected turn. He should have known his Russians better. No sooner was the regular order of business completed than Zena was asked, "Well now, give an account of yourself?"

Her moody gaze boiled over them. She was sick, and what affair was it of theirs, anyway? People here were too nosey.

"Is that so! Hoity-toity miss, you know holding up production is no private affair!" Pankrevich, who had his own reasons for doing so, came to her aid. He was able to explain, he said, at least one of these absences: the woman had requested two days off, and he had granted it, so that she might bury her child. With reawakened sorrow Zena put the corner of her shawl to her eyes.

A quick hush blanketed the meeting. Only for a moment. Leda, an older woman near the back wheezed across the benches, "Her child dead? Humph. That's a good one! She only has one, and it's home this minute cutting up the mischief with my young brat." Her smirk reached to the far corners. Countenance falling, she added. "Poor kid, maybe he'd be better off if he was. His mother's a rotter, but I never held that against her brat." She had seen Zena, she said, on that particular day of the supposed funeral starting off on a lark with—well, check up on the timecard of a certain dieman by the name of Ivan Nazarov, they'd find him off to the same funeral! Not Zena's only one either. She had plenty of lovers, that slut.

Loose bosom heaving, Zena broke her way to the front. "It's a lie I tell you. All lies!" Tigress at bay, she snarled at her accusers. She was no bad woman. That was done with, long ago. Filthy-mouthed hussy, this Leda, yelloweyed because her old man didn't care where he hung up his pants.

Her arms jerked uncontrollably as she slumped by the table, voiceless, shivering with chill. Her eyelids and whole body twitched, stripped bare. Her head dropped. Lower. Lower. Shame poured over the room, drenching them all in her quick hot flood. Philip wanted to rush outside into the fresh air, but he couldn't move. Like a distraught triphammer Natasha was knocking her fists together in her lap.

189

Maxim, always slow of speech, was laboriously gathering his words as he would gather steel pigments for his work when the gaunt frame of a turner rose from her place. "Well?" she demanded. "What're you gaping for? Isn't it plain? The woman should be fired. No place for such elements in our shop." Think of the example she set the youth! Liar, whore!

Cries of "That's right!" "No! No!"

Maxim drummed on the table. Order! Ask the floor before speaking. And think. Think first, what it was necessary to say.

An old toolmaker took the floor. He agreed, Zena must go. Let her be an example, that the dieshop meant to have real labor discipline. What Zena chose to do after work-hours was her own affair. But to hold up production, lie to them—that was wrong. She had been given her chance in a government school, taught a good trade. If she wasn't an honest class-conscious worker by now, she'd never be. An end to sloppy ways! Send her off.

As he took his seat, young Kolya stepped over benches through the crowd. Neck and hands flushed, he pleated his cap, waiting for Maxim's nod to begin. Zena started. That lad was the one friend she had in the whole shop.

With hoarse fury he told how Zena had been made the butt of coarse jokes. "Not even Leda can say she's not good to her boy. Right? Right! There's good in Zena, plenty. But you fellows tormenting her, chasing her! You're murderers, I call it. Driving her away!" As for the youth, Zena knew they were on her side. Let some of the older ones ask themselves where they stood.

Benches scraped the floor, several spoke at once. "No doubt she's got her side to it!" "Rubbish! Send her off, and be done." "What about the men running after her?" "Sons of bitches, send them off too." "What do their kind care for our Five Year Plan!" "Such carryings-on right in our factory! The slut!" "Think of her going off, leaving our whole shop in the lurch!" "Liar! Cheat! Getting us all on the blackboard!"

Maxim saw Natasha raise her hand, come forward. She

half-ran, her countenance drained of color. By the red cambric-draped table she turned, put her hands on Zena's low shoulder. Philip leaned closer. What was the girl up to? His eye caught on the silver hammer and sickle beside her. "Comrades," she shouted, "are we crazy! Who's guilty? That's the point. Only Zena? Nonsense. Shame, shame on us all! Fourteen years after our revolution, think of it! And one of our workers selling her body! Shame! Rotten shame!"

Her listeners stirred uncomfortably. Her gaze was level, searching. "Leda, you worked hard to get rid of red lights, bad houses, didn't you? So did I. And you Marya—Maxim—"

"What on earth are you driving at? White slavery's gone."

"Quiet! Quiet!"

"What am I driving at? Oh, you! Swell bunch of workers you are. So you think we can wash our hands of the Zenas! I tell you we're the guilty ones!"

"Nonsense!"

"That, slut—she never wanted to be one of us!"

"You're wrong," the girl retorted. "When Zena came to us, she came for a new life. Has she found it? Oh you helped her a lot, you did!" Her voice slackened. "And the same with me."

Zena sat hunched, twisting her blouse.

Her shopmates sobered. "Well? So what do you want?"

Natasha raised her arm. "Those skunks who lured her, acting the same as White Guards. They're the real criminals! It's them I accuse before the whole shop!"

Maxim's heavy bulk loomed beside her. His voice carried the deep rumblings of the fire-draught he stoked. "Natasha's right." He had found speech at last. The eyes beneath his shaggy brows grown fierce, his stubbed forefinger pointed at the benches. How any worker could have so forgotten himself! Such a man was a traitor, exploiting this woman. Who were they? He looked questioningly at Zena. She merely jerked her head. *Svolitch,* the lot of them.

"If she won't talk, I will!" Leda spat out the names of Lebedev, Turin, Stepanov. "As for you Karl Bougnov, trying to sneak out the back door, you're another!" His exit blocked, he pulled his cap over his eyes.

"Well my brave men!" Maxim demanded. "What you got to say for yourselves? Speak up Karl, Lebedev. Maybe you gave her a bag of candy Mark, for her favors? And you Karl, bought her a silk scarf, bit of ribbon? Silent? Well, what can you say! Fine lads! Betraying our new life, that's what! We'll deal with you later in our comradely court."

In Zena's lowered eyes was hid a peculiar triumph. They'd be fined, disgraced before every one. She lifted a defiant head.

Maxim's brows drew together, like poles of a battery trying to complete the circuit, let the current flow free. "Come Zena," his voice was gentle. "We're all workers here. That's how it is, one the same as the next. Take our word for it, things'll be otherwise from now on."

Zena shrugged, bit her lips, eyes on the floor.

"Let any one so much as dare bother or torment you," Maxim persisted, "we'll make him answer for it."

Natasha, who hadn't moved from her place, stooped to talk with her. "Zena! Don't be ashamed." Come, see the look on her shopmates' faces turned toward her. They were sorry, ready to start over. "Zena, your boy ... You're a working woman. Don't act stubborn, turn your back on the past, march with us."

A curious change had been going over Zena. Her gaze crept up by slow inches, shifted from Natasha to steal a quick look at the benches. It was true. Those looks were friendly. But if they thought they were going to—

Hooking her under an elbow, Natasha jumped up. "Before the whole shop I challenge you, Zena, to a socialist competition. What about it?" For good work and rate of progress in studies. As for terms, they'd work them out. Each'd be set a task within her reach and at the same time be put on her mettle. "Well Zena? Do you accept?"

Zena broke away. Nothing doing. Hell, they weren't tricking her into a competition. She had enough to buzz her head as it was.

"Zena!" Kolya called, "you're scared. Natasha's as quick as they come."

"Who's a-scared!" Zena's arm drew back. "Ain't nobody quicker on a lathe than me. When I want."

"All the same," Kolya taunted, "you're scared. She'll lick you sure." The shop laughed, tense, waiting. Maxim rubbed his brows toward his nose. "Don't mind the kid."

"Well?" Natasha asked again. "Are we on?"

"Go it Zena!" Kolya suddenly tossed his cap in the air. "Go it!"

"Go it!" others shouted.

"Let's have it!"

Natasha held out her hand.

Looking neither to right nor left, Zena met it with her own. Men and women jumped to their feet, clapped, shouting, "Bravo! Hurrah!" That Natasha was a girl now. When she took you on, there'd be something to watch.

Not waiting to speak with any one, Philip rushed outside.

Natasha held the raspberry-colored glasses up to the light. They were beautifully clear. "Not bad, Mommy." She walked past the tiny humped figure to wrap the glasses in fresh newspaper, button on her jacket and stoop to peep into the glass, push a strand of hair under her cap. It was a new one, gorgeously red. Caps were her weakness. Whimsically her reflection smiled back at her. Well, admit it, you are primping for that American.

She turned from the mirror abruptly. Silly girl, nothing of the kind.

Veined hands clasped across her stomach which bulged permanently with child, her mother watched her daughter's movements with frank curiosity. She was standing near the kitchen stove, her drab blouse hidden under her tightly fastened shawl. Her small eyes were a faded blue, her cheeks puckered toward a full mouth. Bent for decades under heavy loads of wood and fodder, her spine had molded when Natasha was still a little girl, into the patient curves of the burden bearer. Quizzically she bit down on a mouthful of sunflower seeds. Where was Natasha taking that jelly?

The girl answered briefly: to a sick comrade. She hated that sunflower habit, hulls scattered all over the place. Hated it almost as much as the icon in the corner, and the fussy lace curtains at the window. Before her mother could ply her with more questions she whisked by her, down the stairs.

Poor Mamuchka. Why grudge her her sunflower seeds? She had little else. Not even the papers. Natasha had even quarreled with her over that, but her mother held firm. It was sin enough, ah, sin against all the saints, to have your children turn godless. If she was to go to one of those new-fangled classes, they would fill her poor old head with more than letters. With Anti-Christ. She had lived all these years without reading. Better to die so. Ignorant, but blessed. At peace.

The girl sighed. Poor old Mamuchka. Scolding fretful, bound by her teapot and needle....At peace! Poor little mole, fearful of daylight. A setting hen who'd hatched a brood of hawks.

Mama was difficult, no gainsaying that. A dozen times she had asked herself: What are my duties anyway to Mama? What a headache! Why am I failing? Can it be that she's too old to change! Not at all. To give up to her, let her live on in darkness—impossible! To let her go on, cooking sweeping slaving for her children, bound hand and foot with no life of her own—why that's the very thing I am most against.

Is this part of the price of our going over to a new society? That some are left behind, unable to make the grade? Too old or too feeble, rooted in the past?

Nonsense! I'm too selfish with Mamuchka, that's all. Like Papa and brother, just take her for granted. But she is *so* stubborn. Well, I shall be more so!

Natasha's grip tightened about her jars of crimson jelly as she gave her cap a final twist and walked quickly up the hospital's broad steps. Andy was sitting by the window where he had the vantage of a three-cornered view of the street. "So you did come!"

She unbuttoned her jacket. "Of course! Didn't you know

I would?" Suddenly diffident, she slipped off her cap, using it to conceal the jar. Now that she had brought it, it occurred to her that it might seem silly. Perhaps in America, they had no such custom. Well, anyhow . . .

"What a nice cap!" He reached for it. Her sweater matched.

She saw that the jam pleased him. Holding the jars before the window, he admired their clear hue, then placed them carefully on the windowsill. "They're too nice to eat."

"Don't think I made it." She felt shy, not like herself. He appeared thin, lonely. Or what was it? These Americans had a queer trait of staring. Quickly she began speaking about the coming swimming meet, the shop. More at ease, observing him closely, she told him about Zena.

And was their new contest, especially against being late, getting her up! By sunrise, no fooling. It was worth it, to get over that terrible habit of always running five minutes behind. He listened, sunk in watching her changing expressions, and the quick lights in her brown eyes and hair. Sure it was worth it. He agreed. Sure. . . .

A week after Andy left the hospital, Sasha came to take him over to Mikhail's for supper. The belt super had just the family Andy suspected; into everything, from the youngest up. Reckless with their vitality. They lived in three rooms, one of which was lined clear to the ceiling with books. To Andy the library was a surprise, also the fact that Mikhail was author of one book and writing another. For crying out loud. The first had been on motors. The second was his recollections, written at the request of Gorky's committee on factory histories.

The Russian smiled at Andy's comment that he had always thought of writers as a special kind of bug. You know, a bunch of crabs and nuts. Longhaired highbrow college grad and all that. "Stay with us long enough," Mikhail observed, "and you will be turning out books yourself."

Andy laughed. These Russians had their own idea of jokes. The worst of it was, often he wasn't sure when they were in dead earnest. Imagine Morse, listening in on this!

He told Mikhail, "You're the world's best *kidder*." The last word pronounced in English cost him a stiff half-hour. Finally *kidder*, like *Okay* and *Attaboy*, entered into the international vocabulary of the old metallist. These terms he handled with the close affectionate scrutiny he gave to machine parts of a refractory motor.

Standing near him, Andy recalled his last talk with Nat. He had asked her, "You get a big kick out of living, don't you? How is it?" She had puckered her nose. Kick? What was it? He explained. "I suppose you could call it that," she assented. "There are so many reasons—"

He would just put the same question to Mikhail. These Russians had him guessing.

His companion straightened his massive frame, squinting whimsically at him over his glasses. "And suppose you tell me, why you volunteered to work overtime? It comes to the same thing. Or pretty near."

From a table he took an open magazine. Listen to this:

A MATTER OF HONOR

"With us, labor has become a matter of valor, heroism, honor."

> By Magnet Mountain
> We have reared it
> Mighty
> Enduring
> Our steel-ribbed honor!

> Blue glows the morning,
> Emerald the fields;
> Red glow our hearts
> High on the mountain,
> Tipping the sky's roof,
> Crimson flag of the sun!

"All With Our Own Hands!"
Our steel-ribbed labor
  Mounts its bulwarks of
  Heroism valor,
Unfolds its honor
Before the world.

Wrought for all time
In the fires of our epoch
  Reeking with hope!
Ours and the world's April!
  Reeking with sweat
Our songs of travail.

Across our vast land
History has strewn
  Her dragon teeth
  Of Revolution—
We her offspring,
Youth of a young day!

Good old Mother
You are fertile
  Freeing the mind
  Gripping the will.
Travel far!
Bear often and boldly

Until all men know
  Ours and the world's April!
And Labor—that is heroism
   valor honor—
  Ours and the world's April
To seize hold and build!

16

WITH jocular concern, Sasha and Mac saw Andy aboard his train. Knapsack and teakettle deposited in a rack, they turned upon the other traveler in the compartment. Was he going far? Good! Then would he mind seeing after this *Amerikanets?* The stranger, who was making the entire trip as far south as Sochi, agreed readily enough. He would run out with the kettles at stations for hot water, bargain with the peasants for whatever was needed and see the foreigner aboard his boat for Sukhum. Yes, altogether, it would be a pleasant trip.

Andy sauntered out of earshot. Where did Sasha get that stuff! He was out of diapers. Why not tie a green tag around his neck like they did on immigrants being shipped west and be done with it! Guess his Russian and knocking about were good enough to see him a lot further than the Caucasus!

His vacation was being given him early as the doctor had recommended a month in the south. Before he returned the worst of Moscow's winter would be over. He jangled his pocket. Seeing was believing. Here he had it, his month's pay in advance. Getting something for nothing. Well he had never objected to that kind of break. Mac said it was coming to him. Well, maybe.

The little engine rustled her cars, clawed the tracks. Mac and Sasha ran alongside, bantering and offering thankless last-minute hints on the do's and don't's of Russian travel. Balanced on the moving steps, he reminded them once more, whatever letters came be sure to forward them. As the train gathered speed, Sasha's cap and Mac's tam dropped from sight.

Andy went inside. Jeez, he felt queer. But it was great, riding. And a swell month ahead.

The low, spreading city curved and revolved about him. Moscow had a skyline. Not New York's to be sure, but her own.

Once at night he had taken the ferry across to Staten Island just to watch those skysweepers blink their million eyes back at him. Kinda crazy, but someday he'd do it again. Ace-high but something phoney about New York. Like a crowded celery patch going to weed. Manhattan was getting too small. After you dug down, climbed forty stories, what then? Somewhere he'd read the whole thing was sinking by invisible bits into the sea. Probably a lot of bull. Anyway it'd take a million years. All his troubles'd be over before that.

He hummed an old air:

> *Not much money*
> *Oh but honey*
> *Ain't we got fun!*

Moscow had a skyline all her own. Not much reach to it yet but roomy. Well, she had no Atlantic to stop her. All the plains she wanted to play with. No call to climb the sky. Some called her an overgrown village. In some ways she was. Gawky like a boy shoving his arms and legs out of his jacket. Growing fast. Funny, you could see the first tracings of a new outline going up. The Post and Telegraph, Grain Export and government buildings, gigantic plants, apartments and clubs. New dents had shot up in the half-year he had spent here. Anyway, he was glad that the Kremlin's spires and those peppermint oniontops on Saint Basil's Cathedral would stay on in a skyline going modern, continually on the jump.

He looked in his compartment. A young couple with a kid just big enough to crawl over everything had taken over the extra berths. That guy Mac and Sasha had hooked on to him was sure making himself at home. Army cap and belt off, his khaki jacket swung loose as a Russian village blouse. His high leather boots had been discarded for house-slippers. A two-day journey, why not enjoy it? Hard work was waiting for him at the other end.

From his case he produced newspapers. He offered one and Andy spelled out the headlines: ARCTIC EXPEDI-TION REPORTS   SUBWAY TUNNELING SPEEDS UP IMPERMISSIBLE TEMPO ON RAILROADS PIGIRON TOPS WORLD RECORD   DRAMATISTS' CONTEST ANNOUNCED   ACADEMY OF SCIENCE CONVENES IN LENINGRAD   BASKETBALL TOURNAMENT OPENS

He read the day's production figures. Easy reading and over here kinda like the baseball scores. He caught the Armyman's glance on him. Did the *Amerikanets*, he inquired eagerly, by any chance play chess?

Mac arrived home quite late. There had been another long meeting of the brigade. Nan had her storm signals up, tongue buzzing angrily. Her scanty marketbasket beckoned him from the table. After all day on her feet, she'd had to put in an extra hour waiting in queues. And look what she hadn't got! No potatoes no meat no greens. What a store. Only bread cabbage and herring.

As she tossed her packages on the blue oilcloth, he sniffed the herring. "Good enough, let's have a snack of that. I'm famished." Lucy climbed into her chair and reached for the brown loaf. Supper Mummy supper!

Nan rubbed her wrists and hands under the running spigot. "*Dynamo* stores have everything, butter meat candies, and ours are half empty. How's that?"

"Better organization," he answered. "Their supply section has more pep." His head, whole body throbbed. Lucy was crawling over him and munching her bread. She felt a tonweight, he was tired clean through. Say, this tea hit the spot. Not half a bad meal, he told his wife.

She ate without relish. Roast beef with greens was what she had planned. Now she'd spend part of her free day shopping for meat and butter in the open market where prices were fierce. "Mac, you make me sick! Nothing bothers you. You eat their hick grub without so much as a grimace. You're past me."

He extracted a fishbone. "Easy, old girl. Don't rock the boat. You know the reasons for this, what lies ahead."

"Oh, sure I know—what you'll say! 'As soon as the collective farms get going better.' 'As soon as—' a million things more! It's all right for you, you don't wait in the queues." He was provoking, chewing away on that black bread like a contented mule on grass. Swallowing between words—"Greatest changeover for agriculture in all history ... takes time ... Great Scott, Nan! Pass the herring?" Another year, they'd be sitting pretty. Another year ...

Abruptly he broke off, moodily crunched his bread. Sitting pretty, eh. That was it. While back there ... In evening papers there was news of a Pennsylvania miners' strike. Out in Arkansas a bread riot.

"See here, Nan," he asked softly, "maybe you'd like us to be going back?"

"Clarence MacGregor! Are you crazy!" Now he was starting in on that, worrying. As if ...

Quickly she poured his tea, brought out some applecake and veered her sails to a new tack. "Guess who moved into our apartment house today? That funny little couple. He said he knew you. I can't remember the name. Kendrick or something like that."

"That nitwit! That skypilot Heindricks! As if the Chestakovs weren't enough!"

"Why, Mac—and they're so friendly too." (Oh, bother. She was sorry now she'd asked them down for tea.)

Pungent odors of eau-de-cologne drifted in on them from the hallway. Her wet hair in curlpapers, Berta Chestakov passed their door. Mac winked at Nan. A sure sign. The Chestakovs were going to theater. Leon had bathed his face hands and entire crown in the damp fragrance of violets until his head emerged gleaming sleek as a wolf's. To become cultured: every one's aim, yes? Lace curtains perfume highheeled slippers gold watch chain: all these were the outward symbols at which the Chestakovs snatched. Mac laughed. Too bad they lacked the gum. Leon was a long streak of misery. Forever grumbling over how many state loans he'd subscribed to, how hard he must work. Lazy bookkeeper. Always poring over state lottery numbers. The lout had won four times. A radio bicycle and whathaveyou.

"Nan," he asked, "you're not falling for the Chestakovs' grouch?"

"Of course not! Only ..."

Lucy pulled his arm. "Papa, what's that?" Their neighbor Olga's strumming on her balalaika had broken off. Angry voices, then something knocking against the wall. "She's thrown it at him again," Nan observed. "Hope she busted the damn thing. Honest Mac, if that creature doesn't let up I'm going to the House Committee, that's all. And the sink is full of her dirty dishes, this minute." And was she jealous. As if anybody'd give a second look at her old husband!

The Chestakovs rapped on the wall, then at Nan's door. "You heard it? Olga Pankrevich is at it again. We'll demand from the House Committee that he move. I don't care if he is a super, they can't behave in this house like cats on a fence. It's not cultured." Bertha Chestakova's hanging wrists followed her eyes ceilingward. "Is she jealous? My dear! I told her so too. And more, I told her if she'd keep things decent, leave off that balalaika, maybe he'd stay home more. Was she mad! And I told her—but come, darling," she pulled on her furred gloves, "we must hurry." With a sideglance at Nan, "Do we look all right? Yes, to the Opera."

But they stayed long enough to make the acquaintance of the Heindricks who had come down for their promised cup of tea and evening of reminiscences about America.

Nan cut more applecake and went for fresh boiling water for the tea. "Well, Heindrick," Mac asked quizzically, "I hear you're transferring to *Red Star?*"

"Yes," the toolmaker answered, "we thought the rooms better. Well now, to tell the truth, I couldn't work in that place any longer. And they call it Socialism!"

"If I just had my perc—" Catching Mac's eye on her,

Freda's voice trailed off. In undertones she continued her saga of the lost trunk to Nan. Mac turned to her husband. "Still bellyaching about that? Your lost Utopia. Honest, I can't see why you stay on at all."

Gus Heindrick cracked his knuckles. He hardly knew himself. But he had nowhere to go. Nowhere. He had sold everything, given every extra penny he had to the movement. Maybe Freda and he should have bought that little farm in the old country instead. To live their last years there, yes, near nature. The world revolution seemed so far off. But he'd given every penny. And to get a job again, at his age?

Suddenly he turned on the Scotchman, "And you? What about it? Why don't you go back?" At his question Nan looked across, startled. Mac was frowning. "Now what would he be wanting to go back for, I'd like to know!" she spoke hurriedly. "How'd we ever raise Lucy? Give her the things she gets here?"

Mac winced. That's where the shoe pinched. The kid might go under. "I tell you, Mr. Heindrick," Nan rushed on, "we're planning on staying right here."

Freda took Lucy on her lap. Blessed child, her son Gilbert—but what was this! The infant was babbling Russian. What, forgotten English! Oh no, that'd never do.

After they had left, Nan cleared the table, turned on the radio. Mac yawned loudly, "Well, that's over," and removed his coat. He set the clock.

Nan came over to take it from him and reverse the alarm. Tomorrow was free day. "Mac, you're wearing yourself out. Too much of a good thing is enough. Don't go to that meeting tomorrow." Her eyes filled. She had counted on their taking Lucy sledding in the park.

He put an arm about her, stooped to loosen his shoes. "Sorry, old girl. I must, this time." Doggedly he reset the clock. When you trailed an enemy there was no letting up till you'd got him. This foe took no rest, gave his brigade none. Underhanded old sabotager, Waste, throwing every tenth truck to the whirlwind, distorting engine heads, ramming motors. Easy enough to spot his handiwork: but to get your hands on him, to rout him, that was another matter.

While he slept heavily, Nan sulked over her mending basket. Mac was unreasonable. He had turned into a machine, was killing himself. She was as keen as he to see things go ahead. But there was a limit to all things. Evenings free days everything, swallowed up by meetings, studies, social work. He called her oldfashioned, a housefrau. "Go ahead," he had told her, "strike out for yourself more. I can't do any way but what I am. For the next five months anyway, and after that, maybe it'll be something else." He had expected that her going to work would change her faster than it had. She had always depended on him too much, he said, to make their friends, their whole life. It had been that way in Scotland, then in America. Time she came out of her shell, found her place.

She patched his workpants with hot fingers. Was Mac growing hard? Since a child, she had been diffident of all but old people and children. She liked to sit by Mac in a group of his friends, listening quietly, preparing the tea. Gradually as she became more friendly, she'd put in a shy word here and there, but in the main just listen. Life at the plant for her was hard ... She liked her work, yet at brigade meetings she couldn't open her mouth. Mac was counting on her, she knew, expecting things of her. But somehow her voice choked her. When there had been a mistake in her pay envelope she had asked Mac to come straighten the matter out for her. And he teased her about it, yet.

As for their going back, she dismissed it. Mac'd never! Still ...

Gloomily she reorganized plans for tomorrow. All right, after marketing she would take Lucy with her to that meeting at the nursery. Maybe some of the women, afterwards, would be willing to go with them to the park.

Mac was home when they returned. "Want to run down to see the Waltons?" he invited. Nan skipped to the wardrobe to pull out her best frock. The Chestakovs were back from the matinee and would keep an eye out for Lucy. Mac was like that, mulish, until he had won a point. They were both like that. Too stubborn to give an inch, heckling, arguing, then all at once both giving in. Mac, like a boy, sorry he'd hurt her. And he knew she especially liked going to the Waltons.

Galya Walton, a little dark thing with black eyes, was as lively as Edgar, her redheaded English husband, was reserved. They lived at the *Rivera*, with other foreign journalists representing workers' papers abroad. Nan, like Mac, enjoyed their talk, for they had traveled wide, knew several languages and countries and many good stories. In addition to the Waltons there was the Parisian just returned from Central Asia, who perched his round bulk on the edge of his chair like a robin on a limb and trilled exotic descriptions of the awakening East; Henri Gerber, famous Hungarian author who had recently been *incognito* to Japan and China, read them chapters from his latest book; and Johnson, the American correspondent, had been covering the Ukraine. Walton had been making studies in Siberia for his paper. All were good talkers and good listeners, a rare combination. The wife of the Berlin correspondent was working with Clara Zetkin on her autobiography, and Nan liked most of all hearing about this old veteran.

She felt rather shy in such company, and wondered at Mac's free way of taking issue with this one or that. Still, she noticed they listened to him closely and questioned him about many matters at the plant. Walton made a practice of visiting *Red Star* and sitting in on their meetings, his redhead cocked to one side, his sharp little eyes taking in everything.

The Waltons seemed glad this evening that Nan and Mac had come. Galya dropped her book, Edgar cleared his papers from the table and plugged in the electric teakettle.

With a warm twinkle of appreciation in his half-closed eyes for Galya's gay mimicry of her *Intourist* charges where she worked as interpreter and guide, Edgar pulled leisurely on his pipe. He had heard most of them before, but her rollicking mood tonight was irresistibly funny. Nan soon forgot her disappointment that they hadn't been asked to go downstairs into the restaurant for coffee, where the gipsy orchestra moaned dreamy weird music. Galya possessed an inexhaustible ready supply of these anecdotes, but Mac suspected her of touching up the high spots with a true artist's brush.

Her latest group, she said, hailed from Liverpool and points north. Among them was one aspiring Scotch middle-class gentleman in kilts. The kilts appeared to be a principle with him. A bit unaccustomed and selfconscious he seemed, but untiring in telling other members of his tour about his MacDonald clan and its celebrated history. As guide, Galya had been honored with more than her share of his family's chronology. The plaids, nevertheless, proved a source of embarrassment to the English ladies traveling in the same tour. Several times they hinted broadly that it would be wiser if he adopted ordinary street costume. To this, Robert Burns MacDonald turned his deaf ear.

However threatening the weather, however the wind might whistle down Leningrad's Nevski Prospect and across the chilled Neva, he never permitted himself to weaken. Gaping passersby, smiling at his gnarled knees and goose-flesh bristling the hair on his legs, irritated him to the extreme. Rude people, these Russians. He had come to stare, not be stared at. Galya, nevertheless, detected behind his ill-humor a secret pleasure in the stir he created as he strutted along the Boulevards, chest arched, his green and red plaids kicking alluringly with each step.

Despite all remonstrances of his companions, the Hermitage, Winter Palace, marble lions and Opera all witnessed the loyal Scotchman in the sacred robes of his clan. Only when he had contracted a severe cold in his exposed knotty members did he regretfully fold his kilts, like the Arabs their tents, and condescend to prosaic nonScotch trousers.

His cold, which lasted until the group arrived in Moscow, made MacDonald more belligerent than ever. With inquisitive condescension, he put the question to his fellow-travelers: Why had they chosen this two weeks' tour through Russia? As for himself, he had gone into the matter thoroughly. Scotch, of course. Perhaps unwittingly on their part, they had made the most sensible choice of all trips offered by Cook's, Lloyd's, or any other agency. Armed with maps and railroad tables, he had given several days to working out this problem. At last, with several sheets of bowlegged figures spread before him, he had solved it absolutely. Probably the rest of his company had gone about it with less intelligent foresight than he? Nevertheless, their decision on Russia, rather than Italy France or the Mediterranean, was a wise one. On the basis of exact computations, he was prepared to state the following: taking into account all factors such as mileage, length of stay, and accommodations, this two weeks' trip in Russia covered more territory and afforded the largest returns on one's investment of all tours offered during this winter season.

Mac laughed heartily. "Galya, no one but a Scotchman will believe your story."

She refilled his cup. "Wait. I'm not through." Some of the English gentlewomen, as she had said, found MacDonald annoying, crude, one of those unsolicited skeletons in the closet that attached himself to you inadvertently. He was forever having to be explained. For Grace Elizabeth Maddox, tall willowy creature who trembled delicately on her slender trunk, he proved a particular trial. A woman of independent means and poetic aspirations, her great passion was "to be fair." To this land of the modern Sphinx she had come with open mind. She wanted to walk unhindered along its streets, breathe in its atmosphere, vibrate to its mysterious Eastern spirit. This encumbrance, this apparition in kilts had proven distracting, a discordant note. Likewise in conferences, he was continually putting the most uncultured insensitive questions. She felt ashamed, for after all they came from the same Isles. What would the Russians think? Greatly annoyed, she confided in Galya.

There was the time when they had gone to the Soviet Municipal Court, later interviewing the Judge in his private study. It had all been so revealing. She had felt she was nearing some new realm. This care for children and reclaiming women was a beautiful thing. Of course, divorce laws seemed alarmingly lax—yet one wanted to be fair. Then this Scotch pawnbroker had broken in, stamping with his rough boots on her very spirit. In his inimitable nasal twang he had rasped, "I also have a question for his honor." The Judge inclined his head. "Please. What is it?" To Elizabeth's horror, MacDonald had craned forward, thumbs in his vest pockets. "What I want to know is, how do you go about collecting, over here, if a man owes you twenty pounds?"

The worst of it was, Elizabeth felt, the Judge had bothered to answer his question!

As the kettle and Galya perked merrily, there was a timid rap on the Waltons' door, then a firmer one. Galya opened, stepped back. Grace Elizabeth Maddox, in person! With her came Doctor Agatha Lloyd, holding her Diogenes lantern. She had heard Walton speak at the Djerzhinsky Club and liked his straightforward manner of reasoning. Elizabeth Maddox, who had decided two weeks was not sufficient, was staying on to get deeper insight. One wanted to be *sure* that she was being fair. Agatha and she were neighbors at the *New Moscow* hotel.

Rather abashed, the table was moved over to make room for its new guests. Extra glasses and a fresh pot of odorous tea were prepared. Agatha recognized in Mac an immediate find, for his answers to her battery of questions were short, to the point.

With quiet reflection, Elizabeth Maddox sipped her tea. Her fair hair formed a radiant halo about her finely molded features. "Mister Walton," she inquired, "will you tell me, do you expect a revolution soon in England?"

He knocked the ashes from his pipe. "No, not in the immediate future."

She relaxed. "That is what I think, too." It was reassuring to hear him say so. With so many unemployed and all, one never knew. Her fingers curved delicate tendrils around her cup. "Then," she queried, "just what does the British Communist Party find to do in the meantime? Stir up trouble?"

Mac gulped as Nan choked into her handkerchief, marveling at Walton's patient explanation. She had been raised to respect the gentry. But this woman, why, she was daft!

The English visitor poised her cup. "I see." She grew pensive. "One more question. Do you personally feel, Mister

Walton—you know one wants to be fair—that your British Party has any one in it capable of being a dictator of our United Kingdom?" She herself was a liberal.

He pressed fresh tobacco into the bowl of his pipe. "Hardly. But we don't aim to have a personal dictator. Revolution brings about a dictatorship of a new class, not a person." He developed his thought.

Astounded, she put down her saucer. "Then you don't expect, assuming that sometime a revolution might take place in England, to establish a system like that of Soviet Russia?"

Mac jumped up, bounding in the air like an acrobat in his net. "I can't stand it," he said quickly. "Make her stop!" Nan pulled his coat. Repentant, he leaned his head against Galya's shoulder. Forgive him, he'd never doubt her stories again.

Galya and Edgar exchanged glances. The woman *was* hopeless. Agatha interrupted. "Let me explain to her. I've been all over this ground, so I ought to know."

When the gathering dispersed, Mac was still mimicking, "And Mister Walton, don't you think—one wants to be fair —" Gasping herself, Nan was afraid his loud guffaws might draw a crowd (the easiest thing to do in Moscow), and some militiaman want to take him in charge as a drunk.

Misha found Mac bending ruefully over a lathe he had dismantled for repair. Worse luck, it needed reconditioning throughout. "Come on," Misha told him, "this noon we're raiding the supply shop." With their notebooks and inquisitive noses trailing down sources of holdups, the repairmen were considered impudent scourges by more than one department. Assembly blamed motors, motors the tool and die shop and foundry; and all blamed the supply depot. What, they wanted to know, were the exact facts?

As they entered the office, door swinging to after them, the man behind the desk gave scant notice except to sink his bulbous nose further into his ledger, his thoughts far away. Misha thrust his notebook across the page. "We want some information." Leon Chestakov started. "And who might you be?" He was not pleased at seeing Mac. Misha answered briefly. Members of *For Soviet Machines* brigade. And he, who might he be? Chestakov put a protecting arm across his ledger. "Assistant to the chief."

Misha produced their credentials. "In his absence, you'll do. The foundry reports that you delivered only eighty per cent of their quota last month. Is this true? And what about your supplies for the dieshop? No verbal statements, please. Show us the books."

As they scanned records, Mac sniffed a fading odor of violets. Cold, detached, Misha made notations in his book. When they returned to their sector, his ugly face creased until Mac thought of dried apricots heaped in a burlap sack. Well, they were sure collecting the lowdown, right? Had Mac seen that young Kolya today? Sure, his mate answered, Kolya and his Comsomol pals in other departments were doing a swell job, checking up supplies received, number machines operating, absentees, daily breakage, and all the rest. Jolly well making department managers sit up and take note, that's what.

Yet one thing had them stumped. A ton of first quality steel—gone up in smoke! Unaccounted for. "Devil's mother, nobody ate it," Misha said irritably. "That lousy supply depot says they sent it to the foundry: foundry says they never got it. Records too jumbled to know what to believe. The thing was too bulky to filch. Dammit, where's it gone?"

They reported this to Maxim immediately after work, also, in guarded undertones, their discovery of an hour earlier: a key bolt on one of the MAGS had been unscrewed, thrown aside. Some dirty bastard! If Misha hadn't found it in the nick of time, their beauty would have thundered herself into a scarecrow! The men looked at each other. Dirty work: sabotage. But whose? There were a couple of disgruntled repairmen, but neither would think of going to such lengths as that. But whoever removed that screw knew MAG well. Some dirty rat, not one of theirs. Who?

They were standing near the warehouse, as Alex Turin rolled a truck into the yard. Aha, my fine fellows, so you're worried, eh? Maybe I can guess what's on your mind, no? What a "shock brigade" you are. Everything anarchy, no order anywhere. You and your kind are running the country to hell.

Well, my brave clowns, we're just a little too clever for you, that's all. Never fear, my darlings, a day will come. (Unobserved, he reëntered the plant.) Just wouldn't you like to see the letter I got only this morning. Foreign stamp too—only it didn't come through the regular mail.

Alex was still smarting from that fool trial over Zena. He'd square accounts yet.

Mac, when mulling it over later at his work, thought of Peter, the blockhead he had quarreled with over smashing a MAG. But the louse'd been transferred to common labor in the foundry, hardly likely that he ... Still, worth checking up. The way everything was now, all kinds of things might happen. And Peter had been a bad egg. Well, this meeting with Vronsky from the Moscow Party Committee ought to do a lot to help tighten things up.

He sat between Natasha and Vasiliev and, as the meeting opened, riveted his attention on Karl Vronsky, trying to decode every subtle motion of his lean shoulders and the fine network of muscles around his mouth and eyes. What was going on in that old Bolshevik's head? And how could he sit there so calm, with fireworks cracking all around him! That swine Pankrevich had preferred charges against their brigade. The brass that guy had, dubbing them "disruptive elements," claiming they'd spread discord throughout the plant. Did this pain in the ass think he'd put it over on Vronsky and the Moscow Committee? Just try it.

Mac cast an uneasy glance at Misha's glum mask. (Although a non-Party man, as an active brigader his friend had been asked to take part.) What'd Misha think, he whispered, was the rake getting away with it? Seeing his wry grin, Mac puffed more cheerfully on his fag. As Natasha reached for a light he saw her hand tremble. Did him good the way she loathed that toad.

Vasiliev turned on them the slow absurd wink of a canny old owl, as his rumpled head made excited jerks from side to side. Like a seasoned veteran, he was preparing to relish a good fight.

But Vronsky was no baby at these things, either. Sure, Vasiliev told Mac, he knew him from long back: his habits of browsing about Moscow, standing in queues, visiting workers and all manner of citizens in their homes, eating around in their restaurants, going into work shops, listening, questioning, everywhere getting on the inside, until every one agreed that Karl Vronsky had a closer grip on life in the Capital than any person living. A man with a real feel for the masses, and what was on their mind and heart. Sure, he knew Vronsky from long back, and could make a shrewd guess at the thoughts running through his keen old head while this flabby Pankrevich mouthed out his case.

Suddenly the speaker veered to a new climax: "And who is this Misha Popov? One of the main instigators of this famous brigade, who is he? A renegade! Expelled from the Party. Can we trust—"

"Stop it!" "Liar!" Vasiliev knocked against Mac as each sprang to his feet. Misha raised his fist. "You dirty louse!" Vronsky rapped for quiet as the lines about his mouth hardened. "Comrade Pankrevich, you are out of order. Grossly so. It's not a Communist who tries to sidestep issues, hiding behind personal attacks. By such methods you harm only yourself." As quickly as it had flared, the crackling rip in his voice died out. He turned to Misha. "I want to assure Comrade Popov that we didn't invite him here to listen to any such talk, but to help us get at the facts. We ask him to overlook what has just been said." Pausing, Vronsky knocked a pencil thoughtfully against his spread fingers. "But since the question has come up, I want to say that I have known Comrade Popov for some years. I disagree absolutely with Pankrevich. Whatever mistakes Popov may have made in the past do not concern us at this moment. These last months he has proven himself a conscientious fighter for Party principles. And this, I want to remind Comrade Pankrevich, requires courage and political insight, if you get the point." Mac felt a quiver running through

212

Misha, lifting for a brief moment the set mask on his pockmarked sour face.

When Pankrevich shrugged his indifference to say more, Ivan Filatov, the director, and then Maxim, Misha and Vasiliev took the floor. That dieshop manager, the elder repairman said bluntly, was all manners of a fool. Those articles in *For Soviet Machines* about waste in his shop had surely hit home. But the worst of the whole thing, where had the plant's Party and trade-union committees been during the fight? Why hadn't they given their brigade any real backing? As for management, only a few like Mikhail had come through as they should. This was what he wanted to call to the Moscow Committee's attention. True, Filatov, in the name of self-criticism, had posted the articles about *Red Star* on the bulletin board. But how far did that go? What they needed was action, better organization, not a pious admission of faults!

As he saw it, Ivan Filatov was as honest as the day was long, hard-working too, but a round peg in a square hole. Fact was, *Red Star* needed a director with more drive.

When Natasha began reporting, Mac pulled his nose with glee. How she waltzed into Pankrevich! Told about Boardman, Zena, the waste, everything.

After every one had spoken and heckled, and the room grown heavy with spiraling clouds of mulberry smoke, Vronsky rose to give a terse summing up. Mac saw Vasiliev straighten, Natasha's color come and go. This was the soundoff. Either . . . or!

Pankrevich's charges, Vronsky said, were unfounded. The brigade was on the right track and would get, he was sure, full backing of the Moscow Committee. Natasha squeezed Mac's arm. Oh boy, that meant . . . ! Her smile spread from face to face. "Your brigade's fight," Vronsky continued, "goes far beyond *Red Star*. You're one outpost of our hard two-fisted struggle to overcome every inner weakness in our class. Understand? Put our industries on an efficient basis, make them wellrun comradely strongholds of Socialism." He looked around. "Our whole country honors those workers throwing themselves into this fight. Your brigade, comrades! Hold to it, wield it.

"As for those who stand aside or hinder, we say—you can't block the path! Pankrevich, you're going to seed. Unable to keep up with the times, you've become an ordinary bureaucrat. A phrasemonger. Well, the Party and Government that put you in your post can also remove you. As for Comrade Filatov, yes, Vasiliev is right. A good man but for a different type of job." Regarding the weak factory committees, was it the opinion that annual elections take place this year three months ahead of schedule? And let *Red Star* see to it this time that she pick a better lot.

Winter in Central Russia breaks suddenly. Piercing through the gray sky, the sun clasps the snow in his ardent embrace and a thousand gushets go shimmering over cobblestones and asphalt, coursing into the sleeping Moscow grown turbulent beneath her ice blanket.

Snow, like charity, may cover a multitude of unpleasant facts. And so the brigade found—rather, the supply depot. As the brigaders crossed the plant yard toward the wide exit, Natasha lifted her head, threw back her shoulders and breathed in the exciting air. First hints of crocuses under the snow. Spring! Great blocks of cinder-grimed ice, which had stood in the yard all winter, were beginning to melt. Soon the river must break, and Andy would return.

For that tremendous moment of the river's breakup she'd go with her comrades to watch throughout the night, until iceblocks churned and ground angrily and the swift black monster beneath them leapt free. Would the Moscow overflow this year, or the dynamiting that had been done up upstream prevent it? Families living on ground floors of streets bordering the river had already moved out. She smiled to herself. In two short months she'd be swimming its brown currents, diving into its heart.

Maxim and his companions felt in particularly good mood. After weeks of careful study they had summarized their findings on waste and drafted their report for the Moscow Committee. It would appear in *Pravda,* mark their

214

word. From one proposal alone there'd be a saving of two million. "No mean item eh?" Mac thumped his workmate. Steel and brass shavings sold as salvage for a fraction of their worth could be melted down and re-used, right at the plant. This would help relieve the chronic shortage of those very metals.

"Sure, not bad," Misha growled, "but what about that ton of lost steel?"

Mac turned to Natasha. Say, he'd had a letter from Andy. Her step quickened. So had she. And had she puzzled over his sprawling letters!

She gave a light spring across a pool formed in the yard by melting snow. Wait! What was that glitter? Reversing her jump, she prodded under the snow's edge with her foot. It struck against something hard, harder than snow could ever be. Something that gave a metalic ring. What the ...! "Maxim! Vasiliev!" She held up a loosened bar, flashed it at them.

Incredulous, shouting, they joined her to claw with hands and feet. Ned ran for a shovel. What a find! Natasha's rusty bar swung against the blackened ice. Cleared edges revealed a solid mass of unused high quality steel. Misha scowled happily. Over a ton. What careless bastards they were in that supply depot. Imagine! No wonder they couldn't account for this steel, left all winter to rust in the snow!

Mac was chopping with an improvised pickax. Tomorrow in the paper—oh boy, that supply department'd never know what hit them.

This was going to be a rousing old Russky Scan-*dal!*

17

THE Black Sea, after a windtossed day, lay at rest. Its glassed surface heaved gently, flushed with the slanted rays from the sun, which, like a fullblown poppy, drooped toward the earth's rim.

From the mountainside where he had halted in his uphill tramp, Andy could see far up the valleys, across green and brown hills surrounding, to the purple ridges of the snow-capped Caucasus. Distances mounted and glowed with the hazy blues of Manhattan bridge at dusk.

Fishing boats were tracking in single file to the mainland. Near them flying porpoises sported, securely dogging their trail. Their glistening dark bodies made joyful arcs along the quiet waters: frolicking seapuppies who lacked only the bark. Not even steamers plying from Batum to Odessa could frighten them. Only the wicked swift schooner with its harpooner crouched by the prow could send them scurrying into its treacherously clear depths. White wings of a sloop that spread near the horizon crept toward the harbor as the sky fluttered her colors over mountains which marched to the very brink of the sea.

Andy drank in the fresh salty tang of the air, the odors of mimosa, early violets. Although Moscow was still buried in winter, in this country it was full spring. Sub-tropical. Russia's Palm Beach and Switzerland in one. Hillsides around him were massed with yellow.

In the city and lowlands, rose bushes and magnolia trees were budding, and snow had been brushed for the last time from the palmtrees' lean branches. Banana trees had put out fresh shoots, and the palms, released of their winter sacks, stretched their stiff joints toward the kindly sun. Mountain-streams were tumbling headlong into the sea.

What a land, Andy thought, for Mickey Mouse to play in. Apes and monkeys in the zoo park nearby were allowed out to gambol as they liked with no fear of their sneezing and coming down with the flu. Andy often walked over with his roommate, Habib Mohmed-Aliev, to watch them. Habib was a brownskinned lively vacationer from Baku. Uncanny creatures these apes. Too near human. Not comfortable.

Andy shaded his eyes from the rays of the wilting sun as his gaze circled the horizon. This was his favorite hour for a climb. His ankle was strong again, though not good for the long hikes that Habib liked to make. But this short climb up the mountain overlooking the harbor he made every evening, sometimes with companions from the resthome, oftener alone. Long conversations in Russian tired him. Besides, he had plenty he must think out, alone.

The smoke rising from farmers' huts dotting valley and hillside was bridging the river. Nearby, sheep and horned cattle grazed lazily as their great horns swung from side to side.

This place had got him, no denying it. Made him want to say, do things he didn't savvy. He felt washed clean, inside out. Making ready, gathering steam.

For what?

Days ahead; what did they hold? He loosened a rock, flung it far below into the valley. Crap, why spoil a good walk puzzling over that!

Beneath him, as though sighted from an aeroplane, spread the flat crystal white housetops of Sukhum. Their latticed balconies and fringed roofs reminded him of paper trimmings on an iced cake. The kind that had stood in the village bakery window when he was a boy. With his pals he had schemed how to storm the citadel, bind the baker, and carry off the prize as their own. His gang had wanted to celebrate Lame Willy's birthday in style, but that tight-fisted baker had spoiled the day.

Peaked helmets of churches down here looked more eastern-like than Moscow's. Wakened at sunrise yesterday by weird chantings of the faithful and churchbells' ringing, he had gone out on the balcony to find a golden ball rising over the sea. The mournful dirge was soon half-drowned in the familiar airs of a martial song as marching columns of Redarmymen wound along the road and their full male chorus echoed along the shore. They'd seemed so carefree and resolute, he'd wanted to step out, fall in line. Crazy notion.

One Sunday, he had gone to a local church service. Just to see. Priests in blue and silver robes were chanting through their noses some Greek jingo while their darkskinned congregations bowed and crossed themselves and placed petitions and coins before pictures of the saints. Some glanced at him sideways.

As smoky incense swung from the altar across the room, the wailing chants grew louder. Recalling a smutty joke about incense pots, he made a quick exit. What a pickle if he'd spilled a laugh. Those guys looked wicked. Plenty with knives. Sure, they'd hang a guy to a sour apple tree!

Outside in the cool garden the dirge sounded far off, as unreal as the ancient brown faces which had been turned toward the altar. He thought of the lonely graves decorated with sacred patterns of white stones that stood near the highway running parallel to the sea. Queer country, this region. The whole Russian thing, queer. But natural too. Like being shut up in a sweatbox and just when you'd quit hoping, getting out into the open and great chestfuls of air.

Yesterday Habib and Andy had wandered all afternoon over the hills to gather bluets, mountain daisies and a fragile pink blossom they called *felke*. Habib said he was going to press some of them overnight in a book, send them off to his wife and son in Baku. Andy liked the idea. But should he send them to Elsie or Nat? He slipped them back in his Russian Grammar. It didn't seem quite decent to send them to both.

Topping the highest hillock, Andy stretched himself against the cool ridge. His thoughts drifted with the clouds across peaks and valley. In four months his contract was up. What then? What was going on in the States? Morse's note, for all his big talk, sounded down in the mouth. And not a word about the oil station. Tim, he'd mentioned, had gone west to look for work. Andy blinked. Good old Tim. That was the boy he missed. Dirty shame, he'd jammed on that rotten brake. And tramping again. There was talk, Morse said, of a pickup in summer. And Hotcha, what a swell party they'd slung when they hit New York. In Detroit too. He knew them. An oldtime blowout for the gang. Everybody asked for Andy, was he going bolshy or what? And when in hell was he coming home?

Andy flipped an ant from his neck. Sure, he'd better head for home. Forget this Russian girl and all her ideas. Jeez, he liked her too much as it was.

Funny, the things you could see in clouds. Uncle Jem smoking his corncob. One of these Caucasian mountaineers riding his donkey. Old Mikhail in his specs and loose workblouse puffing a light. Sasha ... Mac ... Damn if he would! Gotta wise up. Savvy the works. Something to swing by. Besides, he had a good job.

These clouds looked so near you'd think you could reach out and snitch one. Like a daisy. Sure, a quick affair with that girl'd been one thing. Taking her on for life, something else.

Conceited ass, think she'd give you a second thought? You, a greasy machinehand, and she starting in fulltime next fall on her engineering course. For all her Communism, you can't get around that. Don't kid yourself. She's decent to you because you're a foreigner. A Ford worker. What you got to offer a girl like that? Her job tops yours. Or nearly. Doesn't fall for pretty things. That is, not like Elsie. But in other ways, she must expect something! Everybody does. Sure, we have a peachy time swimming skating and all that. A real pal. I like to talk with her, get her ideas. Maybe she likes me some. But not that. Nuts! The girl's head is too full of campaigns, books. And whathaveyou.

A fellow ought to feel a girl needs, depends on him. Looks up to him sorta. This one was too smart. Too sure of herself. Not a Smart-Alec, though, had to hand her that. Can't get sore at her. Fact is, admit it, you lousy sucker. She's got the goods.

No frills on her. Nails clipped short as mine. Streaks of machine grease when she's in the shop. But that saucy tilt to her nose, cutest thing this side the Atlantic. And her eyes. Look clean through me. Wonder what she sees?

Say, those trucks down there tooting up the valley might be from their plant. Sure enough. Don't I know their lines! Attaboy, you got a rough road. One thing this country sure needs, good roads.

Now get this straight, baby. The man Nat hooks up with'll never be the center of her universe. Not her. Always come second, her damn work first. Lot of men that way, but in a woman. All right. Maybe I am. Old-fashioned. Just don't like it, that's all. Sure, a girl should be a fellow's pal and all that. But too much of a good thing's too much.

Andy, you gimme a horse laugh. How you gonna burn your gas and have it too? But how you'd get any home life with a woman forever chased off to some meeting? Be like Nan and Mac. Elsie now, she'd doll up for me every evening, meet me with a smacker at the door. Cook my favorite dish. Act right.

But she'll be a nagger. Forever after me about getting ahead. Dough. How could I? Over here, fellows like me got a chance. Look at Kolya, Sasha. On the up and up. Look at Nat.

Maybe I'll start in studying myself. Like they say. But she's got a year's start on me, the young buzzard.

Wonder if my Detroit flapper'd fit in here? Or supposing I go back to the old USA, would a Russian girl go along? Likely not. Can't blame her. Aw, what the hell. In a few years Elsie's nagging and chatter about clothes'd get me fed up. I'd razz back. Is that what I want?

Jesus, am I changing too?

Take Nat. She needs somebody home to greet her. Fry her bacon. Listen to her doings, say, "What a guy!" Be a new shuffle with a girl like that. Her man'd have to fish pretty much for himself. Bare room, two cots. Not even a teapot, I bet. Thataway, home's not the real thing. But how you know you got her right? One thing, with her a fellow'd never get bored. Something new all the time. Something to swing to. And no grouchy sulks. Jeez, what a headache!

And about kids. Well, you gotta think these things out, ain't you. I don't even know how she looks on it. After all, I don't know her so good. Guess I never will. Maybe she's against marrying, altogether. Like that song she sings, "Here today, Tomorrow there!"

This earth's rocky and damp, think I'll go. Well, old puffclouds, shall I stay on or go back? Ask me another! Jeez, this place is too pretty to be by yourself. Just lamp Nat here, stretched out, watching the clouds. Nuts!

Shall I? I'd never stomach the breadline. Most I've got to hope for, back there, is that speedcrank, Feldman. His lousy mouth. Jeez, if we'd just take the US and Russia, shake them up together. Take the good, let the rest go. As things stand, not much question where things are moving. Gotta think about that.

Hell, am I reasoning in circles, or getting somewhere?

Standing up, Andy reached his hands over his head. The earth's moist warmth had been seeping through his clothes. He gave himself a vigorous shake and started down. Another week and he'd be heading north. Not sorry, either. You got enough of lazing pretty quick. Even when there was something doing at the Rest Home all the time; from seven on, when Habib woke him for setting up exercises on the volley-ball courts with the sun topping the white pillars of *"Asia"* where they were staying, to the evening of games or movies in the dining room with tables pushed to one side.

Mail was the exciting event of the day. Andy wrote post-cards to every one he knew in Detroit and Moscow and hoped at least for a few answers. Their neighbor, a *udarnik* from Sverdlosk, made the air miserable with endless thumbing on his guitar: "Dunya, Dunya, Oh my Dunya," and the Georgians were ready to sing and dance half a dozen times a day. On the balconies, in the rooms, up the mountain, it made no difference. What amazed him, they never seemed tired of it. Well, neither was he. Especially their sword dance, done in native costume with stomping rhythm and wild leaps in midair. Everybody kept time, striking their palms together and joining in the dancer's shouts. Following this always came a dance of a black-eyed girl to wild staccato music. Jeez, what a flirt. It was swell.

These Georgians were rowdy and happy as kids. Proud too. And you could tell they got a big kick out of Stalin, Ordjonikidsie and other Big-Shots coming from their part of the country.

Andy had entered into vacation life wholeheartedly. Never mind that bum ankle. He became one of their crack volleyball players, starring on the team that defeated all other Rest Homes in Sukhum. On rainy days he won at dominoes, a game he hadn't played since a farmboy. They made him clog and sing jazz until he begged off, with a faked limp to prove he meant it.

Jolly sociable crowd they were: railroaders, miners, *udarniks* from Siberia to Dneiprostroi, a couple of aviators, doctors, teachers, armymen, and many engineers. His kind. It had given him a jolt, though, to find out about his croquet companions. A small wizened fellow with his front teeth gone was a court judge from Kiev, and the other, a gray-bearded jolly ham was a member of the Georgian Republic's Central Government!

After supper everybody'd gather on the veranda, with the evening going blue and cool. The fireflies were coming out in the grasses and sky and the earth was relaxed and free. Waitresses, government officials, mechanics—it made no difference. Comrade this and *Tovarisch* that, and plenty of joshing all round. They'd brag about their kids, and what was doing in their town, and "We finished our Plan in three and a half years!" The girl sitting next to him was a pippin. But he only sparred. Up to his neck as it was.

The next morning a big crowd started off on one of the daily hikes, this time to an old villa lying off the east of town. He joined them. Some said the road had been built by the Romans. Its bed was as firm as ever. They marched in semi-military fashion, their heads covered with towels wrapped turban-wise to protect them from the already hot sun. Now and then they sang, until the heat took their breath.

About a mile out of town was the community bathing beach. Written on the stone breakwater in huge seafast letters and four languages (Greek, Russian, Georgian, and Abhasian) were the regulations. Here women were to bathe à la nature, if they chose, and no man dared come near. A hundred yards further was the men's beach. Between each, a no-man's land. Farther on was a stretch where couples attired in proper garb might swim together. The whole thing amused Andy very much.

Too bad the sea was still too cold for a dip. A Siberian vacationer tried it, but one glance at his purple skin decided the rest. Leave that swimming with icebergs to the movies!

As they tramped on, village horsemen from the hills and carts drawn by foul-smelling oxen passed them on their way to market. The hills were spotted with Rest Homes, former millionaires' villas taken over by the State. To reach the villa, they had to walk through a large park, where jasmines from the East, rubber plants from India, palms from Africa and California redwoods and cactus were planted helter-skelter. The old Croesus who had owned this place before the revolution had a hobby for collecting shrubs and curios from all parts of the world. So Habib told Andy.

The villa itself rested on a fuzzy mountain close to the beach. Its slanted roofs and peaked red-and-green caps tilted skyward. Within, they found a spiral iron stairway running from ground floor to roof. Its porch faced east. In the wide dining hall the banquet table and mantel over the hearth were made of heavily carved mahogany; on the sideboard stood the former owner's hammered silver service, and upstairs, his library in five languages. Nothing had been touched. Andy didn't fancy the plush and gold furniture in some of the rooms but a little handpainted table top from Spain caught his eye. In the large bedrooms were four cots each and vacationers' belongings hung in neat rows, nearby. Habib said it was good, all this wealth and culture socialized. Andy looked over some of the books and grew downcast, thinking of all the lingos in the world. So many books, and still old Mikhail was writing more.

In the sideyard were pheasants and a cunning baby bear, as tame as a housecat. He was taking a suncure, too.

Before breakfast the next morning, Habib and Andy went to market in search of those famous golden-skinned apples. When Nat flared up, or kidded, her eyes flashed spots just that color.

As they crossed the seaport's few main avenues, its hot pavements yellow with dust, Andy stared openly at the mounted donkeys, slung with gunny sacks and baskets and their straight-backed riders with skins darker than burnished copper. Beneath their caracul turbans gleamed fierce black eyes. Their regular features bore a haughty look. Pleated cartridge pockets breasted their tightly belted jackets from which swung a dagger or sword in decorated sheath. Some had discarded their turbans for a summer handwoven head-dress of a type that Andy remembered having seen in pictures of the East. Arabs.

Dulleyed animals, which the Russians termed "beefaloes," but what he thought a sorry cousin of that grand beast, swayed homemade wagons over cobbles, as they patiently bore produce to market. Native women wore shawls much more highly colored than any he had seen further north, and fullgathered dresses that swished as they walked. Their beauty was compelling. Greek. He wished he could speak with them. But many knew far less Russian than he.

Mountaineers on black highspirited steeds, with studded bridles and saddles, dashed by the slow line of carts and donkeys. Something about these natives reminded Andy of the American Indian. These Abhasians, so they said, were descendants of the Greeks. To his inexperienced eye they and the Armenians and Georgians all looked alike. Yet, he learned, each considered itself a distinct people with its own traditions and language, and Soviet Republic.

Of their little country the Abhasians spoke with all the fervor of Habib in describing his Baku, or the Georgians their Tiflis. This was the land to which Jason was supposed to have come in search of the Golden Fleece. The magic

224

country sung by Homer. Abhasians related their country's past sorrows, extolled its resources and natural beauties, took the *Amerikanets* on excursions to their historical museums and new schools in the native tongue (something which the czar had forbidden), to their new power station, concerts of native music, and olive and orange farms run by their young republic. "Come back in five years," they begged, "and you'll see Socialism's Golden Fleece!"

Andy was bewildered. He spoke with Habib. He'd thought Russia proper was the one and only republic making up the USSR. How was it? Habib gave an amazed laugh. True, the old régime considered only Russians human. The rest, only beasts of burden to swear at and flog. The way Negro people were still treated in the States. "It is fourteen years since we put an end to that!" His scorn was hot as the gummy pavements. "Tuirks, Georgians, Russians, now it's all the same."

Andy must come to Baku. Return to America before seeing their marvelous City of Black Gold? Impossible! Their forest of oil derricks running out into the Caspian Sea, their eastern women only now removing the veil. Camels, stone huts, electric railways, and new workers' towns like "Stenka Razin." Come to Baku, see what a freed people could do. Besides—Habib's dark eyes danced—Andy would see his wife and small son.

His boy was less than five months. When he had first come, Habib had refused meals, worrying about his child. The post brought no news from his wife. When her letter finally came, laughing, he showed Andy the sheets of delicate Tuirk script, all curls and dots, read him news of his boy, and opened a bottle of wine to celebrate.

To Andy, his roommate was a new world in himself. This son of a Tuirk shoemaker, until ten years before, hadn't known how to write his name. He'd slept on straw because his family was too poor for beds. Hated Russians, spat after them in the streets.

Yet three years ago Habib had graduated from Baku's Oil Institute and done postgraduate work in Leningrad. There he had met his wife, a Russian girl who was studying to become a doctor. Now he was on a big job set him by the Party, helping organize the cotton farmers in his native villages around Baku.

Andy was ashamed to admit it, even to himself. In Detroit, if he had met Habib on the street he'd have passed him up as just one of those wops.

They had reached the market. As they passed the muddy entrance to the stalls, a gypsy shook her lobed golden earrings at them. "Come, darlings, let me tell your futures!" Her matted dusky hair was plaited with saffron ribbons. Dirty rabbit-eyed children clutched at her skirts as her bare feet stepped uncaring through the mud.

The men pushed by her, through crowds of turbaned peasants and their sternfaced women, past the basket women and cornplaster man with his lurid encased models of tortured feet. Beyond the stalls of radishes and early potatoes, freshly slain hogsmeat, butter and egg women, morose bearded farmers were crouched by their sacks of walnuts and golden apples. These apples, so the legend ran, had proven the undoing of the fair Greek, Atalanta. Dropped along the way by her suitor, their bright hues had caused her fleet steps to turn aside once too often during the race.

While Habib bargained, Andy witnessed an amazing encounter. With their ferocious mustaches and swords dangling, two native mountaineers stealthily approached one another. What was up? Abruptly they stepped back and, with outstretched arms, alternately and with slow dignity, implanted mild kisses on the open space beneath their chins. Jeez, they were harmless as pigeons! But get them in a brawl, he bet those swords'd fly. Look at the neat slice to that fellow's dagger as he halved an orange.

Munching their fullmoon apples, the vacationers made the round of the bazaar. This municipal market, Habib said, was one means of bringing new life into the mountains and countryside. Free medical advice and books on scientific farming, politics and many other subjects, as well as much-coveted manufactured goods were centered here for their use. Slogans and banners ran over the stalls. Such a motley display of goods swarming with buyers, pickpockets and beggars, Andy had never seen. Oriental carpets and shawls had few customers, but shoes, dress goods, and such precious items as nails and tin buckets drew a continual throng.

Habib was critical of the market, especially the mud. They had much better in Baku. On their way back, they stopped by a local photographer's contrivance. He was original, to say the least. The sidewalk had been appropriated as his studio. Against the outer wall of a hardware store reared canvas on which had been painted a lifesize dashing Cossack. There was no face; only a gaping hole. His sword waved above his turban as he spurred his black charger up a perilous cliff.

"Come, citizens," the photographer invited, "have your picture taken for your sweetheart." A solemn-faced country lad stared with round meek eyes while the photographer disappeared under his musty cloth to focus the lens.

Convulsed, Andy and then Habib placed their heads through the gaping hole in the canvas. With hurt dignity the photographer waited until they assumed correct expressions. Andy strove to match the wicked stare which the town's artist had contrived to impart to his flying steed. Elsie would sure giggle over this world's fair exhibit.

At Andy's plate, when they reached the Rest Home, was a letter. From Nat. In funny English and very short. Big news. *Red Star* was getting a cleanup, new director. And when was he coming back?

18

PHILIP BOARDMAN asked Natasha to go with him to the supply shop. (The kid sure seemed happy, these days.) Since her brigade was checking up, here was something to add to their list. Down a rear aisle he led her behind some crates of broken junk. Her lips pursed. Dies!

"Yep. Bought for a type of work we discontinued long ago." Wiping dust from their copper plates, he said to her, "Read 'em and weep." She touched the English lettering: from Cincinnati. Imported dies—and never used! But why?

His brows arched. Better ask Crampton, he'd bought them on his last trip abroad, nine months ago. He ought to know.

Natasha bit down on her thumb with her little even teeth. The wrecker! "No, you got him wrong," Philip told her, "it's just good business. If you can put it over, fool 'em and get away with it, it's legitimate—as he sees it." The thing was to stop his putting it over.

She turned without a word and started for their shop. As he walked by her, Philip wondered what was passing in the girl's mind. Did she think him little, mean-minded, or did she know why he'd... At the doorway she extended her hand. "Thank you, *Tovarisch* Boardman."

He hastened toward his press, the warmth of her handclasp tingling through him. *Tovarisch*. He sprang lightly on the electric crane which stood ready waiting to reverse a half-ton die. Now if Mary... Well, Mary was Mary, and his wife. For better or worse. (This crane needed oiling.) Since Mark Koshevnikov had led him to shoot off his chest, he felt spruced up. What Mary needed, Mark said, was work, new interests: to be a person on her own. What were her abilities, training? Philip had thought, shaken his head. Damn if he knew. Maybe something with kids. And she was a good cook. Outside of that, jazz or bridge lessons! Over here worth as much as a snowball in hell.

The crane responded quickly to his varying motions. He relinquished his place to young Kolya, who was restive for his turn at the levers. The lad's skillful handling was not to be begrudged. Die in place, Philip went to examine some pieces of finished work. Not until lunchtime was there time for his thoughts to revert to Mary.

Last night had proven a jolt, a nice one at that. At the Koshevnikovs' repeated urgings he had brought Mary with him. He hadn't relished the visit at all. Mary might find them boring, while they, for all their tact, would be hard put for common subjects for talk. He had misguessed on Mark's wife, Vera. There was a woman for you, a chemist in her own right and a real woman to boot. And maybe he had misguessed on Mary too?

When Mark had taken him over to his worktable to show a miniature model for a Soviet-made machine of the MAG type, Vera and Mary had begun talking about all those things women and mothers always find to say to one another. Later on, when they regrouped for tea, he glanced repeatedly at his wife. No two ways about it, this wasn't her polite visiting expression, but what he called her easy movie-going smile.

Going home, Mary had slipped her arm confidingly through his, as she used to do when their oldest boy was still little, and said she would like to go again. And they must have the Koshevnikovs over. What charming people, so cultured and refined. Why hadn't Phil taken her before? His friend must be very prominent, wasn't he: had he really designed that machine himself? Mrs. Koshevnikov had said such lovely things about Phil, and asked her to serve on a committee with her to inspect children's nurseries. Mary's poor Russian would not matter, she said, as she'd translate for her. Mary rather liked the idea, and what did Phil think? He pinched the soft flesh above her elbow. Hop to it, why not? Surprising, what a difference it made having Mary in better mood. If only she would let up about going home.

He gulped his lunch. Yes, maybe he'd misguessed on Mary. Loping over to Kolya, his trained eye watched the youth's supple motions as he duplicated a pattern on the Keller machine. He manipulated this clever mammoth twice his size with the dexterity of a tennis player, varying his stroke to meet the changing angles of a fast charging ball. Not a smarter more complicated machine on the market than this one: able to do everything but say hello. As for Kolya, give him six months and the country a hundred thousand of his brand, and all hell couldn't hold 'em.

Philip felt a cool scratching on his sleeve. It was Katia Boudnikova, as crisp in her lavender frock as if she had just stepped from her bath. Graciously she handed him a roll of drawings which, she informed him, Mister Crampton had sent, for a plate to be made at once. Her polished long fingernails tapering over the sheets put Philip on edge. Impatiently he unrolled the blueprint. Time Crampton had sent it, the plate was badly needed. He ran over the specifications. Of all the goddam ideas, what was that gasbag thinking about! The drawing called for the plate with its twenty-four punches to be made in four sections, uneven ones at that. Why in hell did he complicate a relatively simple problem! Let any one section be off by a millimeter, and the whole blessed business was no good. Worse than that, it'd be the very devil to correct.

Weight thrown carelessly on a silkclad hip, Katia listened to his fuming with growing uneasiness. These technical questions she had ceased trying to understand, yet she sensed that Henry Crampton was rapidly losing his prestige. And he had grown strangely irritable when she pressed him about the State Trust approaching him for a renewal of his contract. What was in the air? And was her power over Henry waning? Could she prevail on him to desert his family, take her with him to America? Or must she resort to Alex Turin? At least, until they reached France. Ah, Paris! City of dreams. With her beauty and cleverness she could go far. How sad life was. She, an emigrée from her beloved Russia.

Oh, Paris, Paris. (Unconsciously her arm weaved a tragic arc. She thought it a particularly eloquent gesture adopted from a Chekhov character as rendered by the Moscow Theater of Art.) Paris, will you comfort me, love me enough?

Forcing her mood, she tripped after Boardman who was off to find the chief engineer. She loathed this man even more than her stupid tub of a Crampton. Empty-hearted empty-headed, these foreigners. And flourishing off the lean fat of their land, profiting through her country's recent years of misadventure! She longed to strike out at them, yet did not dare. Well, when this Mister Boardman discovered his proposals rejected by BRIZ, and for such reasons! It should send him backstage, perhaps off the set altogether.

The superintendent and Henry Crampton were seated by their desks, their papers spread before them while they quietly pulled at their cigarettes. Ashes dropped on the sheets had not been brushed aside. Henry was worrying over his girl Bella. She was getting out of hand, sneaking out to meet Russians...

Philip slapped the drawing. What the hell did this mean? Why shouldn't the holes be punched like they always were in America, on one solid sheet?

Their bitter voices, as they argued, grated on Katia's finer sensibilities. These Americans, when it came to scratch, were not gentlemen. They lacked breeding, finesse.

Crampton held firm. Make the plate as specified: one solid piece was unthinkable. If one hole was off, the whole die had to be remade. That meant wasted labor and metal. Philip swore hoarsely. Nonsense! Didn't they always make them in one piece in the States? There was far less chance of error in the spacing of holes where they were stamped simultaneously, on one sheet. Four sections multiplied the chance of mistakes by several dozen. In fact, it was ten to one that the die'd have to be junked and restamped. Talk about waste of metal and labor! This was the way to get it.

What about it, when a hole was punched wrongly, or was worn out? Crampton demanded. If in four sections, only

231

one piece had to be remade. Boardman squinted. What about it? His chief knew as well as he. They'd put a neat piece on the plate, as always, that was all there'd be to it.

Pankrevich, to whom they appealed, preferred to remain neutral. This was their affair. Crampton was chief engineer and should be quite competent to decide the issue. As superintendent, he was occupied with drafting his report to the new director, and he was letting nothing interfere with his intention to make the facts appear in as favorable a light as possible: a matter which became increasingly difficut. (Neither of the *Amerikantsi* knew it yet, but next month he was ... er, being promoted to other work.)

With his thumb caught under his vest and cheeks puffed, Crampton's fingers beat an angry tattoo on his taut shirt. Goddam it, make the die as directed. What was this, anyway, anarchism! Subordinates questioning their chief's orders! Boardman would never dare such a thing in the States.

Philip rolled the drawing into a narrow tube. "No, by God, for once you're right. There my job depended on my being a good yesman. I took orders, not giving a damn so long as I wasn't the goat."

"And here?" Henry Crampton demanded. (He knew this fellow's game: after his job. Well, he'd have a run for his money.) "What in hell is it to you, to get so hot under the collar about?"

Boardman winced. Was he going to tell this blowhard something he'd never clearly expressed even to himself? Anyway, this guy'd never believe it, that a person could get a new slant. That—ah, hell. "That's my affair," he replied with sudden emphasis. "Enough that I do care, get me?"

Sure, orders were orders. Gripping the paper tube of blueprints as he would a lever, he vanished below stairs. Orders were orders. For the moment, the sour cheese had stumped him. Orders. All the same, he was not going to make that die wrong. There had to be a halt to this, somewhere. What to do? Crampton was pigheaded, the kind that never admitted a mistake. Pankrevich, with the spine of a jellyfish. What must he do?

All his past training cautioned him to drop the matter, make the die and let its poor working prove the facts. Waste, more waste. Damn if he would. But what to do?

His hand revolved quickly over his mouth and chin: a habit which Mary often scored. Where to turn? Crampton had the drop on him. Singlehanded, he was licked. But to make that die. What would his friend Mark do in a pinch like this?

He rapped on Kolya's shoulder. "See here, if anybody wants me in the next half hour, say I'm with Maxim, in the Party Office." The toolmaker was helping a learner with his blueprint. The broad charcoal smudges over his deep-set eyes screwed downward as he examined the sheet Philip gave him. The engineer had been right not to make the die. Leave the drawing and matter with him?

Kolya wondered why his swearing *Amerikanets* went about his work the rest of the afternoon with his lips framed in a dry whistle. Just what steps Maxim planned, beyond talking with Crampton and Pankrevich, Philip did not know. At any rate he was sure the wrong die would never be made. And that bluffer trying to pull his dirty chestnuts out of the fire was going to get more than his fat paws burnt!

Baku, which Andy visited on his way to Moscow, proved all Habib had promised. After spending a few days with his friend, Andy took the train for Moscow. Oh boy, his tappets were doubletiming it. He felt like Old Pete when Uncle Jem, after all-day-meeting, turned her nose homeward. Racing to go!

Three days on a train can be unbelievably long. Yet a Russian train is never boring. He wandered through to third class, termed "hard," and sat where he could listen in on the dirty stories some of the train crew were using to speed the journey. Some words were unfamiliar but he couldn't fail to get the main point.

"And he said, come on, *davai!* And she said, 'Say, wait, youse. What about—' " and the rest was drowned in loud guffaws. This went on and on. The girl, it seemed, was exacting.

Up the aisle, he noticed two men enter the train carrying a lidded wicker basket. They seemed out of breath. One of them, holding a handsome caracul coat bundled under his arm, went immediately to the toilet. When he returned, the coat was minus its brown fox collar. The man's companion shifted his gaze about, as he took the fur piece from his pocket and stuffed it quickly into the basket. Andy caught the sheen of a dagger under his jacket. He lost interest in the stories at once, and sauntered up the aisle.

He wasn't the only one, he found, who had been watching. A flat-nosed woman with worn hands sitting near them commented, "A beautiful coat. Why'd you rip off its collar?" The man answered her glumly: to sell it. Her other questions received equally scant reply.

She sat a moment, looking out of the window, then went into the next car. When she returned she brought with her a quiet-faced man in uniform. Andy stared: the O.G.P.U.!

"Come with me," he told the men quietly. They objected. "But we've done nothing!" "Then," he answered, "you have nothing to fear." Seeing their exit blocked by two railwaymen, they took their basket and preceded the government man down the corridor. The woman and Andy followed.

In a sheltered corner of the railwaymen's section, the coat was carefully examined. Where had they gotten it? They had bought it. "Are you sure?" the official inquired. "Sure you didn't steal it?" No reply. "How much did you pay for it?" "Two hundred roubles." "Remarkable! I must congratulate you, you're great bargainers. The coat's worth at least a thousand. Why did you rip off the collar?" "To sell it." "Not to disguise your theft?" The examiner's low voice carried a sneer. He demanded their documents.

They had none. The woman clucked her tongue. So she had thought. These men had boarded the train at Alexandrovka. They'd told her they'd come from there, but Kolkova was more likely—a colony of exiled *kulaks*, some twelve miles away. These devils! "So you can't rob and live off the poor peasants any more eh," her face reddened, "now you're looking for new ways to cheat!"

Opening their basket, the examiner held up a heavy silk shawl. Its blue folds rippled in the car's shifting lights. "Suppose you bought this too? And this? And this!" The basket was crammed with miscellaneous finery. Carefully the man repacked it, lit a cigarette.

Standing outside the compartment, Andy whistled under his breath. Two escaped *kulaks* caught with the goods! And everybody to outward appearances, except the woman, as cool as you please. Just carrying on any ordinary talk. The rest of the train didn't even guess anything was up.

At the next station, the government man got off with his two prisoners. Face pressed against the window, Andy scarcely believed his eyes. The O.G.P.U. man, his arms filled with the coat, was walking in front! The arrested men, carrying the basket between them, brought up the rear. Surely they'd make a break for it, maybe stab their captor in the back.

Nothing happened. The three disappeared within the station and as the train started, the government man came out, alone. The flatnosed woman told the American that he had turned them over to the local authorities. This station would call back down the line for some report on the thefts. Her blue jacket adjusted, she resumed her seat. "We have to be on watch day and night for these hooligans, that we do. The class enemy's a tough one," her voice was hoarse, "and fighting now with its back to the wall. Thieving, speculating—look at the Ukraine! Even hiding behind kind faces and smooth words. But don't think we won't catch them!"

He liked her jacket. Like Nat's. She was a weaver from Ivanovo-Voznesensk, she said, on her way back from a sanatorium in the Crimea. She had been there six months because of a spot on her lung, but it was gone now. From his view of Ukrainia's brown rolling plains, Andy turned to study her homely serene features. Jeez, there might have been something in Sasha's boast about the O.G.P.U. having a hundred million pair of eyes.

When the train puffed into Kazansky station, he descended its steps three at a time. He was back! The snow had gone, but there was a chill to the air after subtropical Sukhum. Should he run home, drop his bag and have a washup before going over to the plant? To hell with it. It was noontime, just when he could have a good word with the boys. "But it's free day," *Red Star*'s gateman reminded him. Also, if he took that bag in he'd need a special pass to bring it out. "Need a pass here to breathe," Andy retorted gayly and deposited the suitcase with him. He'd have a look. Just on the chance somebody'd be inside. Mac or Sasha. Or even ... His pulse skipped. He went to the Foreign Bureau. Empty. The Assembly shop. Locked tight. For crying out loud! Why hadn't he wired ahead when he was coming? No doubt everybody was off on an all-day trip somewhere. Jeez, what a break. He rattled the door, wandered off.

Why should he? Well why not? He'd just have a look. In case. Jeez, try and keep him away.

His steps had turned toward the dieshop. Say, the yards were sure spruced up. Stacks of old iron and shavings were gone. Even the trucks cleared out. What'd been happening anyway?

The door swung easily on its hinges. From within came a loud silence of presses and lathes. Giving a nervous jerk to his coat, he crossed the entrance. Voices! He pulled off his cap, crammed it into his pocket, hastily put it back on. Jeez. How would she greet him? With a casual hello, just as if he'd never been away! Anyway, she'd hardly be here. Yes she would too. Anything doing in the shop, catch her missing out on it. Jeez.

Hands thrust into his sidepockets, he neared her machine. Deserted. Voices came from further down the shop. He touched the gleaming side of her lathe, stroked its curves. Gorgeous creature. Even when still, you felt its power. Trim, set to go. What was the use? He couldn't help it. Come what may ...

Swinging her dustcloth and humming a new air, she came full on him. Her cloth fluttered unnoticed to the floor, her wide eyes darkened as she held out both hands. "Andy! Oh, I'm glad!" She leaned one arm over her machine, her palms pressed against her hot cheeks. He gripped the metal. Hard. Her face told him even more than her words. Stupid things rushed to his lips. Instead he said simply, "Sure. It's me." What an idiot he was! *Nichevo!* Had he seen right? Did she?

Some one called her. She rescued her cloth and nodded, again her old self, friendly, assured. Come on, join their cleanup? Kolya and Alex had proposed they freshen up the shop. With an unsteady grin he followed her down the aisle. Smells of paint, glistening windows, and Kolya on a ladder greeted him. Jeez, his head reeled. Had he imagined it? 'Or hadn't she? Well now hadn't she? He caught up with her. "Jeez, I'd do anything for you, Nat. Anything you say. Even clean cellars." Would he paint lockers? Would he! Ask him something hard. He slipped off his coat, donned a pair of overalls.

Afterwards, Natasha, Kolya and he decided on a stroll down Tverskaya, with a windup at a movie. His suitcase they dropped in his room on the way down. Swinging onto her strap, Natasha tilted her saucy nose and firm chin up to him, relaying the news. He flipped his leather hanger, swayed nearer. Had any girl's lips minus lipstick ever been so red?

Natasha smiled back. What a swell tan he had. Had the sea been too cold for swimming, and was his ankle no patched tire but a good-as-new doubletread? What friends had he made there? The bronze points in her eyes flickered. Oh, but she was forgetting the news! After the scandal over the forgotten ton of steel left all winter under the snow, things had happened fast. First, a new director had been appointed, Feodor Pavlov. The State Trust couldn't have done better by them. Before coming to *Red Star,* Pavlov had been assistant manager of Stalingrad. A former mechanic, he knew trucks inside out. And could he organize! Right away he had set out to make things hum. How many conferences! First those terrible supply depots had been reorganized. Their dieshop was next on the list, and how! Yearly elections of their Party and Union committees were due soon, lucky that Andy was back in time for that.

He tapped a ragtime with his left foot. Yep, this was his lucky day. As they left the car at Pushkin Square, he waved a salute to the old man. Pushkin must have been a swell guy, for all he knew. State lottery signs across the square twinkled at him. Breezy gay Tverskaya. Its curved speedway sloping toward the capital's center was in holiday mood. Crowds moved up and down its sidewalks as though on endless pulleys. The first balloons of the season were out, great huckle and raspberries prancing over the promenaders' heads. Andy bought two. Just for the fun of it, to see them bob by Nat's cap as they flowed happily in the human current toward Sverdlov Square.

19

ANDY had a date to keep, modern style. The girl arranging tickets, everything. Even when he'd been on the rocks he hadn't let Elsie do that. And she hadn't wanted to, either.

This Natasha had a way all her own. She had laughed off his idea of calling by for her. Why, her place was quite out of the way, they could meet at the club.

The club! He refused pointblank. Nothing doing. Not superstitious or anything but taking no chances. One miss had been enough and plenty.

She had given him one of her knockout grins. Why, hadn't he forgotten that! Silly boy. All right, come over to her place, for supper. Come early, by five, as the concert started at seven-thirty. They were going to hear Beethoven. She said it with such a swing that he asked, "Who's he? New ivory tickler? String wizard?" Her laugh was sudden, merry. He joined in, not knowing why. Something catching about Nat's laugh.

Quickly she sobered. "I didn't know either, a few years back. Beethoven, Andy, is one of our great men of all time. You'll hear, feel for yourself." Pausing, she added simply that she'd grown to love him and his music very much.

Supper in the Safonovs' tight quarters appeared to Andy more swanky than any banquet he'd ever taken part in. Warming to his frank pleasure, the old mother forgot her stiff politeness in entertaining this foreigner come all the way from that fabulous America. Prim in her black serge and fresh apron, she had annoyed Natasha by whisking imaginary dust off the chair placed for him.

"Don't, Ma! You'll embarrass him. What you think! Treat him like folks." In fact, the girl was the one embarrassed. Ridiculous, for Mama to bow and scrape to people as she'd done a score of years back, in the rich folks' kitchen! Andy exercised his gift for making himself at home. While Nat's father splashed cold water over his head and hands and the women made last preparations for supper, he initiated twelve-year old Felix into the intricacies of a full-rigged camping knife. The boy, in turn, brought his hammer and three-legged stool made in his school shop, explained how he had won his pin and the red scarf knotted around his neck, and Andy allowed him to give a whittling tryout of all the blades to his knife.

While Felix poured forth his avalanche of questions about America, the visitor's glance strayed about the apartment. Five living in three rooms. A pretty close squeeze. Lace curtains and rubber plants at the window were like the farmhouse, back home. The icons in the corner surprised him. Natasha must hate that. Seeing the old mother in her neatly pinned shawl and knotted worn hands which folded, whenever at rest, over her pumpkin stomach, the nickeled iron bed with its crocheted counterpane and tapestry hanging on the wall behind, made him feel closer to Nat. The homely friendliness of the place warmed him, set him at ease.

"Come on." Felix tugged his hand, pulling him toward the other room. "The best thing I've made you haven't seen." He pointed with a pride he did not trouble to conceal to a three-deck bookcase which he had made for Natasha. Wasn't it a beauty!

Andy halted on the doorsill. Nat's room. Felix strengthened his hold, disappointment verging on fury. Say, wasn't he even going to give it a once over, after all the work it had taken! See how carefully he had joined it together. Slowly Andy let himself he drawn inside. The boy, amazed, looked down. Why, the guy was softpedaling just like somebody was sick. Anyway, he was sure giving the bookcase a thorough going-over.

The shelves of books stood next to Natasha's cot. Andy knew this cot was hers, rather than the one opposite, because the dress she had worn that day lay across the end. She shared the room with her sister, Maria. A girl as unlike Natasha as her straight hair which always seemed in need of a haircut differed from his girl's fluffy waves with their dancing bronze tints. Furtively he examined Natasha's books, her photographs of Krupskaya and Lenin grouped with others over her small worktable. Felix, finding interest in his handiwork exhausted, drew his visitor's attention to the girls' *udarnik* diplomas and Natasha's swimming pictures taken last summer.

The room was not at all what he had imagined! Natasha's touch was everywhere. On the windowsill was a flowering plant, set between brightly colored linen curtains. Counterpanes were blue. Now who would ever have suspected the girl of that! The tapestry by her cot was woven in dull rich blues and greens, with hints of purple.

How many hours and months of her life had she spent here? What did she think about, when she put her books aside, turned off the light? Did she drop right off? Hardly. Her cot faced the window. No doubt she looked out on that rectangle of sky, morning and night, just as he. About what did she think then?

Crap, maybe he had no business here. He turned to leave. Natasha was standing in the doorway. She swooped on Felix with an ardor that nearly cost him his sturdy balance. Supper was ready. But why the deuce, Felix protested, should she get so excited over that!

Andy forced down his food. Everything was extra good after restaurant fare. But something had happened to his appetite. His throat and entire chest felt strange, swollen. Yet fear of incurring her mother's disfavor prodded him on. This was agony, yet there were people heartless enough to joke over it.

Mrs. Safonova made him accept a second bowl of soup. Like his old grandmother, she never accepted a guest's refusal but calmly refilled his plate. Inwardly he cursed himself. What a boner. Honest-to-god porkchops, and you full to the gills. Just before leaving with Natasha he slipped his knife into Felix's side pocket. A gift that ought to bear high reward.

Sverdlov Square, as Natasha and Andy crossed it, was shimmering with mist. Warm seething fog blurred arc lights and electric signs flashing over *Mostorg,* Eastern Kino, and House of Columns. Snatches of gay talk, a woman's scolding drifted by them, then some one peddling cigarettes.

When he took her arm she didn't draw away. She could not, even if she had wanted to. It was like a current pulsing through them, she was welded fast. They scarcely spoke.

The cloakman who took their wraps, a man of patient sideburns and cutaway uniform, nodded after them with a reminiscent smile. He bundled wraps for hundreds of couples, like them, every Spring. Once it had been fine ladies, even princes and counts. These last years were more pleasant. True, tips were less, but he no longer depended on that.

The drama went on, and still he bundled wraps.

Their seats were in the center. Andy veered his gaze around the horseshoe tiers of balconies dotted with human faces which diminished to mere specks at the very top. Natasha waved to acquaintances, then pointed out to him the boxes where royalty had once sat.

Hundreds of transparent crystals quivered in brilliantly lit chandeliers swung from the far ceiling. The orchestra was tuning up. Quietly the lights faded. The audience stirred, hushed. Belated conversationalists were roughly and promptly shushed. Natasha, lips parted, set her gaze on the spot where the conductor would mount his stand, lift his baton for the opening notes. Andy felt her expectancy, and the suspense of every one waiting with them in the darkened hall.

His chest hurt him, contracting until he couldn't take a free breath. His senses strained for he knew not what. He was uneasy. After all, this classical stuff was a new one on him. Natasha said that Beethoven in his Fifth Symphony had put all the big feelings of man in his struggle with life and death. Like an epic, she called it. Maybe he wouldn't get it. Let Nat down. Was she testing him? He sat stiffly, muscles taut.

The conductor, his swallow tails flying, bowed right and left as a swift clapping of hands swept from floor to galleries. His baton lifted. Again the audience hushed, waited. Natasha slipped lower into her seat, her head resting against its back. In the darkness Andy could gaze at her, undisturbed. Her eyes were closed. She seemed to have forgotten her surroundings, everything. He wanted to grasp her arm, call her back. Tell her this wasn't fair. Take him along. He wondered. Was he going to be sorry he had come?

From the darkness the opening notes struck their sharp claps of thunder in clean downward strokes. Fate, or was it life, knocked her devastating blows against man's breast. Again, like a warning. A challenge. Open up! You! No denying me. Come on, catch hold! Then, answering sweep of violins that surged and rose to a crashing impact of cymbals.

Andy's wet palms gripped the arms of his chair. He must understand, follow through. He must.

He was back in the open fields as a boy in Virginia. Caught in one of the Atlantic Coastline's fierce storms. Alone, surprised with his tin can of fishing worms, on Sunday. The Lord was sending his wrecking powers to punish him. Terrified, he cowed by a patch of briars. Blinding flashes seared the weeping air. He winced lower, covered his eyes. His earthy hands clapped his ears in a fearful waiting for the bolts to come. Halfcrazed, he had fled before these wild elements that threatened to strike him down like a broken rag-weed.

Only later he had learned to love storms. Tramp through them, drenched to the skin. Take each clap as it came with clean fierce pleasure. A grand, fearful sight. The whole earth racked in labor and him a part of it.

The music rolled on. Chords and counter-themes swelling, rounding out with horns and drums; now descending, their deep rumblings burrowing beneath the earth. All the while the main theme was repeating its majestic tattoo on man's bared chest.

Andy was back on the belt. Speeding, speeding, fighting

to keep up. Suddenly flung off. Pounding Detroit's streets, searching. The question *why? why?* beat on his hungry stomach, his burning head.

With a start he realized he had been pressing hard against Natasha's arm. Her fingers circled his wrist. In the dim light he glimpsed the brown sheen of her eyes. "You like it?" she whispered. Her eyes closed, but she didn't take away her arm.

The first movement was over. Then the *Andante*, breathing deep as a sea swell. And the *Finale*, tearing through your chest.

It was finished. They blinked at the harsh lights, startled to find themselves within four ordinary walls. They joined the procession circling in the outer rooms, but the light talk and buffet with its iced cakes and tea seemed queer, off-key.

As they found a quiet corner she looked up at him. "Well?" Her blue silk and wool sweater brought out all the copper glints in her skin and hair. "Well?"

"Great," he answered. "Only I don't know whether I got all he was driving at." He told her about his time in the storm and later, in Detroit. How the music had brought them back, but in a different way.

That was natural, she thought. Beethoven too had been a man who loved storms. He tramped in them, they said, and wrote some of his best music that way. Some of his great themes had been taken direct from nature. Of what had she thought? The hard years of Civil War and famine, when she was still a little girl. Then these last years, the heroics of their *Pyatiletka*.

"Beethoven," she confided, "is one of ours. That's how we feel. He's not afraid of big themes, and to build on a vast scale. Think what he might have written for our time! He was a thinker, a revolutionist. One of our own."

Not even their Russian composers like Tschaikovsky and Rimsky-Korsakoff were known and loved so well. It wasn't too much to say that the workers in the big centers these last years had come to know Beethoven. Concerts of his music were given regularly not only in the main auditoriums

244

but in factory clubs as well. Always they explained the man and his work. That was how she had come to love Beethoven.

The Fifth and Ninth symphonies were her favorites. She had heard them over and over until she knew each phrase as it came. To her too, they were creations of the storm. The whole world, as Andy said, rocking. Rocking with crisis, death of the old order, birth pangs of the new. You could almost see man, all of laboring humanity struggling back from a dreadful hell. Wasn't it true? Summoning courage to dare all. And in the *andante* and *finale* movements he did find courage. One grand *finale,* way cleared for the new!

Anyway, that's how she saw it.

The warning bell sounded and they reëntered the amphitheater as the orchestra assembled and began tuning up.

This time it was Brahms. Again the music charged into him. Like a rough sea mauls a swimmer. He put his mouth close to her ear, her warm hair brushed his cheek. What was it he heard? Not exactly the notes the orchestra was playing. Now he heard it and now he didn't. Something he couldn't say what. Deepdown yet so high, almost out of sight.

She smiled. Overtones. "Good, I hear them too."

They walked the long trip home. Who wanted to rustle a crowded car, after that! She had forgotten all her practical objections earlier to his seeing her home. The misty night had lifted, filled with great music. And she and Andy were together, walking, arms locked, under a star-crazy sky.

He'd never been to opera? Oh, they must go. To *Faust, Eugene Onegin,* and *La Bohème.* He'd like it, he said. In the States, working stiffs like him didn't go in for opera. They left that to Millionaire Row. Say, if he'd tried to crash the Metropolitan the boys'd ragged him stiff. Not that he ever thought of it. They'd guyed him he was going highbrow or wop. Of the common people, only kikes and dagos stood in those long lines for rush seats in the peanut.

Since the depression these had dropped off. Breadlines taken their place. Sure, he'd try anything once and when could they go?

He found himself talking to her about things he'd never said to anybody, not even himself. Girls sometimes got you that way. Even about his mouth harp and wanting to play a fiddle.

"Why not?" she countered, join an orchestra class at the plant.

"You forget," he told her, "I'm going in for big game." Engineer. Boy, for once he was going in for what he liked. No more grammar but machines. He had visited technical classes with Sasha and Mac. They dealt with motors trucks and the things that he'd fooled around with since a kid. That was no dry-as-dust study. More like play. Higher mathematics, from what Nat said, was a tough one. But then he'd never been so punk at figures.

"Andy," she asked him, "you think music'll make you a bad engineer? Stupid! Perhaps I'll join the class myself."

He parted with her on her doorstep, wondering why he hadn't the nerve to tell her goodnight proper. Better wait than risk being too soon. But not long. Why hadn't he told her about Elsie? Would she understand? They still had a lot of things to talk over. But he was certain it was going to work out.

He neared the factory. Its sheer cliffs loomed high in the splotched green night. *Red Star.* Old buddy that never slept. Beating out a new life for them all. *Nasha,* that's how his pals put it. *Nasha,* ours. He knew now how Nat or Mikhail felt when they said it. *Nasha.* His warm glow when Sasha had told him, "You too—*nasha.*"

How was it he'd ever felt alone here? An outsider? *Ours. . . .*

He felt something stir in him. Deepdown. His mind, heart, body reaching out. He was twenty-eight. Queer, for he was just beginning to grow up.

As he switched on his light, the dull tint of the cablegram leaped at him from the rug. He walked around it, stared fearfully. What? Elsie? The old folks? No, Elsie! He knew, even before reading it, what was there. The zigzag patterns of the rug plucked at his eyes.

At last he reached for the square of paper, tore up its side. It read:

LOST JOB DESPERATE COME HOME OR SHALL I COME THERE
ELSIE

20

SASHA had troubled over his friend all morning. Andy wasn't like himself. Reddened eyelids smarting for want of sleep, he tightened bolts and adjusted steering gears with such listlessness that his partner forgot the jaunty spring outside.

"Andy, you feel sick?" he inquired anxiously. The laconic tone of his mate's, "Nope, just a touch of spring fever" was no bracer. With a cheerless whistle, he fell silent. This was no matter of nut-dropping, a lost hammer. His comrade was in a real funk. Probably bad news from home? There was that Italian working on motors who'd wept over the letter telling about his little sister's accident in the saltmine. And the German, Fritz, storming because his brother in Hamburg had been cut off the dole. Now, Andy. And he, Sasha, not knowing what to say. "Bad news from home?" he ventured. No answer.

Sasha rallied. Had to bust through, somehow, devil take it! Next week, he reminded, was shop elections. Had Andy written up his proposals and list of candidates, put them in the box? Again no comeback. Strange, for only yesterday his workmate had been keen on it, asking dozens of questions. And they'd chawed on about the race to go over by the holidays.

As they sent their righted chassis on its way and received the next, Sasha tried once more. "I miss our old Mikhail, don't you?" Andy nodded. He actually did. Guess managing the whole assembly shop kept him on the jump. He had to spread his time, the conveyor saw less of him. Must say, though, the works were running smoother. Jams on the belt nearing zero.

Old Mikhail. Tired pits beneath his eyes. Driving his body beyond the last ditch. Maybe he should talk with him? Unload everything. Like to Uncle Jem. The cable burned through Andy's pocket into the flesh. Elsie. Poor little kid. She had played straight with him. In her own way. She wasn't to blame, was she, if her ideas were crankwise, and he ... (Damn this automatic, trying to leap out of hand. Guess he'd been giving her too much pressure!) Elsie. Poor baby. Couldn't let her down, now. But wasn't there some way?

Hunger. Hunger canvassing America. Elsie caught. On the breadline. Down and out. The breath fluttering in her soft baby throat. He just couldn't. Nat was able to stand on her own.

At Sasha's reminding cluck, he fastened iron clamps of the sling on a fresh chassis. He couldn't. That was all. He wanted the cream, everything. Leave the kid not so much as skimmed milk. Hadn't she stood by him? Her Big Time. What could he do? If his brains'd only come out the fog, let him think! Today he must tell Natasha. Decide the right thing.

Lunchgong. He sensed his mate slipping an arm through his, giving it an affectionate squeeze.

Mikhail's stooped look, as they met him in the passageway, startled them. "See here!" Sasha urged, "you ought to take off for a rest. Quick. We can't have you sick." The very thought frightened him. If need be, he was going to the director about it, himself.

Mikhail dismissed it with an abrupt shake of his head. Rest now? Ridiculous! Feodor Pavlov, the director, had already suggested it. He had refused. To leave just then when things were getting under way, in proper fashion? Poppycock. Tired? A little. But he was not such an old fellow. He had more pep in him than these young chaps thought. After May first, with seventy trucks running off the conveyor, fine! He'd be ready to take his month's rest with a will.

Sasha's arms wriggled helplessly. What to say? But to risk losing him. Outside the spring was jaunty. To the devil with it! His pal, in a funk. His old comrade, washed up. In short, he was going to speak with the director himself. Put it straight. But who'd quit now, right at the crux!

Mikhail was waddling hurriedly into the motors assembly.

And Andy, where was he off to? Refusing lunch, saying he had to see some one, and quick. Outside the spring was jaunty but— Suddenly Sasha's eyes whole face twinkled. And to think he'd been worried! Blockhead. His beltmate was heading for the dieshop. That's how it was. Nothing but one of those lovers' quarrels that came with the spring. Lydia and he'd had their share of them, too. They soon blew over. Wheezing a breezy trill through his rounded lips, Sasha raced ahead for his tardy lunch.

Andy drew Natasha aside. Overhead, while the air sang under her breath, the clouds were playing tag with the sun. "I gotta talk to you. Right away. No, it can't wait."

His misery seized hold of her. Beneath his tan he was uncommonly pale. She braced herself for she knew not what.

Behind rows of trucks waiting to be taken for their test run, they found a secluded corner. Their polished grayness and nickel trimmings gleamed restlessly, as though saying, "Mind you, it's high time we were off." Along brick walls fluttered red streamers, lively with slogans. Natasha slipped her headscarf free, to catch the glorious beat of the returning sun. Her bared head shone with rippling fired lights, her cheeks flushed with the first marks of summer brown. High spirits of healthy youth coursed through her, driving out the fears Andy had raised. It was spring, spring! All morning, at her lathe, she'd been humming themes of last night's music and fingering gently the fine texture of their homeward walk.

Her glance traveled with quick sympathy over his haggard face. That lock of his was straggling over his eyes, tempting her to brush it back, muss his towhead which gleamed like white silver in this harsh glare. Well, what was it? Why did he stand there, staring that queer way, not saying a word? Secretly she felt nothing could be really bad on a day like this.

Andy jerked at his collar. He wanted to tell, ask her a million things. But his throat had gone dead on him. Closed tight. Wordless, he held out the cablegram. She read slowly, then raised her glance to his with an instant warmth that smote him through. "Elsie. Your sister. Poor girl, bring her here. We do everything to make her happy."

Her breath caught on his hoarse words. Not his sister?

She slumped to a seat on the running board. Not his sister. Then...

Wordless, miserable, Andy braced himself against the fender. Natasha had hit it right off. Bring her here. She must think him a skunk. As he was. *Bring her here.* Smells of fresh paint and gasoline were making him choke up.

Not his sister. Painfully her thought grappled with it. Why had he never told her? Last evening... She must have been mistaken. She had thought. Oh, that odor of gas was insufferable... After all, what had he said or done to make her think. Suddenly she loathed him, wanted to run away. Not his sister. He loved this Elsie!

Overhead the clouds were playing tag with the sun.

Andy moved closer, seeking her gaze. "What shall I do?"

She kept her eyes averted. She must be calm. Her voice . . . She couldn't make the words come. "Tell me about Elsie."

It was hard to follow him. His words were all mixed. She must think him a cad. He wanted to do the square thing. Elsie, poor kid. If she stayed in America, anything might happen. If Nat was in that fix, she'd buck up. Take it fighting. Not Elsie. The kid had stuck by him. Still, he had hoped... Again he sought her eyes. "Oh, Nat, you know how I feel, don't you?"

She kept her eyes lowered, afraid of the foaming sea within. "Yes...I understand." (Why should she feel so tired. Sky, buildings, life, turned a mud gray. Like a blotting paper run over them.... Andy hadn't played straight. Just a flirt. She should have known. Cocky Yankee. She must get away from here. This gas...Oh, to be by herself. Get away. Swim hard, against a stiff current. So hard that nothing mattered. Just to pit her strength against its running force.) "Why do you need to ask me?" she said, cold with fury. "Bring her here."

He colored resentfully. So it was as easy as that.

Faltering, Natasha tried to repeat her earlier phrase, "We will do everything to—" broke off . . . Would this girl fit in, she wondered dully, be good for Andy? . . . After all, why was she sitting here. Why didn't she leave?

He slipped closer. "Aw, but Nat!"

She rose, walked aside. He came nearer, touching her shoulder. "What about us, you?"

Natasha misunderstood. Damn his nerve! Head up, her short laugh cut him across the eyes. "About me? Don't worry. Thank you. I manage quite well by myself."

She was gone. He wormed the toe of his boot in the gravel. The air's joyless ditty swirled around him. Spring, damn bitch . . . Nat expected it of him. How could she take it . . . She didn't care. Not like he did. Too many big things in her life. In a month she would have forgotten him, while he went on . . .

Aw, hell. He must do it. Quick. Before his courage gave out. Even if he had to ask off, go right away to the post-office. No, he'd stick out the afternoon. If she could.

Thoroughbred, Natasha. A real friend. Better if he went away. Asked for a transfer to Nizhni. Or Stalingrad. Any place, but where she was.

Andy returned the cable to his pocket, tossed his unlit cigarette aside. Reëntering the assembly shop, he had to face Sasha's teasing smile and broad hints about these quarrels that come with the Spring.

Natasha fixed her blurred sight on her whirring lathe. Not his sister. What a young fool she had been. But last night, she had thought. She had been so sure. Even before that. Trusting fool! Gullible, an easy mark. Well, he'd see.

Mechanically she examined her finished work, and started. The last five bolts she had threaded were simply *brak*—ruined. This would never do. She was making damage like some raw beginner. These would go on the blackboard. And she could never explain them, never. Neither to her brigade, nor to herself. Fool! Fool.

She felt numb, ill. Perhaps she should ask to go home. By tomorrow, she would have herself in hand. Five bolts *brak*, her record spoiled. If only she might swim, swim hard all afternoon, this numbness would go, her brain clear. ...Not his sister.

Her lathe frowned at her. Self-centered girl! Mind wandering, careless, spoiling state goods. Come, come, the way out is not that. Buck up. Work! Work!

Natasha beat impatiently on its drum. Her machine knew only work. She was human. But she'd not ask off. She wasn't really sick. What was one person's problems? Besides if she once gave way ... That madonna-faced girl in the picture, no wonder Andy loved her. And she needed him. Natasha, you little fool, you got to be sensible. Take it standing, get on with the job.

Her flowered blouse shaking, Zena came over to her friend's lathe. Natasha was coming to the meeting at the nursery tonight? Ashamed, the young woman slipped her machine rag over the spoiled bolts. Zena would surely win the competition today.

Everybody had noticed the change in Zena. Her surly defiance had slipped off little by little like an old coat. No mistaking it, a new quality was creeping into her face. And now this nursery business kept her in a perpetual stew.

No, Natasha said aloud, she couldn't come. She had a blinding headache, and was going immediately to bed. Just this once ... (She must be alone. Think, weep it out: get hold of herself.)

What, Zena exploded, such questions coming up, and Nat letting a headache keep her home! Rubbish. Some good arguing would help drive it away.

"I know." Natasha answered miserably. "But there *are* times ... Oh well, you are right," she amended hastily. "Sure, I'll come." Good. Lathe, Zena, the whole shop not leaving her a brooding minute. Good ...But how could she get through the afternoon? Long evening?

In a month, May Day. She had even imagined they might

march through the Square together, part of thousands cheering, singing. His and their first May Day. The best of them all. Now ... Well, what of it? She would march, as always. And he—maybe with the other.

The drip-drip of the golden machineoil sounded awful today. Her head was screwing tighter, tighter. How was she going to get through the long afternoon? Would the sky and earth ever give her back their colors? Every day sing its old heady tunes? Well, such things happened. She wasn't the only one. People, life went on. By tomorrow. Perhaps it would be better if she went away. Spent her summer repairing tractors in the Ukraine. If the Party agreed it was wise to send her. She'd tell them. ... Well, what would she tell them? If need be, she would tell them straight out. Maxim, Mikhail, would understand. Drat it, her sight was smeary, she couldn't judge whether the bolt's thread was true, or not.

Swearing affably, Philip Boardman rushed by with the new superintendent, Boris Kornev. This man knew men and dies by God, and how to work.

Natasha nodded after them. The dieshop was pulling out of the hole. Her lathe turned the next thread with beautiful precision. She took up a fresh bolt, fastened it in place, threw on the power. She could never go to hear the Fifth Symphony again. But she was beginning to swim.

Andy walked immediately from work to the telegraph office. Three blanks were spoiled before he had a clear message: NOT RETURNING COME HERE AWAIT MY LETTER CABLE ANSWER COLLECT. The telegrapher took the fatal slip from him as though it were a mere wiring of birthday greetings!

His letter took him most of the night. Elsie must come with her eyes open. Prepared to make it a go. There were long pauses, spoiled sheets, dashes of cold water over his wrists and face, and long swigs of hot coffee toward morning.

DEAR ELSIE:

I got your cable. By now you got mine. It's tough you lost your job. I know. Before you decide on coming here

254

or not, I want to put all the facts before you, Let you add the pluses and minuses, strike the balance for yourself.

For get it straight, Kiddo, I don't plan on coming back. That is, any time soon. Maybe not ever.

I'll tell you why. Not so much I got a steady job here I like. Three meals a day, and a sure roof over my head. That's a lot, but not the main thing. Not even that I don't have to worry over old age in the poor house, doctor's bills, and all that. No, when you come right down to it, it's not just that.

There's something going on here. Big. I want to stay in on it.

But I didn't mean to start off this way. Because these ain't the things you'll notice, right off. What will hit you are the pesky nuisances, red tape and a whole carload of little things that'll take time to shove them all in the ashcan. (He spared nothing. Better to let her find it not so bad as he painted, than come unprepared, then raise scenes.) We won't have a house to ourselves like you planned on, just a room, and later on, a small apartment, soon as the building program is carried through. And when! Anyway, it'll be ours for life, nobody can give us the air, and you can doll it up any way you like. That is, with such stuff as there is in the stores. There ain't much choice. On grub either. No grapefruit, bananas, but kid there's ice cream. And movies, circus, radios, but not much jazz or dancing our kind. Plenty of sports. (Jeez, Elsie'd think them old-fashioned as all getout. He broke his penpoint, swore, fitted in another. Hell, these things came first with the kid. Well, she better know now than later.)

One thing, Elsie. When you get a closeup on it, everyday, you'll find working stiffs like me count here. No kidding. Office girls, too. You won't have to sling the dog to make a splash. I'm starting in to train as an engineer. Honest, no kidding.

Who knows, plenty my kind are running entire works. But don't think this will mean our own car, and things like that. Autos over here belong to the state. Anyways, a guy can live not so tough and every year a little better. And have a swell of a time to boot. That is, if you take to it, laugh off the bumps. There's a Big Kick in it, but you gotta be here to find out about that for yourself.

(The letter, when he read it over, struck him as pretty bum. Cold. He must end it off, right. Unsteadily he wrote)

If you come, honey, I'll do everything to make you happy.
With lots of from your BigTime.

ANDY.

P.S. Don't bring a trunk.

He slipped it into the mailbox, set his alarm for six. So what? Was he doing the right thing, or being a plain fool? Yet if he hadn't given her her chance, he would have felt a rotter all his life.

Natasha tossed on her cot dreaming of bolts spinning crooked threads, Beethoven's music pounding the stars, and Andy jeering at her over his shoulder as he jigged the Charleston with the madonna-faced slip of a girl.

The days dragged by on leaden feet. Every evening Andy opened his door with growing dread of what he might find. A week went by. Any day now. Any day.

He wanted to go over to Mac's, and he didn't. He worked overtime, furiously, until even Sasha objected. "Say, what's the rush?" "Well, we gotta swing it, ain't we?" "Sure, but what the devil!" Afterwards, wandering along the polished ebony river, putting off going home, he met Gus Heindricks and his wife Freda on their way to visit friends. "Old Hothead, by Jeez! And just the same." But tonight he had no time for the guy's agitated dirge about "Is this Socialism?" His muddled features gave him the pip.

After a bristling halfhour of give and take, Gus told Andy he was the kind that'd beat the drum wherever he was, and Andy retorted that his friend's *anti* habit would see him into his grave. The chassis man humped his right shoulder and looked at the toolmaker with fresh eyes. "Say, Hothead, you're a swell chap and all that. Know what's the trouble with you? I told you before. Your feet ain't on the ground."

"Is that so! You! Of all things, you! You telling me!"

"Yep, buddy. That's it. Straight." Too tired to notice their arguing, he walked on. Poor hams. It really was tough. Gus was a swell guy.

That night, there were no fatal white squares under his door.

Andy filed into *Red Star's* club auditorium with Sasha and a couple of other conveyormen. A local band puffed lustily. Damn if the place wasn't broke out with banners, the stage all decked out with palms and posters of big shots. Floor and galleries filled to the brim.

Mac, with his pals Vasiliev and Pavel, took seats right in front. Lotta women and girls too. Mac was beaming like a clown. "Another high-water mark. Say boy, here's where we finish our cleanup."

"Oh yeah?" But Andy knew his comeback lacked punch. For once he was jolted out of himself. Swept along with the rest. Shop elections and him one of the belt's delegates. Imagine, him.

Old Vasiliev buffed his glasses. Ahead of them was a long day's work. This past year's record had to be mulled over thoroughly before tasks were set and men and women selected for the one ahead.

Andy strained to locate Natasha. Yes, there she was. Sitting between Lydia and Maxim. Out of the sea of faces hers swam toward him. She smiled uncertainly, turned away. His chest pounded. Sunk. Here they were. In on the same thing but as far off as hell.

All through the long hours of reports and discussion he tried hard to keep his mind from slipping. Sometimes Mac leaned around to translate a point he thought Andy might have missed. But Sasha's beltmate was letting nothing by him. Were they lighting into the old union committee! Talking cold turkey.... Anyway, what was it? Not so much what these men and women were saying. The slant behind it all. The Plan. It jumped at you from their eyes, put edge on their kickbacks, punch in their fists. "Five Years in Four." Soon done too. After this, a whole string of Five Year Plans. Phoney how it got you. Took your mind off your troubles. (But Nat, what about us, you?) Set your jaw.

Intermission for supper and smokes. Delegates stretched

their cramped muscles and bunched in excited groups. Finally elections. Andy heard Mac's name called, saw his friend go white. But say, he'd vote with a hurrah! For old Vasiliev too and Nat. Some of the others he didn't know, have to take Mac's word on that.

When Misha was put up, several took the floor against him. He was too gruff with workers. Let him work in the rationalization department, he'd do a good job on BRIZ. But on the shop committee, no. Vasiliev and Mac defended him roundly but he was voted down by a good margin. Andy saw that Mac was more disappointed than if he'd been knocked down, himself. "Never mind, *tovarisch.*" Mac pressed Misha's arm. "On your new BRIZ job, you'll show us all." He knew now why Misha had been expelled from the University and Party: for high-handed methods of dealing with the peasantry when sent to the village on his practical work.

Misha's reply carried no rancor. The vote was correct. "Our masses are no fools. They're right to demand I prove myself to them." Maxim and other Party men had spoken with him often, of late. He had been entrusted with important work in BRIZ. In time, with his comrades' help, he'd conquer his nasty ways, make a full comeback. Yes, the vote was right.

Elections over and the new committee installed, Ned Folson said solong to Mac and the gang, pulled his cap over his closely cropped head and ran for a car. Tomorrow night he was giving a party for his friend Wilcox to celebrate his opening in "Othello." Lucky the foreign store remained open until late, for he needed supplies for their pow-wow.

Standing in line for the cashier, he wrote up his list: cigarettes, wine, candies, iced cake. Whew, this party'd cost a pretty rouble, just when he needed to save. Well, opening nights came once in a lifetime. In front of him stood a man whom he knew by sight, an American engineer from the dieshop by the name of Crampton. With him was a sour apple, must be his wife. That pompous kind made him want to jab a sliver into the seat of his full pants. Pity no banana peels in Russia.

He started to drop back in line, just to get away. Catfish, why should he? It was late, and a crowd of lastminute shoppers flooding the store.

"Henry," the woman was saying, "don't you think you ought to talk with Bella again? I can't do a thing with her."

"All right." The engineer looked around impatiently. "Oh I say, George," he called, "run over and get me a box of cigarettes will you? I'll hold your place."

Ned's head spun. George! Errand boy. He gave no sign of hearing, but bent lower over his list. Henry Crampton repeated his demand in a louder voice. "Oh I say, George—"

Ned's notebook cracked with a bang to the floor. Two black coals flashed up as his voice boomed across customers' heads and counters. "Who in hell you calling George!"

The engineer stepped back. Edith smothered a low cry. This black ape dared insult her husband. And Henry was apologizing! "Now look here, I meant no offense. Just a civil question. How'd I know your name wasn't George?" (Everybody was looking their way, better not have a scene. He had enough on his hands as it was, his position too risky. You never knew when these damn Russians would make a scandal over nothing. In Detroit he'd have given this dirty nigger what was coming to him. Knocked him down, had him locked up. But in this lousy burg a white man got no support.)

Ned was not letting up. George eh? With his kind, it was George shine my shoes, George hustle my bags, George hoe my corn. A blanket name for a pair of black arms and a loaded back.

Edith pulled her husband out of line toward the door.

Ned's voice trailed them, "My name's Edward Folson and don't you forget it, Mister Henry Crampton! You dumb fish, in this country that George stuff don't go!"

On his way home the funny side of the thing struck him. Mac and Wilcox'd think it a scream. Of course maybe he shouldn't have lost his temper on that fat buzzard but....

As he passed near the plant entrance, he noticed Alex Turin leaving by a side gate. Phoney, not the fellow's shift.

Ned caught up with him to ask casually what brought the Russian to the works so late?

Turin veered to one side. Just his fortune, to have that charcoal face pounce on him out of the dark. He had wanted particularly to keep this night's visit a secret. His reply was taciturn: he had come to bring a promised parcel to a friend, that was all.

Ned inquired further. (Somehow he had never liked this bug.) Funny, delivering it so late, wasn't it? And where did his friend work? Had he come recently or been there a long time? Alex Turin answered in monosyllables, at random. This black devil meant no good. Clearly, he was becoming suspicious. Most inconvenient. All must be ready in the next days. Katia seemed more open to reason, and now this fool was poking his thick nose into affairs not his concern. It was better, he decided, to go over to the attack, carry on some questioning himself. Where, he asked aloud, might the other be coming from, loaded with bundles? "Oh you live well, you foreigners!" And this was his corner. He bade his companion a cool goodnight, walked off rapidly, keeping within the dusky shadows patterned along the walk.

Ned emptied his arms and pockets on his desk, his brow furrowed. This fellow bore watching. What could he have wanted about the plant, this late at night? Lame excuse, about the parcel. Of course, if it had been Sasha or Mac, he'd not give it a second thought. Alex Turin though never gave a hang for anything, as far as he could see. He had never liked the man, for no good reason. Nothing tangible against him, but his hide was too thick. Too damn polite!

Lately several motors had stalled: sand in their filters, or pistons mysteriously broken. It had never been Turin's car, nor he involved. Still, somebody was responsible. They had to find out who. Mac had told him about the loosened bolt on MAG. Some underhanded work was sure going on somewhere. Evidently a handful of bad declassed elements had crept into *Red Star* who needed weeding out. But who? Tomorrow he was going to report Alex's visit, have the guy checked up.

It was some time before he was able to fall asleep. Just

dozing off, he jumped up, hurried into his clothes and over to the plant. None of the men on the night shift whom he asked had seen Turin about. The foreman was certain that he had not been around. One blind alley.... Remembering an acquaintance in the supply shop, Ned went there. Yes, a man similar to Turin's description had come around midnight to see a laborer named Peter who worked there. Turin had been in several times in the last week, the men seemed close friends.

At cross purposes, Ned went for breakfast. Alex Turin's story, queerly enough, was a straight one. Maybe there was nothing in his hunch. Sometimes your imagination ran away with you. After all, you couldn't spot a crook by the shape of his nose! Still ... And this Peter, could he be the same one that Mac had told him about, who was taken off the machines for spoiling MAG!

In the shed's runway he passed Andy. The chap looked seedy, off his wind. Well, he felt the same way, after a letter from home. Things were going from bad to worse with Mammy and his brother's family. He had to push arrangements to bring them here.

Just as the conveyor began its measured click forward, Alex Turin appeared. Ned caught his eye on him when he thought he wasn't looking. A sly one! Up to something, sure as his name was Ned. He was going to keep his eye peeled for this baby, catch him with his pants down. Trying to lame their trucks, was he, play a fast game, hold up the Plan? They'd boot him a fast one to where he belonged.

> *Oh say can you see*
> *By the dawn's early light?*

Edith Crampton quavered uncertainly on the high notes. Sternly belligerent, she eyed her two offspring. Henry Junior piped with gusto but Bella's lips barely moved. They were parched, stiff. She kept thrusting out her dry tongue in an effort to moisten them but it did no good. Leaning over, Edith took her young daughter by the arm. Sing, or she would be made to feel it. Sing, repeat the Lord's Prayer, salute the flag. (The stars and stripes had been draped near her favorite icon.)

During those years which she never liked to recall, years when she had served as grammar school teacher in the charred plains of Minnesota, Edith Crampton had led forty tow heads through the service each morning until she knew every phrase and motion by heart. Even on the words of that octave-jumping hymn she never faltered. But her daughter! "Sing, Bella!" Obstinate child, in danger of God knew what! She scrutinized the girl's blotched set countenance. This queer ungainly child, just beginning her teens, had become a foreigner to her. She must break her stubborn will, teach her a lesson, however belated, that she would never forget.

Gracious heavens, could it be too late! Edith's nerves were still quivering from the chance discovery: disobedient Bella had secretly joined that Red Boy and Girl Scouts known as Pioneers. What had she done, she inwardly moaned, why had God sent this on her? Had she been neglecting the children? She twisted her damp handkerchief into a rumpled ball. "Now, Bella, the Twenty-third Psalm. You are to repeat it alone, unaided, until you have done it perfectly, without mistakes." She waited while Bella swallowed hard.

Henry snickered, gleefully jabbed his sister with his fist. Served her right, the Bolshie. Tatler! He had squared accounts. Bella's head jerked like a balloon on its stem. Her mouth opened, shut, but no sound came. Her mother's grip on her wrists tightened painfully. She winced, moistening her lips. "The Lord is my Shepherd—" Try as she might, the words would not come. Humiliation and stark fear bowed her slight frame. She had wanted a good time, to go to camp. "The Lord is—" Coward! Wasn't she big enough to have any rights? Suddenly the words came. She whirled on her mother, eyes streaming, "I hate you!" And on Henry, "You nasty toad!"

Edith's hand flew out, catching Bella on the ear. "I'll teach you to be insolent!" Sobbing, the girl stumbled across the hall and locked herself in her room. Oh, was there no one to help her? She'd run away, anything. Her mouth tasted of black ink, copper pennies. She could never face them at the club again. A turncoat. Squealer! She detested herself most of all.

Her brother smirked, slinking off before his mother's anger reached to him. He was quits. Bella was in for it, sure.

Stretched face downward on the divan, Edith tried to regain her composure. It was ghastly, to feel hate for your own child. They must leave this terrible country. Even desolate Minnesota was preferable to this. Her first born, such a sweet trusting baby ... bewitched, turning into a Red!

Yes, even Minnesota. There at least were Sunday Schools, civilization.... The cords above her eyes drew tighter. She called Berta. Let the woman bring her aspirin from the bathroom, dip her handkerchief in camphor. No answer. Another calamity that momentarily she had forgotten. Berta had given notice and left that morning. Now Edith must begin all over again with some fresh-cheeked girl from the country who, in six months' time, would learn Moscow impertinence and take herself off to the factory.

After all she had done for Berta! There was ingratitude. These Russians said a great deal about labor, yet the servant problem was worse here than anywhere else in the world. She would get the aspirin herself.

As for Bella: the young miss should have no food until she had apologized to her mother. Her mother, who had gone to death's door to bring her into the world, suckled her, taught her to walk. Her own mother, sworn at, defied! How horrible the world was. Just wait until Henry Senior came home. He would know how to deal with Bella. God, what a tragic muddle was living....

Henry Crampton swung his ponderous body through the die shop. Where was that skunk? His jowls shook furiously as he walked, his pale eyes blanched to a murky white. Each man he asked said that Meester Boardman had just been there but gone. Their swearing *Amerikanets* was all over. The engineer no doubt would find him down the line. Crampton snorted. Hiding, eh? He'd smoke him out. (To think what a cool turndown he'd just got. That new superintendent so damn polite, but talking cold turkey. Thought they'd get away with it, eh? He'd show 'em.)

Philip had gone to the supply depot to verify the specifications of some particular steel he required. Henry Crampton shook the plant's latest paper under his curved nose. "This is your business!"

There was no pretense in Boardman's surprise. What did he mean? The other sneered. Playing innocent, eh? Here, look his treachery in the face. He smacked the paper. Philip stared. There at the top of the second page, the title leaped at him: IS THIS THE WAY TO WORK? Rapidly he ran through it. The whole matter was there: useless dies purchased, wrong drawings made, and his own crankshaft proposal that had been botched beyond use, the whole works. So that's what Maxim.... An irrepressible grin lifted the corners of his thin mouth. "I didn't write the article. Those initials, M.K.V., are not mine. But what's wrong with it?" The facts struck him as pretty straight.

Crampton snarled. Of course Boardman had written it. "If we Americans are going to play this dirty game, I've a few things to let out against you, myself."

Philip shot a contemptuous glance over his superior's bulging figure. "Pure bluff," he retorted. Crampton had nothing on him. No telling, though, what low tricks he might try. "I told you I didn't write the article, and I didn't. But I agree with it. What are you going to do about that?" Swerving, he walked off before he took his fists to the ass. He was anxious to get at making the correct die.

He made a gay hi-sign at the trucks lined up, leaving soon for their test run. Swell trucks, needed like the deuce. At last things were moving. This ought to mean Crampton's finish. Whew, work free of that jackass would be great.

Edith sprang to meet her husband as he came through the doorway and poured out her story. His scowl darkened, lips sucking rapidly on an imaginary cigar. He couldn't believe it. His Bella. Red, was she! What the impudent girl needed was an oldfashioned dressing down. Some sense put into her. He knocked on her door. "Bella, it's Father! Open at once." Edith drew herself together haughtily. When the door opened, Bella should look full upon her mother.

Drumming the panel Henry turned to his wife. "Well, you're getting your wish, we're leaving. Quick, in two weeks. What? What in hell you think! Plain enough, I'm fired. Through. Damn it, Bella, unlock this door! My contract not renewed. I tell you! Well, what's the matter? Grin, can't you? Holy—" He rattled the doorknob, placed his boot against the frame. "Bella, open up. It's Father. Have you lost your mind? Open, or I'll break in." The kid was pretty big for it. He hadn't touched her in two years. Little Bella. He couldn't believe it, cursing her own Mother! What she needed ... He had to. The only way to get any sense into her. Take her across his knees, wallop her, thrash the Red Menace right out of her. Forever.

God, in the States this'd never happened.

Suddenly the door gave. Bella's terrorized face was pressed against the doorsill. "Stop, stop! I'll open." She fled to the far corner, her father in pursuit. Edith placed her frail palms over her ears. Perhaps she shouldn't let him—

"Oh, don't, Papa. Don't! How can you? Oh, I hate—"

"What! Bite me, will you, you young savage!"

"Oh—Please.... Papa. Please!"

"Bella." His voice broke. "What made you—"

"Oh, please, Papa.... Only stop. Yes.... No, no! Never again."

21

SNARLING, bodies swinging, the massive line of trucks were beginning their fifty-mile test run. They rumbled through the plant's gateway along the boulevard and over the asphalt like a herd of well-trained beasts starting a hunt. Ned brought up the rear. He sat with one foot on the clutch, his hand idling over the gear shifts. Echoes of last night's party seethed through his tired brain, but his gaze ahead was clear, alert. In the truck preceding him was Turin. He had arranged this with Moissaye, their leader, who headed the convoy stretching four blocks in length.

The thick fumes from Alex Turin's exhaust spread directly in his path. Ned cursed him. The fellow was doing it on purpose. Choking his engine, giving her too much gas.

"Damn it, it'll take more than that, old boy, to peel my eyes off you. For once I got you where I want you. I'm gonna keep you there."

He honked angrily, signaled. "Speed up! We're falling behind. And lay off that gas!"

Alex humped his thin shoulders, slowed down a notch. For once he had that black ape where he wanted. Through his reflector, he watched for the thing to happen. Any time now. There! Grimacing, he thumbed his nose, speeded ahead.

Ned threw on his emergency brake, switched off his engine. What the hell! No mistaking that wheezing clank-clank. Jumping down, his tongue ripped in two languages. Both front tires gone flat! What the, defective inner tubes, blowouts? Hardly. This meant an hour's delay to change tires and overtake the convoy. Lucky his truck carried two spares and he knew the highway for which they were heading.

Punctures! Nails had been skillfully hidden near the rims, to work their way in as the wheels revolved. "Goddam you, Turin, this is your work!" He drew them out, put them as evidence into his watch pocket. Was this just spite work? Or wasn't it more? By Christ, this time that son of a gun should get what was coming to him.

As he loosened bolts and braced one foot against the axle, preparing to yank loose the stubborn tire, a sailor with a Baltic insignia on his cap stepped from the sidewalk. Tough break, eh? How about lending him a hand?

Turin's brittle grin narrowed as his truck raced down the blocks. His plans were working out to a T. At the next corner he'd make his getaway, pick up the load as scheduled, get his wallet, then make for the dead country. With the truck stranded on a backroad within easy reach of a wayside station, he'd meet Katia for the overnight flight to the border ... and freedom! Yes, she had at last decided to come.

What if her courage gave out at the last minute? If she failed him! But no, tickets, everything was arranged: surely she'd come.

Only one matter caused him regret. He'd not see the flareup. How he might have relished it, from a secure distance. That miserable crew wailing like frantic ants over their dunghill, scrambling over their smoking madhouse of a factory. Well, even in Paris he could sniff, relish the fumes. Ah, Paris! White arms, languid depths of Katia. Friends whom he hadn't seen for over a decade, whom he'd nearly lost touch with, except by devious routes. Compatriots, ready to endure all to restore Russia to her place among nations.

In Paris lived *Red Star's* former owner. He'd know how to appreciate ... also he possessed certain confidential information that some people would find worthwhile. Yes, Katia and he'd not fare badly. And some day these dogs should pay well for their treachery, and his misery, degradation. By Christ, they should pay through their coarse *muzhik* snouts.

With the convoy's sharp turn to the left, they entered

heavy traffic on a main thoroughfare. With a quick swerve to the right, Turin sped through narrow side streets onto an avenue running directly west. Ned out of the way, there was no one to see. Two o'clock. At seven his train left. At eleven-thirty ... well, he hoped his worst enemies were working the late shift. Mikhail, Natasha. When the paint shop went up, there'd not be enough pieces left of them and their damn Plan to fill a coffin. For once their ludicrous Red funerals wouldn't have so much as the grace of a corpse. Quite a fitting end to their pretentious adventure.

Holy Mother, his engine was snarling. That's what came of having to use a new car, you couldn't even trust these filthy Bolshevik trucks. What if she stalled on him? Angrily he gave her less power....

With a hasty grip to the sailor who had helped him and a "Come over to *Red Star* club while in town," Ned vaulted into his truck. He was off, set on overtaking the convoy, his motor's even hum a lullaby in his strained ears. He dared not push her too hard. Besides, who knew what other mischief that man had done? Maybe the old girl would break down with a new kink. But Jesus, to creep along this way! The miles'd never end, the trucks loom in sight. "Come on, old girl, just this once! Let 'em have it."

As Ned forced her speed, inky clouds tossed in the sky's net and threatened at any moment to blot out the green fields and russet furrows of new-turned loam.

When he overtook them after two hours, they were parked along the highway, giving their motors a ten-minute rest. Where had he disappeared, the brigader demanded, and what about Turin? Their absence had been discovered only now. He assumed the two were together, one had had difficulty and the other stopped to help. But why hadn't Turin signaled ahead, as agreed?

"Oh, yeah?" Ned gave a nervous hitch to his elbows. Turin had made off! No one could say when, or in what direction. Other drivers doubted it: was the fellow really such a scoundrel? He wouldn't dare. Perhaps he'd had some motor trouble.

"Oh, yeah?" Reaching into his watch pocket, Ned exhibited his nails.

Cutting short angry outbursts and conjectures, the leader dispatched Ned to the plant for a report and immediate checkup. The remainder of the convoy must finish the journey, for the trucks were due to be shipped out that night.

With uneasy fury, the gray beasts and their drivers reformed their procession. As Ned's truck rolled into *Red Star's* yard, the ancient towerclock pointed its hands to five-thirty. Hearty globs of rain pelted against hood and windshield, blinding his path. Just as he knew, no word of Turin. The fellow was up to some game, sure.

Old Mikhail, when he heard, became a supercharged battery, crackling beneath his timed resolute moves. Phone calls and couriers were dispatched to all parts of the city. *Red Star truck number 22983 and its driver running amok!*

The sky, which had completely lost her temper, beat distractedly on all within reach. Cursing the downpour and the rat scurrying somewhere through it, Ned methodically combed the district assigned him. Not so much as a clue of the piker.

When the drenched convoy, after finishing its test, returned, the men sought out Mikhail, joined the search. This devil thought he could make off with one of their trucks, eh! One they were sending to Nizhni Tagil. They'd show the bastard. A wolf in overalls. Wait till they caught him! Devil's mother, what a downpour. And where had the louse gone?

Andy was sauntering aimlessly through the shed, undecided whether to go home or postpone the thing by a visit to Mac's. Better go over and talk with him about Tim. His pal was down and out, asking to come back. Morse, he wrote, had gone in for the bootleg and stickup racket. (That'd be one too many for cautious Tim.) Poor old guy, he had muffed it once. Still, for Tim he'd do what he could.

What was all the flurry among the drivers? He edged in. So that was it, eh? With a whoop, he sprang on the running board of a truck. After that fourflusher? Damn the rain, take him along. A good chase'd just set him right. Race the jitters right out of his brain.

As they slowed for the dip at the exit, his heart whanged in his throat. Rain-splotched cheeks and leather jacket braced against the pelting steel, Natasha was coming through the entrance. Like a young birch, she rose stark clean through the gale.

Impulsively he leaned out to wave to her, drew back. Hell, that was over with. Maybe at home there was word from Elsie. Maybe she had sailed. Maybe ... Once, under a night jammed with stars, they'd walked and ... Once.

"Say!" he jabbed his companion unmercifully, "Let'er have it, can't you. Never catch that thief, at this rate." Guess he couldn't give him a turn at the wheel?

Before entering the shop, Natasha halted under a dripping eave. Her wet face raised toward the bellowing night. If only she might walk for hours in this storm, drench her thoughts ... drain them. Beethoven had loved storms. But she couldn't listen. Not yet ... Beethoven. Great things had been born of his suffering. But hers, a loadstone bearing her down. She must wrench herself free, and no looking back.

She must push her request to be transferred. They *must* understand. Without being told. Rain ... sometimes she loathed it. Tonight, she must prove to Zena and her brigade that she could top her old record. That she could ... Why, when there was so much else, should love matter so? Why was it, that all she had studied didn't help her now? One person, out of all the millions. And yet ... Silly idiot! There were bigger things to worry over. Tonight, she must show Zena— After rain, there would be a star-pricked freshly starched heaven. There always was. An intoxicating lilt to the air.

A heavy burden, Spring.

Philip Boardman nudged her elbow. "What are you mooning over? Come on in, out of the rain." What a girl. Junior, lucky rascal, should grow up to mate with a woman like this. Mate and work in a startling new world. "Notice the bulletin board?" he asked brusquely.

Giving herself a rude shake, she preceded him into the shop. "Seen the board?" he repeated. "Looks like our shop is going over the top. You ought to feel proud. Put plenty of elbow grease behind it, didn't you?"

Cheered by the shop's din, she wiped the rain from her face, ran a quick comb through her wet hair. Yes, she had seen the board. Great, wasn't it! She turned with a sense of home-coming to her lathe.

Coughing dejectedly, a sneeze in its wet sparkplugs, the truck bearing Andy drew up by its rain-groomed mates back at *Red Star*. Intermittent jabs of lightning seared the group of trucks. Incoming phone calls and dispatchers all brought the same report: no trace of the stolen truck nor its driver. Shivering with damp and exasperated at their failure, Andy drifted about Mikhail's office, waiting for news. Why go home? Maybe there there'd be ... Rattlesnakes, this skunk was getting away with murder.

A foreboding quiet in his stoop, Mikhail was phoning outlying districts. It was already plain that Turin had not stopped at Moscow. "What? What's that?" he rasped suddenly into the telephone. Andy crowded with others around him. "Well, I'll be— Rammed in a ditch, eh? The son of a bitch. Why in hell didn't you call us? Never mind excuses. Put a guard over that car, a rescue crew is leaving at once. What? To hell with the bad roads, we're after that truck. Hello—wait a minute! What about the driver? D-R-I-V-E-R. You don't know! What the hell you mean you don't know! You think he must have jumped the seventen train? Damn your— What? Nothing. Listen, see that a guard— Hello! hello!" The receiver clicked to with a bang. Mikhail looked up. "You heard?"

Gleefully Ned rubbed his palms. Sure thing. A couple of extra tires, tow rope, jack, directions, and he'd be off. Andy begged, "Let me go with him." Mikhail shook his head. "Too bad, my boy, can't spare you from the morning shift. Ivan'll go with Ned. Well boys, it means an all-night job for you. But when you've brought in number 22983, you can sleep happy. Wait! Get a couple of dry coats and hot drinks inside you first." He jiggled the receiver. "Hello, hello.

Central! Drat you, gone to sleep on the job! Hello. Give me the O.G.P.U."

Ruefully Andy saw Ned and Ivan underway, began his homeward trek. Near the dieshop he must pass, near the very place where he had shown her the cable. And she had said— Bull. An end to all that. He was going home, and to sleep. Two weeks it was since he had sent his cable and letter. Still no answer. What could it mean?

His footsteps sounded their hollow taps along the hall. Every night to come home and not to know if or when.

Natasha. There had been no chance to talk with her alone, since that day. Yet he couldn't rid himself of her. Day or night. Maybe if he and Elsie went to Siberia. But picture the kid in Siberia!

Natasha. She was friendly enough, but avoiding him. She was right. What could they have to say to each other, now?

He blinked in the sudden light of his room, passed a rough hand across his eyes, and slumped into a chair. No mistaking it. There, on the cube-splashed carpet, lay two deathly white squares of paper. What if he tore them up, never read them? What if ... Oh, Nat, why did you tell me to! Say, get a hold of yourself, jackass. Pick 'em up.

Gingerly he hitched his chair toward them. The letter was addressed in his friend Bill's uneven scrawl. The other— what if he struck a match to it, never read it. Was she coming? Already sailed? He stared at the cold lettering of his name on the cable, unable to touch it.

Baby! Yellow! Pick 'em up. What you scared of? Two little squares of paper, and you!

Anything was better than not knowing. Couldn't be worse than these last two weeks.

He reached for Bill's letter. Rigid fingers unfolding the sheets, his glance ran mechanically down the page.

> Don't blame you for hanging on there. Wouldn't mind giving it the onceover myself. Since we got our Auto Union started, things been getting hot. You'd never know the old berg, how things, people are changing.
> (His eye raced ahead. Why in hell didn't Bill come to the point?)

You asked me to write you about Elsie. I got some bad news for you, buddy, you might as well know straight out as keep dragging on. I hope you won't take it too serious. Because when a girl pulls a lowdown like that on a friend of mine, well—

Dropping the letter, Andy snatched the cable, tore it open with a force that ripped it across. Its five words stared back at his blanched face and suddenly blurred eyes. At a young man whose crooked mouth was twisting between a good bawl and a whoop, standing, stupidly reading and re-reading, as though he couldn't believe his own two eyes.

Bareheaded, Andy ran down the stairs, out into the rain. Natasha. Where was she? Damn the hour. Damn everything. Oh boy, this was one on him. What a sucker he'd been. She was working late shift. God, what a break. Would Nat listen? He'd make her.

The downpour was over. The sky sobbed fitfully, like a child whose temper is spent. From huddled roofs a violet mist was seeping down alleyways and lanes. Before morning the stars would be out.

Five words. Cable balled in his fist, Andy rounded a corner. Scarlet forked tongues were lapping the fuzzy skyline above the plant, smoke rolled in low clouds toward the east.

Red Star—afire!

He ran toward the gates. Locked . . . What could he do? Try the side gates. No good, they'd be locked. Jeez, *Red Star*. *Nasha*. Nat, Nat! Let me in! Should he try skinning the wall? Crazy fool, and get it in the neck for a sneak thief.

"Heigh, keep your shirt on!" A guardsman took him by the shoulder. "Can't you see it's about over?"

Andy shielded his face from the heat, looked up. Right. They had it licked. But how had it started? And where was Nat? He couldn't stand here! . . .

At last the gates opened, releasing a flood of strained faces, orderly ranks. Where was Nat? In this jam he'd miss her sure.

"Anybody hurt?" he heard them ask.

"Not to speak of. Three kids with a few burns." "The

blockheads must've thought they could choke out the flames with their bare claws. Young fools!" "Sure, we caught the traitors. Redhanded. Three rats in the foundry." Bodies jostled by him, smells of fresh smoke and charred wood on their jackets. Where was she?

"How much damage! Lousy bastards. And us working so hard to—"

"Somebody was asleep to let them get away with it!"

Andy spied Mikhail and plunged recklessly through the loosening crowd toward him. Had he seen Natasha? No, but as for Turin, yes, they'd caught him and the woman with him, headed for the border! They were bringing them to Moscow and—

"Attaboy!" Andy gave him a whack on the shoulder, rushed on. Jumping spark plugs! Where was his girl? Glimpsing her in the rear of the crowd, he forced his way through, took her arm. Her face was smeared, her leather jacket snagged, and her head scarf gone. "Nat! You're not hurt? Come quick, I got news." Laughing shakily, he tightened his grip. "No, it can't wait. Come on. What a break. Read it." Jeez, he couldn't help the crowd.

"What you bothering me now for!" she demanded, twisting her arm free. (Idiot. Bothering her now.) She took the cablegram.

Slowly she unknotted the crumpled sheet, held it under a lamplight. He looked strange. Queerer than before, when ... Damn the man, why should he come now ... She choked back a bitter retort. To tell her that Elsie was on the way! Well, he expected too much. He looked ... Had he no sense, no care for how she might feel? Did he ... She felt worn out. Old. Wearily she read the words through. Spring. Their plant safe. She, twenty-four, yet ... Why was he crowding her so? Fool. Everybody could see. Her whole body was trembling. She must be drenched. Chilled through, that was it. And this young fool! Old themes were racing her blood. She'd go home. "What is it?" she asked desperately. "The thing doesn't make sense." (THANKS KEEP THE CHANGE ELSIE) Why *would* he crowd her?

His shoulder bore hard on hers. "What you mean you can't

read it? She's given me the raspberries, that's all. For that Mortimer bum."

"And you?"

"Nat—darling!" Well, it wasn't his fault if there was a crowd.

Shadows moved by, and the plant reared its bulk in the wet April darkness behind them. Its belts clicked forward on metal plugged boots, assembling two-and-a-half ton trucks for Nizhni Tagil.

22

MIKHAIL was waiting for his assemblymen at the foot of the conveyor. Through the skylight the morning sun gleamed jubilant after the storm. As it lit on machines and dark overalls and the women's red scarves and black cambric aprons, few bothered to heed. Not today.

Mikhail appeared before his mates like some horrible cartoon of himself. How many days, Sasha wondered, before the man'd cave in? A dirty shame.

"Mates," the super blurted, "you know the answer?"

"Sure thing!"

"Don't you worry Mikhailovich!"

"Dirty lice, we'll show 'em!"

Sure, *eighty a day!* The record so far was sixty-nine off the belt. And May First only two weeks off. "Tell those tool-slackers to step on it!" "And that dieshop, damn them!" "Them keeping us waiting around here on our hind legs for them spare parts!"

"Say, Mikhailovich, it ain't the main line holding up the works!"

Mikhail grinned. "So eighty'll be a cinch eh? Big talk! We'll see."

As Andy raced Sasha, their terse jibes stung them faster, faster. The twelfth skeleton. The thirteenth. They needed twenty-five a shift.

The first day they made twenty-two babies, the next seventy-three. But yesterday there was a drop back to seventy. A hitch in bodies. Sasha blurted, "I'd like to bust those snails in the ass." But today they'd clear seventy-five easy. As for eighty—well!

Andy eyed the rapid motions of the beltmen. No greenies now. The mainline could do an even hundred, and not feel it. Up to the rest, to feed in the parts. "Think we'll make it by the Big Day?"

Sasha fumed under his breath. "We gotta!" As he ran through his circle of slings screws and jackups, Andy lost himself in the happenings since the fire. The evening after, Nat and he had gone for a long tramp up the river. To talk things out.

Damp biting smells of April stung their lungs. The heavens sprawled over them, like a yellow beach left ridged by the tide. Rowboats swarmed up and down stream, accordions and balalaikas hummed tunes old as the Kremlin walls, and other tunes as new as the young grass pushing up on the banks. Groups of all ages wandered along the river joking and singing, tipsy with Spring. Children scampered and leaned over railings, until their elders tugged them back. Young couples passed close by, swinging on to each other, and speaking low.

Sure, he and Nat'd talked it out. And planned, and you know. Jeez, what a swell kid. "There's no place at my house," she'd said, "where we can stay, so I'll move over to yours." Simple as that. Her Dad and little Felix had helped them cart over her clothes and books. And the old lady, gruff and sniffling over Nat's going and the want of a priest, had cooked them a big feed and offered her best skillets and teapot.

Surprised him plenty, how Nat liked pottering about. Fixing things up. And he'd put up extra shelves and hooks in the closet. Right off they'd taken out shares in the housing coöperative. No telling how long they'd wait to get a place. Plenty ahead on the list. Well, where Nat was was okay with him. So long as they'd no kids, one room wasn't so bad.

Jumping sparkplugs! What a howl the bunch'd made, when they heard. Sprung a powwow on them. Mikhail and Mac had made toasts, and Gus. Well and who hadn't! Everybody a high time. Even that old crow Misha had loosened up.

"Attabuoy!" Sasha reminded him. The chassis flipped over like a turtle from a rock into the pond. "Diz ez how!"

The Detroiter's eye was caught by his mate's pin. *Udarnik,* eh? Once he'd called it soft soap, a racket. Nat and Mac had one too. Nearly everybody but him. Well, who cared? Once Sasha had asked him, "Joining us?" and he'd come back with a "Who, me!" Guess he'd been a ham.

At lunchtime, a slicklooking fish who said his name was Spenser, a writer for *Land of the Free,* came mosing over. "I want a story, boys. That is, my paper. You know, about *Red Star's* record. Splash the front page and all that. A real pippin!" His voice trailed off. The beltmen stared at him, sent him to Mac. Mac knew how to deal with heels like that.

Work done, Andy went by the dieshop for Nat. For once they had the same evening free. Sasha and his girl came with them and they took a boat at the wharf reserved by *Red Star,* for a fast row up the river. It was Andy's first trip. How the river curved on herself, looped the loop. Swift too. As her brown waters gave deep throaty gurgles, Natasha, anticipating her dip, dragged a hand over the side.

Over the peaks of the Kremlin and St. Basil's Cathedral hovered a rosy mist. Under bridges and past blocks of gray and salmon-colored mansions (quarters from which mechanics and their families now leaned), they pulled up the river. In the windows were flower pots and plants, and down by the flat stone edge of a wharf some women and girls were rubbing and rinsing their wash. Near their boat a pair of lazy gulls swerved and dived for fish.

They kept on until they reached the Lenin hills, where they'd tobogganed in winter. Now they were huge clouds of all shades of green. They pulled rapidly into shore and the girls donned their bathing suits behind a clump of bushes while the men held the boat and shed all but their trunks. Pushing off again, they dived overboard in midstream.

Natasha came up near Andy. "Come on!" Shoulders level, they stroked toward the hills. But it was too cold for more than a brisk turn. From the flatbottomed boat, they shouted over Lydia's repeated tries at crawling aboard. "Honest, Sashka, you've got a terrapin for a wife!"

Back in their room, Andy set the old alarm while she foraged for something to eat. Ignoring the sandwich she held out to him, he caught his girl by the waist, swung her out and then close. And who minded the cheese smearing hard against his neck.

The days went fast. Seventy-six, seventy-seven, the record climbed. A week to go. Andy whistled. Would they? Everybody from the new director to the sweeper was jamming the gas. Boardman swearing and romping on it. Old Mikhail game but stripping his gears. And he and Nat dead tired nights, but not too flat for a swim.

Seemed like the earth was heaving with them. Andy felt the pull. "A thing of Honor—" Well, he was in it too, no fooling. He no longer asked why? He was in it and that was that. *Ours.*

"Well, what say?" He looked across at his buddy.

Sasha nodded. "We gotta." Why, the floats were all ready, also the wooden giant statue for the public square. Only the boasting figures were waiting to be splashed in. *Eighty a day!*

Daily papers carried the news: DNEIPROSTROI TO BE READY SIX MONTHS AHEAD SCHEDULE. KHARKOV WORKERS PRESENT EXTRA LOCOMOTIVE AS MAY GIFT COUNTRY. And a whole list of items: Sasha read them off to Andy at lunch. COLLECTIVE FARMERS OF THE TARTAR REPUBLIC WRITE OPEN LETTER TO STALIN, "We celebrate May Day by Completing Our Sowing in Advance...." They laughed over its ending, "And Comrade Stalin, we invite you, when you have a free day, come and have buckwheat cakes with us." Carloads of tomatoes and apples had been shipped as a present from Turkestan to Moscow workers.

Andy read them over Sasha's shoulder. Jeez, this was more fun than Christmas.

But what about *Red Star?* Would they make it?

They had! "All With Our Own Hands." Proudly they

marched into the Grand Theatre. The evening before May First. "Let's sit near the front," Natasha urged. Say, Andy felt queer. A lot was going to happen. And he wasn't sure. If . . .

Stage and galleries were decked out with miniature trucks and banners. Everybody was shined up. Nat was sporting the new watch Andy had gotten her. And was her face red! After speeches and awards, there would be an Act from *Red Poppy,* so the Actors' League announced, "in honor of the victorious proletariat of *Red Star.*" Mac and Nan, carrying Lucy, took seats by them, with Sasha, Kolya, Lydia and Zena alongside. Just in front were Gus and Freda Heindricks. "Hi there, Hothead!" Poor boob, Andy thought. Lapping it up. Sure, for a couple of days. Then he'd start yelping for fairies again!

Down the aisle Natasha spied Boardman coming in. Was that frizzled woman by him his wife? Philip brought Mary over. "Meet some of my friends." At sight of Andy, she stuttered, held out her hand. (Life here was upsetting, relations mixed. But if Phil wanted.) Her hand hung in midair. Natasha nudged her companion. Quickly Andy seized it until she winced. Okay, he'd give Boardman's snoot a break. "Slide over," Philip asked, "make room." Andy saw the spetz had the jitters too. What was eating him, he wondered.

While his wife and the girls made small talk, Philip fidgeted around. He'd had to hint like all getout for Mary to come. Mac had his kid. He'd wanted to bring Junior, but she'd put her foot down. He wished Mark was here, but he had his own plant's doings. Every theater and hall in town tonight was jammed to the gills. All over the country there were big doings, hurrahs, even in the stuffy village halls. Well, they had it coming. As for him, he'd be glad when it was over.

"Thought you'd be on the stage?" Mac asked him.

"I begged off," Philip shrugged. Wasn't it bad enough as it was! He really didn't care for these three-ring shows. God, was he forgetting! He squeezed his pocket. No, there

it was, all written out. But he wasn't pleased with it, not
at all.

I want to thank you for this great honor. This premium.
I feel the lads in the shop deserve it more than I do. I ...

Hell, it sounded flat. But he'd really like to tell them about
the boys. And how the bigwigs in Europe and the States
were saying science and technology were a joint Franken-
stein. Spengler ... It wasn't so, and here they'd been prov-
ing it!

He'd like to say these things. But he wouldn't. He'd muff
it for sure, get stagestruck, come up for air.

"You oughta be up there," Nat reproved. Solidarity and
all that.

"Say, I'll take mine here." He imagined a change in
her. Under the surface, but there. And in that Anderson too.
Or was it just his imagining?

Philip turned to gaze up at the balconies around him.
Into the sea of human faces.

He felt the old stirring passion. He had probed it deep,
was probing still. Remarkable. A whole people fired by the
thing. His restlessness was centering, pointing up. Science
and planning, that was the thing. Science and humans.

Lines from a play he'd liked at college came back to him,
in fact, they'd never quite left him:

What a man wants in life is a course and a star
A star to steer her by—

It hooked up somewhere with this crowd singing:

A new world in birth!

Mac and the others were craning to recognize their
friends among those on the stage. Next to Ivan Pavlov,
their director, were Maxim, Ned, a girl turner and old
Vasiliev. The toolmaker was sitting by the man he'd gone
to see in the Kremlin, in a ripped work jacket—Loganov.

On their left must be the German Metal Workers' Delegation, their plant's special guests for the holidays.

Andy craned too.

But where was Mikhail?

Reluctantly Sasha told them. He had keeled over on his way home. The doc said he needed a long rest, and come off lucky at that.

Andy turned his program. Over and over. The old sucker. And to miss out on the big doings, tomorrow's parade. Wasn't right. And the belt, who'd manage that?

Why did Russians make such damn long speeches? All fired up. He flipped his shoes until Natasha shushed him. Crap, he'd never thought. And all over eighty babies a day. They'd do a hundred easy. Lotta waste motions on the belt and hitches, still. When they got rid of those ...

But say this Dutchman had the stuff. Couldn't savvy his lingo, but his punch and "Heil Moskau!" had 'em all on their feet.

Now the real thing. The awards. His triphammer had stalled on him. Would *he?*

Jeez, he knew how Boardman felt, standing up there gawking. The crowd cheered, waited. The engineer's lips moved, not saying a word! Gulping a "Thank you!" Philip started off. Then, with a sudden loud "Hurrah for Science and the Five Year Plan!" he hurried down the improvised steps to his seat.

"Old swearing *Amerikanets!*" Kolya breathed. And Mary wondered what on earth he had said.

Now they were calling names, shop by shop. Nat squeezed his hand. Yes, there it was. *"Udarnik* Frank Andeerson."

Sasha pulled at him. Atta buoy! Get a move on, was he deaf!

Andy found himself going down the aisle with the rest. But his brakes were jamming and his ears hurt. Was he going right? Somebody from behind pushed him on. Up the steps and half across the stage. He chanced a look at the faces next him. Hell, they were grinning jittery too. It braced him. The shouts out there sounded a long way off.

He straightened up, while the director clipped on his pin

and handed him his charter. *Udarnik*—brigade member. On the sheet was written his name and in red letters:

With us, labor has become a thing of valor, heroism, honor.

He looked down at the paper. Once before he'd stood up to get a diploma. From Grade School. Well. This time he had it.

The last thing before they turned in, Nat went to the window. "Oh, bother! It's cloudy." Honest, she couldn't bear it, if tomorrow it rained.

At daybreak she came over to his cot and tousled his head. Sleepy-eye, roll out. "May First to you, Andy!" She was dancing. May First all round the world. Berlin Moscow New York Shanghai! Imagine!

She broke loose from him. "Come on, hurry. We can't be late!"

She ran to. the window. A heavy fog curtained everything. Would the sun rift it? Swallowing a hasty breakfast, they made for the plant. Everywhere people were hurrying along. Troops of school kids, whole families.

Through the slowly drifting fog they could see runners flapping on the houses and lettered "Hail May First." "Hail the World October!" Flags were out, houses emptying, streets filling.

Lines were already forming when they reached the plant. Placards of all shapes and designs in bright colors were raised in the air: miniature motors, trucks, cartoons of slackers and fascists, and what-have-you. Everybody had on his best dress or suit. Here and there groups had formed circles and were passing the time with games and dances while the faithful accordions hummed. Jeez, Andy thought. Jeez, what a day.

Boardman was there, with Junior. No, his wife hadn't come, she thought it too long a hike. Six miles they'd tramp, to reach the Red Square. (Truth was, she thought parades vulgar.) She had gone with some friends in a car to tour the decked-out city. Color schemes and layout had been in the hands of the best artists, and they had done a good job. As for him, he was going to take in the whole show, from the inside. Trot Junior on his shoulder, pass the reviewing stand and shout with the rest.

Mac, Andy thought, looked funny. Solemn as hell. "My next'll be in Chi, buddy." Nan didn't say anything, just stood there, patting Lucy's hair.... Just when the queues were shortening, and they were getting ahead. She didn't quite understand Mac.

"Jeez," Andy told him, "gonna be tough, if you go back." Mac joked it off. But Andy was glad when the lines started moving.

All the main arteries of the city were flooded with endless human columns, a forest of red banners and placards flapping over their heads. Eight hours it took, Nat said, for all the lines to pass through the Square. Close to two millions would be marching and streets everywhere would be banked with watchers.

All traffic was stopped or re-routed. Blocks ahead they had begun singing, moving on. The full chorus of human voices echoed along the stone buildings down the avenue toward them:

The earth shall rise on new foundations

What a holiday! A people's holiday, Boardman said to himself. Not even the carnivals and festivals of the Middle Ages could have equaled this.

He lifted Junior to his shoulder, fell in step.

The boy pulled his collar. "Look, Pop!"

"I see, son."

"Gee, it's blocks and blocks. Ain't there no end?"

"No, son, there's no end."

Just the beginning—

Near him they were singing one of the marching songs born during the Civil War:

> *Out of the past*
> *March we forward ...*
> *Endless the way of the millions ...*
> *Bright glows the morning ahead!*

And echoing along the highways, intermingling with cheers and the sounds of thousands of tramping feet, the refrain:

...Shall be the human race!

23

SPRING had given way to midsummer.

Looking up from the row of potato plants he was hoeing, Andy caught the gentle roll of the chocolate brown earth heaving its slow breath under the torrid glare of high noon. Jeez, these acres of spuds they were working would give *Red Star* soup and hot jackets for some weeks to come. Recently on free days, groups of volunteers from their plant had traveled out to *Ilyitch,* one of the state farms attached to *Red Star,* to give them a timely lift during the height of the season.

With his knuckles rubbing the small of his back, he loosened his muscles cramped from long stooping and stole a moment to watch Natasha. Her face was puckered over a plant which some careless hoe had chopped almost in two. As she glanced up, her pucker faded. "Lazy!" she challenged, "see how I'm beating you!" "Oh yeah?" He tossed a clump of weeds to one side and smiled back at her as she looked up at him, squinting a little comically from the harsh sun. "You telling me!" (Hot dog, if he didn't watch out he'd be finding some excuse to run over to her row again, and Sasha'd start kidding.) He leaned down to disentangle a wiry weed from his plant. Her glance carried all the warm sureness of August fields and sky. Of their last months together.

As he turned the fresh loam, his thoughts ran back, mingling with clicks of hoes, insects' buzzing, and moist smells of teeming earth and growing things. Things familiar since boyhood, that made his entire life until now seem not a jumble of senseless parts but working toward some new whole.

He loved the soil, and so did Nat. Pity that town life

cut folks off from it. And country people had a pretty dull time. Well, they said it was gonna be different. The new life they were making would unite city and country and everybody would enjoy the best of both. Be jake with him. This farm was pretty citified at that. Big movie, dining room, place for the kids.

He hoed with a dash until he passed Nat, then relaxed his speed. "You bragged too soon!" "Oh did I?" They scratched merrily until Sasha laughed outright.

Only one thing had bothered Andy. And he'd been ashamed to let on to Nat. Yet it just didn't seem right. Such a fine girl and all.

Plenty did it that way. Nobody seemed to mind. Except oldtimers like Ma Safonova.

Over here they sorta figured if a man and girl liked each other and wanted to live together, that was their business. And only when kids came along the State took a hand. To look after the rights of the child. Pretty sensible and all that when you thought it over. Still. Hang it, that's how he felt. But not a word to Nat.

What was it? Not that he wanted to put strings on her. Or himself either. Not needed. Kind of insulting to say it was. He got Nat's slant. Love wasn't something you could guarantee by laws or bargains. Stamp with a seal. Free as the air you breathed. Or it just wasn't. Depending on how you lived worked it out together. Sure, he got her slant. But there it was. He couldn't help it.

Then one freeday morning she'd come over to him with one of those kidding grins that always warned him something was up. "Well now, out with it, Andrushka!" she'd said. "Come on, own up... Well, I don't mind. If you like, we'll go down this morning and register." And that had been that.

Sensible girl, Nat. And human. Jeez. She wanted three kids but not right off. Not until they got further along in their course. Sure, there were nurseries and things, she said, and she'd get four months out with pay. Still, babies took plenty looking after. They were young enough. Plenty of time. But maybe in two years. A May baby. Think of counting 'em up ahead like that. Three.

Andy broke a clump of earth between his fingers. Jeez, talking about kids and him just growing up.

When the last row was weeded and the ground freshly broken around each plant, the sun was dipping at a forty degree angle. The weeders scattered for a welcome rest on the grass. Natasha wound a slender blade around her thumb. She was ravenous, was supper ready? Tonight they were guests of the farm.

Mikhail, back from his three months' rest, pushed off his cap to mop his wet forehead. "Sasha, this farm work is showing us city guys up, eh? Look at you, sneaking a feel of your muscles! And you claim to come from a farm!"

"Is that so!" Jumping up, Sasha began tossing ball with Ned.

During supper Philip Boardman leaned across to ask Andy, "Your wife tell you how she razzed me yesterday?" Natasha laughed. "I razz our chief engineer? Never! Now would I, Maxim?" Philip winked at Andy. "You telling me! She thinks I'm against more women on the machines. Some stiff argument, and I don't need to tell you who came off the winner."

"Come on," Kolya called to them. "Aren't you through yet! Come on for the games." Within a circle of clapping palms and timing feet while an accordion sung an old village air, a young farmer and his girl partner were giving a lively version of an old folk dance. With a final curtsy she ran out and he beckoned in another. Later when he too disappeared into the circle the girl chose a new partner, and so it went on and on, until the accordion player's fingers were stiff and the circle had applauded the last original step. With a shout his neighbors thrust Ned Folson into the ring. He clogged until dust clouds danced at his heels while his bared arms flapped like a black crow's idling over a ripened corn field.

"Go on in with him," Mac urged his friend. Andy hung back. Why should be? Doubling up. Besides he'd make a poor second. Suddenly Ned slid toward him. Andy felt a quick push from behind, and they were clogging it double-time, each playing up to the other's new steps and sidetricks while the crowd whistled and beat tattooes on their knees and flat palms.

By the time they had started homeward the stars were coming out, the long evening fading, and a mist gathering over the river. As they wound along the path between the white flecked trunks of the tall shifting birches a half-wistful feeling lay hold of Andy. He was thinking of Mac. His pal was leaving soon for home. Just about broke them up when he'd told him. Well, they had sent for him, Mac said. Things were getting hot and after all he'd learned a lot here, guess his place was back there...So he was going. But imagine *Red Star* without Mac. Jeez, would the time come when he too...Something heavy kinda sobering about dusk.

Natasha slipped a hand through his arm. "Smell the birches." "Uh-huh." A star zigzagged across the heavens. August was the month for shooting stars.

"Andrushka, what you thinking?"

"Oh, about things. And Mac."

In the sleeping village through which they were passing two rowdies bumped against an old well, caroling:

> *Oh you can talk all you want*
> *About your Five Year Plan*
> *But give me five links of boloney*
> *And fill up the glasses, man!*

"Shirkers!" Natasha bit down on the long grasses she was carrying, to draw out the cool taste in their veins. Up ahead Sasha and Kolya had begun singing:

> *Mighty and strong*
> *Our song of labor*

Unconsciously their step fell into rhythm. Andy brightened. Tomorrow he was going to spring one on Nat. Sort of casual-like, Sasha and he were going to take her over to their *Conveyor* Reading Room and let her get a slant at it. All of a sudden. Wouldn't it jolt her seeing their mugs and write-ups on the Board of Inventors! Yes, his pal and he had worked out a new type of bolt for the upper frame. Meant a big saving in fine steel. Nothing to get swelled up over. But all the same. And they had better schemes underway. But they weren't bragging. Not to anybody. Least of all to Nat.

Down the night a train sent its low wail, rising to a shrill staccato, calling ... calling ... to what? Glory, ever since a boy one of those sirens at night had set something going in him.

These tracks ran back to the world from which he had come. Jeez, millions back there ... "Some world, eh Nat?"

"Yes, Andrushka. Ours for the taking."

From ahead came warning cries, the whirr of an approaching train. Pulling Andy's arm, Natasha ran with him over the moist earth, between flecked birches, toward their workmates gathering in the station.

GLOSSARY OF RUSSIAN TERMS

Amerikanets—American

Amerikantsi—Americans

Babuchka—a village grandmother

Bezprizorni—homeless waifs who took to the roads in large numbers following the years of war and famine

BRIZ—the Department for Workers' Suggestions and Inventions

Chom delaet—what is the matter?

Comsomol—the League of Communist Youth

Comsomolets—a Comsomol member

"Davai!"—"Come across! Let's have it!"

Droshky—an old-fashioned horse and carriage

Durak—fool

Gayechni Kluch—a wrench

Kvass—a coarse peasant drink

Kulak—literally means fist: a term used to denote the rich farmer who opposed the collective farm movement

Muzhik—a peasant, benighted and illiterate, typical of the old Russian village

Nanya—a nurse or housemaid

Nasha—Ours

Ne ponimayu—I do not understand

Nichevo—a much-used word of many meanings, such as, Never mind, Who cares? Forget it! Nothing of the kind

O.G.P.U.—the Government Secret Police

Pyatiletka—the Five Year Plan of Soviet Economic and cultural development

Shto?—What?

Symchka—the term used to designate the alliance of workers and farmers, also any joint action or social gathering of the two

Soviet—a Council, city, state or national, composed of elected representatives of workers, farmers, and other occupational groups

Spokoini nochi—goodnight

Spetz—a specialist or engineer

Svollitch—scum, swine

Torgsin—a chain of government stores operated solely on a basis of purchases paid for in foreign currency, silver or gold. Its goods are of high quality and much in demand

Tovarisch—comrade

Triangle—a committee of three, found in every department of all institutions and places of work, and composed of one representative from the trade union, another from the Communist Party, and the third from management. Their task is to assist in the daily running of a plant or institution and to raise questions of general concern

Udarnik—a shock brigade worker, one who voluntarily takes the lead in setting standards in industry, education or agriculture. *Udarniks* are everywhere publicly honored, in the press, civic parks and clubs

Valuta—foreign currency

Vot !—Here!